DARRAN M HANDSHAW

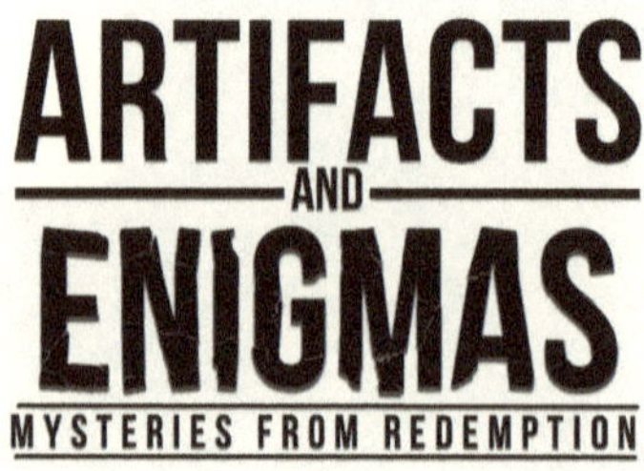

ARTIFACTS
AND
ENIGMAS
MYSTERIES FROM REDEMPTION

The
Engineer's
Press

To Ed Barkan, who taught me to never cease being curious.

Table of Contents

Map Of Redemption

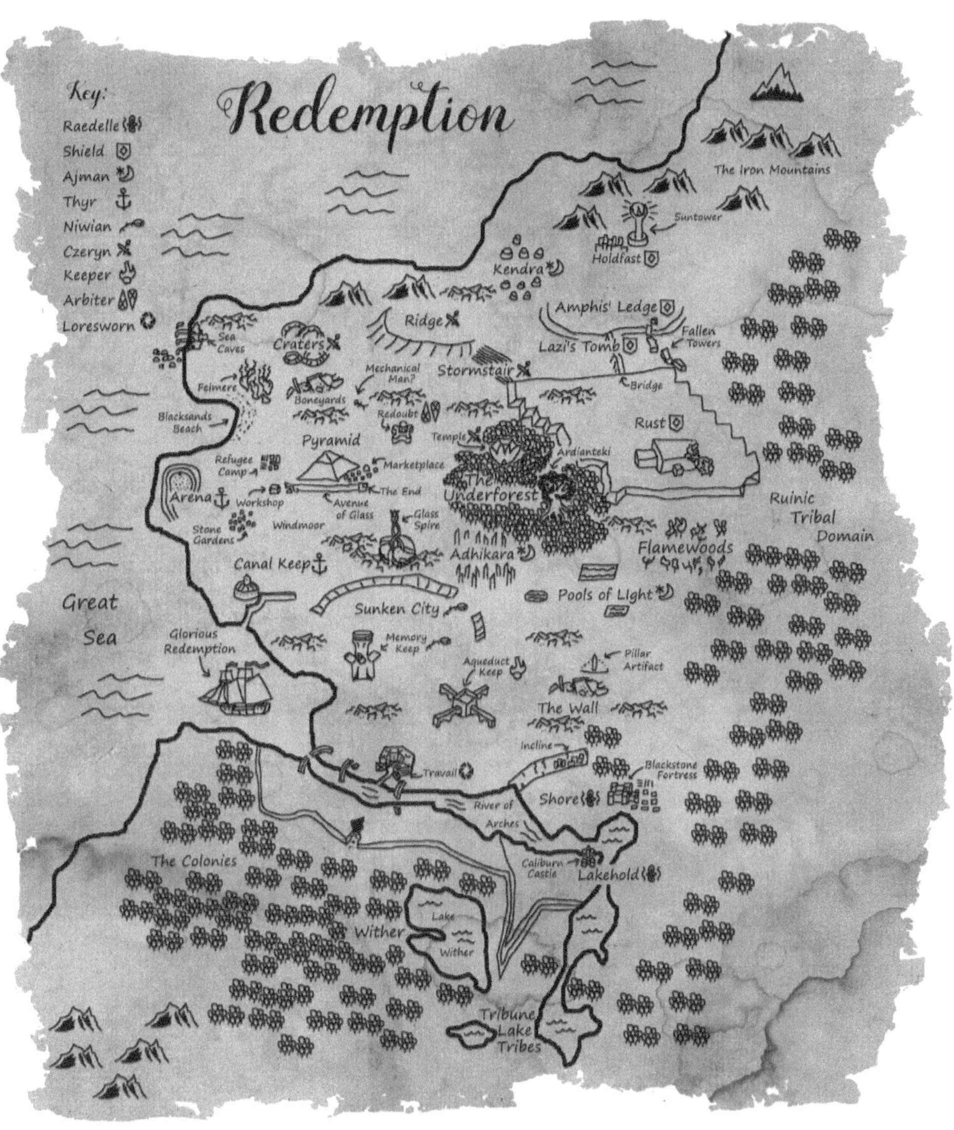

Dramatis Personae

MAIN CHARACTERS

Aethelgard sof Leaf: a Knight Investigator with the Order of Arbiters

Actaeon Rellios Caliburn: Prince Engineer of Raedelle Dominion

Eisandre Rellios Caliburn: Princess of Raedelle, former Knight Arbiter, and Actaeon's wife

Yanelle: Companion of Raedelle and bodyguard of the Prince Engineer

Lauryn: Engineer, woodcarver, and Actaeon's friend and associate

Ruinlock: Criminal mastermind, Aethelgard's nemesis

THE ARBITERS

Mitrius sof Cignith: Sentinel Arbiter

Corvin sof Haringar: Sentinel Arbiter and Technical Specialist

Jauvis sof Oriburt: Knight Arbiter

Matine sof Fystra: Knight Arbiter

Schlefer sof Jauvis: Initiate Arbiter

Bergum sof Matine: Initiate Arbiter

Elmerth sof Matine: Initiate Arbiter

THE ALTHEANS

Seraeta: Healer and Matron of the Altheans

Shard: Herbalist

OTHERS

Aedwina: Actaeon and Eisandre's daughter

Wave: Actaeon's friend, associate, and bodyguard

Ithelie Faris: Voice of Raedelle

Jezail Vren: Bard, Archer, Captain of the Wall Breakers warband and childhood friend of Actaeon

Faschin vor Steubick: Lord Protector of the Niwian Dominion

Jurlan ris Minovec: Captain of the Niwian Reds

Indros Zar: Prince General of Shield

Enrion Zar: Shieldian Lord and son of the Prince General

Gaemri Ip Monjata: The Raja of Ajman's Portent

Calisse T'ra Coletka: The Raja of Ajman's Warrioress, Yanelle's lover

Maerdia Bazardjan: Ajmani artist and Actaeon's friend

Cassanthia: Proprietor of the Song of the Sisters in Pyramid

Rin: An artifact dealer in the Warrens

Grameera: A blacksmith in the Open Markets

Arvin sof Balur, aka Leaf: former Knight Arbiter and Aethelgard's once mentor

Death from Above

THE WORKSHOP DOOR SLAMMED OPEN with such a resounding crack that Actaeon nearly fell from the top of the ladder. He'd finally gotten around to trying to decipher the problem with the ventilation system at the peak of the building's vault – it hadn't been quite the same since the fire and kept getting stuck when he tried to crank it open from the workshop floor.

"Where are you, Engineer?" came an unfamiliar voice from below. "There's been a murder. I need your aid."

"Last I checked, I am an engineer, not an investigative agent of the law," called Actaeon as he steadied himself on the ladder and started the climb back down to the second floor loft that stood above most of the central workshop floor. "It would be best if you spoke with the Arbiters about the matter. You have come to the wrong place."

"On the contrary, my new friend," countered the voice. "I'm precisely where I need to be, for you are the exact expert I require with this type of murder."

Actaeon started down the stairs to the ground floor with its scattered inventions and partially dismantled artifacts covering the many workbenches. He was genuinely surprised at the person who waited for him.

The tall man was shaved bald right down to the pate. A pair of lenses in a crude frame was perched upon his crooked nose, behind which were shrewd, cobalt eyes that scrutinized everything around him. Dark brows accentuated his gaze and was complimented by a straight brown beard the length of a hand – shot through with white in two places. He wore a gray cloak over a plain gray tunic, black vest, and gray trousers that were tucked into knee-high leather boots. The red armband on his right arm was emblazoned with the interlocking shields of the Order of Arbiters. With his right arm, he leaned heavily upon a cane of polished wood and at his right hip was a ceramic scabbard that confirmed what the faint smell of ozone in the air suggested was the presence of a writheblade.

"Apologies, Your Grace. He insisted on speaking with you immediately," said Companion Yanelle from the doorway. The red-haired warrior leveled her striking eyes on Actaeon, giving him a look that said she'd remove the man immediately if he wanted. The Companions served as the guards of the royal family of Raedelle Dominion, and Yanelle had been assigned to Actaeon since the Second Invasion War. In fact, she was one of the reasons he was still breathing.

"No need to apologize, Companion Yanelle," said Actaeon with a grin. "The Arbiters are our friends and allies, after all. I am sure that this gentleman has a perfectly good reason for nearly startling me off of a ladder."

The man arched his brow and smirked. "Perhaps if your Companion truly valued your well-being, she would have been up there footing your ladder instead of trying to interrogate Arbiters on official investigations."

Yanelle scowled and opened her mouth to voice her displeasure, but Actaeon forestalled her with a gesture.

"I presume this murder you speak of was committed with some form of artifact or invention, or else you would not be in my workshop, Knight Arbiter," theorized Actaeon.

"Knight Investigator Aethelgard of the Order of Arbiters," he corrected with a wave of his cane. "And quite astute of you, Engineer. If you care to join me, I would show you the scene of the murder."

"That's Prince Engineer to you," snapped Yanelle. "You're speaking to His Grace, Prince Engineer Actaeon Rellios Caliburn of Raedelle."

"Bah!" scoffed Aethelgard. "I don't care about the Prince part. It's the Engineer whom I seek."

Actaeon grinned. "Well then, you know what the important part is, Knight Investigator. Please, lead the way. I shall do what I can to help."

The murder scene was just below the Pyramid's pinnacle, inside a room that opened up like the jagged maw of a wild beast to the broken Northern Descent. There was a long wooden table with a disarray of chairs scattered about it on both sides. The remnants of a large feast were left on the table and were now surrounded by buzzing flies. Some of the food had fallen to the floor and more than one tankard had been spilled. The pool of dried blood upon the end of the table and floor closest to the open northern face of the room suggested that the victim had died there, although the Arbiters had removed the body earlier that day.

The pair of Arbiters guarding the entryway parted to let Aethelgard and Actaeon through. Companion Yanelle joined the Arbiters outside.

Aethelgard gestured with his cane for Actaeon to follow him. He righted a chair that had been on its side near the bloody mess and spun it around so he could sit leaning forward against its back. "Alright then, Engineer. Tell me. What do you see in the scene before you?"

Actaeon narrowed his emerald eyes and looked around the room for a few long moments before replying, "The person who was killed was standing at the head of the table, perhaps speaking to everyone else? However they were killed, it appears to me that nobody present expected it, because they all moved away from the table in a rush, spilling drinks and overturning chairs."

"A rudimentary but accurate assessment," said Aethelgard, his eyes flicking about the room intently.

"Care to enlighten me further?" asked Actaeon with a grin. He leaned forward on the shaft of his halberd expectantly.

"Of course, my good Engineer," said the Knight Investigator. He stood then and began to point with his cane as he explained. "The killer, who was much shorter than the victim, approached from behind and fired a single crossbow bolt through our victim's heart, at near point-blank range. The victim then fell upon the table and bled out. Those present, who had been listening to an impassioned speech from the victim, at first recoiled with the horror of the murder that unfolded before their eyes. Then many of them stood to pursue the killer. But, being prepared as they were, the killer fled to the north and leapt from the room to safety in a manner wholly unexpected by those present."

"A manner wholly unexpected?" parroted Actaeon. "What makes you certain?" He made his way over to the broken edge of the room. The shattered steps of the Northern Descent were visible far below and out beyond that was the ruinous expanse of the Boneyards, stretching toward the mountains of Czeryn far to the north.

Aethelgard stood to join Actaeon, where he lowered himself to a crouch. "See these bloody streaks? Partial bootprints from two men who ran through the blood that had spurted from our unfortunate victim's wound. The marks on the floor before them show that they were running toward the killer, in pursuit no doubt. The last marks are streaks because they slid to a stop after the killer leapt into the air and took off like a bird with some manner of artifact."

Actaeon took a step back, astounded. "A flying artifact? While I suppose it is possible, nobody has ever seen nor heard evidence of such a thing. What makes you surmise such a possibility? And while we are at it, how could you know that the pursuers were men and not women?"

The Knight Investigator barked a laugh and shook his head. "You surprise me, Engineer. I surmise precisely nothing. Everything I have said to you thus far has firm evidence to support it. I have studied such things for a lifetime and so it is simple for me to see that the length and spacing of their strides are indicative of men. A woman's stride would generally be shorter, and almost always narrower, as a matter of commonality to the fairer gender. Perhaps it is to keep pace with men, who typically have longer legs? Anyway, it matters not, for you will observe this in most all cases. Additionally, in the taking of their narrower strides, women also rotate their hips more, which can be evident in increased lateral drag as their foot presses against the ground."

Aethelgard paused then, looking about, while Actaeon narrowed his eyes upon him in what could only be described as a conflicted combination of interest and skepticism.

Before Actaeon could speak, the Arbiter clicked his tongue and pointed to the left side of the opening. "That's the one I was looking for. See those marks? Those were made by a woman who also stepped in some of the victim's blood. Notice how the marks are closer together and how you can see a smear toward the centerline of her gait. You'll observe that she stopped well before sliding off the edge. Many of the fairer sex are also the wiser sex as well." He laughed at that and used his cane to regain his feet.

"I can see that your hypothesis might hold correct with these limited examples. Provided you found the person associated with each," said Actaeon. "However, I still cannot fathom how you determined that the killer flew off on a flying artifact. Care to explain that?"

Aethelgard shrugged. "You'll see the truth of it soon enough. I suggest you watch people's gaits as you travel the city, if you're truly interested. As for our little killer birdy, that is even more clear. When you look down to the level below, you'll observe the blood stain from another pursuer who leapt after our killer and plunged to their death below. They leapt so far out over the Northern Descent that the only conclusion is that the killer ran off at a great speed and continued at least beyond the distance that their unwise pursuer leapt to. And judging by the early testimonies of the witnesses we've detained and the fact that there are no additional bloodstains down there, I can only determine that our culprit took to a flight of sorts as part of their escape."

Actaeon leaned carefully over the edge and spotted the place where the person had died in the broken portion of Pyramid far below. He straightened and turned to look up into another broken room above the one they stood in. "So the killer dropped down from above then?"

Aethelgard's lips curled into a thin smile and he nodded with a satisfied tug at his beard. "Indeed. Now you're thinking, Engineer. And there's evidence that they had camped out in the room above for quite some time – waiting for the perfect opportunity, no doubt. So, you've no thoughts on what could've been used in the escape?"

Actaeon unshouldered his recurve bow and put its scope to his eye. With it he slowly swept the Ancient ruins in the distance. Once he was satisfied, he slung the bow back over his shoulder. "There are one or two locations where a person using a flying device might land. Of course, it depends on the method of flight they achieved. If they glided upon the winds like a bird as you describe, then they would need a relatively flat landing location to dissipate their momentum, lest they break their legs upon landing. It also strikes me that the killer might have been waiting up there for the perfect wind conditions to arise for a flight to enable their escape."

Aethelgard pushed his lens frame up along the bridge of his nose. "The Sentinel Arbiter was right that I should contact you. I'm glad of this. So should we venture into the Boneyards to examine your potential landing sites?"

Actaeon shook his head. "First I would prefer to gain a higher vantage than this."

"The Song of the Sisters?" asked Aethelgard, speaking of the inn and restaurant at the Pyramid's pinnacle.

"Even higher," said Actaeon.

"Higher than the top of the Pyramid?" Aethelgard cast the Engineer an astounded look.

"Aye. And I think I know how to accomplish it," said Actaeon with a grin. "But first, do you have a witness who I can ask some questions of?"

"I've just the one, in fact," said Aethelgard. "We've detained the woman who was intelligent enough to stop when she realized what was happening. She was clearly possessed of the greatest power of observation present at the time. Shall we see what we might glean from her?"

Actaeon smiled and nodded. "Lead the way."

On the way back down into the Pyramid, Aethelgard explained the rest of the details of the case.

The group of people present, twenty-seven in total, during the murder were all Czerynians – members of the fallen Dominion to the north. Most surviving Czerynians had joined the new Hold of Wither in Raedelle, through an agreement which Actaeon had brokered, and these people were ones that he hadn't heard of before.

The murder victim was a man named Kragin who was a Czerynian Shield Warden, one of the right-hand men of a Warlord, before the Cataclysm of the Blue Sphere, as it was coming to be known. The witnesses who Aethelgard had interviewed all called Kragin their Warlord in Exile, but they wouldn't say much else about him or why they were there.

The witness who had been detained was a Czerynian woman named Gertiz. She had not been quite so forthcoming as Aethelgard had desired during the first interview.

The Knight Investigator led Actaeon and Yanelle down through the Skyspiral along a twisting staircase that arced high above the Sun Chamber below and eventually curved its way into the Pyramid's great Western

Tunnel. The way led past the Sea Lounge, which Actaeon was altogether familiar with, and down farther until they reached the entryway to a chamber that had always been sealed shut.

Aethelgard lifted his cane in front of Actaeon to halt him before he could go inside. "Hold. There's something you must know about the Rainbow Room."

"The Rainbow Room?" asked Actaeon. "I have never heard of such a room in Pyramid."

Aethelgard smirked. "That's because I hadn't wanted you to know about it. Now, listen carefully. The room changes color based on the emotions of any persons inside, which, in short order, will include ourselves. Thus, you must endeavor to eliminate any semblance, however minor, of emotion from your mien. Instead, become a study in stoicism – something which, as an engineer, you should have little trouble with. If you can manage this, then we shall see how the colors of the room will change, and it will reveal our witness' feelings in response to what we say to her. Since she has thus far refused my every effort in interrogation, we must now incite her to emotion to see what insights we might capture from her reaction."

"Fascinating," said Actaeon with a grin. "By what mechanism do you suppose the room uses to determine the emotion? I wonder if it is similar to how the Veiled One and Yonniker manipulated minds. It would be interesting to study this further."

"It matters not," said Aethelgard. "And no study of the room will be permitted beyond that of the emotions of anyone being interrogated inside."

"Matters not?" exclaimed Actaeon. "The knowledge could save the people of Redemption from future instances of mental manipulation! You do not care about that?"

"My only interests lie in solving the crimes committed within Arbiter-protected territory," explained the Knight Investigator. "Anything else is outside my purview."

Actaeon blinked and ran a hand through the disheveled, black hair behind his goggles. "Incredible. Lead on then. I shall endeavor to avoid asking you anything that requires too much of a digression from your interests."

Aethelgard laughed at that and pushed his lens frame farther up the bridge of his nose. "I shall lead on... when you control your present emotion." He narrowed his dark brows and offered Actaeon a pointed look.

The Engineer realized he'd been staring at the Knight Investigator in wide-eyed disbelief. He grinned and shook his head. "Very well. Consider it done." With his off hand, he gestured for the Knight to proceed.

The bald Arbiter nodded in satisfaction, and any sign of amusement vanished from his face. He assumed a blank look that penetrated his expression right down to a dead stare from his cobalt eyes. Aethelgard became the embodiment of indifference – the paragon of apathy. And then, lifting his cane, he rapped it against the door three times.

The door slid open and an Arbiter emerged and saluted. "Knight Arbiter Aethelgard."

"Knight Investigator, thank you," corrected Aethelgard.

"Aye," responded the Arbiter. "The witness waits inside as instructed."

"Very good," said Aethelgard. "You may wait out here."

The Arbiter nodded and stepped outside to join Companion Yanelle, who offered him a bewildered shrug.

The Knight Investigator led the way inside, and the Prince Engineer followed.

The Rainbow Room was a nondescript, conical-shaped room about twenty paces across. It terminated in a rounded point at the very top which appeared to stretch an impossible distance above their heads. Its walls were a uniform light pink color, but quickly changed to a mild orange hue. At its center was a single chair where sat the witness. There were no other furnishings to be seen.

Aethelgard came to a stop several paces before the woman and Actaeon paused at his side to lean on his halberd.

The witness was a Czerynian woman with dark skin and piercing black eyes. Her head was shaved with the exception of three strips of very short hair that ran from front to back. She wore simple brown leather armor and sturdy boots. She tried to stand but failed when she was quickly reminded that her hands were lightly tethered to the arms of the wooden chair. Her eyes narrowed, and she fixed them on Aethelgard with a glare that could shoot daggers.

The room shifted to bright red. Actaeon noticed that the color drifted down from the top of the cone to replace the previous orange.

"Glad I could assuage your boredom, Gertiz," began Aethelgard. He rapped her knuckles lightly with his cane, as though making a point. "You wouldn't be tied up here if you'd cooperated with my investigation. For all I know, you were working with the killer all along. After all, we already know that you were the least determined to pursue the killer. Or else why would your footprints show that you hesitated while everyone else rushed forward until the moment the killer made their leap?"

A sickly brown color washed down to fill the room.

It made things dim, but not dim enough to see Gertiz lean forward and spit at Aethelgard's feet.

"Such guilt, Gertiz..." goaded Aethelgard. "It reads clear upon your face. I see I must have struck a nerve there. You must have helped kill Kragin. Even if we don't catch the killer, at least we'll have one guilty party for the chopping block." He offered her a thin smile then.

Gertiz struggled against her bindings and kicked out, which shifted her chair.

The room flared red. A dark hue this time, which cast an eerie light upon them all.

"I didn't kill Kragin, you p'kin fool!" spat Gertiz. "I'd not 'ave killed my Warlord! Any guilt I feel is I couldn't run that bitch through with my blade!"

Aethelgard leaned upon his cane and looked up at the point of the ceiling far above. "Your Warlord. I thought all the Warlords in Czeryn were dead. The last Czerynian Warlord died in battle at the side of my friend here – or at least, that's how the story goes."

The color shifted to a deep shade of purple and Gertiz bit her lip until it bled. "Kragin was..." She paused then and shook her head.

"Kragin was going to change that?" suggested Actaeon, breaking his silence. "How? By retaking Czeryn with twenty-seven warriors? You have a place in Raedelle, you know. In Wither. We made a new home for you – it was one of the final things Warlord Berk did before he died."

The room turned a dark shade of pink and she spit this time on Actaeon's boots. "We'd sooner drown in a shit-filled latrine than live under the thumbs of you southern sods."

"And so, you fell in with this Kragin," said Aethelgard. "The man who would be Warlord. To restore that which you all lost."

The pink shifted to a deep, healthy green color that cast a verdant light upon all of their faces.

"If ya knew Kragin, you'd've understood," said Gertiz.

"But a woman who flew from the top of the Northern Descent prevented that," said Actaeon. "She took your leader from you."

"And with that your dreams," added Aethelgard.

The room returned to the deep shade of purple that Actaeon guessed was grief. But just as quickly the room changed to a sickly magenta hue.

"You're angry. So what?" chided Aethelgard. "It's clear you won't do a thing to help us with it." He turned his cobalt eyes on Actaeon and nodded to the door. "Let's go, Engineer. We've more important things to attend to."

When the men turned to walk out, Gertiz cursed under her breath. "Fine!" They paused at the word. "Fine... wait, I'll tell ya what I know. So long as ya do everything in your power ta catch Kragin's killer."

Aethelgard smirked and tapped his cane on the floor several times before turning to face the Czerynian woman once more. "Catching killers is what I do. What can you tell me about his killer?"

The colors shifted again – this time to a yellow-orange.

"A tiny one. Maybe a girl, even," said Gertiz. "Dark blue robes that she pulled the crossbow from. And a hood that hid most of her cursed face. Saw a lock of blond hair though."

The yellow-orange shifted to a light pink color.

Aethelgard shot Actaeon a look and the room shifted in color once more – this time to a dull reddish shade.

"What can you tell us about how she flew from the ledge, Gertiz?" asked Actaeon after offering the Knight Investigator a shrug. "Any details you can remember may be important."

Gertiz shook her head. "Bitch leapt like a bird to air. An' when she opened her arms they got longer. That an' her robes got longer with her arms. Like wings of a bird. She glided right off on 'em."

"And did she do anything before that happened?" asked Actaeon, intrigued. "Did she touch anywhere on her body or make any strange gestures?"

The woman shot him daggers with her eyes. "Are ya deaf? I said she jumped off an' opened her arms. They got longer. That's what I know."

Actaeon shook his head at her response and opened his mouth to ask another question.

He was stalled when Aethelgard tugged at the sleeve of his jacket. "Let's go. We're done here."

"Done here?" repeated Actaeon, confused. "But..."

Aethelgard offered Gertiz an apologetic look. "Perhaps he is deaf, as you suggest."

The Czerynian woman barked a laugh.

The room turned a faint shade of green then.

Actaeon grinned. "Point taken."

"Who would want to kill a Czerynian Warlord?" asked Aethelgard.

The pair of them walked back through the Skyspiral to the eastern side of the Pyramid with Companion Yanelle lagging behind. At Actaeon's suggestion, they were going to visit Shard, the Althean herbalist, in the Terrace of the Stars, a massive, open-air garden that occupied a large portion of the Pyramid's eastern face.

"A Shieldian or an Ajmani? Someone afraid they would come to take their lands back, no doubt," suggested Actaeon.

"I'm afraid it's much simpler than that, my dear engineer." The Knight Investigator tugged at his beard.

"Simpler how?" asked Actaeon.

"You'll see soon enough," was Aethelgard's enigmatic response.

"I do not suppose you could just tell me?" suggested Actaeon.

Aethelgard smiled thinly. "And what would be the fun in that?"

"You have a strange idea of what is fun, Knight Investigator."

"I investigate crime and murder every day. Would you expect anything less?"

They found the Althean herbalist toward the bottom of the Terrace. With a rake, the herbalist battled a thorny garden of hardy plants found along the bluffs of the Thyrian coast. The androgynous gardener turned toward the two men as they approached and regarded them critically with eyes sunken into a mass of wrinkles.

"Best ye be here'n help ol' Shard," said the Althean. "Else, off wit ya!"

"I'm sure a sister of the TriForge wouldn't mind helping a Knight Investigator with his investigation?" said Aethelgard. "My engineer friend here has some questions for you."

"Ain't nowns sister!" snapped Shard, waving the rake toward them threateningly. When the two men didn't leave, Shard lowered the rake and sighed, turning those beady eyes on Actaeon. "All ya do's ask questions, eh? Spit 'em out then. 'Fore I make ya weed this damnable garden."

"We are curious as to the weather yesterday. What can you tell us about the conditions? In particular, we need to know which way the wind was blowing," explained Actaeon with a grin.

Shard squished their eyelids together in the struggle to recall the conditions of the day before. When the Althean's eyes opened, they lifted the rake and pointed. "Out the north. Blew all day like that. Clouds spoke a rain, but none was shown. Just strong wind blowin' south."

Actaeon looked surprised at that. He leaned heavily against his halberd. "A northerly wind... one could not fly into that so easily. The technology used must have been able to overcome it. Interesting..."

"Ain't no bird gwon ta fly 'gainst wind like that," argued Shard. "No point to it. Waste a energy. Birds'll go with the wind or not at all."

Actaeon turned to Aethelgard. "An artifact that could fly into strong winds like that must have had some manner of propulsion."

"Gertiz said the killer had glided. Glided... not flapped wings," mused Aethelgard.

"Aye," said Actaeon. "I wonder if the artifact was similar to the projector orb that Kryo uses," he suggested, mentioning the leader of the Loresworn.

"That's what you're here to figure out," said the Knight Investigator.

Actaeon narrowed his eyes. "Perhaps, next time you might allow me to finish questioning the witness instead of cutting me off?"

Aethelgard settled his shrewd, cobalt eyes on the Engineer. "You'd not have gotten any further with her. Besides, even if you had – she hadn't the eye that you have. A discernment of detail toward artifact technology isn't something that comes naturally to most in Redemption."

"A light... a shape... a noise. All of these things might have provided me a clue to the artifact which, despite any lack of understanding of technology, would have been simple matters to an ordinary observer." Actaeon shook his head and gazed up at the sky.

"Point taken, Engineer," said Aethelgard. "I'll not cut you off in the future."

"Please, do not."

"Out my gardens!" snapped Shard, again waving the rake at them. "I an' got no time fer dis nonsense. Ya got no more questions, den begone! I've work ta do!"

The herbalist turned about and strode off, headed toward the next challenging patch of garden.

They watch as Shard hobbled away on stumpy legs.

"So what does Shard's stride tell you, Knight Investigator?" Actaeon grinned.

"You've got me there, Engineer," said Aethelgard. "I'm as stumped as those legs."

It took the better part of the next day and several dozen tests of miniature models to construct what Actaeon had in mind.

Yanelle and Wave, Actaeon's mercenary friend, were sent in search of supplies from the Open Markets.

Meanwhile, in the workshop, Actaeon put Aethelgard to work helping him sew massive sheets of brightweave together. The material couldn't be cut by normal implements, and so, Actaeon had Aethelgard use the tip of his writheblade to pierce the sheets at intervals so that a thin glass rope could be threaded through to join the brightweave sections together. In addition to being woven together, folds between the brightweave sections would help prevent air from escaping easily.

While the Knight Investigator was so employed, Actaeon set about constructing a frame with help from Lauryn, his engineer-in-training. As she used steam to bend thin bands of light wood to the shapes that Actaeon had drawn up, Actaeon worked on making an investment casting that would form the shape of a sturdy bracket to hold one of Lauryn's light lances. The lances were long pole artifacts that, when activated, could emit an intense orange beam of light that would destroy nigh anything it passed through.

In the past, Lauryn and her Light Lancers had turned the tides of a war with the artifacts. But now, Actaeon intended to use one of the light lances for a completely different purpose – as an engine for flight. Or so he hoped.

The frame was constructed in several rings that could be assembled on-site, and as Lauryn finished each section, she rolled it over to the waiting cart, driven by a boy named Salif, the grandson of the old carter they had used on many occasions.

After pouring the molten metal into the mold, Actaeon set to work on the final component while he waited for it to cool. He lifted his goggles from his eyes and began to sketch out the details. It would be a circular bench with a floor where one's feet would be. The size would allow up to three people to sit comfortably together as the device was in flight. The back of the bench would also double as a railing in case any passengers needed to stand to tend to the lines or the light lance. Actaeon sketched out grab handles periodically and added cleats to the outside for the tying off of ropes.

The next day, when everything was assembled in front of the workshop, quite the crowd gathered to see the strange apparatus that the Prince Engineer was building in the Outskirts. Even the Princess of Raedelle, Eisandre, had come to see her Engineer take flight, accompanied by a contingent of Companions and their infant daughter, Aedwina. She stepped forward to embrace Actaeon and wish him well.

"I think I'll stay on the ground," said Companion Yanelle, looking up at the device skeptically.

The circular passenger carrier sat upon the ground. It was made from woven materials and some light woods that Lauryn had selected to keep the weight at a minimum. To one side of the carrier were the rings of the craft, surrounded by a small fortune in brightweave. The resulting shape looked like a gigantic, inverted cone. At its narrowest point was an opening with a metal bracket ready to accept the device that would power it.

"Well, I'm not missing it for anything in the world," proclaimed Lauryn excitedly. She leapt into the carrier and inserted her light lance into the bracket before closing the latches that would secure it.

Actaeon grinned and gave Eisandre and Aedwina each a kiss before climbing into the carrier to join Lauryn. "Rope minders, to the ready!" he called out. "Everyone stay clear. If this fails to work properly, the wind might drive it in any direction." Thankfully, the air was still at the moment and the skies were clear. It was a good day for this test.

"Best of luck, Engineer," said Aethelgard from where he stood near the edge of the crowd. He tugged on his beard as he leaned heavily on his cane.

"While I appreciate the sentiment, Knight Investigator," said Actaeon, "You must needs be joining us as well."

The Arbiter smirked and removed the lenses from his face to clean them on his vest. "Oh no. I've no need to risk myself on this trial. After all, who would solve the crime if your invention does fail?"

"You needed me to accompany you on the inspection of the crime scene and interrogation of the witness, did you not?" asked Actaeon.

"Precisely," began Aethelgard. "Because you might have observed something that I had n..." He trailed off as he realized Actaeon's point. "I'll join you for the actual flight of course. No need to risk a trial."

"And if something happens to me during the flight? Will you know how to work all the controls?" asked Actaeon with a grin.

Aethelgard replaced his lenses and offered a thin smile in reply before shaking his head and limping over to the carrier to climb within.

"And so, for the second time in known Redemption history will humankind attempt to grace the skies with our presence," announced Actaeon to those gathered. "Lady Lauryn, will you please do the honors?"

"Proudly!" exclaimed the young woman. She touched the pair of activation panels on the light lance that extended horizontally into the brightweave cone. The lance crackled to life and a beam of energy extended into the brightweave. Lauryn began to count.

After she reached eleven, the cone began to lift into the air. By twenty it was nearly vertical.

Lauryn shut off the lance and reset her count to one. The cone began to drift toward the ground slowly.

"We should have created a bracket that allows two lances," said Actaeon.

"If this works, we'll be able to do that quickly," said Lauryn. "Just don't ever mix up which lance is cooling down."

"What would happen if that were to occur?" asked Aethelgard.

Lauryn finished counting to thirty and touched the panels. The lance crackled to life again and filled the air around them with the scent of ozone – their hairs rose up in response. "We would explode," she answered matter-of-factly.

Aethelgard's cobalt eyes widened and he looked back at the ground outside the carrier in consideration. Before he could move, the carrier jerked and he was thrown down onto the bench.

The hot air float lifted into the sky and bounced as the tethers that held them to the ground stakes became taut.

"Give it a few rounds of beam light, Lauryn. I want to make sure we have enough lift before we let out the tether," Actaeon instructed.

"Aye aye, Act," said Lauryn, following his orders.

After the fifth operation of the lance, the ropes were beginning to creak and stretch under the strain.

"Rope minders, release the ropes!" called Actaeon and the ropes tethering the lift cone to the ground were released to hang free from the apparatus.

Actaeon untied one of the three ropes tethering the carrier to the ground and fed it through the two sets of double pulleys that were hooked to the bottom of the carrier and the light lance bracket respectively. The rope was anchored to the ground and ran through the center of the carrier basket to a neat coil under one side of the bench. He tugged the free end of the rope through the last pulley on the bottom and pulled it taut before tying it to one of the inside cleats. The pulley system would give him a five to one mechanical advantage to better control the ascent.

That done, he untied the other two ropes and the lift began to bob to and fro along the single remaining rope.

"Ready?" Actaeon asked his fellow passengers.

"Am I ever!" said Lauryn, beaming. She activated her lance again.

"If I must be," responded a less enthusiastic Knight Investigator.

Actaeon began to untie the knot from the cleat. He left it wrapped around the cleat once for extra friction and let out rope slowly.

The apparatus rose into the air and the gathered crowd gasped. Nothing of the like had ever been witnessed in Redemption – at least not by those currently residing there.

As Actaeon let out more and more rope, the lift continued to rise until it was even with the observation walk along the top of the workshop's vault. And then, short moments later it was above even that. He continued to let out rope until they were about twice the height of the workshop above the ground.

"I can see to The End, Act!" said Lauryn, referring to the tavern at the far end of the Avenue of Glass. "And to the Great Sea on the other side!"

Aethelgard gripped the seat of the bench so hard that his knuckles turned white. "Are we ready then, Engineer?"

"Yes," smiled Actaeon as he waved down to his wife and daughter far below. "Yes, we are."

It took another day to set up the tethered hot air float lift back at the murder scene.

Aethelgard had numerous Knight Arbiters present to act as tenders. They struggled to prevent the cone from sliding down the side of the Pyramid until Actaeon showed them how to tie off the ropes in various places within the murder room.

Once that was done, the process of assembling the lift went more quickly. Starting with the top of the frame and working their way downward, they carefully slid the parts into place within the brightweave skin. When the assembly was completed, the float lift cone hung upside down from its tethers atop the jagged edges of Pyramid's broken northern face. Actaeon was glad he'd decided to make the float skin from brightweave – the material of the Ancients was nearly indestructible and wouldn't tear as it was pushed against the broken fragments of elderstone and shards of elderglass below.

Aethelgard tugged at his beard skeptically and reseated his lenses upon his nose. "What now then?"

"We right it, of course," said Actaeon with a grin. He slid the extra light lance that Lauryn had lent him into the bracket and clamped it into place. "Since the float lift is upside down, we shall need to make sure the hot air doesn't escape until it is righted."

He unfolded a nearby section of brightweave that he'd fashioned for just this purpose. In it he stepped, like a child ready to run a sack race, before shuffling over to the bottom of the cone beside the passenger bench.

Actaeon offered a grin to Aethelgard's arched brow and then disappeared as he pulled the brightweave sack over his head. He coupled that end to the opening of the cone and fastened it in place with a few spring clips.

Aethelgard turned to Yanelle and tugged at his beard. "What in shattered Redemption is he doing?"

The Companion smirked. "Act's got a plan – he always does. You'll see."

Inside the giant brightweave cone, Actaeon interlocked his fingers and stretched them before pulling his goggles down over his eyes. "Here we go," he said to himself as he reached out to grab the two activation areas on the light lance.

The heat that followed and funneled up from the cone toward him was wholly unanticipated, but painfully obvious in hindsight. The blast of hot air singed his hair and eyebrows, nearly causing him to lose count of how long the lance had been on. Once he realized what was happening though, he steeled himself and, even though wave after wave of heat washed over him, he could feel the cone's entrance tilting – which meant that the entire cone must be lifting up as well.

In addition to the incredible heat, there was ozone – a byproduct of the light lance beam. As he breathed in the gas-filled air, he coughed and felt his chest begin to tighten in reaction to it entering his lungs. He bit down on his lip and held his breath.

After the hot air filled his sack, it pushed downward to fill the brightweave cone – offering aerial buoyancy to the lift.

And no sooner than the cone floated to a horizontal orientation did he feel tremendous relief as the hot air and ozone from the light lance's beam began to fill the large volume of the rising structure instead of relentlessly assaulting him. He hazarded a breath and was rewarded with warm, but infinitely more breathable air.

While the cone continued to rise, he undid the clips of the sack until it fell at his feet. He reached a count of twenty lifebeats a moment later and shut off the light lance.

Yanelle stepped forward to steady her charge. "Your Grace, are you alright?" she asked, concern evident in her striking green eyes.

"Aye, Yanelle," said Actaeon with a grin. "Victim to a poorly thought out idea, but nevertheless, I persist."

"And yet, your idea appears to have worked," observed Aethelgard.

"Quickly," said Actaeon as he hopped into the carrier basket. "We ascend at once."

Aethelgard limped over to join him and climbed in himself. "Are you coming?" he asked Yanelle.

"Oh no," she answered. "Somebody has to find you two if you splat into the ground or go flying out to the Great Sea."

"Comforting," answered Aethelgard. "Here, hold this." He handed her his cane and then held tight to the back of the circular bench with a white-knuckled grip. Actaeon activated the light lance again and the basket jerked upward.

The hot air float lift was soon straining against the tethers with the two men dangling beneath it in the carrier. The Knight Arbiters unhooked the tethers at Actaeon's command, leaving the device dangling upward against the final tether that ran up through the center of the basket.

Actaeon wrapped two loops of a safety rope around his waist and tied it off to one of the cleats. Unsteadily, Aethelgard did the same.

"Ready?" asked Actaeon.

"Let's get on with it, Engineer," said the Knight Investigator. "Try not to get us killed."

Actaeon grinned and unhooked the main line from its cleat. With care, he began to let it out through the pulleys, and they started to rise into the air. The ascent hastened further as he activated the light lance again.

The great elderglass face of Pyramid's peak angled away from them as they climbed upward. The midday sun gleamed off one side, throwing up a coruscant veil of light that made them avert their eyes. To the west, the Great Sea stretched far into the distance – an endless expanse of rolling blue waves. To the east, the Underforest stood tall – its tremendous trees jutting upward from the very ruins of the city. To the north, the mountains beyond the former Czerynian Holds loomed like jagged teeth.

It was from that direction that came the wind. It was sudden and unexpected. The speed with which the Pyramid rushed toward them was astounding.

A crack sounded as the brightweave envelope struck the elderglass. Less than a lifebeat later, the carrier basket hit the glass and one of the benches broke free and slid off to the right.

Both men clung to the remainder of the carrier and one another in desperation. In the chaos, Actaeon lost his hold on the rope and the float lift began a runaway, wind-driven ascent up along the slope of the Pyramid.

As they slid along their uncontrolled path on the outside of the Ancient structure, they could see inside the Pyramid clearly. The shocked faces of people climbing the various stairwells near the top of the Skyspiral sped by at an alarming speed as the wind buffeted their backs. Actaeon saw an Arbiter point to them and pull out her whistle to blow it before they'd passed her by as well. The wind pushed them sharply to the right and then they were up above the Song of the Sisters, a restaurant and inn near the top of the Pyramid. Noble men and ladies leapt up from their restaurant tables as the strange device came hurtling up past them. Many of them opened their mouths in a scream that couldn't be heard from the outside. A waiter dropped a tray of drinks on the table in front of one group of nobles, soaking them all in a calamity of broken glass and alcohol. Then they were past the restaurant and sliding their way past personal rooms.

A naked noblewoman powdering her nose in the elderglass wall of her room stumbled backward in shock. In another room, a pair of entangled men in mid-coitus beneath the slanted elderglass wall of their room threw themselves from their bed in terror. After a lifebeat, one of them covered his manhood while the other lifted his hands to hide his face.

Aethelgard laughed. "Bet they didn't expect us to come flying past them!"

"Indeed," said Actaeon with a smirk. "It would be most interesting to be a fly on the wall to hear the conversations this will inspire."

"We'll be a smashed fly against the side of the Pyramid if you don't stop us, Engineer!" reminded Aethelgard. He began to shake Actaeon with the hand that was clutching his jacket, urging him to take action.

"Ah, right," said Actaeon. His eyes drifted down to the rope that was flying through the double pulleys as the wind drove them upward. He thought about squeezing the rope lines together in the center with his fingerless glove-covered right hand, but then thought better of it at seeing how fast the ropes were moving.

At that moment, they cleared the peak of the Pyramid and the wind whipped them back and forth as it pushed relentlessly. Both men experienced vertigo as they watched the massive building fall away beneath their feet.

"I advise action," said Aethelgard.

"We shall certainly have to add a braking mechanism in case this occurs again," said Actaeon as he considered his options to stop the wild ascent.

"A bit late for that, don't we think?"

"Perhaps not," said Actaeon. He had a sudden idea.

Unsheathing his hooked dagger from his belt, he cut through the fabric of his vest on each side of his upper chest between the front opening and the arm holes. He returned the dagger to its sheath and yanked the vest free. "Steady me, Aethelgard."

The Knight Investigator did as instructed, hooking his legs under the bench and clutching the Engineer's jacket on either side.

Steadied thusly, Actaeon leaned forward and carefully looped the fabric of his vest around the four rope sections that were racing through the pulley system. He was careful not to let the vest touch the fast-moving ropes just yet. When he was ready, he pulled the fabric of the vest tight around the ropes and twisted.

There was a snap, and the vest was torn from his hands. The pulley assembly ripped free from the underside of the brightweave sack frame and crashed down through the floor of the carrier, breaking the remainder of the bench assembly in two.

Actaeon nearly fell after it, but Aethelgard yanked him back against him.

Together, they climbed up onto the remainder of their bench until they were straddling it.

"Please remind me never to do anything like this with you again," said the Arbiter. His face was pale. Somehow his lenses were still perched upon his nose.

"At the very least, it has been a major success," said Actaeon, smiling.

"A major success?" blurted Aethelgard. "We've lost half of our seat, were smashed against the Pyramid itself, and now we float untethered above the Avenue of Glass. If we were to fall now…"

"I do not plan on falling. Do you?" Actaeon didn't wait for a reply before he continued. "Perhaps you are correct though – we could have surmised what we learned here without leaving the ground."

"What *did* we learn here?" demanded Aethelgard.

"Birds might not like to fly into the wind, but they take off into it in order to gain more lift," Actaeon explained.

Aethelgard stared at Actaeon for several long lifebeats as though he were an idiot, but then he slowly began to nod. "So you mean to say that the killer flew into the wind to take off and then back in the wind's direction?"

"Precisely," started Actaeon, mimicking the Knight Investigator. "Shard was correct. No bird would fly into a wind like that, but they could use it to gain lift faster, without requiring as much speed while on the ground. And once in the air, they could turn quickly to change direction, gliding upward along Pyramid's slope much as we did."

Aethelgard grabbed Actaeon's shoulder and shook him again. "Nicely done, Engineer. So our killer didn't fly out to the Boneyards after all."

"No. They flew in the exact opposite direction." With that thought, Actaeon unclasped his recurve bow from the back of his jacket and lifted it to gaze through the scope. Using it, he swept the terrain on the other side of the Avenue of Glass. "A nice flat clearing in the Windmoor." He pointed. "Like there. That is where we should look for signs of our killer's landing."

"Agreed," said Aethelgard. "Excellent deduction. But how do we get down?"

"I have an idea," said Actaeon.

"I'm hoping for more than just an idea."

"We shall see if it comes to that."

Normally, Actaeon would have wanted his halberd for something like this, but having left it with Yanelle back at the launch site, there was only one other option. He reached up to release the clasp that held the light lance in place and pulled it down until it rested across his thighs. "Alright, I shall require your writheblade for this."

"Why can't you just use the lance?" asked Aethelgard.

"I would prefer if we did not inadvertently cause our wayward vessel to rise again."

"If you say so." The Knight Arbiter pulled the violently crackling weapon from its ceramic scabbard and carefully handed it to Actaeon.

Actaeon accepted it and placed it so that its hilt was at the end of the light lance. "Would you hold this in place?"

Aethelgard held both the light lance and the hilt of the writheblade in place against Actaeon's thigh.

The Engineer then pulled out a length of glass rope and bound the writheblade securely in place to the lance. When he was satisfied, he lifted the light lance and couched it in his lap. "We had best commence our descent, lest we fly all the way to the Great Sea as Yanelle feared we might."

That said, he lifted the lance and used the writheblade to pierce the brightweave balloon on either side to begin letting air out. Without any recent bursts of the light lance to heat up the air, the apparatus had already stopped rising and was just blowing in a southerly direction. Now that there were extra places for the hot air to escape, the lift started to descend. When he was sure of the rate of descent, he opened up two more holes to double it.

"We shall have to create a more permanent system for descent control flaps before our next flight," said Actaeon, as he looked down toward the ground to try and judge their speed.

"Ha!" snorted Aethelgard. "There won't be a next flight for us. I'll wait for you on the ground in the case that this sort of insanity ever becomes necessary again."

"That is most unfortunate, given that you are now one of the two most experienced air navigators in all Redemption," said Actaeon with a grin.

They approached the Windmoor rather quickly. Actaeon unlashed the writheblade and handed it back to the Knight Investigator who muffled its incessant crackling by sliding it back into its ceramic scabbard. The expanse of the plain was growing larger and larger as they rushed toward it. The wind was beginning to push them a bit westward now in addition to their southward trajectory, bringing them closer to the strange and varied ancient statues and clustered rock formations of the Stone Gardens.

Actaeon lifted the light lance up and activated it to slow their descent.

The wind carried them closer to the elderstone sculptures as their impact with the Windmoor was postponed.

"Get ready to leap clear from the float just before we impact," said Actaeon.

Aethelgard grunted, but perched himself up on his good left leg to be ready to do as the Engineer instructed.

Just before the balloon struck the ground, Actaeon tossed the light lance to the side and both men leapt clear of the apparatus.

Actaeon rolled onto his side while Aethelgard landed on his bad leg and cried out in pain before flopping onto his back.

The remainder of the float lift's bench broke in half when it hit the ground. The brightweave bubble continued to drag it until it wrapped around a nearby cylindrical statue some three hundred paces from them. The wooden substructure beneath the brightweave bent and cracked.

"Shattered Redemption! My leg. I landed right on my bad leg!" shouted Aethelgard, tears rolling down his cheeks from the pain.

Actaeon rushed to the Knight's side and felt his hurt leg, causing Aethelgard to pull himself up to a seated position to shove him away angrily.

"Darkest Hour take you! What are you doing?" he cursed.

"Just checking to see if it is broken. It is not. You must have just strained it," explained Actaeon. Reaching into the inside pocket of his jacket, he withdrew a half-through vial and handed it to the Knight Investigator. "Drink this – it should help the pain."

"You always carry that with you in case you bust up an old man's leg after flinging him over the Pyramid?" griped Aethelgard.

"Precisely," responded Actaeon as he fell back onto his elbows beside the Arbiter and pulled his goggles up to rest on his forehead.

Aethelgard regarded him skeptically, but popped the cork and quaffed the medicine anyway.

In the distance, the fabric of the brightweave fluttered violently against the stones. The sun started to set to the west, stretching long shadows from the stones onto the plain before them.

After some time had gone by, Aethelgard laughed. "I haven't had that much fun in cycles."

"That is the drug speaking," said Actaeon with a grin.

Aethelgard slapped Actaeon on the back. "Maybe so, but it still stands true."

"So you will go on the next flight with me after all?" asked Actaeon.

Aethelgard gave Actaeon a playful shove. "Don't push your luck, young man. Now help me up and let's go see what remains of your flying machine."

After Actaeon helped him up, Aethelgard leaned heavily on his left shoulder and the two men walked toward the looming elderstones.

"Stop!" commanded Aethelgard when they were but halfway there.

Actaeon halted and arched a brow. "What is it?"

"This way," said the Investigator enigmatically. He yanked Actaeon to the west, using his companion as a crutch.

The Arbiter led the way into the field of stones, weaving the way from shadow to light and from light to shadow. And when he stopped and leaned heavily upon his companion's shoulder to gaze upward, Actaeon gasped at what he saw.

Impaled atop the sharp point of a conical elderstone pillar was a winged figure. She was a slight woman wearing a simple woven shift that was fastened around her waist with a hide belt. Her body was locked in the fetal position around the spike where it entered her belly and an expression of excruciating pain was frozen upon her features. One of her shoes was missing and in her hand was held a crossbow in a white-knuckled death grip. Her scalp was clean-shaven, but her features were clearly Shieldian. Below her body, the stone was stained red with her lifeblood, which ran down to a dried pool at its base.

The most shocking part of the scene though, were the shimmering wings that extended out on either side of her body. They protruded from an artifact backpack that was strapped onto her shoulders and hips. A rainbow of colors reflected from elements on each wing, glimmering in the sunlight like the scales of a fish as they rippled in the wind.

"Poor girl," said Aethelgard. "She tried so hard to kill herself after ending up in this predicament, but to no avail."

"How do you know?" asked Actaeon, bewildered.

"Observe how worn the fingers of her left hand are." Aethelgard pointed up with his free hand. "She worked them raw trying to pull the stirrup of the crossbow to load another bolt. In the end, she didn't have the strength. With this sort of injury, it might've taken her a long time to die."

"Circumstances brought to her a just end then," said Actaeon.

"I'm not so certain," said the Knight Investigator. "If my suspicions are correct, it was likely that she was justified in this killing."

"If it was justified, then why try to solve this murder?" asked Actaeon, genuinely confused.

"Justified or not, it stands against the laws of the Pyramid," he explained. "There is only one acceptable manner in which to resolve such conflicts, and that is in a declared duel, in the public eye, under the supervision of a Knight Arbiter. Allowing a violent conflict resolution in any other way invites war, combat, and assassination to the neutral territory of the Pyramid beyond what the Order of Arbiters could ever hope to control. And thus, the killer must be punished."

"That makes sense," said Actaeon. "In either way, it appears that a punishment is no longer necessary."

"The public must still have an answer to this case," insisted Aethelgard. "Here, help me get her down from there."

The stars had come out by the time they managed to bring the dead killer down.

It had taken Actaeon some time to pull out some of the broken support structure from the brightweave balloon and fashion a ladder from it.

It took even longer to dislodge the corpse, frozen in rigor as it was, from the elderstone. It was an unpleasant operation that Actaeon had to conduct entirely on his own, given Aethelgard's injury. He'd been around death plenty of times, but handling a body like this was different and markedly disturbing.

When the dead killer was finally on the ground, Aethelgard hobbled over to inspect her body. On it, he found an artifact and a folded note.

Once he was done reading it, he handed it to Actaeon. "We have somewhere we need to go in the morning."

After he finished reading, Actaeon offered him a somber look and nodded.

The next morning, the unlikely pair found themselves in the Open Markets outside of the Pyramid. Aethelgard leant more heavily on his cane than the previous day as they traced their way between the colorful stalls and past noisy shoppers hauling wares and haggling over prices.

Actaeon unfolded the note again to review it. It read:

Unira,

If you're reading this letter, then I have failed.

My hope was to make sure that history could never repeat. The artifact I found was to be the key. But, alas, it was not to be. If our detractor ever does come to power, then promise my fallen soul that you'll go somewhere far, far away.

What I did, I did for you. Please remember that.

I'm so very sorry...

-Anchelle

After a quick stop at Grameera's shop, Actaeon's old blacksmith friend told them where to find an Unira in a small tent near the Warrens where she sold pottery. Grameera insisted that they stay for a too-warm ale to toast her late husband, Balin. Both men gulped it down with forced smiles and thanked her before heading on their way.

The young woman sat beneath a low tent in a deep-seated chair before a table covered with a variety of pottery bowls and bottles. Her features were clearly Shieldian and she had ear-length black hair and curious dark brown eyes. She wore a simple brown shift.

"Might I interest you gentlemen in a carafe? Or perhaps some bowls?" she asked, flashing them a smile stacked with faux charm.

"Unira, I presume?" began Aethelgard. He leaned forward heavily on his cane to inspect the wares and the girl. "Your back is broken. I didn't know."

"Yes, I..." she paused, unsure at first what to say. "Why would you... Uh. How do you know that? All of it."

"I am Knight Investigator Aethelgard, with the Order of Arbiters," he said, placing a hand on his chest. "And this is my associate, Actaeon. He is helping me with an investigation. Your condition is obvious by the dirt at the bottom of your dress, the size of your biceps, and the fresh dirt under your fingernails. Not to mention your lack of ability to hold posture and the design of your chair."

At the mention of the Order of Arbiters, Unira's eyes fell to her lap and she brushed a lock of hair from her face. "Then Anchelle is caught, or worse?"

"It is my deep regret to inform you that both are true," explained Aethelgard. He pushed his lenses up along his nose as he regarded her. "Anchelle was to be apprehended for her crime, but, in finding her, we discovered that she had died. I'm sorry for your loss. She was your lover, no?"

Unira's eyes filled with tears and she tried to hide her face against her right shoulder.

"How could you possibly have ascertained that?" asked Actaeon, incredulous.

"Why, it is quite simple, my technically minded friend," said Aethelgard. He turned his head toward his companion and lowered his voice to give Unira a moment to take in the news. "The signs were everywhere. In the note, where Anchelle lingered on her lover's name with her hand, taking the time to get it perfect. It was also neater than the rest of the words in the note, because she took special care to get it right. There are a number of observations to be gained from the handwriting. The deep regret she felt when writing that she failed and the anger she felt as she wrote about their detractor was made with more pressure that cut deeper into the parchment. On the other hand, the fear that she felt as she told Unira to go far away and the sadness in the final words was left with wispy, lighter strokes. Not to mention that Unira here blushed when her partner's name crossed her lips."

Actaeon arched a brow and looked back toward the young woman.

Unira used the sleeve of her shift to wipe the tears from her eyes before she looked back up at the two men and nodded. "The Arbiter speaks truth. She and I are... were lovers. I cannot say that I'm surprised. I warned her against this foolish task, but she insisted. Can you tell me, at least, did she succeed?"

Aethelgard's lips curled into a sad smile and he nodded. "Kragin is dead."

At his words, Unira's head fell back and she clutched both of her hands to her chest. "A weight has been lifted from my heart. Thank you, Knight Arbiter."

Actaeon offered her the note and the artifact, which she accepted.

She clutched the artifact to her chest. It was a palm-sized, metallic disc with a hexagon of prismatic elderglass at the center. Holding it brought tears to her eyes again. "I can't thank you enough for bringing this to me."

"It would be thanks enough if you allowed me to design you a chair with wheels," said Actaeon. "You could use it to propel yourself without having to crawl or carry yourself on your arms. I can send a wagon to come pick you up and bring you to my workshop in the Outskirts for a fitting."

Unira smiled sadly at him. "You must be the Prince Engineer that I've heard about. I'd not normally take you up on such an offer, but I've heard of the things that you can do. I'd be a fool not to." She spread both hands to gesture at the marketplace around them.

"It will be done then," said Actaeon. "In return, I would ask that you keep me apprised of any issues with the device and whether there are any improvements you would wish."

Unira nodded. "Thank you."

"We shall let you be then, to mourn your loss," said Aethelgard, tugging Actaeon's sleeve.

"Before you go," started the Shieldian. "May I tell you our story? The story that drove Anchelle to kill that evil man? It is important that you know... that she was a good person."

Aethelgard paused and nodded. "I believe I know most of it already, but I would like to hear some of the details directly from you to assess the veracity of my conclusions."

Unira set the note and artifact upon her lap and began to recount her story.

"Anchelle and I were both from Rust," she began. "We were the closest of friends as children, growing up together with the lessons of Shield, working in my parents' pottery shop, and learning blades from Anchelle's parents, who were soldiers. It was a simple life, but a good one, and I loved it. It wasn't until we began to come of age as young women that we began to realize something was wrong.

"Our parents both started to daydream aloud about who we would marry to strengthen our households. It left a knot in my stomach thinking about how it would change everything and that I'd not be able to spend so much time with my dear friend. I didn't know what to do though. It was Anchelle who took the first step – she was always the strong one. She brought me to an old, rusted structure where we used to play fort as young children. There she told me that she loved me, not just as a friend, but as the person she wanted to spend the rest of her life with. At first, I didn't understand what she was implying. I loved her too, and I felt a growing attraction to her, but Shieldians are duty-bound to pair off as men and women in order to produce the next generation of warriors to fight for our people. Anything else is seen as a failure of that effort, and so, a relationship between two girls would never be accepted in our Dominion."

"So you ran away together to the Underforest," said Aethelgard.

Unira and Actaeon both looked at him, surprised.

"An easy deduction," said the Knight Investigator. "You both have discoloration and scarring on your feet and legs and in that case, on your forearm," he said, pointing. "Caused, no doubt, by jungle rot from your extended time there, coupled with poor nutrition and cleanliness. Plus, it was the obvious close place to flee to, and the location you were likely abducted by the Czerynians and sold into slavery, given their presence in the Underforest at the time as the Children's Protectors."

"We survived there alone for many months," nodded Unira. "We built a small tree house, held our own joining ceremony, and learned to hunt and snare animals. But in the end, the rains of the monsoon season were too much. Our tree house wasn't able to withstand the torrential downpours. After it collapsed, we began to struggle with being constantly wet, often sick, and with never enough food. When I was out checking snares one day, I came across the band of hunters and decided to approach them. It was stupid, but I was little more than a child, plus miserable and desperate. In my mind, I'm not sure what I'd hoped for. I had nothing to offer them in trade. But I had never encountered anyone before outside of the safety of Shield.

"These hunters were nothing like that. They took me captive immediately, bound me, and made me do all the work at their campsites as they continued onward, away from our home in the jungle. I came to learn they were Czerynians – the boogeymen that I'd heard about who captured children, and even lost adults, and made slaves of them. I never expected that they'd be in the Underforest, but I learned that these ones were travelers from a place called Temple, where they had finished serving a watch over the Underforest. The men, and some of the women even, joked about using me, but there were two women among them who kept everyone from doing so. They told the other Czerynians that I would be more valuable if they didn't do that. At one point, one of the men grew frustrated and tried to take advantage of me in the night, but one of the women fought him and ended up crippling his weapon arm."

"That is awful that you had to live like that, and were taken away from your partner," said Actaeon.

"Yes, it was," said Unira. "I'd never before lost all hope. I shouldn't have though."

"Anchelle was captured following you then?" asked Aethelgard.

"Hold on," said Actaeon. "How could you know they were both Czerynian slaves?"

"You mean aside from it being the entire motive behind the crime?" asked Aethelgard with a knowing smirk. "When we found Anchelle, she was missing a shoe. Did you notice anything about her foot?"

Actaeon thought for a moment, and then shook his head.

"Czerynian slaves are marked – typically on their feet," he explained. "I noticed the tattoo on Anchelle's foot immediately, a pattern undoubtedly belonging to her former owner. Unira here is wearing simple sandals, and so you can see the markings on her feet where she sits."

Actaeon leaned forward to peek over the table full of pottery and noticed that Unira's feet were indeed tattooed with a pattern of triangles. "I see."

"That's how I concluded the killer was justified in the killing as well. Kragin was one of your captors, was he not?" Aethelgard tugged his short beard and turned his attention back to the Shieldian.

"You are quite the observer, Knight Arbiter Aethelgard," said Unira.

"Knight Investigator," he corrected. "My job is to observe."

"Yes, Kragin was the leader of the group that captured me, a Shield Warden, they called him," continued Unira. "And not five days after I'd been captured, the same Czerynian woman who had protected me against rape caught Anchelle tracking us through the Underforest. They bound her too and tried to make both of us serve them. When Anchelle refused, they beat her. I convinced them to leave her be and worked twice as hard to make their travels easier. While Anchelle was kept bound, I worked to set up their camp, cook their food, clean their clothing, and break their camp at the beginning of the next day. Anchelle was furious with me for it, but I couldn't bear to let them hurt her again, so I did my best to make them happy. Often she was kept gagged, but in the rare moments that I got to speak with her, Anchelle would tell me of her plans to escape and urge me to steal a knife for her. I was too scared though. I didn't have the courage of my Anchelle. She would keep fighting no matter what, but all I could imagine was the horror of having to watch them kill her – take her from me.

"And so, they took us like that all the way through the ruins to Craters. I overheard them speaking once that they wanted to sell us far away from Shield to prevent someone we knew from ever encountering us again. Once arrived, we were both sold off and I didn't see her for cycles after that. A terribly mean man bought me and made me his wife. He was handsome for a man, and I did my best to fit into my new role. His other wives explained to me that if I did not give myself to him fully, I would not be treated kindly. And so, I tried... I really tried. But when the night came that he decided to bed me, I couldn't... couldn't do it. That was not for him. It was only for Anchelle. My refusal triggered his anger, and he beat me so badly that he broke my back. I still remember the feeling of his boot slamming into my back – the sharp blast of pain that travelled up to my skull and caused my ears to ring. It was the last time I felt my legs.

"His other wives took care of me and nursed me back to health. After that, he was not interested in me. He'd make me lie in the corner and throw me table scraps like a dog. I was in charge of cleaning the floor and massaging his feet when he came home. I did this for cycles. During that time, he killed two of his other wives in rages that he fell into – there had been five wives in total, including me. I started to recognize when he was close to his trigger point, and I'd find something to do well away from him. It kept me alive."

"Until Anchelle rescued you," said Aethelgard.

"Need I even tell the story?" asked Unira.

"Please do," said the Knight Investigator. "There are details I wish to hear if I've gotten the truth of."

"Anchelle had escaped her enslavement within weeks," she continued. "But it took her many cycles to find me and formulate a plan for my rescue. My master was eating his evening meal while we served him. I had just finished filling a basin with warm water and slid it over so he could soak his feet when I noticed the water had turned red. When I looked up, there she was, my Anchelle. The man who had broken my back and so tormented me all those cycles was staring down at a bolt that protruded from his chest. Anchelle reloaded the crossbow and had the other two women move to the corner and lie on their stomachs, where she bound and gagged them. After that, she hugged and kissed me, and wept about what had been done to me. I felt a relief wash over me that I didn't know would ever be possible again in my life.

"'I'm here for you, Neeri,' she said. 'I'm so very sorry I couldn't stop him from hurting you.'

"After I reassured her that it wasn't her fault, she set the remainder of her plan into action. She loaded me into a wheelbarrow and emptied a sack of potatoes atop me until I was well and buried. Then she rolled me away. When we reached the Boneyards, she rolled me a ways into the ruins until it became too rough, then she pulled me out and bound me onto her back. And thus, my brave, strong Anchelle bore me off into the wreckage of Redemption and away from our tormentors. It took us days journeying like this, but Anchelle had found places for us to camp out at intervals all throughout the ruins where she had stashed some food for us.

"Four days into our journey, Anchelle was knocked from her feet and we both tumbled to the ground as the very earth beneath us shook. A tremendous blue sphere expanded to our north – from whence we came. It grew to fill the entire sky over Czeryn and then shattered into a million glittering pieces that rained to the ground. We'd later learn that the blue sphere had destroyed all of the Czerynians and their slaves. Anchelle had come to rescue me not a moment too soon. Had she taken any longer, then I would have been annihilated with the rest of my tormentors.

"Eventually, we found ourselves in the shadow of Pyramid. From there we made our way to the Warrens, where we hid and celebrated being back in one another's arms. When word trickled to us that the Czerynians were dead, we had even more cause to celebrate. Anchelle helped me open up this shop. We thought we were free at last.

"That was, until Anchelle heard from her connections in the Warrens that our former captor, Kragin, was bringing together scattered Czerynians to try and restore the Dominion that had taken so much from us. I tried to talk her out of it, but in the end, I knew it was futile. My Anchelle would never rest until this threat to us was eliminated. She showed me an artifact she had found more than a cycle ago in the Boneyards while searching for places for us to camp safely during our escape.

"The flying suit," said Actaeon.

"That's right," said Unira, before continuing. "Before she left, I told her that she didn't have to do this – that she could just stay here with me and hide. The words she said next still hang in my mind like she said them just a lifebeat ago: 'We shall never be free to live our lives so long as men who would take everything from us exist. And that is why I must kill him.'

"I didn't know what to say, and so I wished her luck and sent her off with love. But how I wish now that I had argued with her. I would have told her that there were other heroes in this world and that I needed mine at my side. I know she could not have accepted that, but I might've tried harder. I know that now." There were tears in her dark brown eyes.

"She killed him in the end," said Actaeon. "To protect you."

"Yes, she did. And in doing so, left me forever alone," she spoke through a sob.

Actaeon reached out to touch her shoulder and she placed a grateful hand atop his as she cried.

Aethelgard pointed to the artifact in her lap. "The artifact she stole from Kragin. It had meaning for you both, didn't it? What was so special about it?"

Actaeon arched a brow at his companion.

"What?" asked Aethelgard. "The fibers on it are obviously from Kragin's tunic."

"Of course they are," said Actaeon. "In the future, I shall have to pay better attention to tiny fibers on artifacts that I find."

"I should certainly hope so!" Aethelgard spat back.

Unira wiped the tears from her eyes and lifted the disc into the air in one palm. When she waved her other hand over the elderglass prism in the center, it lit up in a bright blue luminance and two life-sized figures appeared in the air floating above it.

Several nearby bystanders gasped. A few people fled while more gathered around behind the two men to watch.

The two figures were Unira and Anchelle, Actaeon realized. Anchelle's projection knelt before Unira's and held her partner's hands within her own.

"I love you to the ends of this world," pronounced the projection. "And I will ever be your shield."

Unira swiped her hand over the prism and the projections disappeared. "I love you to the ends of this world," she whispered. She regarded the device in her palm for several long moments, in disbelief that she was holding it. "Kragin took this from me after he captured me in the Underforest. I'd never thought I would see it again."

The crippled girl smiled sadly up at Actaeon and Aethelgard. "This was her final gift to me. I'm free!"

Capsule

CTAEON RAN HIS FINGER ALONG the smooth stone over the name. 'Hargum,' it read simply – and he flashed back to the Captain's lifeless eyes looking up at him. All of their names were listed there. *All or none, Prince Engineer. We'll be going.* He could hear the warbander Captain's voice in his head as if it were yesterday – as if it hadn't been nearly two years ago.

The simple monolith of carved names had been raised at the edge of the Open Markets. It was appropriate, given that the men and women listed there had given their lives so that the allied forces trapped in the Underforest could break free and go on to help liberate Pyramid and end the Second Invasion War.

All hands had been lost that day from Raedelle's Eastern Rim warband and the Keeper 2nd Division. Actaeon's mind was back there suddenly – hiding beneath the Czerynian Schiltron shield turtle. He could still remember the clattering crash as the Keeper Knights –

The hand on his shoulder brought him back to reality.

"Too many good men and women – gone too soon," said a familiar voice.

"Aye," said Actaeon with a sad grin. He turned to face Aethelgard, who peered through his lenses down his crooked nose at him. "And no matter what logic tells me, my mind always wanders to whether I should have been there in their place, or at the very least, stood beside them."

"Nonsense," said Aethelgard with a smile. "They died so that you and I could solve all the problems of the world. And that's just what we're going to do."

"Oh?" asked Actaeon, arching a brow.

Aethelgard clapped a hand on his shoulder and guided him back toward the Pyramid. "That's right. We've got a missing person to find. And intuition tells me I need an engineer for this case."

The Song of Sisters had been completely remodeled since the last time Actaeon had been there. New cerulean blue carpets lined the halls and the walls had been thoroughly scrubbed. It was almost as though a battle for life and death hadn't ever been fought there. And yet, it still was as fresh in the Prince Engineer's mind as if it were yesterday.

Aethelgard led him to a room that was only several doors down from Actaeon's old room. There he paused.

Actaeon's eyes were immediately drawn to the dried blood that had soaked into the otherwise deep blue carpet before the door. He felt himself freeze there as the memories poured back in. Memories of stacked bodies filling the hall.

The Knight Investigator placed a gentle hand upon his shoulder. "Perhaps this was too much to ask. I am sorry."

Actaeon grinned and shook his head, pushing the thoughts to the back of his mind. "Nonsense. When confronted with one's fear, we must face it head on. Go on then. Show me the rest."

Aethelgard nodded and squeezed the other man's shoulder before he withdrew the key from his cloak and inserted it into the lock. There came a buzz, followed by a low whirring sound as the door unlocked. He slid it open and led the way inside.

The room inside was typical of those in the Song. The far wall consisted entirely of slanted elderglass that was the outer wall of Pyramid's pinnacle. Beneath it was a bed that was splashed with blood. The blood had stained the new carpet in various places around the room, amidst the furniture, which was strewn about chaotically. Only one nightstand was upright. On it was a cylindrical artifact that had been cleaved in two. Both halves were covered in blood.

Actaeon made his way over to it and squatted to get a better look.

It was made from a shiny black artifact metal. There were lenses inset into its curved walls at intervals along the body, with two larger elderglass windows at the top and bottom ends that had been shattered during the artifact's destruction. Inside had been arrays of smaller lenses. Actaeon could discern from the few that still remained attached to the housing halves that they had been cleverly arranged to focus the light onto an assemblage of hair thin glass ropes that were attached to a black, rubbery disc.

"Have you ever seen an artifact like that, Engineer?" asked Aethelgard.

"Plenty of them," admitted Actaeon. "Though none so perfectly divided."

"What do they typically do?" asked Aethelgard.

Actaeon shrugged as he narrowed his emerald eyes to inspect the artifact more closely. "Of that, I can only conjecture, for I have never found one in working condition – at least not that I was able to discern. If I were to guess, this artifact could look at scenes in all directions about it – perhaps to make decisions on its environment, or perhaps to record scenes around it. The elderglass ends may have allowed a projection to be emitted. Is it possible that someone destroyed this artifact in order to erase something that it had recorded? Perhaps they killed someone in this room who stood in their way? Or alternatively, they destroyed the artifact in order to erase the evidence of the murder that took place here?"

Aethelgard pulled at his beard and considered the idea. "Hmm. And to your knowledge is there any possibility that a body could be hidden inside?"

Actaeon laughed aloud at that thought. Then he noticed that the Knight Investigator was looking at him in seriousness. "Oh, I thought you were joking. My apologies. No – not that I have ever encountered. Though, in my experience, I am loathe to discount any possibility, however strange."

"On that matter, we could not agree more. Didn't you once encounter an artifact that trapped Raedelle's Prince inside of it?" asked Aethelgard.

Actaeon considered the suggestion. "That is true. However, the artifact was much larger than the Prince was. Never in my travels have I encountered an artifact that could conceal something larger than itself. Although, if it were some sort of transport mechanism..."

Aethelgard shook his head and began to pace the room, scrutinizing every corner. "Could the artifact have caused someone's blood to scatter about the room like this? If the person was reduced to their component parts, for instance? Would it be possible for nothing to be left except for the instances of blood spatter that we see?"

Actaeon straightened and bumped his goggles against the slanted elderglass wall. He rubbed his forehead in pain. "One thing that is true is that I sincerely doubt this was split in two here."

"Aye," seconded Aethelgard. "No space to swing a sword. I've already deciphered that much. No, the artifact was split here." He pointed to the top of the other nightstand with his cane.   The nightstand had found its way to the center of the room, where it now lay on its side. A deep groove had indeed been cut into the wood surface.

"The assailant scooped up the pieces and laid them there," said Aethelgard. "Interestingly enough, it was placed atop blood that was already there. The blood that is on the artifact itself was old – you can tell because it is significantly darker and the stains have begun to crack if you observe closely."

"Curious," said Actaeon as he backed up against the door to survey the entirety of the room.

"Precisely," said Aethelgard. "Almost as though they wanted attention paid to its destruction."

Actaeon shook his head, "No."

"No?"

"No, regarding your question from earlier," he clarified. "I do not believe the artifact could have feasibly scattered blood in such a manner. At least, not in a way that could have left blood outside of the room like that, as well. It is almost as if it was –"

"Poured?" interrupted the Knight Investigator. "Yes, it most certainly has been. Observe, if you will, the spatter patterns of the blood in each location. They were not created by blood flying off of an individual during a struggle. Note the spines that extend from each spattering of lifeblood. Generally, they will extend to their lengthiest in a position directly opposite that of the impacting blow which caused them. This is often so consistent that the full sequence of combat might therefore be discerned. But not in this case."

"Ah yes," said Actaeon. "I see now. All these patterns show a radial symmetry, as though they were poured from a container and fell directly downward. I imagine the stains in the hall outside will show the same thing?"

"Actually, that is the one exception," said Aethelgard. "The pattern of the stain shows that it was thrown against the door, almost in haste. So what does all this tell you, my observant Engineer?"

"That the person was not killed here?" guessed Actaeon. "Perhaps they were killed elsewhere and their blood was brought here to make this look like the scene of a crime."

"Very good. Or, that they bled themselves to create this scene and therefore the appearance that they'd been killed," said Aethelgard. "Which could explain why they splashed the blood against the doorframe at the last – perhaps they were nearly caught in the act and panicked. And all of this is precisely the reason we are searching for a missing person, because until we find a body, we don't know that a murder has, in fact, been committed."

"So whose room was this then?" asked Actaeon. "I assume you already know more about the full story here?"

"Indeed, I do, my perceptive friend. This is the room of none other than Vichaen vor Steubick, Niwian artifact hunter and nephew of the Lord Protector himself. You see, the Lord Protector is very interested to see my Order solve this case quickly. In fact –"

Aethelgard's line of thought was interrupted as he noticed a glint from beneath the sheets. He pulled them back to reveal a metal cloak clasp. When he lifted the clasp, it glinted in the sunlight. It was cast in the likeness of a blazing sun.

"Well, that changes things," said Actaeon.

"Indeed, it does," said the Knight Investigator, turning the ornament over in his hand. "The blazing sun of the Allfather. And in the room of a known artifact hunter."

"There is your motive," suggested Actaeon.

"Perhaps..." mused Aethelgard. "Come. Let us speak with the proprietor."

The owner of the Song was an old woman named Cassanthia. She had the angular features of a Shieldian, though she wore the overly ornamented and impractical dress of a Niwian lady.

She thumbed through her records book as Actaeon and Aethelgard waited.

"Yes," she said finally. "A Keeper Knight did find comfort with us. A Nathis Carrillum. By my recollection, she had dark skin and armor of impeccable ornamentation. It would please me if where you came about this information did not come out."

"Most certainly, Cassanthia," promised Aethelgard. "You've my word."

She smiled coldly at him and strode off.

He turned to Actaeon. "Come. We've a suspect to locate. I'll have an Arbiter deliver the artifact to your workshop for later analysis."

The line of questioning led them out of the Pyramid and along the Avenue of Glass, where they stumbled, quite literally, into a bit of luck.

As they neared the entrance of the ramshackle tavern known as The End, where they intended to continue the line of questioning with its proprietor, a figure burst out of the doors and nearly bowled over Aethelgard.

The Knight Investigator stumbled and his cobalt eyes lit up in recognition.

"Excuse me!" he called out to the woman.

"Apologies," the dark-skinned woman said over her shoulder as she rushed off. She was clad in ornamented armor of silver and gold, inlaid at the pauldrons and vambraces with colored facets. Her black hair was pulled back into a tight braid, revealing the shaved sides of her head, one of which was marred with an old arc of a scar, the skin drawn tight about it. The cloak across her shoulders was held in place by a simple leather thong.

"I mean to speak with you," said Aethelgard.

"Can't you see I'm in a rush?" she snapped without slowing her pace or even turning.

"Aren't you missing this, Nathis?" Aethelgard held up the cloak clasp he had found.

The Keeper Knight spun and her eyes widened in recognition.

Without another word, Nathis assumed a battle posture and slid her sword free of its scabbard.

Actaeon had a small moment to notice that the arming sword was inlaid with the same-colored facets as her armor. He lowered his halberd to stave off her advance, but she deftly sidestepped it and, with her off hand, grabbed the shaft and yanked it sharply.

The Prince Engineer was pulled along with his halberd and met her extended arm, which knocked him onto his back so hard against the elderglass that the breath was knocked from his lungs.

Above him, he heard a buzz, a crackle, and then a snap.

The Keeper Knight clattered to the surface of the Avenue beside him, her sword cut neatly in two. She still held the hilt of the sword – the tip of its remaining blade glowing red. Before she could lift it, the tip of Aethelgard's cane pinned her hand to the ground and he knelt on her shoulder to prevent her from moving.

Aethelgard made a point to slide his crackling writheblade back into its ceramic sheath as the Keeper squirmed and winced beneath him. "Now, now. It's not very nice how you treated my friend, is it? I do believe you owe him an apology." Then, with a practiced maneuver, he flipped her over, pulled both of her arms behind her back, and knotted a glass rope tightly about her wrists.

He waited a long moment, tapping his foot impatiently next to her head.

"No?" The Knight Investigator yanked his quarry unceremoniously to her feet. "I guess you can think on it then, while we take you back to the Pyramid for questioning about why your missing clasp was found at the scene of a crime in the Song of the Sisters. Don't worry – a representative of the Niwian Dominion will be contacted on your behalf."

Actaeon gasped and coughed as he climbed to his feet and struggled to catch his breath.

"You alright, Engineer? Looks like you got the air knocked out from your bellows there."

"Aye," said Actaeon with a grin. "I shall be fine."

"Right then," said Aethelgard. He gestured to Nathis, giving her a small shove forward. "Lead the way. will you?"

The following day brought one of the first heavy rains of the monsoon season. The patter of big droplets on the stone vault above echoed throughout the spacious workshop.

The guts of the bloody artifact were laid out on one of the many workbenches.

And there Actaeon sat, trying to make sense of the bundle of glass wires.

The interrogation had led nowhere. The Keeper Knight admitted that she stayed at the Song, but she adamantly denied everything else. Thankfully, the victim was the nephew of the Niwian Lord Protector, and the Niwians were the Dominional patrons for the Keepers – although many saw it as the other way around. Whatever the case, with the Niwians calling for the investigation, it meant that the Arbiters were free to hold Nathis Carrillum for a longer period of time while they searched for more hard evidence.

That was where Actaeon now came in. He had suggested that the artifact itself might contain the evidence they were looking for, or at least some clue. The optics were what led him to believe that possibility. The artifact had sat in the room in the Song during whatever violence had taken place. Arrays of lenses were positioned at intervals all around the cylinder like tiny eyes facing every direction. And so, if those tiny eyes had recorded any of the proceedings – an ability he'd seen before with other artifacts amongst the ruins, then he might be able to access those recordings. However, this artifact was utterly inoperable in its current state.

There were several simple artifact projectors of various styles in the workshop which he had collected over the years. If he could figure out a way to input the core of the broken artifact into one of the working ones, then perhaps he could see what its eyes had seen.

After opening several of the projector artifacts and finding nothing that could be used, he finally found one that might work. It had a black disc of its own that looked very similar to the one to which the bundle of glass fibers was attached.

With a grin, Actaeon used a small, wooden pry tool to work the disc loose. Once it was out of the socket, he inserted the one from the crime scene artifact. Then he touched the symbol to activate it.

A transparent scene rose from the top polished surface of the replacement projector artifact and shortly filled the space above the workbench before him. It was flickering in a sickly manner, but the scene was clear. It was a view of the ruins of Redemption from high up in the air. The mammoth trees of the Underforest sprouted from the technology of the Ancients. Beyond it, the pale red architecture of Rust framed even the largest of the jungle trees. It was the view through the slanted window of the room up in the Song.

On impulse, Actaeon stood and walked around the artifact. The projected image changed as he moved, as though he were rotating in the room itself. Everything in there was intact – all the furniture in the correct places and no blood anywhere to be seen.

It also didn't appear that anyone was in the room.

Perhaps the image was static – a snapshot in time. Actaeon tried tapping the symbol on the front of the artifact, then tried waving his hands in front of it, an action he'd seen have an effect on many different pieces of Ancient technology.

He frowned, but then leaned forward to look more closely.

It was small, but he could make it out, just barely. Through the slanted window of the Pyramid, birds fluttered by. Then the projection flickered and the birds started again from their original location in the sky.

Actaeon grinned and paced about the workbench in a slow circle, watching for anything else of interest. Inside the room was completely still. But when he got within view of the door, he noticed something just before the flicker.

The door began to slide open. He thought he could make out a brief flash of red, but then the image was already reset and the door was closed once more. He leaned forward and squinted to try and make out any more details before the scene reset again.

The door opened all the way then. Only, it was the door to the workshop beyond the projection. Gloomy daylight filtered in behind Aethelgard as he limped inside.

"Any luck?" asked the Knight Investigator.

"Some," said Actaeon. "Although, I am not sure it amounts to much."

Aethelgard walked over to join him and adjusted the lenses on his nose to better analyze the scene.

"Do you see that flash of red?"

"Aye, though I wish I could see more. Is there anything else you can do?"

"Nothing I can think of immediately. I am not certain why the projection would end before the culprit cleaves the artifact in two. Perhaps the act damaged the memory of the device," suggested Actaeon.

"It is a possibility," said Aethelgard, before slamming his fist on the top of the workbench. "Blast it! So close to the identity of whoever was about to enter the room."

"True. However..." Actaeon began.

"There's no one in the room at the time," interrupted Aethelgard. "You're quite right, my engineer friend. So the scene we view now might not have even preceded the crime. Unless Vichaen and his attacker entered together. Is there nothing more you can do to salvage any other recordings from this artifact?"

"As I said earlier, nothing that leaps to mind," said Actaeon. "I am curious though, whether whoever discovered the scene of the crime saw any activity from the device. Even when catastrophically broken, some of these devices made by the Ancients continue to operate at times. If anything was glimpsed, it might give us a clue as to how we might render it operable again."

"Ha! We'll make an investigator out of you yet!" said Aethelgard, clapping Actaeon on the shoulder.

Actaeon laughed at that. "I will stick to the investigation of artifacts, thank you. They are much more predictable and repeatable than humans."

"Ah, but that's the fun, isn't it?" said Aethelgard.

"Perhaps the discoverer might have even gotten a glimpse of Nathis as she entered the room," Actaeon added as a sudden thought.

"Don't be so sure that Nathis was the culprit," corrected Aethelgard.

Actaeon offered his companion a dumbfounded look. "She did openly attack us on the Avenue of Glass, did she not? And after we confronted her with evidence from the scene at that."

"Which certainly could be precisely the reason she attacked us. Or, it could be that she attacked us because two armed men confronted her, both bearing various artifacts – anathema to the Keepers," countered Aethelgard. "Have you not heard the stories of Keeper fanatics attacking people on the street to destroy their artifacts?"

"I have," admitted Actaeon. "In fact, I have lived through them doing just that to me."

"See then?" said the Knight Investigator. "Don't allow your bias against our Keeper friends to bring you to false conclusions about this case. Until we have solid evidence that Nathis committed the crime, she remains just a suspect. The right evidence will bring Vichaen's attacker to justice, and the right evidence always rears its head, even if it seems impossible to find.

"Without the right evidence, the Arbiters are no better than the Dominions – using political machinations, contrived evidence, and manipulated facts to convict enemies. Er... no offense," said Aethelgard with a smirk.

"None taken." Actaeon grinned. "Your advice on bias is sound. I shall not allow it to cloud my judgement in this matter."

"Of course you won't," said Aethelgard as he tugged at his beard. "Shall we then?"

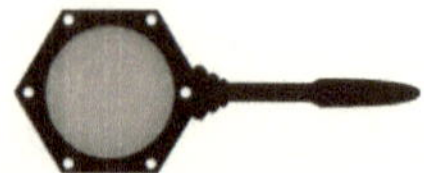

Arbiter Pyramid Command felt nostalgic to Actaeon. He would often wait just outside to meet Eisandre for their walks into the ruins of the Boneyards, while she was still an Arbiter and, of course, before they were married.

They sat down in a spartan room with a table and a few chairs. The man who sat across from them was extremely old. He wore the red armband of the Arbiters on his right shoulder, but that was where his appearance as a member of the Order ended. He hunched forward heavily in the chair, supported by a cane fashioned from artifact metal. Thick wrinkles nearly obscured his eyes, and only a few grayish wisps remained of his hair. Instead of the typical garb of the Arbiters, he wore a loose-fitting gray robe that was belted about the waist. Sheathed on that belt was a standard Arbiter arming sword. And on his feet were slippers that one might wear to bed.

The old man offered them a big smile and gestured broadly. "How may I help you, brother Aethelgard?"

Actaeon offered Aethelgard a sidelong look and arched his brow.

"Ah, I see introductions must needs be made," smiled Aethelgard. "Actaeon, this is Knight Arbiter Gaenwiel sof Balur. He is retired – as much so as one does from our Order anyway. He is no longer required to walk the patrols, though he does help out from time to time. His experience is a boon for which we're all thankful.

"And brother Gaenwiel, this is my associate, the Engineer Actaeon. I'm sure you've heard of his many exploits. I've enlisted his help in the case you discovered for us. He'd like to ask you some questions to hopefully glean some clues that will be useful to our investigation."

"Of course!" said Gaenwiel. "Always happy to help out you young fellas. Anything at all, just ask away."

Aethelgard smiled at Actaeon and gestured for him to begin.

Actaeon grinned. "Thank you, Knight Arbiter. When you found the room did you notice anything in particular about the artifact near the bedside? Any glows from it or projections above it?"

Impossibly, Gaenwiel narrowed his eyes upon Actaeon and leaned forward more to peer at him. "What's this you say? An artifact near the bedside? The luminary, no doubt."

"No no, not a luminary," said Actaeon. He placed a small cloth bag upon the table and opened it to reveal the bloody, broken pieces of the cylinder artifact.

Gaenwiel scrutinized the object for some long moments and then rapped his knuckles on the table. "Yes, yes. That was on the bedside table. In a pool of blood, if I recall right. No, not a glow or anything like that. Not sure what these jeck shuns you're talking about are."

"It would appear as an image above it. Did any sounds or anything otherwise anomalous come from it?" Actaeon reached out to touch the artifact but then thought better of it and returned his hand to his lap where he scratched the fingerless glove of his right hand.

"A noma what?" asked the old Arbiter. "You're gonna have to speak up, lad. I ain't got the hearing I used to."

Actaeon resisted the urge to smirk and endeavored to clarify. "It would be a strange –"

Just then, a round, young Arbiter with a youthful, exuberant face and long blond hair burst into the room. "Knight Arbiter Aethelgard!"

Aethelgard looked at Elmerth down the bridge of his crooked nose and shot him a look that could kill. "Initiate, I hope you have a good reason to interrupt our conversation."

"I... um, the Sentinel Arbiter sent me, uh... sir." The young man stumbled over his words. "He told me to bring you this at once, Knight Arbiter."

"I am a Knight Investigator, Elmerth, and you'd best remember that," Aethelgard chided him.

"Ah, uh... yessir, Knight Ar- Investigator, sir," replied the Initiate.

"Now, what did the Sentinel Arbiter send you to bring me?" asked Aethelgard.

The Knight's words gave Elmerth a sudden recollection and he reached down to fumble with a dagger that was stuck into his swordbelt.

When he pulled the dagger out, Gaenwiel snatched it out of his hand and held it up to the light that filtered down from the top of the Pyramid through a prism inset into the ceiling. The blade was etched with the likeness of an artifact tower with a sword extending upward from it, pommel up. Inset into the blade at the etching of the sword pommel were jewels of emerald, ruby, amethyst, and citrine.

"Jewels the colors of the Niwian Dominion, for sure," muttered Gaenwiel. "But no way of knowing if it belongs to our dead man. Could of been from any careless Niwian Lord or Lady."

Aethelgard held his hand out and after a moment Gaenwiel deposited the dagger into it. "Indeed, the jewels represent the colors of the Serene Dominion. But it indicates the wielder was located centrally to power. Most of the Lords and Ladies would choose one color or the other."

"Like the military units?" suggested Actaeon.

"Aye, 'tis true," said Aethelgard. "Competition between those colors are fierce in Niwian. One would be unlikely to flaunt colors other than their own, unless they were in charge of all four. Thus, our next step is clear, I think." He turned to Elmerth. "Where was this found, Initiate?"

"Um... the, uh... I found it on patrol in the ruinous northern bowels of the Pyramid, Knight Investigator," stammered the Initiate Arbiter, growing redder in the face by the lifebeat. "When I showed it to the Sentinel Arbiter Corvin, he recommended I bring it to you."

"He did well to guide you so." Aethelgard levered himself to his feet with his cane. "Well then, gentlemen, are you coming?"

"Coming? Uh, all of us?" asked Elmerth.

"I don't see why not," replied Aethelgard. "After all, we're all involved now, aren't we?"

Shortly, the four of them sat within one of the private conference rooms at the back of the gaudy Niwian Hold within the Mirrorholds of the Pyramid. At the head of the table sat the Lord Protector himself, Faschin vor Steubick.

The Lord Protector wore his dark brown hair in a big loop that started at the top of his head and curled around to end in a clip on his collar just below his chin. He glared daggers at Actaeon.

The Prince Engineer just grinned back at him.

"Good afternoon, Lord Protector," said Actaeon, dipping his head forward politely. He held no lost love for the Niwian leader, who had proven himself to be quite the fool, by Actaeon's experience.

"What is this *Raedellean* doing here?" Faschin asked the Knight Investigator, sneering the word as if it were an insult.

"Now now, Faschin," said Actaeon. "Is that any way to speak with your friends from Raedelle?"

"The Prince Engineer is acting as my associate in this case and in no way represents his Dominion in the matter." Aethelgard folded his arms across his chest.

"You must think me prisoner-kin that you expect me to believe such a thing." Faschin looked at Aethelgard incredulously as though expecting a reply. When he got none, he changed the subject. "Please tell me that you've made progress toward finding Vichaen."

Aethelgard nodded and unwrapped the dagger on the tabletop. "We have. And I believe this is his dagger. Can you confirm that for us?"

The Lord Protector offered it a fleeting glance. "I'm sure it is. What does this have to do with finding him?"

It was Gaenwiel who spoke next. The old man shifted uncomfortably in his chair where he hunched over. "And how could you know for sure? Why, there must be dozens of similar daggers amongst your nobility."

Faschin glared daggers at the old Arbiter from beneath his floof of hair. He reached out and snatched up the weapon. "I said it was, did I not? Dare you question the Lord Protector, himself?"

Aethelgard spread his hands. "My colleague is merely expressing his concern, because you appeared to be so blasé in your assessment of the dagger. We wish to ensure that your identification is certain. It may well be important to the case."

The Lord Protector scowled at the group of them and adjusted his hair where it was attached to his collar. "Have I not told you what you wish to hear? Do I need to put on a performance for you to believe me? The four jewels of Niwian, the symbol of Memory Keep etched on the blade – it is Vichaen's dagger! How will your finding a dagger in his room be of help?"

Faschin was practically shouting now.

"I heard that you made an arrest of someone suspected in my nephew's murder. So why not go get the gallows ready for them instead of yammering your useless questions at me?"

"Until we find a body, this is not a murder, but the case of a missing person," corrected Aethelgard. "Of this, I must insist."

"Better that you find him alive, but I have little hope after hearing the reports of his room from my retainers," said the Lord Protector. "Go then, and do your jobs. Find out what happened to my nephew."

At Aethelgard's bidding, Initiate Arbiter Elmerth led them next to the place where he had found the dagger in question.

As they proceeded toward that location, Aethelgard stroked his beard and addressed Gaenwiel. "Old brother, you are, of course, welcome to continue to accompany us, but if all the walking is too much, we can take it from here."

"Oh, balderdash! I reckon I know the ins and outs of this old wreck better than you. Besides, an old man needs something of interest to tide him over." Gaenwiel smiled at him and continued along, hunched over his ruincane as it clicked and clacked along the floor.

When Elmerth finally stopped, he pointed to a side of the corridor where an old collapse had rendered one of the branches inaccessible. "This is where it was."

"Show me precisely where you found it," Aethelgard said.

The Initiate knelt and pointed to a small crevice where the collapsed materials nearly met the floor. "Just under there, sir. I saw it gleam out the corner of my eye as I strolled... er, marched past."

Aethelgard handed Actaeon his own cane and, with a wince, settled down to his knees to examine the location. "I'm surprised you saw it there, Initiate. Sharp eye."

The Knight Investigator then withdrew a large lens from his pocket and proceeded to run it all over the area, his eye brought close to the glass. He then lowered himself to the floor until he was all but lying face down and scrutinized the surface thoroughly.

"What are you looking for?" asked Actaeon, leaning heavily on his halberd.

"Shhh!" scolded Aethelgard. "I'll know it if I see it." He then continued to crawl along the floor until he nearly collided with Actaeon's toes. With the lens, he swept the area around the Prince Engineer's boots and the butt of his halberd and then proceeded to circle around behind him and do the same.

Actaeon grinned. "Are you investigating my feet?"

"Let no clue go unseen, Engineer," said Aethelgard before he continued on, so much like a worm, to the other side of the corridor. There he repeated his onerous task.

"There's naught of interest down here," said Gaenwiel. The old Arbiter leaned heavily against the wall and stretched his back. "Just ruin and wreckage."

Aethelgard snapped his fingers there and climbed back to his feet with a wince. He slipped the lens into his pocket then and dusted off his pants before retrieving his cane from Actaeon.

"I'm inclined to agree with you on that. He must've dropped it while poking around here for artifacts, but I see no signs of struggle or that a body was dragged through here." Aethelgard pushed his lenses up his nose and peered at Elmerth. "Unless..."

The young Arbiter looked back at him with no uncertain horror in his eyes.

Aethelgard reached out a finger and poked the boy in the center of his chest. "You didn't kill him, did you?"

All of the color drained from Elmerth's face, and his jaw dropped open. He looked to Gaenwiel and Actaeon for help and began to shake his head rapidly, backing away from Aethelgard. "Uh... I, um... I mean, no sir. I'd a... never." Then he steeled his shoulders and stood up straighter. "I'm to be a Knight Arbiter. I'm here to... to... protect, not to kill... uhm, sir!" He nearly shouted the last words.

Aethelgard laughed and patted him on the shoulder. "Relax, Initiate. I know it couldn't have been you. Or else, why would you bring an important piece of evidence back to me?"

Actaeon and Gaenwiel both began to laugh as well.

"Oh, thank the Fallen, sir! You had me there." Elmerth himself began to laugh then, joining the others as the color gradually returned to his face.

When the laughter died down, Aethelgard turned and began to head back toward the Pyramid's central Sun Chamber. "Oh well. No point in lingering any further in this dead end. Come gentlemen. We must now seek other avenues for this investigation."

They followed him out to the Sun Chamber. There, the Knight Investigator paused to look up at the stairs of the Skyspiral that wound in helices far above them through light that trickled down through the elderglass pinnacle. The area was full of activity, as merchants hawked wares to passing nobles, demonstrators shouted rhetoric, and bards filled the air with a dozen different songs in search of copper bits to buy their dinner with.

"Thank you both, brothers young and old. Your help with this investigation has been appreciated. Come, Actaeon. Let us retire to your workshop and think on this some more." Aethelgard saluted Gaenwiel and patted the Initiate on the back.

On their way out, and after they were a good distance away from the other two, Actaeon grinned. "So, what did you really find during your prolonged excursion on the floor?"

Aethelgard smiled, but the gleam in his cobalt eyes was a giveaway. "Not so much. But enough to solve this case."

"Enough to what?!" Actaeon for once was at a loss for words. "How can that possibly be? Was the killer an insect?"

"That you shall see soon enough," said Aethelgard. "Meet me in the Sun Chamber at nightfall and I will show you everything. Oh, and bring that Companion of yours. We may well need her help with this, and I know she will not hesitate to act."

Actaeon just shook his head, completely baffled that the Knight Investigator could have solved the crime. "Very well. Yanelle and I will see you at nightfall."

When Actaeon and Yanelle arrived, they found Aethelgard in the center of the Sun Chamber. Dim moonlight filtered down through the pinnacle above to light the lenses over the man's eyes and gleam off of his bald scalp as he looked upward, lost in his thoughts.

The Knight Investigator spotted them as they neared and offered a thin smile. "My good sir, do you have any more of that pain medicine you had given me on our last case? My prolonged excursion on the floor took a toll on my injured knee."

Actaeon smiled and tossed him a half-through bottle of his home-brewed medicine, which the man quaffed quickly before tossing the empty vessel back.

"You've my thanks," said Aethelgard.

"It is nothing. I shall concoct up some more for you this week. You can drop by the workshop to pick it up," said Actaeon.

Aethelgard placed a hand on Actaeon's shoulder and nodded. "You are a friend." He turned to Yanelle. "Now, ready yourself, for I already see our quarry. But we must not reveal ourselves just yet. I will let you know when and you can apprehend them."

"Why not have another Arbiter along to do this?" asked Yanelle.

"I do not trust my Order to carry out this plan," said Aethelgard cryptically. "You shall see. Now come – follow me, but maintain a distance behind so that we do not alert them to their tail."

Actaeon and Yanelle let Aethelgard get far enough ahead so that he was nearly out of sight before they followed. Actaeon caught a glimpse of a limping, cloaked figure that hobbled along into one of the lesser-used corridors that branched off from the Sun Chamber.

The going was slow from there given the pace of the subject they were following. It wound from one dusty, disused hall to another, each one more progressively broken and rusted than the next. In this way they carried along, until, at last, they arrived in the corridor that Elmerth had showed them during the day.

Aethelgard waved them forward to join him then. When they did, they peeked around the corner and Actaeon noticed a lump squirming around on the floor. It was the cloaked figure from earlier, down on their knees searching for something.

The Knight Investigator stepped around the corner and stood in the center of the corridor. "The game is up Gaenwiel sof Balur. You've been caught." He motioned for Yanelle to apprehend him.

The figure discarded the cloak, revealing the old Knight Arbiter. As Gaenwiel scrambled to his feet, he nearly fell, but he managed to use his ruincane to stabilize himself.

When Companion Yanelle drew her sword and approached him,

Gaenwiel began to slide his arming sword from his sheath but then thought better of it and slid it back into the scabbard with a click. "I'll not resist. But I don't see the problem with a fellow Knight Arbiter investigating the scene of the crime."

"Not normally," admitted Aethelgard, as Yanelle relieved the old man of his cane and swordbelt and bound his hands behind his back with a cord. "But there's certainly a problem when a Knight Arbiter returns to investigate the scene of their own crime."

"Bah! Must I really have to listen to this nonsense?" scoffed Gaenwiel, turning his head to the side to spit upon the floor. "I was patrolling these halls when you suckled at the teat of your Althean wet nurse."

"Age guarantees not wisdom," said Aethelgard with a thin smile. "And I shall shortly prove how you were the man behind the disappearance of Vichaen vor Steubick."

Gaenwiel tried to walk back the way they came, but Yanelle yanked him back. "Let go, lass. We'll go speak with the Paladin Arbiter and clear this up at once."

"I don't think so," said Yanelle.

"The Companion is correct," Aethelgard said. "We're not yet done here. Follow me, and bring the guilty party along."

"But what if he speaks the truth, Aethelgard?" asked Actaeon. "How do you know he was not simply investigating the scene?"

Aethelgard made a disappointed click with his tongue. "Come now, Actaeon. Do you really think that the same man who earlier said, 'There's naught of interest down here. Just ruin and wreckage,' would return to scrutinize the scene? No, he's the culprit, and I'm about to prove it. Hold your remaining questions, for they will all be answered soon."

That said, the Knight Investigator once more handed his cane to Actaeon and lowered himself to his hands and knees. He led the way down that corridor, and around the next bend. When he reached the halfway point of that hall, he paused near a severely damaged location that had partially collapsed. "This is the location of the crime."

"What led you to believe that?" asked Actaeon, handing him back the cane. "Something on the floor, no doubt."

"Precisely, my dear Engineer," he said, regaining his feet. "You see, I noticed one key piece of evidence earlier today. Your halberd's end cap is made of an ordinary cast metal, which does not scratch or otherwise mar the artifact metal that the Pyramid's floor is made from."

"Ah," said Actaeon with a dawning realization. "So Gaenwiel's cane –"

"Right!" said Aethelgard excitedly. "Was made of a metal from the ruins. Thus, hard enough to scratch the floor wherever he passed. And I could tell that he had travelled this way on numerous occasions, first this way and then back. You see, the marks left upon the floor by the cane make clear the direction of travel."

"So, you know I've walked patrols here. What of it?" snapped Gaenwiel, shrugging off Yanelle's grip from his shoulder.

"Odd patrol," countered Aethelgard. "The marks from your cane indicate that you've stopped here every time and then turned around to leave after loitering quite a bit. And it's telling that there is a break in the dust right here. It bespeaks something on the other side – something that has been accessed recently enough to have evacuated the typical dust that would gather at the sides of a corridor. Anything you'd like to admit before I figure out a way to get in here?"

"No," said Gaenwiel, suddenly cagey. "Carry on with it."

"Actaeon, care to give me a hand?" Aethelgard said.

Actaeon leant his halberd against the opposite wall to free up his hands. "Based on the scratch marks on the floor, I would conclude that the debris swings out to a point right here. Which would put the hinge point just over there and the opening right..." He found a crevice with his fingers and pulled. At first it didn't budge, but then he felt along farther and felt the catch.

There sounded a click, and a makeshift door built from the debris swung outward, into the hall. It had blended into the rest of the collapsed area seamlessly.

And what was hidden behind it made them all gasp in surprise.

A number of people were inside a room, twenty or so at first glance.

But that wasn't what made Actaeon's breath catch in his chest.

The massive bulk of a deathcrawler dominated the center of the room. It was in the process of lunging at several of the people within, its pincers thrown wide and dripping with paralytic poison.

Yanelle wasted no time. She drew her sword and rushed forward to defend them against the creature.

"Yanelle! No!" shouted Actaeon with a sudden realization.

But it was too late. The Companion leapt into the room and charged the beast, the point of her blade forward.

And she nearly reached it. The tip of her blade came within a mere arm's length from one of the creature's beady eyes.

That was as close as she got, for she was now frozen in place along with all the other inhabitants of the room.

Aethelgard made a move to step forward after her, but Actaeon snapped out his hand to stop him.

Behind them, the old Arbiter had backed away from the room to the opposite wall and took Actaeon's halberd in his bound hands. He oriented the weapon horizontally behind him and rushed his captors as fast as his aging form could carry him, intending to knock them both into the room.

Had he not stumbled halfway there, he might have succeeded.

Instead, Aethelgard caught the movement out of the corner of his eye and spun to crack Gaenwiel in the side of the head with his cane.

Blood trickled down the Arbiter's face and he collapsed to the floor, stunned.

The halberd clattered down behind him and Actaeon rushed to retrieve it and to pull Gaenwiel away from the room by the collar of his robe.

Aethelgard knelt over him. "Thought you'd get us out of the way too? Eh, old brother?" He patted the unbloodied side of Gaenwiel's face. "Your guilt is now clear by your actions."

Actaeon returned to the entrance of the room to take a better look.

The room had metallic purple, triangular panels on the walls and floor alike. From what he could discern from the narrow view he was afforded, there were three walls that extended upward until they met far above in a point. The room must be a tetrahedral shape. One of the bottom corners was broken open toward a path in the ruins that led downward. Inset into one of the walls was an alcove in which stood a short pillar with flashing symbols of the Ancients on it. Just beyond the alcove, and apart from the rest of the room's occupants, stood an androgynous bald person dressed in a brightweave outfit – the person lacked even eyebrows, their mouth open mid-scream. The other occupants of the room all appeared to have either stumbled or rushed into the room from the direction of the ruin door that Aethelgard and Actaeon had found or from the opening that led downward into a ruin tunnel. Among those frozen were people who appeared to be from nearly every Dominion and Order.

"What do you make of it, Act?" asked the Knight Investigator, remaining beside the old man, lest he try to push them in again.

"They appear to be frozen in time somehow, Aeth," he said, scratching the back of his right hand through his fingerless glove. "And judging by the styles of clothing I can make out, I would surmise that people have been getting trapped in here for a very long time."

"Agreed," seconded Aethelgard. "The styles of Niwian dress I can see might account for forty years, or more, alone. The most recent style is on our missing man Vichaen right there. But the question is, why?"

Actaeon shook his head. "I have never encountered an artifact effect quite like this one. There was an artifact on the Wall near Raedelle that generated some sort of invisible field with a similar shape – though that shape's reflection also carried along underground. It stands to reason that this room could have elements underground which we cannot see."

Aethelgard nudged Gaenwiel in the ribs with his boot. "Better start talking. You've nothing left to lose, and everything left to gain with your cooperation, starting now. What do you know about this room?"

Gaenwiel turned his head to the side and spat blood that had filled his mouth when he'd bitten his tongue during his fall. "Very well. You young fellas are sharper than you look. But I don't know much about it. Just that it freezes people still as a statue when they walk in there."

"Is there a way to turn it off?" asked Actaeon.

"None I know of," answered Gaenwiel.

"How long have you known about this place?" asked Aethelgard.

"Oh, longer than you lads been around, I suppose," said the old Arbiter, spitting more blood upon the floor.

"And how many of those people are in there because of you?" Aethelgard pointed back at the room with his cane.

"None of the people," said Gaenwiel. "Just the monster ruinstalker over yonder. Trapped it here when it pursued me once."

"So, you know how to get to the opening over in the corner then," said the Prince Engineer, noting that the deathcrawler had entered from that direction. "Will you draw us a map?" He dug out a folded piece of parchment and a sharpened stick of lead from one of his jacket pockets.

"Don't see no use to it, but if you insist. You'd best untie my hands for it," said Gaenwiel. "There's nothing more to see from there. And you need to go through the Warrens to get to it."

"I would still prefer to examine it myself," said Actaeon.

Aethelgard untied the old Arbiter's hands and twisted one arm behind the man's back so that he could draw with the other.

Gaenwiel winced, "Easy there. I won't do nothing stupid."

"Your track record does not indicate as such," said Actaeon, placing the parchment on the floor in front of him.

"Start drawing," said Aethelgard, twisting the arm more.

Gaenwiel's eyes opened wide, even through the wrinkles, and he began to hastily scrawl a map on the parchment. When he finished, Aethelgard tied his hands behind his back once more.

"Come," said Aethelgard, standing. "Help me close this up. We don't need someone else to stumble in here while we're gone."

Actaeon hesitated, looking at Yanelle, frozen in the middle of her attack on the deathcrawler.

"I know," said Aethelgard. "But if anyone will figure out how to get her out, it's you."

Actaeon nodded slowly, but then drew his bow to string it. He fired three arrows into the room. Each one passed through and into the alcove. Two of those bounced from the walls to land upon the floor and roll while the third tumbled out of the alcove and froze mid-tumble.

The Prince Engineer grinned. "We shall return, Yanelle. And with a plan."

Together, they closed up the room and brought Gaenwiel to Arbiter custody.

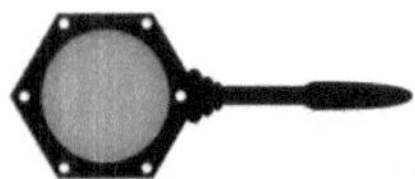

The large cadre of Arbiters that marched through the Open Markets enroute to the Warrens was quite the sight.

Sentinel Arbiter Corvin sof Haringar led the way. With them was the new group of technical Arbiters he had begun to train. They were all laden with supplies that Actaeon had specified before they left.

"This could well be a trap, you know," said Corvin.

"Indeed, it may be," said Aethelgard. He gestured to Gaenwiel, who was being led along by another of the Arbiters. "That's why we have him. Anywhere we're uncertain about, we toss him in first. If he lied to trap us, then he bears the brunt of his own trap."

Corvin nodded grimly.

There were no traps in the end. The map led them right through the tunnels of thieves and vagrants, past Rin's artifact junkyard, and farther into the maze underneath Pyramid until they reached the blocked entrance to the Freeze Room that was indicated on Gaenwiel's crude map.

The section of tunnels there looked like it had been on fire a long time ago, an event which had melted the pile of debris together.

"Clever way to keep people from snooping around here," said Aethelgard to the retired Arbiter.

Gaenwiel grunted in reply.

Actaeon pulled down his goggles and used his halberd to lever the debris loose, cracking pieces free one at a time. A cloud of old ash rose up to fill the tunnel, causing everyone's exposed eyes to tear and Aethelgard to fall into a fit of coughing. The Arbiters helped move the debris aside until they could see up into the Freeze Room.

Illogical relief flooded through Actaeon when he saw that Yanelle was still in the same location they had left her.

"Do you really believe that he is only responsible for the deathcrawler in there?" Actaeon whispered his question so that the old Arbiter wouldn't overhear.

"Most certainly not!" exclaimed Aethelgard, not bothering to keep his voice down. "A person who used that room as a simple tool need not hide it as such. A person using it as a tomb, however..." He turned to level his cobalt eyes disdainfully upon the man.

"Balderdash!" spat the old man. "I'll not listen to the gobbledygook coming out of your mouth, lad. I've never hurt a man beyond my duties."

"Never hurt, perhaps. But you imprisoned them against their will," said Actaeon.

"Not to worry," said Aethelgard. "I've enough information to pin the disappearance of Vichaen on him. And I imagine the rest of them will tell us the truth once Actaeon manages to unfreeze them, isn't that right, old chap?" The Knight Investigator patted his elder on the shoulder and the old man just grumbled in reply.

"Best that we get to work, then," said Actaeon. "Sentinel, could you have your men set up the rigid supports here and here?" He indicated the locations with his halberd. "I believe there is enough space for us to lodge them on either side of the opening."

"Yes, sir," responded Corvin. The Arbiter directed his men to lodge two iron bars into crevices in the broken tunnel on either side of the opening.

When they were in place, the Arbiters tied a rope to each one and everyone lined up to tug it to see if they would come free. One of them shifted slightly, and Corvin directed them to place wedges around it, which they pounded in tightly with a maul. Once that was done, they tied elastic straps, which had been salvaged from the ruins, around each bar.

"How long?" asked Corvin, as the Arbiters unrolled the coils down the tunnel away from the Freeze Room.

"Let us try right here to start," said Actaeon, tapping the bottom of the tunnel a short distance behind the bars.

At that distance, they knotted the elastic cordage to mark the location.

In one of the Arbiter's packs was a leather seat that Actaeon had sewn together at the workshop. He withdrew it and tied the straps into holes reinforced with metal rings on either side.

"Who has the test subject?" he asked.

Aethelgard let his hand fall upon Gaenwiel's shoulder. "Right here."

The old Arbiter's wrinkles widened and they could actually see his eyes, for once.

Actaeon laughed and the others all joined in. Even Gaenwiel laughed nervously along with them.

"You should know better," said Aethelgard. "You'll have a fair tribunal with the Order before we go launching you anywhere. How about the real one, then?"

"You mean the fake one?" Actaeon grinned.

"Over here," said Corvin. He lifted a particularly heavy pack and dumped its contents to the floor.

Out spilled a dummy stitched out of burlap. It was roughly human shaped, with all four limbs and a head. Actaeon had stuffed it with straw, dirt, and stones until it weighed similar to him, using a balance in the workshop to confirm the weight.

"Ah, there is the test subject," Actaeon said, smiling.

"We shall call him Sacktaeon," suggested Aethelgard.

Actaeon laughed. "Perfect. Load him up, gentlemen."

When they had the dummy seated in the leather chair, Corvin nodded to him. "Sacktaeon loaded and ready, Your Grace."

Actaeon nodded and pointed his halberd toward the opening. "Commence launch!"

Corvin tied one of the ropes they'd used to test the bars to the leg of Sacktaeon and then directed two of his Arbiters to pull the dummy back. They flanked it on either side, each grasping an arm and a leg while facing away from the opening. They marched backward down the tunnel's slope until the tension in the bands ensured they could go no farther.

"Fire!" said Corvin.

As they released the dummy, it flew through the air, rotating slightly. Its legs caught the opening as it passed by, which caused Sacktaeon to spin wildly. It arced across the Freeze Room before landing hard and sliding into the alcove to jam against the pillar console.

"What caused him to hit the opening like that?" asked Corvin.

"One of the Arbiters released earlier than the other," said Actaeon.

"Sorry," they both muttered, looking at the floor.

"Not to worry," said Actaeon. "I do not believe you could have possibly released with the simultaneity required to control the rotation. We shall instead adapt to the lessons learned by Sacktaeon's unfortunate flight and will create a single release point. While I work on that, see if you can retrieve our test subject."

He knelt and drew his dagger to carefully cut a hole in the base of the seat. Through it, he passed the free end of the rope, where he tied a large knot so that it would act as a stop.

The Arbiters took hold of the rope and attempted to yank the dummy out. They tried several different speeds, angles, and motions, but the rope was solidly stuck where it had landed on the floor – frozen in place with everything else in the strange room.

Actaeon cut enough length from it so that a few men could grip the section now attached to the seat. Then he withdrew a steel helm that was padded on the inside from one of the packs. He placed it over his head and fastened the strap under his chin.

"Are you sure you want to risk this, Act?" asked Aethelgard.

"Indeed, I am," he replied. "Even if Companion Yanelle were not trapped in there, those people deserve rescue. Matter does not appear to freeze in the alcove. If I can make it there in the launch, I will interact with the console to try and alter the laws of the room."

"And if you don't make it?" the Knight Investigator asked.

"Then the rest will be up to the Sentinel Arbiter. Though I would recommend you also reach out to Engineer Lauryn for help," said Actaeon.

"We also have a few more willing volunteers to launch after you," said Corvin, looking at his cadre of Arbiters.

Several of them shook their heads and more than a few took a step back.

"That is right." Actaeon grinned and set his halberd aside before removing his bulky jacket to lay it nearby. He then settled himself into the leather seat and nodded. "I am ready." Normally, he'd like to run many more iterations of testing, but this was a risk that he was willing to take in order to free Companion Yanelle. After all, she'd saved his life more times than he could remember.

Corvin nodded to the Arbiters. This time, they began to pull the single rope backward to stretch the straps.

As they pulled, Actaeon aided them by backing up along the tunnel. "Release on my command," he instructed.

The Engineer continued to back up gingerly until the straps were fully tensioned. Then, he took a deep breath and tilted his body forward and his legs back.

"Now!" he cried.

And, with a rush of acceleration, he was flying through the air and into the room. The charging deathcrawler raced past him and he slammed his shoulder into Yanelle, feeling a burst of pain in his right arm. The impact threw him off course and he slammed hard into the floor and spun sideways before sliding the rest of the way into the alcove.

At least, most of him made it there. His right leg was still outside in the freeze part of the room. The sudden pain that flared through him felt as though his leg had been severed at the knee. It throbbed and screamed at him as his lifeblood sought to find his foot and met a sudden dead end.

With a gasp of pain and tears in his eyes, he realized that he was suddenly on a timeframe. If he didn't unfreeze the room quickly, he'd lose his leg.

Eis, are you there? he sent through the Thoughtlink Artifact that was clipped to his ear.

I'm here, Act. Although, I wish you hadn't decided to be a living arrow today. How can I help? replied his wife with her thoughts sent through the artifact.

Unfortunately, that decision has already been made. Actaeon shifted uncomfortably so that he could prop himself up on one knee. From there he could barely reach the illuminated symbols on the pillar before him. *Can you help me translate?*

Of course, came Eisandre's response.

With the Princess' help in interpreting the symbols, Actaeon was able to quickly cycle through the options and access a power down sequence for the Freeze Room.

The feeling of his leg returned with a sudden rush of pain and a scream. It took him a moment to realize that the scream was coming from the strange looking bald person wearing the brightweave outfit. An instant later, the scream stopped and the person vanished.

Yanelle staggered as if something struck her, but then rushed forward to slide her sword into the head of the deathcrawler. It writhed and chirped and shrieked. Its pincers, laced with the paralytic poison, lashed out to stab at the Companion. She was faster though, and managed to dodge their efforts before pulling her blade free to sever them both in a blur of the sword's arc. It lunged forward at her to snap with its powerful jaws, and she sidestepped it to drive her blade home at a different angle through the carapace of the head. The creature chirped one last time and slammed into the ground, once again motionless.

Actaeon's vision began to close in as the severe pain from what had happened to his leg hit him. He clutched it to his chest, his tears pooling at the bottom of his goggles.

Yanelle rushed over to him. "Your Grace, are you alright?"

"I..." he gasped out the words. "I will be fine."

The room behind her was a sudden commotion, as everyone who had been frozen became active and aware of the horrific dead creature in the middle of the room.

She smiled at him and touched his shoulder. "Good. Try not to crash into me next time you go play arrow, will you?"

"You saw that?" he asked, surprised.

"I saw everything," she said.

And, as he looked out upon the others that were moving about, he realized with horror that many of them had been frozen here for decades, and had somehow lived every moment of it.

It didn't take them long to notice that Gaenwiel stood in the tunnel beyond the lower break in the room. Several people drew weapons and began to rush the old man.

The Knight Arbiters around him drew their swords to protect him.

Aethelgard raised his hands and stepped forward into the middle of the crowd. "Wait, wait! Listen everyone!" As they quieted down and paused to hear him out, he continued. "I know that most of you were duped into coming here by the man behind me. Trust me that he will stand trial and punishment for what he's done once we leave here. The Order of Arbiters will take care of that. What I could use from each of you, in due time, is a testimony as to what brought you to this present state."

A man who wore the flamboyant garb of a Niwian stepped forward. His leather outfit was dyed a number of colors – his trousers half gold and half red that faded with wear at the knees and his vest was a shiny purple that contrasted with the puffy green sleeves of his tunic. Around his neck were a pair of goggles and wrapped around his waist was a coiled glass rope that glowed faintly with red light. The artifact hunter's coif of hair was styled in a short swirl as ostentatious as his clothing. Long L-shaped sideburns framed the narrow features of his face. He pointed past the Arbiters to Gaenwiel. "That old Arbiter did it for certain – he lured me here and froze me in place somehow. Told me there was an artifact I needed to see."

"Vichaen vor Steubick, I presume?" said Aethelgard rhetorically. "Can you answer one question for me?"

"I shall, but shouldn't that man be answering questions about now?" asked the Niwian noble.

"He will soon enough," the Knight Investigator promised. "But tell me this: Why was there a container filled with your blood in the room in the Song of the Sisters?"

"How did..." Vichaen shook his head and then spread his hands. "Ah, I suppose you were in my room investigating my disappearance. Well, the dealer who sold me the artifact I'm sure you found upon my nightstand said it might be activated with one's blood under the right circumstances. I was running some experiments, you see."

"And so, Gaenwiel seized the opportunity to frame a Keeper Knight named Nathis Carrillum for what many suspected was your murder," Aethelgard turned to a dejected Gaenwiel. "Care to explain your motivation behind that act? There's no good keeping it to yourself now. You'll be held accountable for the illegal imprisonment of everyone here who doesn't clear your name in the matter."

"Now hold on here," came a voice from the room. One of the previously frozen men stepped forward, dressed in the blood-spattered garb of an Arbiter. A short Loresworn woman bedecked in various artifacts stepped forward beside him. She wielded an artifact spear and her clothes were also spattered in blood.

Aethelgard's face blanched at the sight of the man.

"How long have we been in here?" asked the bloody Arbiter.

"I..." sputtered Aethelgard. "I'm not certain, but the year is eighty-nine A.R."

There was a collective groan from those who had been frozen as they each realized how much time they had lost.

"My word," gasped the Loresworn woman. "Twenty-five years have passed, Arvin. I must inform Travail of this place. Astounding!"

"Travail is no more," said Actaeon. "It was destroyed."

"Destroyed..." murmured the Loresworn. "All those resources... Ancients help us."

Sentinel Arbiter Corvin stepped forward into the center of the Freeze Room. "Alright, everyone. I would ask you to follow me. We'll set you up with some temporary quarters in the Hives until you can get on your feet. I'm sure you all have stories you will want to tell. The Arbiters want to hear them, and we will support you in any way we can with reintegrating into society."

One by one, the people slowly filed out of the room, following the Sentinel. Vichaen led the way, followed by the Arbiter and Loresworn pair. After them came several Niwians, two Czerynians, a Raedellean, a woman who was dressed like a bandit, a pair of Ajmani priestesses, a Thyrian sailor, two more Arbiters from different decades, a small squad of Shieldian soldiers, a pair of children in raggedy clothing, three Althean healers, several unsavory characters who looked like they came from the Warrens, and even a Ruinic tribal who looked dazed and confused as he trailed after the others. The last person out was a young child whose skin was dyed in shades of green and had raised brown ridges that looked like vines – a Kainai of the Underforest. The little one – a girl, Actaeon thought – spoke to one of the Arbiters in her alien tongue before being led away.

Aethelgard shoved Gaenwiel into the middle of the room and waited.

The old man let out what sounded like a halfhearted sob as he leaned heavily on his artifact cane with his bound hands.

"I grew up in the Warrens," he began for Aethelgard, Actaeon, and

Yanelle. "My parents were poor, and I was born into that. Me and my friends used to explore the tunnels down there looking for artifacts to sell for some extra bits. One day, they stumbled into this here room and froze right before me. I couldn't believe my eyes! I went and caught some rats and released them to find the same outcome. And that's how I found I had a secret weapon that none other than me knew about. So, I set to hiding it away. Whenever someone crossed me or threatened me, I'd see if I couldn't trick them to go in there. Most of the idiots would just rush right in upon seeing them all frozen like that."

Yanelle offered him a baleful look and Gaenwiel's eyes dropped to the floor.

"No disrespect meant, lass. I saw you were just trying to help them fight off that ruinstalker. After that damned thing got trapped in there, it was a bit tougher, cause people tended to run away once they saw it. Had to shove them in sometimes. Or come up with some story about it to make them rush on in there. 'Twas still easier than you'd expect. Anyway, after my mum and pap were murdered by them p-kin Keepers in punishment for selling artifacts, the Arbiters came and took me – trained me up and got me to the next point in my life. That's when I noticed them same weird glowy symbols I'd seen hanging in the air in the Freeze Room from down in the tunnels. I figured there must be a way to get there from up top and I set to searching for it.

"It took me a couple years of poking around down here, but after a time, I did it. And boy, was it buried behind a collapse. I must have shifted a small building's worth of debris. But in the end, I found it here, right where I thought it was." He smiled a toothy grin at the memory. "After that, I'd bring people down here on the regular to freeze them. As you know, lad, there's a great many people we meet as Arbiters who deserve getting frozen away for all time. And I'd make sure of that.

"I don't suppose there's any reason to hide it from you now, but later in my years, I figured I could frame one person for the murder of the missing frozen one. Kill two birds with one stone, if ya will. The worst of them I'd frame and the lesser of the bad I'd freeze. Then the Order or the Dominions would take care of them for me, oft by bolt or blade."

"So, what did Nathis Carrillum do that made her the 'worst of them'?" asked Aethelgard, referring to the most recent framed suspect.

Gaenwiel smiled an evil smile at that and leaned back almost proudly.

"Not what she did, but her paps. I still remember his words just after he slew my own pap: 'With the Allfather's guidance, may you not turn out like your father, boy.' Ya see, my pap was a student of the artifacts. He found them and sold them to put food on our table."

"And the Keeper Knights came to kill him," said Actaeon.

"That's right. Them Keepers are a bunch of cowards at the heart. Too afraid to kill an artifact hunter from a Dominion for fear of retaliation. And so, they'd hunt us paupers in the Warrens who dabbled thereabouts — looking to bloody their sword to impress their Allfather, no doubt.

"So, when I saw that Nathis had turned out just like *her* pap, I couldn't help but remember that leering bastard's words, and I set upon the path which you sharp lads have now discovered. That snooty Niwian artifact hunter was getting too close to finding my Freeze Room, so he had to go. When I saw he'd booked a room in the Song, I set my plan into motion. And I'd have gotten away with it too, if not for the housekeeper that caught me as I'd planted the evidence to frame that Keeper bitch. Forced me to spill blood in the hall and report the crime as if I'd found it. Then you caught on to my trail, Aethelgard, with all your damned snooping around."

"I'd have caught you eventually, Gaenwiel," said Aethelgard. "You left too much evidence behind to avoid it. All the signs pointed to you."

"Aye, maybe so," said the old Arbiter. "But for just a bit of time longer, the Keeper girl would be dead."

"All the better that we caught you when we did then," said Aethelgard. He adjusted the lenses on his face and then snapped his fingers to get the attention of a Knight Arbiter that had remained out in the hallway. "Take him away. I've heard enough from him."

"Aye, Knight Investigator," replied the Arbiter, who led Gaenwiel away with a hand on one arm.

"So," began Actaeon as they headed out from the Freeze Room. "Who was that man that you recognized in there?"

"Which man?" asked the Knight Investigator.

Actaeon offered him a skeptical look.

"Ah, yes. That one. Oh, he just reminded me of a ghost from the past," explained Aethelgard.

"I saw the pyramidal pommel on his sword, Aethelgard. And I saw your reaction. I know you well enough to know that you were sure about who you saw," said Actaeon with a grin.

"Perhaps I've taught you too well." The Knight Investigator smiled.

"Perhaps," said Actaeon with a shrug. "When you are ready to talk about it, I shall be here to listen."

"You're a friend, Actaeon," said Aethelgard.

"As are you. Perhaps you can now explain to me how you knew it was old Gaenwiel?" suggested Actaeon.

Aethelgard smirked and nodded as they walked.

"His initial reaction to the dagger raised my suspicions. That, combined with the fact that he discovered the scene, was enough reason to take him with us to see the Niwian Lord Protector. Gaenwiel's reaction to the revelation that the dagger was Vichaen's was telling – he was hiding something. The final proof for me was when we visited the scene where the dagger was discovered. As you well know, the floors of Pyramid are made from alloys and materials that are very difficult to scratch. At one point, as we walked throughout the Pyramid on our way to the scene, I lagged behind and noticed that the artifact metal of his cane left subtle scratches on the floor where he passed. When we arrived at the location where young Elmerth found the dagger, I'd already identified scuffs and scratches from Gaenwiel's cane both entering and exiting the area. They indicated he'd oft continued past the place where Vichaen dropped the dagger."

"He dropped it on purpose?" asked Actaeon.

"Aye. Vichaen is a clever man. I imagine he had his doubts as to whether the old Arbiter was leading him into a trap. A smart thing to do – to leave behind something that someone might later discover as a clue. He could always go back and retrieve it after. As it turns out, he was right to do so. Gaenwiel's terrible eyesight prevented any possibility of him finding it after he froze Vichaen in the room with his other victims. There was one final piece of evidence too, which you uncovered, of course."

"Oh?" asked Actaeon, genuinely curious.

"The artifact you repaired placed Gaenwiel inside the missing man's room. The flash of red we saw before the projection ended – it was an Arbiter's cape! In fact, it was the main clue that made me suspect an Arbiter was involved right from the beginning. Gaenwiel no doubt wore his cape up in the Song of the Sisters – a sign of his authority and a guarantee he'd be left alone in his meddling with Vichaen's room. Until, of course, he was caught leaving it, and forced to report the crime to avoid suspicion."

Actaeon nodded. "A plethora of logical deductions."

"All in a good day's work," said Aethelgard with a smile. "We're a fine team, my good Engineer."

"So, what will happen to Gaenwiel?"

"It's up to the Order now. They'll determine his fate."

The Order of Arbiters enlisted Actaeon's help for the punishment. He was to find a way to freeze just a portion of the Freeze Room. In it stood a collection of freshly wrought iron cages lined up along one wall. They were largely empty, excepting one on the end. In it stood the old Arbiter, resigned to his fate.

When Actaeon sent word that he was ready, a group of Arbiters arrived led by Aethelgard.

The Knight Investigator walked up to Gaenwiel's cage and unrolled a scroll.

"Hail, brother," said Gaenwiel.

"The Paladin Arbiter has convened a council of the Sentinels and they have passed down the following sentence for me to read to you." Aethelgard cleared his throat and tugged on his beard. "As punishment for the wrongful imprisonment of twenty-nine people of Redemption, it has been determined that you will serve a time equivalent to that which you subjected them, in totality. You will remain frozen in the Freeze Room within the Pyramid for a period of no less than seven hundred twenty-nine cycles about the sun."

The cry of anguish that Gaenwiel let out made Actaeon's heart catch in his chest.

"Do you have any last words before your sentence begins?" asked Aethelgard.

"Please, please. Reconsider," pled Gaenwiel, dropping to his knees.

Aethelgard rolled up the scroll and tucked it under his arm before joining Actaeon in the control alcove. "Freeze him."

"Aye," said Actaeon. And he did.

Memory's Edge

'MEET ME IN THE END', read the note. At the bottom was scrawled a hasty signature that indicated it was from none other than the Knight Investigator himself.

Actaeon grinned and tossed the note into a waste bin at the corner of the workshop.

"Problem, Act?" asked Lauryn, pausing from the assembly work. They'd been developing a grenado-launching crossbow and had planned a series of tests for that afternoon. It was a challenging project. The grenado had to be activated after leaving the crossbow, but not a moment before, or else the jerk of the string would trigger the explosion and kill the operator.

"Aye, Lauryn. The tests will have to wait until tomorrow. My Arbiter friend sent me a summons." He sighed at the interruption and shrugged on his jacket.

"Aethelgard? Well at least it'll be interesting, right? Need an extra hand?" she asked.

"No, thank you. I would prefer if you continued on these assemblies, so that we can resume testing as soon as I finish with whatever his latest escapade is. You are correct though – it is bound to be interesting." He snatched up his halberd and sketched a mock bow to his fellow Engineer before heading out.

The End was a bloody mess.

"Ah, the Engineer has arrived!" said Aethelgard as Actaeon strode into the tavern and blinked in surprise at the horrific scene. "Watch your step." The Knight Investigator stood from behind the bar, one lens still held in front of his eye so that it looked comparatively tremendous as he regarded Actaeon at the entrance.

Between them and upon the floor lay a dead Niwian woman dressed in a bright purple, flowing blouse and pantaloons ornamented with gold. She lay amidst a scattering of tables and overturned chairs, many of which were covered in various amounts of blood spatter.

"Lovely place you asked me to, Aethelgard," said Actaeon as he carefully stepped around the fallen chairs to join his friend.

The End was the tavern at the shattered eastern end of the Avenue of Glass on the Pyramid's south side. It had a ramshackle and eclectic look, having been built onto the very bones of a damaged Ancient building. Inside, it was little different – inoperable artifacts of all sorts hung from the ceiling and walls. Holes cut high up into the elderstone walls of the structure housed stained glass chunks that created strange patterns of light throughout the room as outside sunlight streamed in.

A trail of blood zig-zagged all the way from the bar to the point where the dead woman had come to rest. An artifact spear was still lodged in her head gruesomely. It made Actaeon look away. Even with all the death he'd encountered in his life, this was still horrible to look upon.

Instead, he looked at the Arbiter, who had knelt behind the bar and was scrutinizing the floor with his lens.

"Perhaps next time you could ask me here for an ale instead of a murder?" suggested Actaeon.

Aethelgard laughed and straightened suddenly, adjusting the lens frame that sat upon his nose. "I've no need of you for an ale, Engineer. This murder, however... now that's a different story."

"Because of the spear?"

"The spear for certain. And quite possibly more," said Aethelgard with a nod. He stroked his short beard carefully.

"What happened here, exactly?" asked Actaeon, regarding the violent scene with bewilderment.

"Why, that's quite obvious," said Aethelgard. "Someone entered with the large artifact spear you see. They headed straight for the unfortunate victim there, who sat at the bar with her back to the door. Wasting no time, they plunged the spear right into the back of her head. It killed her instantly. The spear however, had become stuck. The spear wielder then dragged the victim backward and away from the location of her death in an effort to retrieve the spear. However, the spearhead had become thoroughly jammed in our poor victim's eye socket. They even tossed her to and fro, exhibiting an inhuman level of strength as they tried to dislodge it. In the end, their efforts failed and they fled the tavern, leaving the murder weapon behind. A stroke of luck compared to their other murder scenes. And one I believe will help us bring about a close to this case with help from you."

"Other murder scenes?" asked Actaeon, surprised.

"Ah, yes," the Knight Investigator replied. "One in the very middle of the Mirrorholds, and one in the Open Markets. Both of those victims were also from the Niwian Dominion. All three murders were similar – a cloaked figure appeared in broad daylight and punched their spear through the center of the victim's head. In every case, the murder had a number of witnesses and, in every case, they were unable to apprehend the killer. Any who gave chase failed to keep up with the fleeing assailant.

"Oril, could you pour us both an ale please? This might take a while." Aethelgard slapped a handful of bits down on the bar.

The bartender and owner of The End stepped out from the back room – a large, busty woman with a shock of raven hair arranged in a giant curl to one side of her head. She smiled a familiar smile at Actaeon. "Int'resting comp'ny yer keepin', yer Grace." She poured them both a tankard of ale and slid it over to them, keeping well clear of any of the blood-spattered areas behind the bar. "Yer bits ain't no good here. You both just figure this out and kill the bastard, 'fore I've got no customers left!" That said, she took one look at the horrifying scene before leaving quickly for the back room.

After Oril had left, Aethelgard took a sip from his tankard and smirked. "So, what do you make of the spear?"

Actaeon shoved his own tankard to the side. It didn't feel right to have a drink while the Niwian woman lay dead behind them. "I would prefer to analyze it after your Arbiters can... separate it from her body. Bring it to the workshop and I will give you my thoughts on it. If you will excuse me though, I believe I have seen enough here to understand what happened."

With that said, the Prince Engineer made his way out of the tavern following the same path he used to come in.

Later that day, Aethelgard arrived with the spear.

"Let us see what you have," said Actaeon, motioning to one of the workbenches. Aethelgard set the artifact down and stepped back to allow the Engineer to do his work.

The spear was like nothing he'd ever seen before. It didn't appear to be a pitted and scarred remnant of the ruins like many of the other artifacts with which Actaeon had worked. No, this instead looked like it was more recently manufactured – all shiny and smooth surfaces unmarred by hundreds or thousands of years of neglect. The shaft had a thick copper winding around it for the full length. The winding was composed of thousands of individual strands that were all twisted and wound together as one around the metal shaft of the weapon. The spear's head flared out from the shaft before it tapered to a narrow point. Behind the flared-out portion were two prongs that were clamped, and ran parallel to, the body of the spear. The winding split into two sections there and each was grafted onto one of the prongs. At the other end of the murder weapon was an activation panel like those which were commonly found on light lances. Adjacent to the panel was a clear window that showed a faintly glowing blue cylinder that looked like a luminary.

Actaeon pressed on the window and it popped open, presenting the blue cylinder. He removed it and held it aloft to inspect it more closely. "How curious. If I understand correctly, this spear is designed to deliver the energy of this cell to the spear's tip. After penetrating the victim's skull, the panel there can be pressed to send the energy from the cell forward. It terminates at those prongs and jumps across the gap to the spear tip. See that whitish material behind where the spear's tip flares out? I suspect that is an insulator so that the energy must jump farther and therefore do more damage."

Aethelgard tugged his beard thoughtfully. "And with that much energy delivered in such a way..."

"The victim's brain would be fried instantly," finished Actaeon.

"If your theory is correct, then the motive might have been more than simple murder, but to destroy the victim's brain."

"Exactly." Actaeon placed the cell back into the chamber and closed it. "I shall be right back." He went down into the cellar and found one of the big green Tomb Melons that Enrion Zar had gifted him. He brought it over to the workbench and placed it down in the center. "The other murder victims you mentioned?"

"Same as the one you saw," said Aethelgard, realizing what his friend was suggesting. "They all were stabbed in the head by a spear like this. The tip penetrated the brainpan and the entry wound was consistent with this diameter."

"This weapon is most likely not an artifact." Actaeon lifted it in his hands to examine it more closely. He ran his fingers along the shaft carefully. "There is no sign of surface wear or erosion of material that most artifacts that have lasted since the fall of the city show. I think there is a high probability that this was manufactured recently, perhaps for this specific purpose."

"And so, the killer has access to manufacturing techniques on the level with the Ancients, and either created or commissioned a weapon that could destroy a victim's brain," said Aethelgard. "This all sheds a good deal of light upon the case."

"It does?" asked Actaeon, arching a brow.

"Of course it does!" insisted Aethelgard.

"You shall have to tell me why," said Actaeon. "For now though, it would be best if you stood behind me. I intend to put my theory to the test."

When the Knight Investigator was in position, Actaeon pulled down his goggles and stabbed the spear into the Tomb Melon. It pierced the thick outer shell easily and squished into the inner meat of the fruit. He touched the activation panel.

The Tomb Melon disappeared before their eyes in a cloud of purplish-red mist and exploding green chunks. Pieces crashed into things across the workshop and slammed into the underside of the loft above before raining down around them.

"Shattered Redemption," muttered Aethelgard.

Several lifebeats later, Yanelle dashed down the stairs barefoot and dressed in only a simple white shift. The Companion's sword was in her hand and, despite her red hair being a wild mess, her eyes were sharp and ready for battle.

It took her a moment to take in the scene around her and then she leaned against the railing and began to laugh heartily. "Saints, Act! If you're gonna go blow things up while I'm taking a nap, could you at least warn me next time?"

"My apologies, Yanelle. I had forgotten you were up there," said Actaeon, offering her an apologetic grin.

"I'm your Companion. It's my sworn duty to protect you," said Yanelle with a bemused smirk. She nearly slipped in some splattered Tomb Melon juice but caught herself on the railing. "Of course, I was up there. I'm either up there or helping you blow up fruit down here."

"If anyone is to blame, Lady Companion, it is me for bringing this to your Prince Engineer for investigation," said Aethelgard.

Yanelle just shook her head and smiled. "I'd best get some clothes on before you two get any other smart ideas." That said, she headed back up to the loft, trying to wipe the Tomb Melon juice off her feet as she went.

Actaeon pressed the activation panel on the spear a few more times and watched as a pair of electric arcs shot forward from the tines to the spear tip.

"Seems your theory is correct, Engineer," said Aethelgard.

"And what does it tell you, Investigator?" asked Actaeon.

"There's another piece of the puzzle that I learned just prior to coming here. Have you heard of Niwian Readers?"

Actaeon set the spear down and raised his goggles from his eyes to rest them back upon his forehead. "I have heard stories. They are Niwians that are granted the privilege to get information from Memory Keep, if I recall correctly."

"That's right." Aethelgard pulled his lenses from his face to wipe the misted melon from them onto his sleeve. "And each of the victims was also a Reader."

Actaeon blinked. "Which means that they must have had information from Memory Keep that someone wanted to destroy."

"Precisely," said Aethelgard, sliding the lens frame back in place up along his nose. "And that's why we'll be going to Memory Keep."

"These disguises are absurd," said Actaeon, tugging at the frilly sleeves of his bright green tunic. He looked down with disdain at the matching puffy pants and shook his head. "I can barely fit any of my equipment in them."

"That's why they're perfect," said the Knight with a grin. He wore his own appropriately flamboyant outfit in purple and green. "We'll fit right in."

They rolled a cart filled with baggage and crates along the narrow path through the ruins as they walked. To their left loomed the massive shape of the Glass Spire, shining in the sunlight. The sight made Actaeon shudder – the last time he had been there, many people had died at the beginning of the Second Invasion War.

Ahead on the winding and treacherous road that meandered south through the ruins was the sunken part of the city claimed by the Niwian Dominion. And farther still, was the mostly intact dark cyan tower of the Ancients known as Memory Keep. It stretched above the horizon like the neck of some great technological beast. The glittering windows at the tower's pinnacle looked like the teeth of a gaping maw extending from the upstretched neck in an attempt to devour the flat roof of the structure. Below that protruded forth a number of shiny, metal cylinders of purple, gold, and red. Actaeon knew there was another green cylinder on the southern side, hidden from their vision. The bottom of the tower was supported by massive fins that rose from the earthworks at its base. Extending between the base and the upper windows were massive luminescent tendrils of purple and pink.

"Speak for yourself, Aethelgard!" said Actaeon with a chuckle. "There is a greater chance of my spontaneously combusting than of my passing as a Niwian noble."

At that Aethelgard laughed heartily. He reached up to adjust the lenses over his eyes but was reminded that he wasn't wearing them as part of his disguise. "Oh, from what I've known you to carry in that jacket of yours, I'd say the former is much more likely indeed!"

"Fair enough." Actaeon grinned and tugged on the handle of the cart to pull it over a particularly difficult pile of scree that had collapsed onto the pathway.

The rest of the trip was mostly uneventful, with the exception of two scraggly bandits who leapt out of the ruins on either side and demanded they relinquish their cart. Actaeon pulled his boltcaster from beneath his vest and shot one of them in the leg and when Aethelgard offered to show them how his writheblade worked, the pair of them fled – one thief dragging the other behind.

Once they emerged from the ruins and descended down a road that ran along the fringes of Sunken City, the going was much safer, and they both allowed themselves to relax a bit. The Niwian city was a colorful mix of densely packed Ancient structures and newer constructions that were built seamlessly between those. Where they walked along at the fringes, the clusters of buildings were sparser and more spaced apart, but the buildings were packed together in larger groups and grew progressively in size as they reached the city center where many were as tall as seven or eight stories. There, the most powerful of the Niwian families vied for power and control.

One thing that Actaeon had always appreciated when he passed through was the diversity of geometric elements on display in the architecture. Circles, hexagons, triangles, and squares. Trapezoids, frustums, pyramids, and spheroids. It was a veritable smorgasbord of shapes incorporated into the buildings, the doorways, the windows, and the rooftops. No one of them was the same, and yet they were arranged almost artfully in an organized fashion that insinuated some greater purpose. And yet, the structures were so perfectly suited to living spaces that he couldn't imagine what other purpose that could be. It was one area of the city that might have captured some insight into the minds of the Ancients themselves – in how they preferred to live.

Actaeon felt almost sad as they worked their way beyond the city limits as they continued onward toward Memory Keep. The modern buildings around the base of the massive tower had been constructed in the same spirit as those in Sunken City, but while impressive, they lacked the harmony that the Ancient buildings there exhibited. The whole effort left him with a feeling of disturbance, as none of the shapes there appeared quite right to his eye, though often it was not obvious why.

Near the center of the sizable town around Memory Keep, they arrived at a many-storied inn with a fancy sign that had curled ends and finely painted cursive that displayed the name: The Ephemeral Night.

"Hrm," Aethelgard murmured, looking up at the sign. "I wonder why they call it that."

Actaeon grinned and gestured to a cluster of ladies that was gathered in front of the inn's entrance. Their flourishing dresses put many of the other Niwian ladies to shame, and their colorful faces were so made up with products and powders that it was difficult to imagine what they'd look like without them. They whooped and hollered at passersby, waving fine handkerchiefs to try and flag down men and women alike.

Just behind them were a handful of men dressed in fine and vibrant costumes that rivaled the ladies – though they were notably less aggressive in their advances than the women. Their faces were similarly made up in diverse colors.

"Er... oh, I understand," said Aethelgard, his face turning a shade of red.

"I do not suppose they expect their patrons to do much sleeping. Thus the name," said Actaeon with a laugh.

"Mitrius said this would be a good place to stay," said Aethelgard, looking suddenly very uncertain.

"Are you certain your brother Knights were not playing a trick on you?" asked Actaeon. "Or perhaps they thought you might benefit from staying in a brothel?"

Aethelgard offered him a thin smile and scratched the hair of the wig that sat perched atop his head. "What better place for hearing the depths of the rumor mill? Don't you worry – I won't tell your wife if you don't say a word to the other Arbiters."

"I am sure she already knows." Actaeon grinned and tapped the Thoughtlink artifact that was clipped to his ear. "But do not worry – I will not divulge your secret that you enjoy booking rooms at brothels when away from Pyramid."

The Knight Investigator laughed. "Shall we then?" He led the way inside as Actaeon tipped a bellhop with a handful of copper bits to make sure their baggage was brought in from the handcart.

The concierge at the front desk had a mustache that twisted and looped so many times on either side that it was surprising he hadn't taken to hanging the room keys from it. He twirled a free end of it with one outstretched hand as he greeted them.

"Evening, fine sir!" Aethelgard swung his cane up to rest on his shoulder and leaned heavily on the counter. "My friend and I would like a room for the next few evenings."

"Aha! At once. And what sort of company shall you two gentlemen desire for your first night?" asked the concierge.

"Oh, none at all. We'd appreciate having the room to ourselves," said Aethelgard.

The concierge's eyes widened and he gave them both a knowing look. "Ah, yes yes. I entirely understand. You are both sure to enjoy our accommodations and you may trust us to maintain the utmost of discretion. Do you have a preference of room?"

"Do you have anything with a view of Memory Keep?" asked Aethelgard. "It's not often I get the chance to visit here, and I would very much like to see it better during our stay."

"Of course, sir," said the concierge, finally unhanding his mustache to retrieve a key from the back wall, which he placed on the counter. "You may have our Minuet Suite – it offers a fine view of the Keep all the way down to the entrance courtyard. What names may I mark down for the room?"

"I am Vibrod vor Crezian and my friend here is Gerizzio Sturmakis," said Aethelgard with a nod to Actaeon.

"Welcome to The Ephemeral Night, gentlemen." The concierge handed the key to Aethelgard. "That will be six hundred bits for the first night, please."

Actaeon's eyes widened. "Six hundred bits! For that amount I could put a new wing on the work-"

"I can assure you that the Minuet Suite is worth every bit, Mister Sturmakis," interrupted the concierge. "Of course, you're welcome to stay at the Vagrant's Dirge down the street if our prices are too rich for your coin purse." He reached out to take back the key.

Aethelgard held up a hand. "That won't be necessary." He shot Actaeon a cross look. "We've discussed this, Gerizzio. I've had my heart set on staying here. Now please pay the man, if you will."

Actaeon blinked at Aethelgard. When the Knight Investigator continued to look at him insistently, he grinned and rolled his eyes while he dug into the pockets of his vest to retrieve the necessary bits.

The Minuet Suite was as grandiose as it sounded. It was furnished luxuriously. Each piece of furniture was upholstered with expensive fabrics and a plethora of fringed cushions that covered nearly every surface one could sit upon.

After the concierge brought their bags in, Aethelgard opened the glass doors to the balcony and stepped out onto it to look toward Memory Keep. "Use the bed – I can sleep on one of the couches."

"We shall have to find a place to stow all these pillows or there will not be space for anyone to sit, let alone sleep!" said Actaeon as he tossed several pillows into the corner of the room.

"Join me on the balcony, quickly," said Aethelgard. He pointed excitedly to something down and out of sight below the balcony. "It is happening before our eyes."

Actaeon rushed over to his friend's side and followed his gaze downward.

Sure enough, far below, a cloaked figure had emerged with the cowl pulled down close over their face so as to obscure any features. The person wielded a long artifact spear just like the one that had been left behind in the murder at The End and raced through the crowd rapidly.

A dark-skinned man with bleached blond hair and a silver-fringed robe had emerged from Memory Keep moments earlier and was striding through the courtyard, a stack of books under his arm. It was clear from the trajectory of the spear-wielder that they were headed directly toward the man.

Actaeon cupped his hands over his mouth and shouted. "Look out!" But the words were borne away by the wind before they could reach the man. Actaeon rummaged inside the pockets of his vest until he found the old prototype Arbiter whistle he'd created and brought it up to his lips. The three shrill notes he blew next had everyone below looking up at him. "Look out!" he shouted again and pointed to the spearman.

"Cut that out," instructed Aethelgard. "You're blowing our cover."

The man with the books was among those that now stared up at their balcony. Distracted as he was, one of the books under his arm slipped from the stack. He said something and bent to pick it up.

"By the Fallen, man! Forget our cover," said Actaeon, now waving his arms frantically and piping on the whistle again to get the man's attention. "No! Get up! Run!"

The man picked up the book and tucked it back among the others beneath his arm before looking up at Actaeon again. He lifted a hand to shade his eyes as he gazed up at the balcony. A lifebeat later, the killer drove the spear into the side of his head and pulled the trigger, sending the man's lifeless body into convulsions.

"Shattered Redemption!" cried Actaeon in anguish. He'd just watched a man be murdered right before him. There was nothing he could have done to prevent it. In fact, his whistling did exactly the opposite and distracted the man from his killer. Far below, people in the crowd began to scream.

The killer put their foot against the man's head and pushed it off the spear before turning and fleeing back the way they'd come, leaping down from one of the courtyard's tall walls and disappearing into the crowd below.

Actaeon's mouth fell open. "I... I helped the murderer. Darkest Hour take me..."

Aethelgard grabbed his arm and yanked him roughly back from the balcony and into the room. He closed the doors and latched them before turning to the Prince Engineer. "Don't be a fool, Act. You saw the speed with which the killer moved. There was no hope for him, distracted or no. We were simply too far away. What you did do though, is break our cover. Once the authorities arrive there, witnesses will undoubtedly tell them about the crazy man blowing a whistle on one of the upper floors of this inn. If we have any luck, they won't recognize its tone as an Arbiter whistle."

That said, the Knight Investigator strode past him and unlatched the door to the hall.

Actaeon nodded slowly, the Knight's words taking a few moments to seep in. "You are correct, Aeth. Thank you. And, I am sorry that the whistle might have blown our cover, but I had to try something. I could not simply watch a man die without acting."

"I understand. Nothing to be sorry about. Are you coming?" asked Aethelgard, holding the door.

"Coming... Where are we going now?" asked Actaeon.

"Why, to investigate the murder scene, of course!" replied Aethelgard with a thin smile.

Actaeon grinned despite himself. "You are concerned that our cover was blown from all the way up here, but you wish to walk right down to the scene of the murder that just happened?"

"Indeed. Nobody would be surprised that two men who witnessed the murder from up here came down to see what happened. It gives us a chance to corroborate our story while simultaneously seeing if there are any discernible details that we cannot see from all the way up here. Just remember that I am Vibrod and you are Gerizzio."

"Very well. Lead on."

A large crowd had gathered at the entrance to the inn when the two investigators arrived at the lobby. They had to push their way through. People were still dashing about, some still crying out in terror. A squad of soldiers in red plate armor arrived, swords drawn. They quickly established a perimeter around the courtyard.

As Aethelgard led the way over, another squad of soldiers, this one in gold plate, arrived. The leader of the gold soldiers spoke to the leader of the reds. They argued back and forth before, finally, the gold officer shook his head and led his squad at a run in the direction that the murderer had fled.

As investigator and engineer neared the courtyard, a Niwian lady in a puffy dress tugged on one of the soldier's arms and whispered something in his ear before pointing to them.

The Niwian Red soldier nodded and rushed over. "You two! Stop right there – I need to speak with you."

"But of course," said Aethelgard. "That's why we came. We saw it all happen! All of it! From right up there in the balcony of our room! It was... it was horrid!" The Knight Investigator's hands shook as he spoke and there was panic in his voice. "The man with the cloak, he... he... just ran over and killed that poor man right before us. Stabbed him right in the head! The blood on the ground. The screaming. My friend and I watched him die! Die right in front of us!"

Actaeon had to admit that the Knight Investigator's performance was convincing even to him. If he hadn't known Aethelgard, he'd have been certain that he was shaken to such a degree from watching the murder unfold.

"Calm down, sir!" shouted the soldier. "Start from the beginning. What did you see?"

"My friend and I were watching from the balcony – a man in a cloak, with a... a spear, yes a spear! We watched as he charged right through the courtyard and he, and he... I can't bear to say it. Gerizzio, please do tell the rest for me." Aethelgard punctuated the sentence with a sob and took Actaeon's arm, squeezing it hard.

The soldier turned to Actaeon as he yanked his arm out of the Knight Investigator's painful grip. "Well, he rushed forward, straight toward –"

But Aethelgard had grabbed his arm again, fingers digging through the thin material of his tunic.

"Straight toward that, uh... that, um..." Aethelgard gestured with his finger in the relative direction of the dead man while averting his eyes. "The uh..."

"The Reader?" finished the soldier.

"Yes! Right toward the Reader and just stabbed him directly in the... the..."

"The head, yes," finished the soldier once more, impatience clear in his tone. He glanced over his shoulder at the others in his squad.

"After that, I couldn't bear to watch," said Aethelgard with another convincing sob. Actaeon flinched as he tolerated his companion's rough grip on his arm. "It was just awful, just horrible!"

The soldier nodded, clearly disinterested in them. "That's enough for now, thank you. What are your names and where can I find you if I need to ask any more questions?" He glanced over his shoulder again and one of the other red plate-wearing soldiers gestured at him to hurry up.

"Oh, yes. Of course! I am Vibrod and this is my good friend Gerizzio. We're staying at the Ephemeral Night for the next few days. Three days, right Gerizzio?"

Actaeon nodded.

"Yes, three I believe, or perhaps four. I forget exactly," continued Aethelgard, rambling on in a manner that had the soldier shifting his weight from foot to foot. "You can find us up on the seventh floor. Or was it the tenth? I was never good with numbers. Gerizzio, do you remember?"

"It was –" began Actaeon.

"Never mind!" snapped the soldier, at the end of his patience with them. "You can return to your business then. I have matters to attend to now." The soldier had begun to turn away before remembering his manners. "Thank you, for your cooperation."

"Of course, good sir," said Aethelgard. "And if you've any need of our help to catch the vile man who did this, please come find us. The killer must be brought to justice! Oh, the horror of it all! Gods help us!"

But the soldier was walking away, ignoring the remainder of the ramblings.

Aethelgard gripped Actaeon's arm again and led him away from the scene.

The Prince Engineer yanked his arm free. "Would you stop squeezing my arm like that already? You can lug that cart back yourself if you do not cease at once."

Aethelgard laughed at that. "I don't intend to bring that rickety thing back past the edge of town. We needed cover in, not out. A fine job back there, Engineer. You're a regular study at this undercover work."

The comment made Actaeon grin. "A regular study? I barely managed to say a word!"

"Exactly. And you were most convincing!"

"I am more impressed that you managed to get him to tell you that the victim was another Reader," said Actaeon.

"Aye," said Aethelgard. "And so, the plot deepens. The killer is here at the same time as us. And kills again."

"What does it mean?"

"It means we are closing in, my friend!"

Afterward, they visited a local eatery where they treated themselves to a fine meal of stuffed longfin, which they each washed down with a tankard of ale.

As the darkness of the evening began to descend, Aethelgard insisted they retire to their room. "We'll give Memory Keep a visit on the morrow to shed more light on this mystery."

As they relaxed on the balcony of their room, the Knight Investigator drew forth a small, fluted pipe and began to play a simple but uplifting melody on it.

Actaeon tried to close his eyes and relax, but, when he did, he could only see the convulsing body of the dying Reader. So instead, he opened his eyes to watch as the sun set along the glittering water of the Great Sea a distance beyond the hulking form of Memory Keep. The sky began to change color to orange. As he watched and listened to his friend pipe out song after song, the oranges faded to reds and then purples and he found himself smiling as he remembered a different sunset four years ago at Blacksands Beach, which he had shared with Eisandre before they were married. Through the Thoughtlink Artifact he told her that and she stepped outside to share the sunset with him from many miles away.

The reverie was interrupted by a sudden and vigorous banging at the door to their room.

The Knight Investigator's pipe music came to an abrupt halt and the two friends looked at each other.

"I told you you'd blow our cover," said Aethelgard.

"Oh, and your incessant rambling at the scene of the murder did not?" retorted Actaeon with a grin.

Aethelgard stood and offered him a thin smile. "Remember now: I'm Vibrod and you're Gerizzio."

"Alright then," said Actaeon, standing. "Lead the way, Gerizzio."

The Knight Investigator narrowed his eyes upon him and shook his head before leading the way to the door. "Ready your boltcaster, just in case," he whispered, checking the cloth-wrapped writheblade scabbard at his hip to make sure his weapon was ready.

The soldier that stood in the doorway when he opened it was a Niwian Red in full shining plate, complete with an ornate red and silver helm that extended down to cover the face with elaborate cheek guards and had a tall, brown-feathered plume rising from it to extend straight up into the air. The markings on the pauldrons identified them as a Captain in the Niwian army. The hilt of a longsword peeked over one shoulder.

"Gentlemen," said the soldier, in a distinctly feminine voice. "A moment of your time, please."

"Oh yes, of course – of course!" Aethelgard reverted to his rambling persona once more. "Is this about the murder? Why, of course, it must be. What a daft question. You must want to ask us more questions. Surely, you do. Well, we're here for that. Anything that we can do to help – anything at all! It was so... so horrendous to witness the –"

"Enough of that already!" snapped the woman, glaring at them with sharp amber eyes. She lifted off her helm and stuck it under an arm. Strangely, the plume remained attached to her head. It took Actaeon a moment to realize that it was, in fact, her hair, arranged in a stiff vertical braid that extended upward from her head and was held in place by a tall silver and red clasp – hair cascading out from the back of it like waves. Her helm had a slot that ran through the back to accommodate her unusual hairstyle. The softly chiseled features of her face were punctuated by a jagged scar that ran down her left cheek and through her lips.

"I know you're not Vibrick and Germizzio, or whatever silly names you told my soldiers down below. You both make for terrible Niwians," she said, pushing past them and into the room. "So, let's get to business, shall we?"

"I assure you, good lady, that we are visiting merchants," said Aethelgard. "My name is Vibrod vor Crezian, and this is Gerizzio Sturm-"

"Shut it, Arbiter," said the Captain. "I'm not some nullwit noblewoman. I'm Captain Jurlan ris Minovec of the Niwian Reds." She tossed her helmet onto the bed and spun to point at Actaeon. "And I'd recognize this man anywhere. Prince Engineer Actaeon Rellios Caliburn, the man who broke Travail, the man who summoned the spirits of Temple to scare off the tribals and turned the tide of the Second Invasion War."

"You served under Wronka, did you not?" asked Actaeon with a grin, suddenly remembering the woman from the war. She'd looked different back then – battered and dirty from weeks of jungle combat.

"Indeed I did, Your Grace. And now, I have the Colonel's old command, where I do my best to bring him honor," she said.

"Of that, I am sure that you do," said Actaeon. "You were a fierce fighter. And you have cleaned up nicely since our days in the jungle."

Captain Minovec smirked at that. "I wish I could say the same about you." She gestured to his clothing. "Honestly though, I do believe I prefer your old outfit over this ridiculous one."

Actaeon laughed and the other two joined him. "You are not the only one, Captain – trust me. It is a pleasure to see you once again. Allow me to introduce my friend, Knight Investigator Aethelgard sof Leaf."

Minovec sat down on the edge of the bed and crossed her legs in a clatter of plate. "Knight Investigator, huh? My suspicions were correct then. So, the Readers who fled to the Pyramid are dead too then?"

Aethelgard abandoned any pretenses of his previous disguise and pulled up a chair to sit across from her. "Aye. Three of them at least, that I know of."

"Damn..." she muttered. "That makes eight total then, including the one from today."

"Then you are performing your own investigation, I presume?" asked Aethelgard.

"That's right, and no closer to figuring it out than I was yesterday," said Captain Minovec. "Which is why I came here. I figured if an Arbiter and a Raedellean Prince Engineer were on the case, then we should pool our resources."

"How, may I ask, did you know I was an Arbiter? Was it the whistle?" guessed Aethelgard.

"That's right. I'd recognize that anywhere. It was foolish of you to blow it if you wanted to maintain your cover," she said with amusement.

"Wasn't even my whistle, nor did I blow it," he said, offering Actaeon a thin smile.

Sudden understanding dawned on Minovec's chiseled features. She turned to Actaeon and nodded, impressed. "How am I not surprised that Your Grace designed the whistles for the Arbiters?"

Actaeon shrugged, blushing at the recognition. He scratched the back of his right hand through the thin suede glove. "You may call me Actaeon, Captain Minovec. And it was just a matter of the right opportunity coming along."

Minovec tapped the scar on her lip several times, regarding him. After a moment, she blinked and folded her gauntlet-clad hands in her lap. "Right, Actaeon. So are we a go on my offer?"

"Indeed we are, Captain," said Aethelgard. "And first thing tomorrow, you can help us get into Memory Keep!"

"Get into Memory Keep?!" exclaimed Minovec, her brows furrowed in shock. "But you aren't even Niwians, forget about the fact that you aren't Readers! None not of the Dominion have ever been allowed within."

"Ah, but you're forgetting, my dear Captain. I am Vibrod vor Crezian and this is Gerizzio Sturmakis. We are specialists that you've brought into your investigation because of our in-depth knowledge of artifacts. Gerizzio, in particular, has a wealth of experience with interfacing with artifact machines. And, that is how you will get us in and get Actaeon connected to the Keep."

Actaeon had to sit down in his own chair then. "She will what now?"

Aethelgard shot him a shrewd look. "How else do you think we'll get to the bottom of the motive here? There's one thing in common with all the Readers, and it is killing them. You need to find out why, Engineer. None better than you."

The Captain's expression changed from flabbergasted to thoughtful. She unfolded her legs and stood. "Well then, gentlemen. It appears we have an arrangement. I will see you first thing at morning's light."

Dawn had barely begun to crack when Captain Minovec showed up at their room the following morning. She tossed them each a jerky stick and then, without delay, led them out and down from the room.

Together, the three investigators crossed the broad avenue to enter the large courtyard that stood atop one of the earthworks bastions that had been built at the base of the tower. Two Niwian Reds saluted sharply and stepped aside for Minovec. She led the way up the stairs that led to the courtyard. The stairs were designed to be removed upward using a collection of ropes and pulleys. In case of attack, the base of Memory Keep was designed to serve as just that, a true keep. It was fully defensible and was surrounded on all sides by raised earthworks and bastions that would allow defenders to loose arrows upon attackers from any side.

Within the courtyard atop the bastion, the books that the Reader had carried were still scattered in the spot he had dropped them upon his death.

Aethelgard gestured to them. "May I?"

"Please do," said Captain Minovec.

The Knight Investigator knelt and began to thumb through several of the books. He withdrew a magnifying lens from his pocket and examined the last written page of each of them. When he arrived at a thick book bound with blue leather, he paused and tapped the page. "The ink in this one is fresher than the others. I would venture that he wrote here on his final visit to the Keep."

"What does it say?" asked Actaeon, curious. He and Minovec leaned close to peer over the Knight Investigator's shoulder.

On the page was scrawled the following, in a panicked hand:

We made a mistake to tempt fate as we did. The gods have turned their backs upon us! The artifact will see to our end!

"What does he mean by 'the artifact will see to our end'? What artifact?" asked the Captain, unease in her voice.

"The spear that the killer uses is an artifact," said Actaeon.

"It *is?*" Minovec looked between the two men and then back at the words on the page.

Aethelgard thumbed through a few more pages before slapping the book shut and putting it in precisely the exact location he'd found it. "True, but that's not the artifact our unfortunate Reader friend speaks of."

"What do you mean it is not?" asked Actaeon, arching a brow.

"Come," said Aethelgard, wincing as he stood. "I believe we'll find more about that within." That said, he led the way toward the entrance of Memory Keep.

The looming doors stood open for them and they passed through to the inside. A short hallway brought them to a large, open, cylindrical chamber whose ceiling extended high up into the tower. Numerous glass rope cables as thick as a man's arm wound and slithered their way upward from floor to ceiling. Pulses of light swept along those transparent cables nearly faster than the eye could follow in colors of purple, red, gold, and green.

No sooner than they could gaze in fascination at the wondrous inside of the building, they were surrounded. Drawn writheblades crackled threateningly as half dozen armored knights closed the gap between them. Actaeon had heard legends of Memory Knights whose task it was to protect Niwian's treasured Memory Keep at all costs. Each of them wore a faceted artifact helm with a glass plate in front of their face. Rainbows swirled on the plates, twisting and turning as the light played across them in different directions – the effect completely obscured the facial features of whoever might be inside.

"Put your weapons away!" shouted Minovec, her words echoing upward along the cylindrical chamber walls. "I'm Captain Jurlan ris Minovec of the Niwian Reds. We're here to investigate the murders of your Readers. I need to speak with the Echo Sounder."

The Memory Knight opposite the Red Captain tapped the side of his helm and the glass plate slid up inside the helm somewhere, revealing the handsome, clean-shaven face of a man with large sideburns and sad brown eyes. "Captain Minovec. You should know that none but the Readers may speak with the Echo Sounder."

"If you want there to be any Readers left alive, I suggest that you take me to the Echo Sounder at once," she answered.

"Is that a threat?" asked the Memory Knight.

"It is the truth," she replied.

The Memory Knight offered her an expressionless look that lingered for longer than was reasonable as he considered her words. Finally, he nodded. "A moment then." He tapped the side of his helm and the rainbow glass visor slid down to cover his face once more.

The sounds of him speaking were barely audible from inside the helm.

"Fascinating," murmured Actaeon. "Another sort of Thoughtlink Artifact perhaps?"

He was interrupted when, as one, the Memory Knights spun and sheathed their writheblades. The smell of ozone lingered upon the air.

The Memory Knight's visor slid open to reveal his sad eyes once more. "You have my apologies, Captain Minovec. You may call me Rudick. I will take you to the Echo Sounder. Your companions may wait here."

Minovec shook her head, her plume of hair wobbling with the movement. "My associates will join me. They are part of my investigation. Both of them are experts in artifact technology and I require their opinions to solve this crime." She looked at Aethelgard expectantly then.

"I am Vibrod vor Crezian and this is Gerizzio Sturmakis," said Aethelgard. "As the Captain says, we have expertise in artifacts that store information and interface with the human mind."

Rudick closed his visor once more and could be heard speaking again. When his visor slid open, he nodded. "Very well. Please step aside."

Minovec looked around in confusion. The three investigators stood in the center of the chamber, surrounded. Perhaps the Knight meant to lead them out from the tower. She glanced at Actaeon, and he shrugged.

She took one large step to the side and Rudick stepped forward to stand beside her and spun an about face. A ring in the floor around them slid upward to surround the four.

"Oh," said Actaeon as understanding dawned.

The floor lifted then, and bore them upward toward the ceiling.

The color drained from Aethelgard's face. "How come I always end up leaving the ground when I spend time with you, Gerizzio?"

"There is a lift like this in Pyramid, Vibrod," countered Actaeon. "In fact, there are two I know of. I am surprised you have not used one before."

"I have not had the displeasure," said Aethelgard with a thin smile.

The lift rose up and before it could smash them into the ceiling, the ceiling split apart and a circular hatch opened above them to allow entry. They passed through to a different floor and were suddenly in the center of a vast library with hundreds of shelves full of scrolls, tomes, and piled sheafs of parchment. The glass cables extended up from the chamber below and ran just below the transparent floor, spiraling and winding until they were organized by the colors of the light pulses to travel along into one of the four large wings of the library.

Each wing was a long cylinder lined by curved bookshelves that were built along the entire circumference. The bottoms and tops of the shelves contained thousands of scroll cases that bristled like the needles of an evergreen tree, all pointed toward the center of the wing – the upper scrolls must have some mechanism to hold them in place, Actaeon thought. In the middle sections were books on level shelves. He had never seen so many in his life. How he wished he could spend a few weeks here – the things he might learn!

Within each wing was a lift mechanism that the Niwians had constructed. It ran upon a central shaft that was affixed along the center axis of each wing. A browser of books could stand upon it and turn one crank to drive the platform along the axis. Another crank spun the platform around the shaft so that they could reach books or scrolls at any height. Three of them stood level with the floor of the central library while another was in use – the operator perusing a scroll before they stuffed it back into the case and shoved it into a socket in the shelf above where they twisted it and left it hanging before moving on.

"Rudick tells me you've come to protect my Readers," came a frail voice.

Actaeon spun to look behind him and saw quite the out of place figure.

The Echo Sounder of Memory Keep was a short and wrinkled old woman with a well-worn brown robe wrapped tightly about her thin frame. Her dark gray hair was shot through with white and arranged in three tight buns against the back of her head. She was remarkably plain for a Niwian, except for the fact that the whites of her eyes glowed purple.

"Oh, don't look so surprised Actaeon Rellios Caliburn," said the old woman. "What did you expect, a handsome man dressed like a pompous ass?"

Rudick's hand dropped to the hilt of his writheblade, but was stayed with a gesture from the Echo Sounder.

"You must be mistaken, madam," said Aethelgard. "This is G-"

"I don't make mistakes, Aethelgard sof Leaf," she returned. "And don't play me the fool. I know what you pair are up to. Now, let us get down to business."

The Echo Sounder turned to lead them farther into the library, but the Knight Investigator's next words made her stop in her tracks.

"If you don't make mistakes, then how did you let eight of your Readers die?" asked Aethelgard, folding his arms across his chest.

The old woman spun and narrowed her glowing eyes upon the Arbiter.

"What are you doing?" Minovec rasped at him. "Are you insane?"

"How could you hold her responsible for the killings, Aeth?" asked Actaeon, dropping any pretenses of their disguises. "She could not have been responsible."

"And yet she is," said Aethelgard.

Actaeon shook his head, flabbergasted. "Explain yourself, then."

"He is correct," said the Echo Sounder. "Their deaths are all my fault, to my great sorrow."

"B... but how, Revered One?" asked Captain Minovec, her voice quavering.

"Because she let a machine man in on the secrets of Memory Keep," said Aethelgard.

The Echo Sounder nodded, hanging her head in sadness.

Actaeon and Jurlan both turned to face him, their expressions demanding an explanation.

"It was a simple deduction really," he began. "I first suspected it when I spoke with witnesses to the murders. They spoke of the speed of the assailant in each case. For the killer to escape each scene in broad view of dozens of bystanders – it was a superhuman task. And when I witnessed it with my own eyes, it made it all but certain for me. Especially when the killer leapt from the high wall of Memory Keep's courtyard. A leap like that would've broken an ankle, or worse, for any regular man. And the last, hastily scrawled words of the latest victim that were written in the notebook confirmed my theory."

"'The artifact will see to our end.'" muttered Actaeon.

"Precisely."

"Did I mention you both make crappy Niwians?" said the old woman with a wrinkled smile.

"I told them the same thing, Revered One," said the Captain with a laugh.

"The thing I haven't figured out though is why?" said Aethelgard, ignoring the jab at his disguises. "What would motivate you to connect an artifact man to the Keep?"

The Echo Sounder took a seat at one of the small reading desks and folded her hands across her lap. "Our new fool of a Lord Protector tasked us with getting information out of Memory Keep faster in any way possible. Reader access is limited, and it takes a toll on their bodies. So, one of them came up with the idea to connect an artifact person that was found beneath Sunken City. It had been brought here for study, and was lifeless for all we could tell. A group of Readers brought the idea to me – that perhaps the machine man, as you call it, could be connected to Memory Keep for longer in order to get more information out and satisfy the Lord Protector's unreasonable demands. I authorized it."

"But when they connected it, something went wrong," hazarded Actaeon.

"Not at first," said the old woman. "At first, it did exactly as we had hoped for. The connection activated the machine man and when we disconnected it from the Keep, it was able to answer questions for us on the wealth of new knowledge it had gained. All seemed well and we reported to the Lord Protector that we had a means to access information faster. He was quite happy with the result.

"But a week later, our artificial Reader disappeared from under our very noses. None of my Memory Knights saw any trace of it. After that is when the murders began. It began killing all of my Readers. I noticed a pattern though. It had begun with the ones who had most recently connected with the Keep. Thus far, it has only killed those who connected with Memory Keep after it did. And so, I have made the difficult decision not to allow any Readers to convene with Memory Keep until this matter is resolved."

"Let me connect with Memory Keep," said Actaeon suddenly. "If there is a reason that the machine man is killing the Readers, then perhaps I can find it in there and it can help us stop it."

The Echo Sounder's glowing eyes shifted to the Prince Engineer. "Absolutely not. You shouldn't even be in here as non-Niwians. Let alone connect with the Keep itself!"

"With all due respect Revered One –" began Captain Minovec.

"Why is it that whenever someone says that, they are about to be most disrespectful?" asked the old woman.

The Niwian Red Captain swallowed and drew silent.

"Well then, woman! Spit it out if you've something to say," demanded the Echo Sounder.

"I served under this man in the Second Invasion War and I can truly say that if anyone who is not a Reader and not a Niwian can connect to Memory Keep and get to the bottom of this, it is the Prince Engineer," said Minovec, regaining her confidence as she spoke. "Look at it this way, Revered One – if Actaeon can get the information we need, you won't have to explain to the Lord Protector that you made a mistake that killed many of the Readers. If you have to do that, then he may feel compelled to name a new Echo Sounder, and we both know that his decision would not benefit our Dominion."

"If only more knew the truth of those words," said the Echo Sounder. She stood then and touched the Captain's shoulder. "You are a brave woman, Jurlan ris Minovec."

The Captain's blush was apparent even behind the red plate of her helm. "Thank you, Revered One."

Next, the old woman turned to Actaeon. "Very well, Actaeon Rellios Caliburn. Let us hope that I'm not making yet another mistake."

She gestured for all of them to gather onto the circle of the lift.

The Memory Knight hesitated though. "But, Revered One..."

"It is alright, Rudick," she reassured him. "I trust that they are here to help us. We are at a point where risks must be taken."

Rudick nodded. "Yes, Revered One." He joined them on the lift surface.

The railing rose up again and the five of them ascended to the top level of Memory Keep.

Disorienting was an understatement for the uppermost floor. Projected images flickered and fluttered by in all directions. The projections morphed as they passed by, from human forms, to creatures, to objects, to mechanisms. They were in a constant state of flux as they meandered across the floor. It was impossible to discern any coherent pattern from the chaos, and once one started to concentrate on any given projected shape, it had already undergone another change.   Beyond these projections were windows, many of which offered views out across Redemption's broken landscape. Those that didn't, however, had images floating across them. The images were grainy and alien and just as incomprehensible as the volumetric projections that wandered the floor.

Amidst the chaos, in the center of the room, stood five artifact chairs on pedestals. Each chair had a hinged hood over the headrest. Before the chairs stood a single desk, fabricated from wood.

The Echo Sounder took Actaeon's hand and led him over to the center chair.

"Now listen carefully," she said. "Reading is a process that will take a physical and mental toll upon your body. Your time will be very limited in there on your first attempt. Despite all the distractions, you must internalize the information you want to know. State it aloud repeatedly, as a mantra. Without such concentration, you will become lost and drift freely within the system until I pull you out. Once I do pull you out, you will be paralyzed for a short while. Following that, your nerves will tingle and buzz for a full day. It is quite painful. Your body will be fatigued, and your thoughts will be foggy, as though you're in a dream. Thus, when you are done, you must return to your room and rest. Being a Reader is not for the weak of heart. Are you still sure you wish to attempt this?"

Actaeon took a deep breath before nodding. "Yes. I believe it is important that I try. If I can prevent more Readers from being killed, it will be worth it."

"You are a good partner, Act," said Aethelgard, regarding his friend with his shrewd cobalt gaze. "I believe you will succeed in this."

"Thank you, Aeth," said Actaeon. "I will do my best."

The Echo Sounder pursed her wrinkled lips together and nodded. "Suit yourself then. I have as much interest in your success as you, but I doubt you will make any sense of what lies within Memory Keep. The Readers have spent their lives training to do this work. Now listen carefully. If you need to exit prematurely for whatever reason, lift your hand to your mouth and bite it as hard as you can."

"Bite my hand?" asked Actaeon, concerned. "The sensations will flood my nervous system and cause a disconnect then?"

"It is the incongruity that will help you snap out of the simulation. The pain will be expected, but the pain will not come. Everything then collapses from there," she explained.

"I think I understand," said Actaeon.

"Good," she said. "Then we begin."

Without waiting for a response, she took his arms and, with surprising force for such a frail, old woman, drove him down into the chair.

Actaeon opened his mouth to object, but bands extended from the chair and clamped him in place. The spikes that entered his spine caused him to cry out in surprise and pain. When the hood of the artifact chair rotated forward, he was thrust into a sudden and deeper blackness than he had ever experienced before.

There was a wet and sizzling slap against the back of his head and he felt his entire body spasm against the restraints of the chair.

There was darkness and there was pain.

Gradually, both began to fade and light came into the world around him.

The pain slowly receded from the tips of his limbs and into his spine, where it grew duller but remained ever-present.

The light slowly took form and the scene around him sharpened.

He was in a vast space that was filled with endless complex imagery. The aerial view of a high-tech city of the Ancients. A pair of lizard-like creatures aggressively mating. An androgynous person in shimmering brightweave delivering a speech in the tongue of the Ancients, which made his head throb in pain. A blue and green sphere dotted with slashes and smatterings of white against a black background with glittering *stars*? A spinning mechanism that drove a series of what looked like chains up and down along a waterfall.

The number of strange things sought to drive him mad. Each one spiked his curiosity and drew him in, but, before he could discern further details, more things would flood into view and distract. A man and a woman, making love. Hundreds of babies in glass containers. A building being constructed by tiny, flying robots. A metal ring with a sheet of glittering blue liquid inside. People being forced into chairs like the one he sat in as they screamed and struggled in vain. A bird drinking dew from the cup of a flower.

Remember the mantra, came a voice. Eisandre's voice.

A mantra! The Echo Sounder had said he needed a mantra.

"Machine man," said Actaeon, ignoring the burst of lightning that struck a great metal ship in front of him.

"Show me the machine man," he said again as a line of colorfully dressed dancers spun past him in a synchronized routine.

"The machine man that connected with this place, show it to me," he repeated. He was in a tunnel and a massive machine sped its way toward him.

"Machine man."

A star exploded.

"Machine man."

Blades spun, chopping trees apart as a family of fuzzy, green creatures burrowed down below them.

"Machine man!"

A hand opened, revealing a field of flowers and crackling spikes. He sat in the palm.

"Machine man! Show me the machine man that connected here!"

A number of red projectiles whipped past him. He could feel the warm breeze from one on the back of his neck.

"Machine man!" he shouted, his voice hoarse.

Then he blinked and there was calm.

He stood atop Memory Keep. The five artifact chairs were in the center of the rooftop. A cyclone of strange visions swirled around him.

Redemption lay spread below, glimpsed between the swirling visions. The city was intact. Where once there were ruins now stood pristine buildings, shimmering in the light of the shifting visions.

Strange that such visions could cast their light all the way across the city. All the luminaries in the city flickered as one, blinking on and off in a pattern. No, not a pattern, but a sequence of sorts.

A hand upon his shoulder interrupted his thoughts.

When he turned, there was Princess Eisandre standing before him.

"Eis. Is it really you?" he asked.

His wife blinked her brilliant blue eyes and looked around incredulously. "I... I am not sure what's happening, Act."

Actaeon stepped forward and took her into his arms, holding her tight. She returned the embrace. "Where are we? How?"

The question hung in the air above them like a heavy anchor.

"Memory Keep must have pulled you here as well through your connection with the Thoughtlink Artifact," said Actaeon. "It is fascinating that such a thing could occur. Every other Reader must needs sit in one of those chairs, but with the Thoughtlink..."

He trailed off as his eyes wandered back to the chairs.

In the center one sat a machine man staring at them with abyssal black eyes.

Its skin was a metallic silver color and it wore a simple black tabard.

The bare, silver orb of its head cocked suddenly and it was on its feet in the blink of an eye.

Eisandre caught Actaeon's gaze over her shoulder and turned to face the machine man.

"Do not be afraid," said Actaeon. "We are here to find out more about what happened to you. Can you –"

What happened next was a blur in his mind.

Faster than he could register, the machine man lunged forward and his wife drew the greatsword Caliburn from where it was slung over her shoulder and brought it to bear. The blade glanced off the artifact's shoulder as it ducked below the swing. It snapped out its arm in an action that sent Eisandre flying to the side and off the edge of the tower.

Caliburn clattered to the floor where she had stood.

Actaeon opened his mouth to scream, but the machine man brought up its knee and forced the air from his lungs. It then grabbed his arms and swung him down to the ground, kneeling on his back in a manner that made it feel like his spine was about to crack. Strangely, it didn't hurt at all.

Around them, the visions twisted and changed as they revolved around the tower.

As each one passed Actaeon's limited field of view, he noticed a pattern. In each of them, a different Reader was connected to Memory Keep. And, in each one, as the Reader went about their efforts to find the information they sought, the machine man stalked them throughout the process, staying just out of their sight.

"So why..." grunted Actaeon. "Why reveal yourself to me?"

The thought dawned on him suddenly as he noticed that both of his arms were pinned beneath the machine man's body.

As if in answer, it tightened its grip on Actaeon's arms.

Actaeon fought for a few moments, before deciding it was futile. He worried about Eisandre, tossed from the edge of this simulated building. How would it affect her? He imagined she was catatonic somewhere in Pyramid. Hopefully Itarik and Tarcy were there to keep her safe. But would she wake up okay after her experience here? He imagined she wouldn't wake up out of the trance at all as long as he was linked. The Thoughtlink was keeping her connected to Memory Keep. He had to find a way to sever that connection.

The machine man was making sure he couldn't do that.

But there was one thing it hadn't thought of.

"Falling," said Actaeon.

The whirling visions fell away. He felt more pressure on his back.

"Falling. Falling down."

The chairs flickered, and were replaced by clouds that drifted away.

"Falling. Endless depth. Falling and falling."

Suddenly, the floor beneath them fell away and was gone and they were tumbling into an abyss as dark as the machine man's eyes.

It made a grab for his flailing arms, but was too late.

Actaeon brought his left hand to his mouth and bit down hard. Warm blood flowed out onto his tongue as the machine man grabbed his arm and tried to rip it free, slinging him about in midair on their endless fall.

He bit harder and harder despite the resistance from the machine. And the fact that there was no pain from something that should be excruciating started a chain of events that collapsed the simulation as the Echo Sounder had described.

The machine man blinked and fell away. Then the void was gone.

And suddenly he realized he wasn't falling anymore, but sitting.

The return to consciousness brought an array of pains and fatigues like he'd never felt before in his life.

There were pins and needles throughout his entire body like those that one gets when they fall asleep on an arm. Nerve pain radiated from head to toe and he felt unconsciousness closing in on his vision that he resisted.

An attempt to scream produced no sound.

To lift his arm did nothing.

Frantically, he searched the room with his eyes.

The Echo Sounder was there, along with Memory Knight Rudick, Captain Minovec, and Aethelgard. They all looked on at him with concern.

The machine man was right behind them, spear raised.

It was Rudick who followed Actaeon's panicked gaze and threw himself between the Echo Sounder and the artifact spear.

It slammed into his neck and arced, killing him instantly. He fell to the floor, his body convulsing with electricity.

"It has come for me, at last," said the Echo Sounder.

"Not by my sword," said Minovec. She pulled her longsword from her back and tossed the scabbard to the side, revealing a red-tinted blade.

Aethelgard pulled free his crackling writheblade.

Together they rushed the artifact man.

It easily parried their blows and knocked them both aside.

Actaeon saw what was happening next and used every bit of effort he could muster to tip himself forward and out of the chair. He fell forward just as the machine lined up its shot and threw the spear at his head. It lodged into the chair and sparks rained down upon his back as he fell face-first to the floor. His nose broke and he rolled, involuntarily, to the side, his nasal passages filling with blood.

Blood trickled from his forehead into his eyes as he helplessly watched the rest of the scene unfold before him.

The Knight Investigator and Niwian Captain kept themselves on opposite sides of the machine man and continued to press attacks.

Toward the top of his line of sight, he watched the Echo Sounder kneel and scoop the heavily armored Memory Knight into her arms. As the fighting went on around her, she sobbed at the death of her protector.

Aethelgard and Minovec continued to press the assault against the machine man with astounding ferocity.

Eventually, it was forced to retreat and it broke one of the projection windows with a punch that shattered the elderglass, before leaping out and away from Memory Keep.

"Is everyone okay?" asked Captain Minovec.

"Everyone is *not* okay, Jurlan ris Minovec," scolded the Echo Sounder.

"It wa- ..." began Actaeon, struggling to speak against his paralyzed vocal cords. "It will... will go for Eis next."

Aethelgard knelt beside Actaeon. "Why would it go for your wife?"

"Be- ... because she was brought into there with me. The machine man maintains its connection with Memory Keep. It will try to kill her next."

"Then we will depart immediately, back for the Pyramid," declared Aethelgard.

"Nonsense," said the Echo Sounder. "The boy needs rest."

"She is right," said Actaeon. "We cannot go yet."

"You want to rest while an artifact man is hunting your wife?" asked Aethelgard, confused.

"Not rest," said Actaeon, blowing some blood free of his nostrils to clear his nasal passages. "Put me back into it. Back into Memory Keep."

"Have you lost your mind, Actaeon Rellios Caliburn?" said the Echo Sounder, lowering Rudick gently back to the floor. "Nobody enters Memory Keep twice in one sitting like that. It will destroy your mind!"

"Lives depend on it. My wife's for one. Put me back in there!" demanded Actaeon from his less than prestigious position upon the floor.

The Echo Sounder looked at Aethelgard and Captain Minovec. They both nodded to her.

She shook her head. "I don't like this at all, but if we are to prevent the Keep's fall, I will do anything at this point." She gestured to the others. "Very well. Put him back in the chair. I hope you are right about this, Actaeon Rellios Caliburn."

As the Captain and Arbiter lifted Actaeon to place him back into the chair, every part of his body screamed at him in tingling nerve pain.

Once he was back in the chair and the Echo Sounder had facilitated his connection back into Memory Keep, the three of them waited.

Captain Minovec stood guard by the broken window while Aethelgard watched over both Actaeon and the Echo Sounder with his writheblade out and ready.

The writheblade sputtered and sparked, the room filling with the sickly stench of ozone.

Blood oozed from Actaeon's nose and pooled upon the green collar of his tunic.

The Echo Sounder wandered between the body of her Memory Knight and the artifact chair, silently fretting.

"How long do you think he'll be in there for?" asked Captain Minovec.

"As long as he must be to find what he needs," said Aethelgard, matter-of-factly.

"If he even returns," said the old woman. "None have gone in so soon in my cycles, and for good reason."

"What's he even looking for?" asked Minovec.

"A way to kill it, I'm certain," said Aethelgard.

"Let's hope he's successful," said Minovec.

They all found themselves nodding at that.

After a long and nerve-wracking wait, where they weren't sure if the machine man would return to attack at any moment, Actaeon began to cough and fell forward in the chair.

The Echo Sounder caught him with strong hands and supported him.

Minovec rushed over. "Did you find what you were looking for, Actaeon?"

Actaeon grinned up at them and rolled to the side, bloody drool dripping down to the floor.

"I take it that went well then?" said Aethelgard with a thin smile.

Actaeon tried to nod, but his head just lolled in the other direction.

"Give him a moment to recover. Please!" said the Echo Sounder. Her words were not a suggestion, but a command.

And when Actaeon finally felt up to speaking again, he grinned up at the old woman. "There is an artifact that Memory Keep told me you have stored here. I hope you might loan it to me."

Actaeon winced as the cart struck another piece of debris. The impact jarred his entire body.

"Be careful! I would much prefer to make it back to Pyramid in one piece, if at all possible," he said.

Knight Investigator and Niwian Captain both shot him daggers with their eyes. The pair of them rolled the cart along through the ruins at a jog.

"You said to go faster!" griped Minovec. She made a point to steer the cart purposely for the next elderstone fragment.

Actaeon winced and grinned. "If you break a wheel, you will have to carry me there instead. I doubt that alternative is much more appealing."

"Or we could just leave you here," she suggested.

"It would be preferential if I was there to oversee the engagement," said Actaeon.

"If I cut his legs off, he'd be lighter," joked Aethelgard with a thin smile.

"You would cut them off just as I am beginning to feel them again?" asked Actaeon.

Minovec smirked at that. "If you didn't have me send my men ahead, maybe I wouldn't be so grumpy." She had sent the four Niwian Red soldiers that accompanied them ahead with instructions from Actaeon to deliver to Lauryn at the workshop.

"Had we not sent them ahead, we might soon be dead, which is much worse than grumpy last time I checked." Actaeon's teeth chattered as one of the wheels inadvertently struck a big root.

By the time the three of them arrived at the workshop, Actaeon was able to walk again.

Lauryn showed him the modification she'd made to one of the grenado launchers at his behest.

Actaeon inspected it quickly and nodded. "A fine job as usual, Engineer Lauryn." He turned to his two investigator companions. "Shall we proceed then?"

"Do you want me to come with my light lance, Act?" asked Lauryn, still blushing from his compliment.

"If I am correct, it should not be necessary," said Actaeon. "However, if there is one thing I have learned over the years, it is to always have a secondary plan in case the primary fails. So yes, bring your light lance. We must be quick now. Eisandre tells me that the machine man has found her!"

They found Princess Eisandre in the Way of the Pillars within the Pyramid. The scene was mayhem as Eisandre fought off the machine man. She was flanked by two of her Companions, Itarik and Tarcy, the First Companion and the Giantess.

Collectively, the three of them were able to fend off each attack of the machine man and his artifact spear. But they were beginning to grow fatigued.

Tarcy Hael, in particular, looked like she was about to collapse as she swung her massive ruinblade to fend off another flurry of attacks from the artifact man.

Eisandre leapt clear of one thrust and ducked another. She wielded her two-handed artifact sword, Caliburn, in an effort to do more damage to her artifact opponent than a normal blade might. In addition to being a sigil of Raedellean power, Caliburn was renowned for its ability to destroy artifact weapons – even writheblades were not safe from it. The next swing of her blade would've taken off the top of any normal man's head, but the killer machine was much too quick and narrowly slid under it.

The counterstrike from its spear was aimed right at Eisandre's face. But she had anticipated the blow, and shifted her head to the side to clear the point. She tried to break the spear's shaft with her sword, but the machine man had already pulled it back and launched himself at Itarik.

The First Companion knocked aside the spearpoint but received a firm kick to the head, which sent him crumpling to the ground.

Minovec and Aethelgard drew their swords and started forward.

"Wait!" shouted Actaeon, bringing them to a halt.

Actaeon leveled the modified grenado launcher at the artifact man and pulled the trigger.

With a sharp twang, the special payload launched toward the machine.

It easily dodged the bulky projectile, but it made a dire mistake by turning to look at it.

When it hit the ground, it began to flash in the special sequence that Actaeon had programmed into it. The one that he had gone back into Memory Keep to obtain.

Once the machine man had looked, it found it could not look away. Its jet black eyes locked onto the flashing artifact that the Echo Sounder had loaned to Actaeon. It stood, transfixed, until the light sequencer ran through the entirety of the sequence it had been configured to flash.

As the light sequencer artifact began to play through the pattern again, the machine man clattered face down against the elderstone floor like a toppled column. There it lay still.

Eisandre gave a questioning look to Actaeon and he nodded. She wasted no time in stepping forward to sever the killer artifact's head from its shoulders with a neat sweep of her sword.

It pained Actaeon to see the machine ended. He would have much rather disabled it somehow and reactivated it later to see if there was anything he could learn from it. The risk was too high though. There was no guarantee he could've kept it restrained, and if it managed to escape, it meant death for him and his wife. Thus, it had to be destroyed. Though, he would still bring it back to the workshop for teardown and study.

Eisandre interrupted his thoughts with her arms around him. He returned the hug.

Aethelgard placed a hand upon his shoulder. "So, that's what it killed so many for? A flashing light?"

Actaeon loosened his embrace to look over at his friend. "A specific sequence of lights that would trigger a shutdown for it. It was protecting itself. Any Readers who connected with Memory Keep after they gained knowledge of the machine man could have found out."

"And, so it killed them all – just to be sure," said Captain Minovec. She stood over the body of the thing, looking conflicted.

"If any of us were confronted with such a fundamental threat to our existence, we'd have done exactly the same thing," said Aethelgard.

"But would we have?" asked Minovec, skeptical.

Everyone gathered around the headless machine, silently considering the question.

It was Lauryn who finally spoke. "Yes. I never knew it until the moment I first had to take a life, but in the instant when it mattered, I killed to protect myself."

"In that regard, it was truly no different than us," said Actaeon.

The Broken Lock

91 A.R., THE 45TH DAY OF TORRENTFALL

LONE ARBITER FOUND IT WHILE on patrol during a break in the rain. A partially folded section of vellum, plastered by the deluge against a shattered column in the Boneyards to the north of the Pyramid. It was only visible because a loose end of it was fluttering in the wind. That alone drew the Arbiter's attention and convinced him to divert from his course to investigate.

The paper was nothing exciting – just a damp and tattered remnant of something more. Nothing of note – just another piece of debris amidst the ruins. And that would have been it had not the Arbiter unfolded the thick parchment to look within. The sheet was partially delaminated in its waterlogged condition and ripped some of the writing from the page.

It was what remained, however, that caused the Arbiter to report it with all haste:

– will kill me in this place. I'm sure of –

The text before and after that part was missing, stuck to the opposing section. The Arbiter dared not open it farther for fear of destroying the writing within. It was a good thing too, for that was how it ended up before Aethelgard mostly intact.

The Knight Investigator carefully slid the vellum across the table to Actaeon.

The pair sat at a workbench in Actaeon's workshop as the torrential rains outside tapped away at the stone vault above like a thousand tiny wooden hammers.

Actaeon poured out two tankards of ale and pushed one across to his friend before leaning forward to scrutinize the vellum. "What, exactly, am I looking at?"

"A piece of evidence in search of a crime," said Aethelgard. He took a sip of his ale and drummed his fingers on the workbench in solidarity with the rain.

"You have yet to open it, I see," said Actaeon, arching a brow.

"Not until I could get your expert opinion on the matter. I didn't want to disturb it beforehand." The Knight Investigator pushed his lenses up his nose and offered a thin smile.

"The folds?" considered Actaeon as he continued to examine the parchment from different angles without yet touching it.

"Precisely," said Aethelgard.

Actaeon pushed back the stool to kneel so that his face was level with the table's surface. He closed one eye and swept his head slowly along the edge as he examined it. After a long moment of that, he grinned and stood, before retaking his seat and sipping from his own tankard. "A paper glider?"

"A paper glider." The smile on the Arbiter's face showed that he was pleased with his engineer friend's conclusion.

"At least, that is what it appears to be. When I was a child, I used to play with my friends to see whose glider could fly the farthest off of Incline. I swear that one of mine flew all the way across the River of Arches one clear, windy day, but you would have to ask my friend Jezail to confirm that particular story." Actaeon smiled at the memory of the glider shrinking to a point on its way beyond the glittering river.

"Aye," said Aethelgard, smiling. "When I was a young lad, my fellow Arbiter Initiates and I would break up the boredom of manning the walls of Redoubt by launching gliders made from stolen pages of texts found in the library there. When the technical Arbiter in charge of the library found out, he was furious. He made us scour the ruins until we found every last page that had been taken from his books. Of course, we'd only taken the most useless pages from them – the ones with superfluous chapter endings, section introductions, and appendices. That didn't quell his anger. He lectured us for days after that on the importance of the written word and the time it took to scribe all those volumes."

"Did you find them all? The pages?" asked Actaeon, genuinely curious.

"Aye, we did. It took four days. After that he stopped with the lectures about it," said Aethelgard with a chuckle.

"Shall we open it?" asked Actaeon.

"Do the honors, if you will," said Aethelgard.

Actaeon brought a halfthrough bottle over from another workbench that was full of sharpened wooden sticks and probes of varying shapes and sizes. Using a pair of wide, chisel-shaped probes, he set to work.

First, he worked them gently between the section of vellum that had stuck to the opposing portion of paper across the fold. Once he made a purchase, he gently pried the two sections of paper apart. Some of it crumbled as he worked, but the majority of it remained intact. This he pulled apart until he reached the next fold, which was still in place. He flattened the fold carefully and began to wedge the tools into it to separate the faces from one another. As he proceeded, a major problem became clear: much of the ink had been washed from the surface by the rains. It had spread from its original intended position to pool upon one side or the other of the folded paper surfaces. Undeterred, he continued to work the folded glider open and apart until it lay fully flat upon the workbench. At its corners, he placed four metal weights to hold it flat. After that, he spent some time simply scrutinizing it again.

"May I use your magnification lens?" he asked, breaking the silence.

Aethelgard snapped out of his reverie, immersed as he was with watching Actaeon skillfully dissect the glider-cum-note. He passed Actaeon the magnifier and the Prince Engineer examined the paper with it.

"Despite the ink being displaced in many places, the indentations from the applicator still remain. If you allow me, I would rub a flat portion of a charcoal stick across them and it should enable us to read the contents of this glider." Actaeon pulled a charcoal stick from one of his jacket pockets and used his knife to cut an angled flat on one side.

"Please do. I insist," said Aethelgard. "Let's see what is revealed to us."

Actaeon rubbed the charcoal stick across the paper, careful to keep the edge parallel to the parchment. It gradually revealed the contents of the letter, and both men leaned forward to read it.

Today is the 35 Reap if I count correct. The year is 88. 94 days now I'm trapped in this damned room. I know not who holds me, but I doubt at this point I will stand beneath the sky again. They will kill me in this place. I'm sure of it. It was after the Monsoon Festival they took me. Someone must have spiked my drink with a poison. I awoke here after. It took me near 100 days, but by some miracle I convinced them to allow me writing materials to keep myself occupied. This one I let fly through a small crack in the corner of the room. With hope, it rides the strong winds of today to my salvation. If you find this, please help me. And tell my dear Alisha that I love her.

-Rognin Thrist, Baron of Suncrest in the Hold of Rust

"Fascinating," said Aethelgard. "Baron Thrist was reported missing shortly after the Monsoon Festival that year."

"He let this letter fly around the time of the first incident we worked together," said Actaeon. "The one with Anchelle."

"Yes," said Aethelgard. "The winged protector. A few weeks before that case, as I recall."

"Strange. Do you suppose that this letter might have been released from a different room in Pyramid around that same time period?" Actaeon took another sip of his ale and considered the words on the parchment again.

"It is entirely possible," said Aethelgard. "Though I doubt it is related. And it might've come from anywhere near the Boneyards, though I agree that the Pyramid is a likely source."

"The Baron wrote that he was in there for a long time. Do you suppose he could still be in there?" asked Actaeon, considering.

"Ninety-four days he was there. It was three years ago, though. To keep a man in captivity in a public building for so long, no matter how much a labyrinth it might be, would be a challenge for anyone. But for another three years?" Aethelgard arched a brow and looked over at Actaeon. "Tell me, my engineer friend. Why would someone keep a Baron against their will for so long a time?"

"The only reason I can imagine is that someone must have wanted something from him. Something that he was unable or unwilling to immediately deliver," guessed Actaeon.

"Precisely," said the Knight. "Or, that someone else was unwilling to deliver."

"I can arrange for us to speak with Enrion Zar about it," suggested Actaeon. "He may have more information about what the Baron might have had that was worth holding him for so long."

"Good idea," said Aethelgard. "In the meantime, I'll have a team of Arbiters scour the Boneyards for more of these paper gliders." He levered himself to his feet with his cane.

"Wait a moment," said Actaeon. "Can the Arbiter who found this one recall the exact location? If so, then perhaps we might have a clue as to where it originated."

The Knight's cobalt eyes lit up and he smiled his thin smile. "Now there's a thought."

When they arrived inside the Pyramid, they found the Way of Pillars filled with a number of merchants looking to escape the torrential rain outside. Hastily built stalls had been thrown together between the massive elderstone columns that held up the ceiling of the entry hall far above their heads. A team of Arbiters that was much too small for the job was attempting to convince the merchants to leave the area, but to no avail. One of the Knights stepped away from the others and blew upon a whistle to summon more Arbiters to help. He looked relieved when Aethelgard approached him.

"Glad you're here, sir," he said. "This situation's getting out of control. They all think they're entitled to space here to hawk wares just because of a little rain outside."

"Actually, I need you to rally a few Arbiters to do a thorough search of the Boneyards for more paper gliders like the one brother Elmerth found," said Aethelgard, pausing to adjust the lenses perched upon his nose as he watched the conflict unfold behind the Arbiter.

"Sir?" There was positive disbelief in the Arbiter's tone. "You want us to search for children's toys amidst the ruins during a monsoon instead of securing the Pyramid against these ruffians?"

Aethelgard chuckled. "That's one way to put it, I suppose. But consider this: those children's toys might result in a saved life. Do you imagine these merchants will kill anybody if you leave them be for the meantime?"

The Arbiter opened his mouth to argue, but then closed it. He opened it again to speak, but then shook his head, rounded up his patrol squad, and left to pursue Aethelgard's orders.

Actaeon grinned and shook his head.

"What?" Aethelgard shrugged and offered a smirk.

"You have an interesting way of tackling problems, my friend."

"The best course of action is always the direct one, if you want to get things done." The Knight Investigator pointed with his cane. "Now let's go find your Shieldian friend. Lead the way."

The Lord Zar merited his own private room in the Pyramid's Mirrorholds, where the Dominional embassies were all located. A rap upon the door brought him about. The young noble peeked out and ushered a small toddler away from the door before recognition dawned on him and he threw open the door. "Act! How have you been? Do come in." He stepped back and led them both to a large settee. Once they were seated he snapped his fingers and a servant emerged from the corner to pour them all a cup of rice wine.

"I see that your lovely daughter is growing quickly, Enrion," said Actaeon with a grin.

"They grow big so fast," the Lord said. "Little Indovo keeps us occupied for sure." Enrion winced then and his left hand leapt up to the pinned up flap of sleeve where half of his right arm was missing.

"Are you alright?" asked Aethelgard.

"I am," said Enrion, his eyes narrowing. "The rains always bring about an exquisite pain this time of the year." His daughter giggled off behind a set of dividers and his expression softened. "So, what brings you gentlemen to my abode?"

"A certain Baron Thrist," said Aethelgard.

Enrion's eyes narrowed again upon the Knight Investigator.

"We found a clue to his disappearance," explained Actaeon. "Any details you could share about the Baron might help us in the matter."

"Rognin Thrist is no friend of the Zar dynasty," said Enrion, his tone hardening. "Shield will not miss him."

"And what did this Baron do to earn such ire from the Zars?" asked Aethelgard. He took a sip of the rice wine and leaned forward expectantly.

Enrion tilted his head to the side and glared at the Knight. "I trust you are not suggesting that Shield had anything to do with this?"

"I suggest nothing, Lord Zar." Aethelgard steepled his fingers. "I'm not interested in implications and conjecture. The only things I am here for are facts. Any that you might share with me may prove pivotal in this investigation. If, at any point, I say something, you may rest assured that it is not a suggestion, but an incontrovertible fact. Now, you were saying that Baron Thrist is no friend of the Zar dynasty?"

Enrion leaned back on the settee, using his stump to prop himself up while he eyed Aethelgard mistrustfully and shot Actaeon a skeptical glance.

"Aethelgard speaks the truth," offered the Prince Engineer. "Often it is baffling how he arrives at his conclusions, even for me, but I have found that he always speaks the truth of the matter. You can trust him."

Enrion let out a deep sigh and finished off his first cup of rice wine before holding it behind him for the servant to refill. Once it was full, he sipped it again before speaking. "If Actaeon says you can be trusted, then that's good enough for me. Thrist is a schemer and a scammer. He embezzled coin from the Shieldian coffers while using that coin to further lies and propaganda against the rule of my father, the Prince General. In the end, the effort resulted in one of the worst insurrections in the history of Shield. Luckily, it was quashed quickly by my sister, but the entire ordeal was an embarrassment of the utmost order."

"If he did this, then why wasn't he wasting away within a Shieldian cell?" asked Aethelgard, adjusting his lenses.

"Shield is a Dominion of law and order – something I suspect you're familiar with," started Enrion.

Aethelgard nodded and rubbed his bad knee. "Continue."

"The leaders of lesser Dominions might hang their enemies with little more than an inkling of wrongdoing. In Shield, we need proof or the justiciers will not sentence an individual for a crime, not matter how likely it is. The missing money was never traced and the source of propaganda never identified. But we all knew it had to be him. None other could've pulled off such an insurrection, and in the capital Hold no less. His dislike of my father is well known among the noble circles. The Prince General is a clever man though... In short order, many in Shield were convinced that the insurrection was not in fact a revolt, but a training exercise gone wrong. An exercise where, after the wrong orders were given and there existed a general failure to notify many of the intended participants, dozens of soldiers lost their lives. Of course, it later became known that the originator of the erroneous orders and the failed notifications was none other than Thrist himself. Even the soldiers directly involved in the clash were convinced of the matter." Enrion smiled proudly and took another sip of his drink.

"The training exercise was just a story to get back at Baron Thrist then?" asked Actaeon.

Enrion narrowed his eyes and clucked his tongue. "Just a story? Of course not. It was quite the tragedy in Shield. Rognin Thrist lost much of his support from that point forward. You see, things have a way of sorting themselves out without even crossing the justicier's bench." He smiled again and ushered the servant over to top off the others' cups.

Aethelgard handed the servant his still full cup and shooed him away. "And since the Prince General had his revenge, what became of Baron Thrist?" he asked.

"Oh, the murmuring of displeasure and rumors of an attempt to create a second insurgence. Nothing beyond that though. Just rumors. You see, he had lost his allure. The glamorous and sharp alternative to my father had become nothing more than a dullard – an incompetent fool responsible for needless deaths of his own people." Enrion paused then. "Of course, people began to wonder what happened to him after he'd disappeared. From what I understand, his wife, Alisha, has managed Suncrest in his stead."

"Thank you, Lord Zar," said Aethelgard. Using his cane, he levered himself to his feet. "If I have further questions, I will seek you out."

"Please do," said Enrion, standing. "Actaeon, please send Her Grace, the Princess, my regards. And give your little Aedwina a kiss on the head from me."

"I shall do just that," said Actaeon. "Tell your Lady wife that I said hello. It was good to see you, my friend."

"And you," said Enrion. "Oh, and Actaeon?"

"Yes?" Actaeon, on his way toward the door, turned back.

"Be careful with this," he said, worry creasing his brow. "Despite my dislike of Baron Thrist and his recent downturn in repute, he is a sharp and resourceful fellow. If you are investigating this matter, then I imagine there was likely foul play. And if someone bested Thrist in such an underhanded way... Well, then they are really quite dangerous."

Actaeon nodded. "We will."

"What did you make of the conversation?" asked Actaeon as they walked along the halls of the Pyramid.

"There's plenty of motive here," said Aethelgard. "The creator of an insurrection, the embezzler of wealth, the scapegoat for many deaths, the weakened leader of a barony – each of them or any combination of them could be a reason to abduct him. Let us grab a sandwich and tea at the Tea Lounge. It will give us some time to allow the facts to percolate in our minds and time for the Arbiters to search for more paper gliders."

"More notes may lead to a location," said Actaeon.

"Or a culprit," said Aethelgard.

Later that evening, a visit to the Arbiter Pyramid Command yielded good news. An Arbiter had brought back the soggy mess of another glider and marked the location on a crudely sketched map of the Boneyards. The parchment was drooping and smashed, but the shape was clearly that which had given it flight – a tapered body with two narrow wings. Aethelgard was about to unfold it, but then thought better of it and handed it to Actaeon.

"What do you recommend, Engineer?" he asked.

"We should bring it back to my workshop and dry it out in the heat of the forge. I would not want to attempt any opening of the document until it is quite dry, lest the writing smudge or the paper delaminate. From there, we see what we might read before attempting another rubbing." Actaeon turned the floppy glider in his hands and a few dirty drips fell to the floor at his feet. "He designed this to fly fast and far, cutting through the wind."

The effort at the workshop yielded fair results. They were able to decipher some of the writing, but part of the glider had disintegrated beyond recognition and that part of the message was lost.

It's 1 Dawn, 89 A.R. Trapped in a crumbly room in the … So little hope left. Every day I surprise myself by continuing to draw breath. All

*my ambitions, all my hopes, reduced to this. I regret that I ever … …
failed this life and lost it all. May I find redemption in the next li...
...ase, if you get this, try to find me. Every day, when the ray of sun
shining into the crack of my room fades, I shout into the ruins. Listen
for me as the sun sets. And if you cannot find me, tell my dear Alisha
that I lo...*

-Rognin Thrist, Baron of Su...

"Perhaps he regrets his efforts to overthrow Indros?" suggested Actaeon as he finished reading the letter spread before them on the workbench.

"Undoubtedly," said Aethelgard before taking a deep drag from his pipe. An impressive, puffy ring of smoke that he blew up toward the loft ceiling rolled along until it broke against the beams and faded to naught. "A man trapped for years with so little information on his captivity. He must have thought it a punishment for his past deeds. Perhaps for some of the very events that your Shieldian friend described."

"What is next?" asked Actaeon.

"Now we wait." The Knight Investigator took another puff on his pipe. "I'll set an Arbiter or two to listen for his shouts at dusk in case that is the correct time. If he yet lives, they might hear something."

"Do you suppose then, that the crack is in a western corner of the room?" Actaeon absently teased a corner of the crumpled paper with a finger.

"Well, Baron Thrist did," said Aethelgard. "And so, we may think he had good reason to believe that."

It was a full week later, when Aethelgard returned to the workshop.

The rains pounded incessantly against the stone vault, making it hard to concentrate on anything. And so, Actaeon was glad when his friend pushed his way inside, pulled back the heavy cowl of his cloak, and dropped a leather bag on one of the workbenches.

Wasting no time, Actaeon rushed over and dug carefully inside to withdraw the glider. It was a soaked, crushed mess. A muddy bootprint atop it revealed its heavily trodden upon fate.

"Can you salvage it, Engineer?" asked Aethelgard. Making himself at home, he filled two tankards of ale from a barrel against the far wall and set one down beside Actaeon before taking a gulp of his own to help warm his bones after his long trudge through the rain.

Ignoring the tankard, Actaeon set to work. He dried the wet vellum of the smashed glider in the residual heat of the forge. It took some time, but he worked the edges of the paper carefully apart and soon had the entire thing flat. There was no visible text left – just a smudge of runny ink on the center of the paper. It was concentrated around what appeared to be a pair of words. Leaving it to dry for a time, he joined the Arbiter at the workbench and finally took a sip from the tankard his friend had poured him.

They listened to the rain in companionable silence for a while. Eventually, Aethelgard set his tankard aside and withdrew a small, fluted pipe that he had at his belt. The song he played was, at once, mournful and hopeful. Bright, resonant tones were punctuated by deep and drawn-out ones to create a melody that reflected the mood of the case at hand. Could a man trapped for years in the ruins be found? Or was he lost to time?

When the song wound down, it faded away into the incessant thrumming of rain, leaving both men alone in their thoughts. With a thunk, Actaeon set his empty tankard down and stood. He felt the vellum, which had been cooling on a tray suspended over some fading coals from the forge. The paper was dry, and so, he brought it over to the workbench along with a sharpened charcoal stick. Laying the paper out, he set to rubbing the side of the charcoal over the center of the ink blot.

Two words leapt from the page as he continued his rubbing: Ruin Lock.

A stool tumbled backward, clattering on the floor as Aethelgard stood with a start. In the rush, he knocked over what remained of his tankard, spilling the ale to the wooden surface, where it ran across the table and resoaked the flattened glider.

"By the Fallen…" whispered the Knight Investigator. The color had left his face and his hand trembled as he righted the tankard again.

"What does it mean?" asked Actaeon, startled by his friend's uncharacteristic reaction.

"Ruinlock…" said Aethelgard, whispering the word.

"Yes," said Actaeon. "That much is obvious. What is a ruin lock?"

The Knight composed himself and righted his stool before resuming his perch upon it. "Not what, but who. I'd... I'd hoped never to see that name again." When Actaeon arched a brow and continued offering him a quizzical look, he began to explain. "A wraith. A hidden force that has steered the fate of much in Redemption for decades now. Master of obscuration and misdirection. Controller of nearly all the criminal underworld in this city. If you ever find yourself assailed in the Warrens, speak his name and all will flee before it – if you dare."

"If I dare?" asked Actaeon, skepticism wrought upon his features. "This Ruinlock terrifies you, does he not?"

"There is not much in this world that does," admitted Aethelgard. "But the great deceptor is an exception to that rule. As I say, speak his name – make it known that he's caught your interest – get his attention somehow, and he will find out. And when he does, your days will be numbered, my friend."

"What did he do to make you this afraid?" asked Actaeon, still not believing the extremity of the Arbiter's words.

"Some time ago, I was not the only Knight Investigator. There were two of us for a while. But that was before a case crossed our path that led to Ruinlock. It was a dead end. My partner wouldn't give us the chase though. When I found him, it was... It was not pretty. To this day it haunts my dreams. The message was clear – that the Order of Arbiters should leave him alone."

"So you gave up on finding him?" Actaeon looked doubtful.

Aethelgard shook his head. "I will never give up. But I must act otherwise, because to do anything else before I have enough information will almost certainly lead to my demise."

"Do we keep investigating this case then?" asked Actaeon.

"A man may yet live," said Aethelgard, leaning forward to rub his bad knee. "Until we find out his fate, we keep on searching for answers."

The next few days showed a break in the rains. Arbiters positioned throughout the Boneyards in the dusk hours turned up nothing. But three more gliders were discovered, each in a different part of the ruins north of the Pyramid and one near Redoubt, the Arbiter fortress.

And so, they met again to dry and to discern the contents.

The first glider's rubbings came out clear, much to Actaeon's happiness.

If my count stands correct, today is 18 of Spur, the year 90. I've lost count how many gliders have flown. My great hope is that people have found them, and are looking for me. I am Rognin Thrist, Baron of Suncrest in Shield. I am being held against my will by someone or someones who I have not seen. I am fed, and supplied with ink and the vellum I use to make these gliders. My piss and shit are taken from this room of mine periodically. A gas fills the room before then to knock me out. When I awaken, everything, including myself, is fresh and clean. I endeavored to avoid breathing the gas one day to try and witness my captors. For this, I wrapped my tunic around my mouth to filter the gas and stood close to the crack in the room through which I have released so many of these gliders. I couldn't help but breath some of the gas in, despite my efforts. So when my captor arrived in a hooded mask and cloak, I was woozy. I flung myself at him anyway, in a futile attempt to rip the hood free and finally see the face of my captor. It was useless though. I was flung to the ground and beaten unconscious. When I awoke, I found myself naked. Thankfully, they left the parchment for me, so that I might continue to record my thoughts – so that I might continue to let the gliders fly. May they reach someone who can save me. Tell Alisha I love her!

"Amazing," said Aethelgard.

"What are you thinking?" asked Actaeon with a nervous grin.

"That he kept his sanity after years in confinement alone," mused the Knight Investigator. "Whatever your friend the young Lord Zar said about his character, there is one thing we can be certain about – Rognin Thrist is a man of extraordinary willpower."

The second glider's rubbings were less fortuitous. While the text at the top of the parchment came in clear, the paper was much too damaged at the bottom and nothing was recoverable.

Welcome 23 Arrival of 89. A good year and a good day. My 53rd emergence day, in fact. Happy me. I'll get to celebrate with the rats that try to steal my food. Maybe when they come today for my evening meal, I should share it with them. What do you think? Why not, right? In fact, that's just what I'll do. Starting today I'll go on a hunger strike. Whatever they're keeping me here for, it won't work if I starve myself to …

The remainder of the text was lost to the damage.

The third and final glider happened to be the most recent. The writing on the dirty vellum was smeared with dried blood and a bloody set of fingerprints was on the upper left corner. The penmanship was noticeably rougher than the other letters, but still had the same characteristics.

They will kill me on the morrow, of that much I'm certain. Kill me! The pain is exquisite. The beatings never end. I only endure them at the thought of what poor Alisha would do if I was gone from the world. Alisha… Poor Alisha. She must think me dead and gone by now. Like my teeth. My teeth are gone. And another of my fingers today. Oh! Today is Torrent 47. Year 91. Ha! The fool, whoever they are. A sodden fool! I know what they're after and they'll never have it. Never have it, you hear that? The secret follows me to my grave. And my unseen torturer can live on with the futility of their efforts to haunt them. Ha! May they choke on frustration.

"By the Fallen," said Actaeon. "That was written yesterday."

Aethelgard pulled a luminary from his pocket and shined it carefully over the parchment. When he returned it to his pocket, he shook his head. "No, it wasn't."

"How could you know that?" asked Actaeon, peering at the paper. He pulled out his own luminary and slid the baffle aside to shine the light upon it himself in an attempt to discern whatever his friend had.

"There are a multitude of reasons why a man in captivity and suffering torture might lose track of the day," explained Aethelgard. "Whatever the cause, doesn't change the fact that the bloody fingerprint left behind by the unfortunate Baron is at least ten days old. And, I'd say with relative confidence, not more than twelve."

Actaeon blinked and grinned, astounded. "You mean to tell me that you can tell the age of the blood?"

"You run experiments on mechanics, chemicals, and artifacts, do you not?" When Actaeon nodded, Aethelgard continued. "Well, do you think it so unusual that I run experiments in my trade? Knowing precisely the details of blood, footprints, wear of materials, and even the characteristics of an aging corpse have solved many a crime for me. I make a study of such things. They tell me more about what happened than any person might. And they don't lie."

"What of the characteristics tell you the time that this fingerprint was left? The color?" Actaeon guessed.

"The color is a clear giveaway. You will also notice, if you look closely, that the ends of the ridges have begun to crumble and fall away." Aethelgard handed over his magnifier hand lens and allowed his friend to examine the prints closely. "Have you heard the theory that blood carries air throughout the body so that the component parts might receive some energy from the ether?"

"Interesting," said Actaeon, after finding the crumbling ridges. He handed the magnifier back. "Yes. It is why the blood is redder when leaving the lungs than when it returns."

"Indeed," said Aethelgard. "Tiny particles of ether, shuttled along to different parts of the body by little carriers in the fluid – no doubt, too small for our eyes to see. When those carriers leave the body, they slowly die. Thus, the loss in color. As they die, they can no longer perform their function, and without the particles of ether, the color fades. At least, that is my theory on the matter."

"There is good sense to it," said Actaeon with a grin. "I cannot disagree. I have attempted in the past to create an array of lenses in order to achieve the effect of magnification even greater than your handheld lens. Unfortunately, the flaws in the lenses compound significantly at that magnitude, and obscure the ability for me to glean such detail."

"If you found a manner to accomplish that, it would help my investigations a great deal," said the Arbiter, leaning forward on his cane. "Even without as high a degree of magnification. For example, just to see the differences in the oils of a fingerprint left at the scene of a crime and one left elsewhere could help me trace the origin of the culprit."

"Then I will do my best to make you such a device." Actaeon's brow furrowed as he began to think on the problem. "If the light of a luminary could be focused through the lenses –" He stopped then, abruptly.

"What is it?" asked Aethelgard.

"What you said – it gives me another idea," said Actaeon, standing up from the workbench in a hurry. "There is a way to trace the origin of these letters."

"What are you thinking?" asked Aethelgard.

Actaeon grinned and, in an imitation of his friend's voice, said, "Patience. You will see."

The garden tender of the Altheans climbed up onto their stumpy legs and brushed freshly turned dirt from their pants before looking at the pair of them with unequivocal perturbance.

Actaeon had led the way up to the Garden Terraces on the north face of the Pyramid, a place filled with the known diversity of plants found across Redemption and even some from beyond, brought home by Thyrian ships. The gardener, Shard, glared at them with sunken, dark eyes that peered out through an ancient mass of wrinkles on their face. The remaining wisps of hair atop Shard's head offered no clue as to the gender of the androgynous Althean. And neither did their voice.

"Can't ya see these plants be needin' me?" said Shard with an exasperated shake of their head. "Ask yer questions so'n I can get back to it then."

"How'd you know we were here to ask questions?" asked Aethelgard.

"The pair a ya both. Only shows up ta badger me with questions. Ne'er ta say hallo. Ne'er ta help pull some weeds. Jus' when ya needs somethin'. Out wit it then!" snapped Shard.

Actaeon grinned and pulled the stack of folded glider remains from his jacket pocket. "You keep a record of the weather on each day, do you not?"

"A course I do," said Shard, looking taken aback at any suggestion of otherwise. "How else'n I be knowin' what my plants do want?"

"And the wind is a part of your record?" asked Actaeon.

"Is wind parta weather, or not? Whaddayoo think, lad? Didna I jus' say

I keep a record?" Shard mashed grubby fists into deep eye sockets to rub them as in disbelief at the stupidity of the questioning.

Actaeon lifted the papers. "I have five dates over the past few years. Could you tell me about the wind conditions on each day?"

With another head shake, Shard turned about and began to waddle away. "Come, come, come."

Engineer and Investigator followed.

When they reached one of the archways that led back into the Pyramid's interior, Shard knelt to rummage within a cabinet set against the wall and eventually stood with a worn, leather-bound tome in hand. "Kay. Dates. Dunna have all day."

Actaeon relayed the dates and Shard looked up the wind conditions on each one for him. Once they had them all, Actaeon thanked the Althean.

Shard threw hands up in the air and punctuated it with another exasperated shake of their head. "As if I waren't doin' nuthin' here. Ya wanna thank me – pull some weeds." After waiting a long moment to see if they would actually help, Shard gave up and stomped off to get back to work.

Aethelgard laughed. "Ah, Shard. Some people never change."

"So, Aeth. Tell me," began Actaeon with a grin. "Is Shard a..."

"A man or woman?" Aethelgard finished the question, a thin smile forming on his face.

"Aye," said Actaeon. "I was wondering so much."

"Isn't it clear?" Aethelgard pointed his cane at Shard's departing figure. "I've taught you about the gait of men and women. About mannerisms and custom of dress. Certainly, the bone structure and degree of skin wrinkling is a clear giveaway!" When Actaeon offered him a blank look and a shrug, he laughed out loud and continued. "Have you learnt nothing from working with me? Keep paying attention and I promise, you'll know everything there is to know about Shard, and anyone else, just by speaking with them for a short while."

Next, they stopped by the Tea Lounge to imbibe some afternoon tea. Actaeon spread a blank sheet of vellum upon the table and sketched out the locations of each of the gliders that Aethelgard gave him on a rough map of the Boneyards that he'd drawn. Then, based upon the direction of the wind, he traced a trajectory from each one. The lines all intersected at roughly the same point, and, when Actaeon checked the magnitudes of wind on each day, the distances also became clear.

It all pointed to a single location, on the western edge of the northern face of Pyramid.

"By the Fallen, man. You've done it!" said Aethelgard. Nearly spilling his tea, he stood and blew his Arbiter's whistle in a clear pattern. The call was answered from some distance away by another Arbiter, and then another. "Let's go. With any luck we'll find him alive."

"There are probably a hundred or more rooms that he could be within," said Actaeon. "It will take a long time to search them all."

"That's why I've summoned help," explained the Knight. "Many Arbiters do make a quick search, after all. Now that you have a location, what is the likely height he's in, Engineer?"

"It would appear that he is around two thirds the way up. Just below the elderglass pinnacle, I would say. Do you know the way to get there?" Actaeon took one long sip of his tea and stood, rolling up the map.

"Follow me," said Aethelgard.

The search took the remainder of the afternoon. As the sun began to set and cast long shadows across the shattered faces of many of the rooms they searched, Actaeon remembered the Baron writing about how he shouted out for help from the cracked corner. Every time that they arrived in another room where the broken northern wall left it exposed to the elements, he wondered if they'd hear the Baron hollering for help.

They never did.

After they entered one room and saw the purple hue to the west indicating the sun's final descent, they heard the whistle of another Arbiter.

Running out into the corridor, they found the Arbiter several doors down waving to them frantically.

Actaeon and Aethelgard ran down the corridor to the Arbiter, who pointed to a door that had been thrice barred across. It now stood open, beckoning for them.

Without hesitation, the pair rushed through, hoping for the best.

But instead, they were met with horror.

Baron Thrist lay atop a wooden table in the rigor of death, his arms spread wide and held in place with daggers that were embedded into the table's surface. His toothless mouth hung open in an expression of horror and wide eyes stared off at a fist-sized crack in the corner as though expecting some succor to come from there.

What was truly horrible though, was his chest. It had been broken open, with ribs splayed to either side like the brutal teeth of some beast. And where his heart once was, an artifact had been placed.

The room felt like it was starting to spin for Actaeon, but he bit his lip and stepped closer to examine the artifact. It was a familiar one – the same type of lock that the doors used up in the Song of the Sisters near Pyramid's apex. Only this one was... smashed and mangled beyond repair.

"Ruinlock..." said Aethelgard, his voice cracking on the last syllable.

Later on, Aethelgard found his way outside through an adjacent room on the level above. There, he found dozens of paper gliders that had jammed into a crevice just outside the small crack in the captive Baron's room. All of them told more of the horror that the poor man had been through.

"No matter what he might have done to Shield, no man deserved that kind of end," said Actaeon.

Aethelgard placed a reassuring hand on Actaeon's shoulder. The Engineer could feel him shaking. "We will find justice for him."

Actaeon nodded, but he wasn't convinced.

It would be many days before Actaeon saw his friend again. Aethelgard insisted on traveling out to Shield to inform Alisha personally, and to repeat to her the same words he'd said to Actaeon.

"We will find justice for him."

The Sapphire Crucible

"IN THE END, THEY JUST laid down to die," said Aethelgard. The Knight Investigator and Prince Engineer stood amidst horrific devastation in an artifact room deep down in the bowels beneath the Pyramid. The journey had taken them a good portion of the morning as they traveled through a winding maze of tunnels beyond the Warrens near the open marketplace.

The bowl-shaped room had sliding doors at opposing sides – through one of which they had entered. A glowing red, prismatic pillar took up the center of the room, radiating heat that flushed Actaeon's face even as he looked at it.

In various places on the floor were piles of ash roughly shaped like supine humans. The only remains were daggers, rings, clasps, and other jewelry that the unfortunate victims had been wearing.

"How did you locate this place?" asked Actaeon, pulling his goggles down over his eyes to protect them against the waves of heat being thrown off by the pillar.

"Gaemri Ip Monjata kept complaining to me about disappearing Ajmani," said Aethelgard, pushing his lenses up his nose. "He insisted upon my delving into the tunnels to find out where they disappeared to."

"The Raja's Portent."

"The one and only." Aethelgard smirked at the Engineer and knelt beside one of the ash piles, wincing at the pain in his knee. "I would expect a person being incinerated to move – thrash about perhaps. Not lie perfectly still. There is a missing piece here. A poison perhaps, or an artifact. It's why I asked you here. Somehow, these people were all brought here and rendered into a state that made them accept their fate."

With the arch of a brow, Actaeon asked the obvious question. "How did you determine they were alive at the time? This could simply be a killer's method to conveniently dispose of their victims."

"A fair question," said Aethelgard. "How do you suspect I found this chamber? I was able to track one of the missing persons here. The passage of a person leaves many signs in these centuries-old tunnels. The scuff of a boot heel, the fleeting touch of a finger found in the dust on a tunnel wall, the scrape of a staff evident in the settled dirt. These six unfortunate individuals made their way here along four different paths. All of them I can account for." He lifted the charred remains of a boot's sole. "All six of the victims. None other came this way in many decades. At least not before the pair of us."

"Fascinating," said Actaeon. "So you could not account for a killer. Which means..." He leaned forward to investigate the nearest pile of remains. When he shined his luminary upon it, several large, metallic blue beetles scattered and fled from the room. "Amazing." He leaned forward more until he could make out the object he thought he'd seen near one of the places in the ash from which a beetle had fled.

Aethelgard joined him over the ash pile and lifted a hollow, charcoal-textured hemisphere. "Good eyes, my friend. I knew I was right to bring you here." Aethelgard handed him the shell. "An egg, right?"

"Yes," concluded Actaeon. "I do believe it is an egg. One of those beetles must have hatched from it. Let us see if we can find more."

They sifted through the ash of the victims until they had the broken shells of more than ten eggs. Actaeon deposited them in a pouch that he then returned to his jacket.

Together, they also gathered any recognizable belongings for aid in identifying the victims.

That was when they both noticed something strange – they weren't alone.

Aethelgard drew his writheblade and the stifling hot chamber filled with the odor of ozone. He pointed the writheblade at the man standing behind him.

The middle-aged, blond man smiled and lifted a hand. "Hello, friend. My name is Garvin." He was dressed in a white cotton tunic stained in places with different colors and leather breeches that were tucked neatly into tall boots.

The Arbiter narrowed his cobalt eyes on the man. "I am Knight Investigator Aethelgard, and my friend here is Engineer Actaeon. What, may I ask, is a dyer doing this deep in the tunnels?"

Garvin looked as though he hadn't considered that himself. "Didn't you also feel it?" He spread his hands and gestured toward the pillar in the center of the room. "It was calling me here. I didn't realize it at the time, but it was." As an afterthought, he sighed and added, "It feels good to be here."

"You shouldn't be here, lad," said Aethelgard. "You aren't even armed. What if a ruincrawler takes to your liking?"

Garvin frowned. "Well, one didn't. Clearly."

Actaeon and Aethelgard exchanged a look.

The man moved off to one side and smiled up at the pillar as he settled down to his knees before it and closed his eyes.

"A different approach then," muttered Aethelgard. He sheathed the writheblade in its ceramic scabbard and stepped between Garvin and the artifact pillar. "The Order of Arbiters has deemed this area to be unsafe. I'm afraid I must ask you to leave at once."

Garvin opened sleepy eyes and shook his head. "You have no authority here. This isn't even a Pyramid."

Aethelgard grabbed the man's arm and received a bite from him that he was entirely unprepared for. He punched Garvin in the head and sent him sprawling at his feet.

"No!" shouted the manic dyer. "I will not go. I just got here. Leave me alone!"

A flash at Aethelgard's back was the first sign that something was very wrong.

"Aeth, we had best go," suggested Actaeon. "Now."

The prismatic pillar's glow began to increase in brightness until it was near blinding. On the opposite ends of the room, the doors started to slide shut.

Halberd forward, Actaeon ran over to attempt to wedge the door open. He barely made it in time and managed to thrust the shaft of his weapon through the narrowing opening. A crack heralded the failure of the halberd as the door snapped the metal-reinforced shaft of the weapon completely in two as it completed its effort to close.

The bowl-like room was closed and the heat instantly became unbearable. They were sealed in their tomb.

Aethelgard leaned down to pull Garvin to his feet, but the man flailed about and kicked at him like a toddler in meltdown. He cringed and gritted his teeth as the bare skin on the back of his head began to burn.

"Forget him," said Actaeon. The Engineer pulled a cloth from his jacket and wrapped it about his head to keep off the radiant heat. Blisters rose on the back of his left hand as he did so. He briefly considered the blue fire concoction in his jacket but realized he didn't have the time and the blue fire most likely hadn't the power to melt through the door.

"Agh!" cried Aethelgard. He dropped his cane and covered the back of his head to protect it, feeling his hands burn. In front of him, Garvin lay still and content as blisters began to rise on his face.

"Get over here now," called Actaeon. "I need your help."

Aethelgard dashed over, feeling the soles of his boots sticking to the curved floor of the room. Actaeon wrapped a cloth around his friend's head. The Engineer gritted his teeth as his left hand and right fingers began to burn.

"It broke your halberd," said the Knight Investigator. "It has been an honor, my friend."

"Cut it out," said Actaeon. The Prince Engineer reached down and drew the writheblade from Aethelgard's scabbard. He directed the crackling weapon toward the door and sliced a vertical swath through it.

A painful glance back toward the dyer showed that the man's clothing was already beginning to smoke and smolder. Garvin was much closer to the glowing pillar than they were and would die quickly if nothing was done. The wooden cane that Aethelgard had dropped had already ignited where it lay closest to the glowing pillar.

Aethelgard narrowed his eyes to thin slits and rushed forward to rescue the man while Actaeon continued to cut their way out. He grabbed Garvin's arm and pulled him toward the door, but the dyer flailed and flopped like a dying fish, tugging Aethelgard even closer to the pillar of death. He kicked the man in the head to try to get him to stop, but it only intensified his efforts to escape. "What are you doing? Don't you see you'll die here?"

"Leave me be," pleaded Garvin.

A rush of hot air flowed past Aethelgard headed in the direction of the door. A glance found that Actaeon had finished the cut and exited the chamber. The Prince Engineer peered through the hole in the door with goggle-clad eyes that poked through the wrap around his face. The top of his hair was on fire. "Forget him, Aeth. Move!"

A big blister on the back of his hand burst and Aethelgard realized that if he kept trying to rescue this man, he would die here with him.

"Rest well, Garvin," said Aethelgard, letting his arm slip through his burning hands.

"Thank you," whispered the dying man through blistering lips.

Aethelgard turned and fled through the door. The shock of the cooler air that hit him on the other side made him pass out. He awoke a moment later to Actaeon dragging him down the tunnel and away from the artifact room that nearly killed them both.

"You both were lucky you survived."

The Matron of the Altheans finished applying the last of the salve wraps to Actaeon's hand. When the men had arrived at the Althean ward, Seraeta had sent one of the junior Altheans to fetch special plants from Shard on the Garden Terrace. Once applied, the salves from the plants brought instant relief to the excruciating burns on their necks, faces, scalps, and hands.

"Aren't we the pair," said Aethelgard as he reclined on the cot.

"Indeed," said Actaeon with a grin. He lifted a hand wrapped in a thick bandage. "I am happy to be here with you, getting wrapped up like a gift."

"A morbid gift." Aethelgard smirked.

"Aye," said Actaeon.

"I couldn't save him," said the Knight Investigator, on a more serious note.

"You saved yourselves," said Seraeta. "That will have to suffice."

"He thanked me... for leaving him to die." Aethelgard lifted his hand, puffy with bandages, to the bridge of his nose to push his lenses back up.

"And I shall thank you for leaving him so that you might live to figure out this mystery and ensure that no one else is incinerated," the Matron countered. "Now get out of my ward, and go save lives. I don't want my work here to be for naught."

"Yes, ma'am," said Aethelgard, offering her a mock salute with his thickly bandaged hand.

Seraeta offered him a slight smile before upending the cot and dumping the Knight Investigator unceremoniously onto the floor. She chuckled and went off to tend to other matters.

"I do think she likes you," said Actaeon, grinning.

"Clearly."

"There is an artifact dealer in the Warrens we should speak with about the trinkets we collected," Actaeon suggested.

"Rin? Yes, I know of her," Aethelgard said. "That might yield a nugget of information we can use. And we should find out where the dyer worked."

"Shall we then?" Actaeon offered his hand and Aethelgard took him up on it.

Before heading back to the open markets, the pair of investigators returned to Actaeon's workshop to consult the master woodcrafter. She was able to fashion a quick cane for Aethelgard and a new halberd shaft for Actaeon while they waited.

"I will work on a new reinforced shaft for when you get back," said Lauryn. "It's gonna take a bit more time though, Act."

"Of course," said Actaeon with a smile as he hefted the refitted halberd. "Thank you, Engineer Lauryn. As usual, your skill is appreciated."

"No problem, Prince Engineer Actaeon," said Lauryn with a playful smile. "I'll be here if you need me. Try not to burn or snap anything else while you're out and about."

Aethelgard tested his quickly furnished cane and started heading over to the door. "Time to go see your artifact dealer friend."

"A moment," said Actaeon. He beckoned the Knight Investigator over to the forge. "Take a look at this." He handed Aethelgard a set of tongs that gripped one of the eggshells from the artifact room in it. "Go ahead – put it right into the fire."

Aethelgard did so. The flames licked it for a moment, but, when he removed it, the shell was not afire. Lowering it into the hottest part of the flames near their base also failed to yield any destructive results. "Not so surprising, Engineer. After all, it survived the crucible room unlike near everything else."

"Yes, yes," said Actaeon, distracted. "Put it down on the anvil now. Go ahead." Once the shell was in place, Actaeon took up the biggest of the forging hammers – a maul with a long handle. Tugging down his goggles, he then lifted the hammer high above his head and brought it down hard. It struck the eggshell directly and sent up a spark. The shell went flying to the side and the hammer hit the working surface.

When they followed the arc of the shell to where it landed, they found it completely intact.

"What does it mean?" asked the Knight.

"Impervious to mechanical impact and to flame. I wish we had captured one of those beetles before they fled. They must produce some sort of chemical that dissolves the shell. It is an amazing material to so resist both extreme conditions. I placed another one in water to see if that might soften it up. No effect thus far." Actaeon lifted the goggles from his head and brought the shell closer to his naked eye. "It is astounding. Think of the applications if we can manage to reproduce such a material. And all engineered by a small insect."

The dark shop of the artifact dealer was a massive underground chamber in the tunnels of the Warrens beneath the Pyramid. It was filled with piles of artifacts and broken debris that rivaled some of those found in the Boneyards in size.

"You never told me how your army of writheblade wielders worked for you, Act," came a gravelly voice.

Their eyes tracked upward until they spotted the cloaked figure atop one of the piles. The red glow of a linreed stick flared for a moment from the shadowy depths of the hood before expelled smoke poured out.

"I imagine them roaming Redemption and meting out justice," the cloaked person continued, followed by another puff of smoke.

"If only so many had survived," said Actaeon, sadness in his tone. He leaned heavily against his halberd's new shaft to look up at her.

Rin tossed back her hood to reveal her cropped hair and the shimmering artifact goggles that covered her eyes. "Unfortunate. Did they, at the least, complete the task you set upon them?"

"They killed what some have called a god." Actaeon nodded.

"Good," said Rin, lighting another linreed stick from the lit one before putting out the butt on the back on her glove and stowing it in a pouch. "Too many of those anyway. But *you* don't call it a god..." She let the statement hang in the air – an unanswered query.

"The Starborn are many things," said Actaeon. "But gods? Certainly not."

Satisfied with his answer, Rin's shimmering lenses snapped to Aethelgard. "And Aeth, who prefers investigation to arbitration. A curious pair you both make."

"An effective pair," clarified the Knight Investigator.

"You both look like cracked Redemption," she rasped out before leaping down from the pile to land gingerly before them. "What do you seek today? More writheblades?" She looked at Actaeon. "More brightweave?" She looked at Aethelgard. "Or something entirely different?" She spread her hands.

Wincing as he knelt, Aethelgard unwrapped a small bundle which Rin also knelt to inspect. "These belongings were from victims of a most unfortunate happenstance. We wish to know if you recognize anything."

Rin lit another linreed stick and offered it to the Knight, who accepted it graciously and took a drag. She snatched a half-slagged pendant from the cloth and lifted it to her nose to sniff. "Same happenstance that left you covered in those bandages, I'd wager."

"Sharp as always," said Aethelgard.

The dealer dangled it in front of her shimmering goggles and nodded. "A man came through wearing this – at least, the unmelted version of it. And..." she snatched up the remnant of a curved dagger. "Yes. A woman had a dagger like this at her belt just a day prior. Of course, it had a hilt at the time. Burned away, I guess." She laid both down almost reverently on the cloth. "May they rest now."

Aethelgard nodded. "Were eith-"

Rin snapped her fingers twice and waved the question away. "Mister

Questions over here. You come seeking answers, of course. Gonna cost ya." She straightened and took a deep drag of her linreed stick before lighting yet another.

The Arbiter puffed on his again and nodded. "Coin is such an obsession for you." He dug into one of the pockets of his vest and withdrew a handful of coins and copper bits.

The artifact dealer snatched them out of his hand and they disappeared into her cloak. "Not all of us have a revered Order that feeds us. Now... you'll want to know that both of them acted like a right pair of zombies. They wandered through here looking for something that they couldn't articulate with words. I offered them a number of artifacts, but they didn't bite on any – though they were interested in one for a moment. Basically had to push them outta here."

"Wh-" began Aethelgard, before Rin snapped her fingers again.

She held up a finger to tell him to wait and deftly scurried back up the pile.

Aethelgard took one last drag on his linreed stick before he squeezed it out with his fingers and held onto the butt.

"Be right back with another smoke," called Rin from somewhere amidst the piles.

Actaeon and Aethelgard shared a look at that.

"Those goggles," said Actaeon at a whisper. "Perhaps they allow her to monitor sections of the room even when she is not present."

Before Aethelgard could reply, Rin did. "Wouldn't you like to know, oh royal engineer?"

Actaeon grinned. "Indeed, I would."

Rin slid back down a different artifact pile to alight beside them. She handed a black cube to Aethelgard. "Some secrets are outside of even your reach, Act."

Aethelgard shifted the cube between his hands before passing it to the Prince Engineer.

The artifact was hot. It was just shy of scalding – uncomfortable to hold for more than a few lifebeats. Actaeon let it rest upon the palm on his fingerless glove. "So, what is this, Rin?"

Rin folded her arms and cocked her head to the side.

Actaeon grinned and dug into his jacket to pull free a small coin pouch. He handed her more copper bits, which made the woman smile.

"Keep it," said Rin. "It wasn't to the satisfaction of your deceased friends, but it did hold their interest for a short while. May it serve you better."

"They were looking for another heat source," said Aethelgard. "Something much hotter."

"And they found it – much deeper in the tunnels," said Rin.

"How did you –" began Aethelgard.

"My job is to know these places," she replied. "The crucible. A terrible place to meet one's end."

"The crucible," said Aethelgard, mulling over the details of their visit as they walked between the rows of tents on their way through the open marketplace outside of the Pyramid.

"So many places that we are not yet aware of," said Actaeon. "There are so many things we have yet to discover. Can you imagine the world we might live in once we understand and harness all of these things?"

"A world where humans still commit unthinkable atrocities, I'd think," mused the Knight. "The technology doesn't change the base nature of the creature that wields it, after all."

"You sound like a Keeper," said Actaeon.

"Perhaps there is some wisdom to their words," said Aethelgard. "After all, the greater the power wielded, the greater the damage that might be done."

"I cannot argue with your logic," admitted Actaeon. "But, I would ask you to consider the potential impact of technology upon the human mind. All power is not that which destroys, but also that which enhances, evolves, and educates. With understanding and restraint, humanity might grow to a point where the powerful technology of the artifacts can be wielded with caution and responsibility, for the betterment of humankind and the world."

Aethelgard arched a brow. "Did the Starborn do that?" The question hung in the air between them as they walked. When the Prince Engineer didn't immediately reply, he continued. "Based on what you have told me about the Veiled One and Yonniker, didn't the Starborn – creatures of an evolved and ascendant condition – use artifacts for evil in the end? As instruments of genocide for their own benefit? What makes us any different? My work has shown me humans from many different backgrounds and walks of life, but one thing is common – when their lives are threatened, they will kill even innocents to protect themselves. Isn't that what the Starborn you encountered were trying to do? To survive at the cost of humanity?"

Actaeon came to a stop as he considered the questions seriously. "I have witnessed what makes us different. The human potential for compassion and self-sacrifice. There is an abundance of brave people willing to lay down their very lives in order to protect others. My friend Trench was one of those heroes – in an instant willing to lay down his life to ensure that others might live. He embodied that ideal until the moment he died. People like Trench are why I believe that humankind can grow to become worthy of the technology contained within the artifacts. As for the Starborn, perhaps there is even hope for them – the sample size of my experience with them is not enough to draw any definitive conclusion."

"A hopeful perspective," said Aethelgard. "In the spirit of which I hope that you are correct about it. However, my own intuition and experience leads me to the conclusion that your aspirations for humanity are rooted in naivety. When backed against the wall, humans, just like any animal, will lash out without any bias or predilection – to destroy, in the end, anything that threatens their survival. I agree that Trench was a hero, but in the end, isn't that what he did? Destroy the things that threatened his survival?"

"Let us suppose for a moment that you are correct, and that humankind only tends toward destruction and chaos in an effort to survive. That there is no hope for advancement because in the end a cataclysm is inevitable. In the face of such inevitable tragedy, what is the purpose of carrying on – of dreaming, and procreating, and pursuing ambition?" countered Actaeon. "If we are to conclude, as the Keepers do, that humankind is incapable of advancement of any kind and can only exist in a sort of sterile stasis, then what is the point of any of our aspirations? No, I cannot believe that. Either we are beings capable of evolution and forward progression, or we should simply lay down and die, for such idealism is unachievable. And if humankind had accepted that as its fate, could it ever possibly have advanced to this point? Could the Ancients have to their point? Could the Starborn? There is always a risk in any endeavor. I have long said that nothing worth doing is ever easy. But is it worth the attempt? Yes, because without the attempt to grow, to dream, and to create, existence is futile and pointless. And so, we continue to strive, even in the face of likely calamity, because that is what it means to be sentient and to be human."

Aethelgard offered him a thin smile and reached out to touch Actaeon's shoulder. "This is why I so enjoy our friendship. Your mind helps mine grow. And perhaps – hopefully – time will show *me* to be the naive one." The Knight Investigator grinned and pivoted. "Now come, let us find Garvin the dyer's shop. I have an inkling based on the colors I observed on his tunic that it is the one ahead and on the left."

"An inkling?" asked Actaeon with a grin.

"Right," agreed Aethelgard, smirking.

The Knight led the way to the large tent, where multiple fabrics and items of clothing were hanging from racks. A rainbow of colors was displayed across the various stands, showing the full capability of the dyers there. Beyond the racks, workers tended to large vats where fabrics were dipped and dyed various shades.

"Can I help ye?" asked a big woman who wore a black tabard in an unsuccessful effort to avoid unsightly staining.

"Yes," said Aethelgard. "Does a man named Garvin work here?"

"Sure does," she said. "Though he's not been in for a few days. He in trouble?" She eyed the red armband on Aethelgard's right arm suspiciously.

"Worse, unfortunately," admitted the Knight Investigator. "Garvin died. We were hoping that you could answer some questions that might shed light on his demise."

The woman's eyes widened. "Gods..." She let out a small sob. "Course I will..."

Garvin was from Thyr. He'd tried his hand at work on a ship under his father, a ship's carpenter, but incurable seasickness kept him from the water. Instead, he found work in Canal Keep making sails. One day, on a run to pick up a bolt of fabric, he ran into a man whose cotton tunic was stained in a variety of colors. When Garvin joked about it, the man laughed and explained he was a dyer. He invited him to visit his shop and Garvin was immediately hooked. He transitioned to the trade of a dyer within the week.

A year later, a fire would change all that for him. The Canal Keep dye shop burned down in an early morning after a fresh shipment of chemicals was delivered. Disappointed, Garvin set out toward the Pyramid to find work in his new trade. He'd found the shop in the open marketplace and was hired on the spot.

Garvin was a jokester and a prankster, bringing light and laughs to the other dyers there. As Aethelgard questioned the woman, Crynn, her co-workers gathered around her to listen and to add in their own observations to the questions. Crynn admitted that she had feelings for Garvin that she had never expressed to him when Aethelgard correctly surmised as such. She began to weep then, and Aethelgard offered his arms. Crynn stepped into his embrace and he held the dyer as she wept.

An extensive line of questioning continued about Garvin's normal routines and habits followed by a rundown on what everyone remembered of his exploits the past week.

That, and the fact that they were hungry, brought them to Pyramid's Sea Lounge, where Garvin had raved about his meal on one of his days off.

Aethelgard shared a nod with the Arbiter on the catwalk above who stood guard over the entrance to Pyramid's control room.

A host approached them. "Welcome, sir," he said to Aethelgard, followed by a half bow to Actaeon. "Your Grace. Are you here for business upstairs or may I offer you a table?"

"A table please," said Actaeon. "And no need for formalities, good sir."

"As you wish," said the host, leading them over to an empty table near the great wooden bar.

Actaeon leaned his halberd against the table's edge and settled into the chair. "You did well with that dyer back there."

Aethelgard winced and sat across from him, offering a thin smile in reply. "Good with telling them their beloved colleague was dead?"

"Not an easy task," said the Prince Engineer. "But you did it with compassion, where most would be too nervous as to what to do or say."

"It's the hardest part of my job," admitted the Arbiter as he settled his cane across his knees. "Many of the crimes I investigate involve death. It is never the victim though, that pulls so hard on the heartstrings as the ones they left behind. The victim's perspective, after all, has ended. Whatever they may have felt in their final moments is now over. But the ones who loved them carry on, in suffering and loss. Their lives are never the same.

The ones left behind never fail to keep me up during listless nights. It is for them that I do my life's work."

"The ones left behind are not ever the same," said Actaeon knowingly. "But a moment of genuine caring shown during such interactions... It does not soften the blow – nothing really can. However, I do believe it serves as a reminder that there yet exists hope in the world, despite the heavy veil of loss."

"Can I offer you our new sapphire drops?" interrupted the waiter. "Many are calling it a delicacy."

Aethelgard shook his head. "No, thanks. I'll have my usual seafood soup, Claury." He arched a brow at his friend. "You really should try it too, Act."

Actaeon grinned and shook his head. "Perhaps next time. I will take some fresh bread and cheese, if you would. And ales for my friend and I."

The food came out quickly and Aethelgard pursed his lips. "The soup's different today."

"Still good?" asked Actaeon, slicing into the block of cheese to pair some of it with a piece of bread.

"Aye. Just different," said Aethelgard.

"Knowing you, the precise origin and backstory of each ingredient is being calculated as we speak, along with the exact motivations of the chef, of course." They both laughed at that.

They ate in companionable silence then, both mulling details of the curious case. Garvin hadn't been described as even remotely suicidal or unhappy. It was almost as if he had been possessed by some unknown force. The idea reminded Actaeon of how the Veiled One had controlled the cross-faced raiders. Could it be that another Starborn was possessing people and leading them to their deaths? Perhaps it was using them somehow. During the battle in Travail, Yonniker had implied he was using something called 'quantum lifestreams' to facilitate their return to the stars – whatever that meant. If that was happening now, it was a highly dangerous prospect. There could be another battle for humanity to come.

"Your sapphire drops, madam," said the waiter as he brought over a meal to the table next to them. "Enjoy."

"I will," said a Niwian lady. "I've heard incredible things about this." She lifted one before her with dainty fingers and used a tiny fork to scoop some of the filling out.

As she lifted it to her mouth, Actaeon stood with a mad realization. The chair fell backward behind him and his halberd clattered to the floor. Two quick strides closed the gap and he slapped the fork from her hand just as it was about to grace her lips. "Do not eat that!"

"What is the meaning of this, Your Grace?" snapped the lady's companion as she let out a scream that brought silence to the room.

Actaeon snatched another one of the sapphire drops from her plate and turned it over.

The Knight Investigator's eyes widened. It was the hollowed-out carapace of one of the metallic blue beetles that had scattered from the ashes in the crucible room.

Aethelgard levered himself to his feet raised his Arbiter whistle to his lips, blowing out a series of notes that would bring reinforcements. "Apologies, ladies and gentlemen, but the Sea Lounge is now closed by the Order of Arbiters. If everyone can please file out. Knight Arbiter Elmerth will direct you." A motion to the Arbiter up on the catwalk sent the man scrambling down the stairs. "I ask that anyone who has eaten the new sapphire drops to please remain."

As the two Arbiters directed the orderly evacuation of the Sea Lounge, Actaeon swept the room with his sharp emerald eyes. In the wall just to one side of the door, up near the ceiling level, was a substantial crack that hadn't been sealed when the room had been repaired following a grenado blast. He approached it warily and as he drew near he thought he saw movement within.

Turning to the waiter, he motioned. "Can you bring me a set of salad tongs?" When the waiter brought them over, he inserted them into the crack and withdrew a beetle with a sapphire carapace. It was a match to the ones they had glimpsed in the crucible room.

Actaeon stuck the wriggling creature before the waiter's face and arched a brow. "You thought it would be a good idea to cook bugs that you found inside the wall and serve them to customers?"

"It was Brodiq's idea," protested Claury, his face reddening. "Our chef. And you can't cook them. They need to be chilled first and they crack open. Brodiq found out when one of them crawled into a drink."

"And where is Brodiq now?" asked Aethelgard.

"He disappeared a few weeks back," said the waiter. "We all figured he brought his new recipe elsewhere."

Actaeon and Aethelgard shared a knowing look.

"All of the victims that I've been able to trace were at the Sea Lounge before they died." Aethelgard strode into the workshop. "All of them about a week before they died. Their families and friends reported increasingly erratic behavior before their disappearance." He shed his cloak and joined Actaeon by the laboratory workbench where the engineer was exposing a beetle carapace to various chemicals to identify one that would destroy it. "Any progress?"

"None yet," admitted Actaeon. "But these things take time. I have eliminated all the likely candidates for the job, which means that I must discover something new."

"How about what Claury told us?" suggested Aethelgard. "Brodiq chilled them first."

"Yes." Actaeon nodded and grinned as he used a dropper to apply a new chemical mixture to the bug husk. He turned to peer at the Knight Investigator through his goggles. "However, we need to find a way to replicate the result without damaging our victims' stomachs."

Seventeen people had been taken into Arbiter protective custody. Many of them were nobility from the various Dominions. One of them was the Lord Protector of Niwian himself.

"I don't need to tell you that the Dominions are up in arms about this," said Aethelgard. "The Niwians are furious with us. Even after we allowed him personal attendants and for him to be confined to his own room, they aren't happy with our decision. The Sea Lounge cooks that I interrogated haven't turned up any new information excepting another crack from which the beetles were emerging. I'm running out of threads to follow for this case." He tapped the tip of his cane against the stone floor.

"The crucible?" asked Actaeon while he began to mix another group of chemicals in a large half-through bottle.

"Under guard, of course," said Aethelgard. "I've got a rotation of Arbiters monitoring it, and another rotation collecting beetles from the crack as they emerge. Do you have any ideas about the mechanism involved?"

"Some ideas," said Actaeon. "But nothing conclusive." Most of his attention remained upon the chemicals before him.

"And how do you intend to vet your ideas?" The Knight Investigator leaned over the workbench to give Actaeon a hard look.

"Please," said the Prince Engineer with a grin. "There is a chance that these chemicals become volatile. It would not be helpful if you allowed some to splatter on your face."

Aethelgard sighed and winced as he took a seat on a stool nearby. He crossed his arms and waited. A sudden cacophony of clucks sounded from an opposite corner of the workshop and he turned to find stacks of wire cages piled in the corner. "Chickens?" He narrowed his cobalt gaze.

After applying the chemical to a clean carapace, Actaeon grinned. "They will be joining our investigative team for this case. If I am correct, they will solve this mystery in the next few days."

"In the next few days, we'll have all the colors of Niwian marching down the Avenue of Glass on us," said Aethelgard. "How, do tell me, will these chickens solve the mystery?"

"You have long showed me the value in avoiding excess speculation in these cases," said Actaeon. He met the frustrated Arbiter's gaze with an amused one. "Until it is proven, it can distort the truth and bias the mind. I recognize my own proclivity toward overt transparency, but in these cases, perhaps it is best that I hold off until those theories have been proven. It is a wise approach, and something that I learned from you."

Aethelgard sighed and drew out his pipe to light it. When Actaeon glanced over, the Knight Investigator was smirking at him.

Two uneventful days passed with Actaeon and Aethelgard making no discernable advancement in the case.

"Your halberd's all fixed up, Act." Lauryn drove the last glowing rivet through the metal reinforcement and rotated the shaft to hammer the other side flat. She pulled the goggles down from her eyes and smiled over at him. "Just don't use it till it cools down."

"Thank you, Lauryn." He shot her a grin from the other side of the workshop, where he worked a bellows to pump some gasses generated by one of his mixtures away from the workbench and out of the building through the chimney.

"Yet another bug-related problem for you," said Lauryn with a chuckle. "Slug monsters, deathcrawlers, monsoon bugs, and now this."

"Yes, I suppose by this point you might consider me something of an entomological expert." Actaeon grinned and paused his pumping to peruse the rack of chemicals thoughtfully.

"Doesn't that bug you?" asked Lauryn with a smirk.

"More than I would carapace for," said Actaeon.

They shared a laugh at that before their attentions turned back to work.

Just then, a knock sounded upon the door and Companion Yanelle opened it.

In burst Aethelgard, followed by round Knight Arbiter Elmerth, who looked quite worse for wear. Both of them struggled with bound prisoners before them – one a rugged looking Thyrian man, and the other a tall Shieldian woman in a scale mail dress. "Fresh in from the crucible," said Aethelgard. "Any thoughts, Act?"

Actaeon considered for a moment, then nodded. "Lauryn, stoke the forge. Get it nice and hot."

"But I've finished your halberd," she said, confused.

"Not for the halberd." He pointed to the pair of prisoners, who were cursing and fighting to get away from the Arbiters. "For them."

Lauryn's eyes widened with understanding. "Oh, right... Aye aye!"

When she stoked the fires of the forge, the prisoners actually calmed down. Under the watch of the Arbiters, they both approached the forge where Lauryn pumped the bellows and promptly laid down on the floor. There they settled somewhat, but still continued to squirm in discomfort.

"Yanelle, Aethelgard, help me shutter the windows and cover the luminaries," said Actaeon.

Aethelgard nodded in understanding. "You're trying to recreate the crucible."

"As best as we can." Actaeon nodded and together they covered and closed all the sources of light except for one luminary near the laboratory workbench that enabled the chemical analysis to continue.

"Keep an eye on them, Brother Elmerth," instructed Aethelgard. "Do not let them move closer to the fires." The young Arbiter nodded and stationed himself with his back to the forge, between it and them.

A raucous started near the cellar door then as the chickens clucked and shook their cages. One of the cages tumbled free from the stack and landed on its side. The door burst open and the chicken raced for the fires of the forge in a manic, clucking dash.

"Fascinating," said Actaeon, watching it unfold.

"By the Fallen," said Lauryn as she watched with horror as the chicken burst into flame. "Is that what they are doing? The people?"

"That's correct," said Aethelgard.

"At least we can snack on some fresh chicken," said Elmerth, looking on with interest.

"I would not advise eating that," said Actaeon. "Lauryn, after it has finished burning, please retrieve the remains with some tongs."

Lauryn frowned at the thought, but nodded at Actaeon.

"Knight Arbiter Elmerth, might I recommend you tether our victims to those rings inset into the wall?" suggested Actaeon. "I would not want another repeat of what we just witnessed." The Knight nodded and set to work.

"I suppose the chickens have confirmed your theory then?" asked Aethelgard. "Care to explain?"

Actaeon approached the remainder of the cages and carried one over to the laboratory area despite the clucking protests of its occupant. "That is correct. With a caustic chemical mixture, I chilled and cracked some of the beetles open after we found them. These I fed to the chickens in the corner. At the time, I theorized that ingesting the beetles would somehow cause a person's mind to be altered. Like a mind poison, the contents of the beetle would convince the person to search for heat in the darkness, and the crucible was the perfect incubator."

"Incubator?" Aethelgard pushed his lenses up his nose. "You mean they go there to hatch the eggs?"

"I believe so," said Actaeon. "The crucible is part of the beetles' life cycle. At the end of each beetle's life, it has its eggs fertilized and then heads off to be ingested. Once it is, it somehow manipulates the mind of the creature that ate it, and steers it to go find a source of heat that can birth its offspring. Thus, the reason the chicken just cooked itself. And the reason our victims all simply laid down to die. Humans, of course, are not the normal part of the sapphire beetle's lifecycle. After all, humans have not existed in Redemption for thousands of years since the disappearance of the Ancients and prior to the opening of the portals. They had to manage this complex lifecycle in other ways. Knight Arbiter," began Actaeon with a sudden thought. "During your time guarding the crucible, did you witness any other creatures heading toward it?"

The rotund Knight nodded, looking nervously at the two victims lying bound on the floor before him. "That's right, actually. I saw a lot of those little slug monsters squirming their way in there. Should I have stopped them?"

"Certainly not," said Actaeon. "It appears you stumbled upon the natural life cycle of these sapphire crucible beetles. The chef of the Sea Lounge unwittingly conspired to create an unnatural version of it."

"If you say so, Your Grace," deferred the Arbiter, clearly confused.

Lauryn retrieved the chicken for him when it was thoroughly cooked. The workshop would reek disgustingly of scorched feathers for weeks, even despite Actaeon and Lauryn's best efforts. In the end they would need to vacate it for a time until the smell dissipated. In the meantime though, Actaeon located the eggs inside the deceased experimental subject. After all, seventeen lives depended on him – nineteen now with the new arrivals. The burnt eggs were placed in a half-through bottle that was corked at the top with just a small air hole. When they hatched, several beetles scrambled out from each egg. Each scoured the bottle for a way out, scrabbling over the other beetles and the cracked pieces of the shell.

The dissection of a living chicken resulted in three more eggs from its stomach that Actaeon set about testing immediately in search of a mechanism to destroy them. He would have to identify a solution that would kill the eggs without destroying the host's digestive system. Hopefully, the inexplicable mind control exhibited by the beetles would end with the death of the embryos.

Dozens of chemicals and other methods were tried, including herbs, sound exposure, vibration, and mechanical impact, which, surprisingly, managed to chip one of the forge hammers. Even after the sacrifice of five more chickens, Actaeon was no closer to a solution.

By the next day, the bound victims were flinging themselves against their restraints to try and reach the fires of the forge, at which point Lauryn stopped stoking it. A day later, their struggle was such that they were hurting themselves in the effort to self-immolate. Actaeon and Lauryn rigged up some sacks that were bound tightly about them with strips of cloth to protect them. The victims had ceased eating and were growing gaunt with the expenditure of energy. Three more were brought in to join them, and while Actaeon worked day and night to find a solution, Lauryn fashioned more of the sack restraints for them.

"I'm going back to the crucible," announced Aethelgard after four more victims were brought in. "There must be something there we missed."

"There is nothing there but death," said Actaeon. "The answers lie in this effort."

"Perhaps," said Aethelgard. "But still, I would feel better checking it one more time."

The Knight Investigator almost made it out the door. Almost. But Actaeon dashed over in front of him to stop him and peered into his eyes. "You are not going there."

Aethelgard threw aside his cloak and let his hand rest on the writheblade at his hip. "Out of my way, Engineer. I'll not have you tell me how to run my investigation."

"*Our* investigation," corrected Actaeon. "At least, it was. Now it is my investigation."

Aethelgard's other hand shot out and his fist caught Actaeon by surprise in the chest, knocking the wind from him and sending him to his knees.

Another step forward brought the Knight closer to the door, but in it stood Companion Yanelle. She leaned against one side of the frame with her hand casually on the hilt of her own arming sword. "His Grace says you are not to leave."

"And what would give him the right to hold me against my will?" asked Aethelgard, tightening his grip on the hilt of the writheblade. "Go ahead. I'm listening."

Actaeon coughed and managed to wheeze out some words. "Your... soup. You said... your soup... tasted different," he said between gasps.

The Knight Investigator's cobalt eyes narrowed for a moment at that realization, but then he made to draw his writheblade anyway. Yanelle was prepared, and she swept her sword from its sheath, striking him across the temple with the pommel.

Aethelgard crumpled to the floor with a groan, releasing the hilt of his weapon, which slid back into the scabbard after releasing a puff of ozone smell that was a welcome relief from the burnt feathers.

Together, Yanelle, Actaeon, and Lauryn scrambled to hold him down as he struggled woozily. They managed to disarm him and bind him before they all realized that someone was standing over them.

"Um," said Knight Arbiter Elmerth. "Let him go, please." His sword was in hand, but he looked quite unprepared to use it against people who were so recently his friends.

"No can do," said Lauryn.

"He is infected, Knight Arbiter," explained Actaeon. "Like the others. If we release him, he will return to the crucible and die."

"And so what?" mumbled Aethelgard. "It'd be a welcome end. Haven't I done enough in this world?"

"Not if I have anything to say about it," said Actaeon, cinching the knot tighter about his friend's wrists. When that was done, he looked back up at Elmerth. "I think the answer is probably clear, but can you go to where the cooks are being held to ask them whether they used the sapphire beetles in preparation of the seafood soup they make? In the meantime, Companion Yanelle can safeguard our victims."

Elmerth slid his sword back into its sheath and nodded. "I will return with haste bearing answers, Your Grace."

"Oh," said Actaeon before the Knight could leave. "And see if you can bring back one or two of those large blocks of ice from the Sea Lounge so we can do some testing with it."

The Arbiter nodded and was off.

Elmerth returned later that day with a cadre of Arbiters led by Sentinel Arbiter Corvin sof Haringar. Two pairs of Knights each bore a large crate between them that leaked out tendrils of white vapor which quickly dissipated into the air.

Lauryn's face lit up and she rushed over to greet the Sentinel with a hug before directing the other Knights to deliver the crates to the cool cellar.

"This is becoming quite the incident," said Corvin as he approached Aethelgard in the corner where the Knight Investigator was bound with the others.

"Sentinel," said Aethelgard, his eyes lighting up. "Let me out of these bonds at once!"

"In due time," said Corvin, spinning on his heel and joining Actaeon near the laboratory workbench to watch him work on the eggs. He considered the setup carefully, with the skilled eyes of someone versed with technical and scientific matters. "We brought your ice, Your Grace. Fresh from some summit within the Iron Mountains from what the cooks tell me. They also tell me that they began mixing some of the cooked sapphire beetle innards into the seafood soup. The day you and the Knight Investigator ate there was the first day they did that. Fourteen bowls were served that day – the Order has been tasked with locating the thirteen remaining ingesters of the soup. You have my thanks for locating and restraining the fourteenth." He gestured to Aethelgard.

"Excellent," said Actaeon. "Lauryn, break free a chunk of ice and bring it here." He returned his attention to the workbench before him. "So now we have over thirty victims of the late Chef Brodiq and his inadvisable culinary creations. We must manage to find a method to return these people to normal without killing them in the process."

Corvin nodded, leaning forward to peer at one of the eggs that was held within a clamp. "We have a battalion of Niwian Golds at the entrance of the Pyramid and I've gotten reports that Thyr has dispatched two ships full of marines up the coast. We're about to have an interdominional incident on our hands. The Paladin Arbiter has assigned me to oversee this directly until it has been resolved."

"Your help is always appreciated, Sentinel Arbiter Corvin," said Actaeon. "With our minds together, we will figure out a solution."

"And my mind," said Lauryn. The woodcarver turned engineer slipped between them and deposited a large chunk of ice on the workbench surface. Tendrils of water vapor rose from it to evacuate through the overhead vent and up the chimney.

"Yes," said Actaeon. "Three minds are better than one." He slid the ice over until it was touching the egg in the clamp.

The three of them leaned forward, shoulder to shoulder, as they watched the little egg expectantly.

"Can I get you three tea while you work?" suggested Yanelle from behind them. Now relieved from her guard duty by the returning Arbiters, she was looking for something to do.

"Aye," said Actaeon. "Please. That would be welcome."

Yanelle put the kettle at the edge of the forge and shortly it was whistling at them.

Lauryn was the first to see the crack, and she let out a tiny gasp. "That's it!"

"A temperature drop breaks it then?" Corvin looked on in fascination.

"And a small one at that. Perhaps we can grind up ice and feed it to them," Actaeon considered.

"That's an idea," agreed Lauryn. "Though, the amount of crushed ice needed would be unappetizing and difficult to force into them. Plus, the little pieces would get stuck to their tongue and lips on the way down."

"Cream anyone?" asked Yanelle, as she poured out several cups of tea.

The three of them shared an inspired look.

"Yanelle, you are a genius!" said Actaeon, spinning to face her.

The Companion's eyes widened in surprise. "I am, Your Grace?"

"You are indeed," said the Prince Engineer. "Hold the cream. In fact, go to the markets and get us more, along with milk, sugar, salt, and vanilla."

Lauryn smiled at her boss. "Act, are you gonna..."

"Yes, Lauryn," said Actaeon with a grin. "We are going to make iced cream."

Once Yanelle and the Arbiters returned with all the ingredients, they all set about making a large batch of iced cream. Lauryn oversaw the Arbiters as they mixed everything in a big pan over the low fires of the forge. Once each batch was done, Elmerth shuttled the bowls of the mixture down to the cellar for chilling atop one of the big blocks of ice. After those had sat for several hours, Yanelle and Corvin took turns churning the contents in their bowls.

After more than a few tastes, the first batch was given to Actaeon for testing. He dumped it atop an egg inside a bowl that had been warmed to simulate the temperature inside of a stomach.

Everyone gathered around in silence as they watched the Prince Engineer observe a bowl of iced cream with goggle-clad eyes.

Yanelle set the kettle on the fire and they all waited.

Actaeon added another two scoops of iced cream and bent to watch.

The kettle began to whistle, but there was no reaction from the Prince Engineer. It grew into a scream, left ignored on the other side of the workshop as everyone watched with bated breath.

"Success!" Actaeon reached into the bowl to withdraw it and placed the egg behind a large apparatus which contained an assembly of lenses that provided microscopic views. There, through the midline, was a clear crack that expanded down its length.

Everyone let out a cheer that mixed in with the screaming of the kettle.

It was all interrupted by a hostile pounding at the workshop door. "Open up at once! By order of the Lord Protector!"

Lauryn shut off the kettle while Yanelle drew her sword and approached the door. Actaeon joined her and touched her arm so she would lower the sword.

"Open up or we'll –" The demand was cut short as the door opened and the soldier in the gold-plated armor found the Prince Engineer of Raedelle before him. "Your Grace... We, ah..."

"You appear surprised that I would answer the door of my own workshop, Captain Kydach," said Actaeon with a grin, noting the man's rank insignia emblazoned upon the gleaming golden helm.

"I..." The Captain was at a loss for words. Behind him stood the full battalion of Niwian Golds.

"Undoubtedly, you are concerned about the Lord Protector," said Actaeon. "Might I reassure you with the fact that we are presently on the cusp of the solution to heal him and the other victims of this unfortunate mishap."

"And what might that be, Your Grace?" The Captain appeared to regain his voice.

"You may call me Actaeon, Captain Kydach. After all, we served together in the war." Actaeon beckoned him inside.

The golden Captain stepped within and looked about in bewilderment at the Arbiters churning bowls of fresh iced cream, the people straightjacketed against the wall, and the stack of chickens in cages clucking in the corner. "I didn't know you'd remember me," admitted Kydach.

"Of course, I do," said Actaeon. "Congratulations on your promotion to Captain. It is well deserved. The solution I speak of is iced cream."

"Iced cream?" The Captain chewed on the words as though he'd heard them for the first time.

"Indeed. At least, we believe it will work based on our testing. The Lord Protector can be one of the first to try it out." Actaeon turned to Yanelle, who had sheathed her sword. "Companion Yanelle, prepare a large bowl of iced cream for these fine soldiers to bring to their Lord Protector. And make sure they have a block of ice to keep it from melting."

"Aye aye, Your Grace," said Yanelle with a barely contained chuckle. Corvin handed her the most recently churned bowl along with a chunk of ice and she passed both things to Captain Kydach.

"Get this to him post haste, before it melts. Force feed it to him if necessary, but get it into his stomach quickly," Actaeon explained. "After he's had time to process it, send some soldiers back here to get more."

Kydach looked down at the big bowl of freshly churned vanilla iced cream and nodded. "Thank you, Your Grace," he muttered before rushing off to deliver the potential cure.

The Niwian Golds retreated down the Avenue of Glass and Actaeon shut and barred the door. When he turned around, he found everyone else watching him in amusement.

"What are you all waiting for?" he asked. "Let us feed the victims – starting with Aethelgard."

"I never want iced cream again," groaned Aethelgard. He lay on a cot in the corner, holding his stomach.

It had taken two days, but, after the time had passed, the victims had all ceased with their urges to fling themselves into the forge. During that period, they received regular doses of iced cream at all hours of the day and night – each time until their stomachs were full. As they gradually returned to coherence, they all complained about brain freezes that resulted from the chilled blood that passed the iced cream in their throats on the way to their brains. After the first complaint, Actaeon ordered his small army of feeders to increase the rate of feeding so that all their patients received a brain freeze each time. If the cold could fracture the eggs, perhaps it could also kill whatever component from the sapphire beetles was infecting and manipulating their minds. Gradually, they all began to show signs of normalcy. Captain Kydach reported back with a similar update from the Lord Protector.

"It is a delicacy that most people do not even get to try," said Actaeon with a grin in reply to his recovering friend. "You should be honored."

"Honored that you prevented me from going up in flames, quite literally," said Aethelgard. "But I don't think I could abide another spoonful of that creamy frozen pain."

"That is unfortunate," said Actaeon. "For I am prescribing one more day of iced cream administration." When Aethelgard groaned, he grinned. "I know, but one cannot be too safe. I would not want some parasite in your brain to regenerate and resume your urges to self-immolate."

The Knight Investigator sighed. "Of course, you are correct. Horrible... but correct."

"Very good," said Actaeon. He offered another spoonful of iced cream to the begrudging Knight Investigator. "This must be, by far, the strangest resolution to a case that you have seen yet."

Aethelgard laughed at that. "You'd be surprised."

When the Sea Lounge finally reopened to the public, they replaced the sapphire drops with a new delicacy on their menu called Engineer's Iced Cream.

Retribution's Maw

ETHELGARD ARRIVED AMID A VERITABLE deluge of water that punctuated the final days of the monsoon rains. He strode through the open door of the workshop and tossed back his hood, shedding a puddle of water to the cool stone of the floor.

"I hope you don't mind," said the Knight Investigator as he wiped his lenses on a dry portion of his vest before perching them back upon his nose. "I've brought the Great Sea with me in its entirety."

"So long as you also brought a ship with you, so that all my life's work is not washed away," said Actaeon with a grin. He set aside his latest project and turned to his friend.

"What is it you've got there?" asked Aethelgard. "Doubtless something groundbreaking."

"It is actually something you may be interested in," said Actaeon, lifting a small hexagonal prism with glass ropes dangling from one end. "As far as I can tell, this is an artifact eye. Wave would have loved it. I may even devise some method of replacing a human eye with it one day." He drew silent at the realization.

Aethelgard reached out to touch his arm. "You miss him."

"Him and Trench both," admitted Actaeon, his eyes wandering off as he remembered the two mercenaries that he'd shared so many memories with. "It was three years ago, last arc of the moon, that Yanelle witnessed him disappear." He shook his head and grinned. "Whatever happened to him, I hope he found what he was looking for – and maybe a spare eye."

"How'd he lose his eye?" asked Aethelgard.

"A slug monster in the tunnels spat its offspring at us," explained Actaeon. "One of them caught him directly in the eye and when he tore it from his face, it took the eye with it."

Aethelgard nodded gravely. "The same incident that took the life of Knight Arbiter Allyk sof Darovin, no doubt?"

"One and the same." Actaeon nodded.

"I'd been investigating those disappearances myself, until a different matter drew my attention away," said the Investigator. "One which I understand you were involved with as well. A man found upon the Avenue of Glass by a meddlesome engineer."

Actaeon arched a brow and then smiled. "Caider."

Aethelgard nodded and leaned forward over his cane to examine the artifact.

"Did you ever discover the details of his sudden appearance?" asked Actaeon.

"Yes," said Aethelgard. "I retraced his steps after he received the wounds all the way back to Adhikara. A damned tough man to make it all that way after the injury he sustained. When I found the site where he had received the injury, I discovered the body of –"

"A Shieldian assassin," said Actaeon, completing his friend's sentence.

Aethelgard's eyes narrowed. "Has anyone ever told you that you know too many things for your own good, Actaeon Rellios Caliburn?"

"Many people," said Actaeon. He spread his hands. "And I always feel as though I know far too little."

Aethelgard sighed and his mouth curled into a thin smile. "Caider killed in self-defense. I suppose you also know the details about why a Shieldian assassin pursued him so relentlessly all the way from the eastern jungles?"

Actaeon grinned. "And I shall tell you everything. But that is a story for another time." He lifted the artifact eye closer to his real eye. "This can see things that the human eye cannot. Invisible light. It may be of future use to us if I can invent a method to easily utilize it in the field. There is something else I believe you will enjoy. Come this way." He led the way to the other side of the workshop and lifted a small, wooden box from one of the shelves there.

Into Aethelgard's hands he placed it. "Go ahead. It is yours."

The Knight Investigator lifted the lid. Inside was a large hand lens like the one he always carried. But this one had an extra ring built into the frame into which were inset a number of miniature luminaries. With his thumb, he swiveled a dial on the handle that opened and closed a multipaneled baffle that could cover and uncover the luminaries on demand. He brought the lens to the lid of the box and gazed through it with one cobalt eye.

"This is an excellent piece of work," said Aethelgard with a nod of satisfaction. "Thank you, my friend."

"You are quite welcome," said Actaeon. "May you solve many crimes with it, and keep Redemption safe. Now come, let us share an ale together."

Once the tankards of ale were poured, the two sat for a time in companionable silence, both thinking about their respective, and quite disparate, problems. For once, the Knight Investigator had come for a visit and not to seek aid in some strange case. There were several investigations in progress in and around the Pyramid, but nothing requiring the engineer's trained eye.

Even so, Aethelgard shared the stories of his latest cases with Actaeon and, in turn, the Prince Engineer shared his latest engineering problems with the Knight Investigator. In so sharing, both found they understood their various endeavors just a bit better, and that bit might make all the difference.

After Actaeon poured them a second tankard, he retrieved the artifact eye and continued tinkering with it as Aethelgard withdrew his fluted pipe and began to play a simple but uplifting melody. The activity helped both of them concentrate, each in his own manner.

All that was interrupted, however, as Lauryn burst into the workshop in a panic. "Act!" she cried out, catching her breath as she refreshed the puddle that Aethelgard had created with more rivulets of water.

Actaeon dropped the artifact eye and leapt to his feet. "What is it, Lauryn?"

"A woman," she said, gasping for air. "She was walking on the Avenue when a cloaked man rushed over and tackled her. It was horrible. The attacker tried to pull her from the Avenue of Glass and she fought and screamed the entire way. Then, just before he managed to drag her over the edge, both of them just... disappeared."

The account had Aethelgard on his feet, the tankard of ale forgotten. "Disappeared? Did he pull her from the edge then?"

Lauryn looked at the Arbiter with wide eyes. "No. They just... uh, vanished, I guess. One moment there, the next moment gone. The only thing left behind was his cloak."

Aethelgard rushed over to her and scrutinized her carefully. "You left it out there?"

"Left what out there?" asked Lauryn, scared and confused.

"The cloak, of course." Aethelgard narrowed his eyes upon her. "It is the one piece of evidence left behind, assuming you are correct about what you witnessed."

"I am," said Lauryn, her eyes narrowing in annoyance.

"There's no time to waste then." Aethelgard seized her arm. "Take us there at once."

The cloak was still exactly where Lauryn said it would be. It was a pool of brown amidst the flooded elderglass surface. Raindrops splashed around it as the three approached.

"She was Ajmani," Lauryn said, answering Aethelgard's question about whether she remembered any details about the victim. "At least, I think so. It was hard to tell in the heavy rain. Her accent sounded like it, I think."

"When she screamed?" Aethelgard asked skeptically, wincing as he took a knee beside the cloak.

Lauryn rolled her eyes. "Anybody ever tell you you're a pain in the ass?"

Lifting the cloak to his nose for a sniff, Aethelgard gave her a hard look from beneath the hood of his own cloak. "In a world where people do things like this, someone needs to be a pain in the ass to them."

Actaeon went to climb down from the edge of the elderglass surface, but the Knight Investigator lifted a hand to stop him. "I want to see if there is any trace of them there."

"Yes, but my skills are better used in that manner before you disturb any traces that are already difficult enough to detect with this heavy rain," explained Aethelgard.

"See?" Lauryn said with a smirk. "Pain in the ass."

"Go easy, Lauryn," said Actaeon. "Aethelgard knows what he is doing."

Aethelgard rummaged in the pockets of the cloak until he located a heavy metal object. He drew it forth and held it aloft. The color drained from his face.

It was a cracked metal cylinder with a slot on one side.

Actaeon knew from experience that an artifact stick could be inserted in the device to activate it. Most often, the device was inset into doors around Redemption. "An artifact lock."

"Ruinlock," whispered Aethelgard, the name barely audible over the splashing of the raindrops.

"Ruinlock?" asked Actaeon. "Again?"

"What, in shattered Redemption, is a ruin lock?" asked Lauryn.

The men ignored her question and Actaeon leaned over Aethelgard as the Knight Investigator methodically searched the other pockets. In the final one, he found a loose sheet of parchment, which he held beneath his own cloak to protect it against the rain. As he unfolded it, a copper bit fell free and clattered to the elderglass surface of the road.

Actaeon snatched it up and peered at it. On its face was stamped the image of a sword piercing a heart from above. He showed it to Aethelgard, who frowned and finished unfolding the parchment. On it was a crude map of Redemption, and a path ending at Thyr Dominion's Canal Keep. The path began at their present location.

"That seems too easy," said Actaeon.

"My thoughts exactly, my engineer friend," said Aethelgard. He folded the map and placed it safely in a pocket before turning to look up at him through the rain-streaked lenses over his eyes. "Because it is a trap."

"Simple then," said Actaeon with a grin. "We ignore it."

Aethelgard winced as he climbed back to his feet. He shook his head sadly. "Ruinlock guessed that would be our first line of thought. He also knows that, as an Arbiter, I cannot ignore the kidnapped victim. This is a lead I must follow."

Lauryn interposed herself between them and folded her arms over her chest. "I asked you a question." She shot Aethelgard a challenging look.

"Best that you do not know," explained the Knight Investigator. "For the knowledge can only lead to death."

Lauryn's expression softened to one of concern. "Well then, thank you for not answering me."

"There are two facts that strike me on this occasion," said Aethelgard.

"The first, is that the crime was perpetrated not only in front of Lauryn, one of your closest associates, but also when we were both conveniently at the workshop she was returning to."

"And the second?" asked Actaeon.

"A cycle ago, on this very day – the forty-fifth of Torrentfall – we first began our investigation into the tragic case of Baron Thrist." Aethelgard wiped his lenses on his vest before returning them to their perch upon his nose.

"That appears to be too much to be a mere coincidence," said Actaeon with a frown.

"Correct," said Aethelgard. "Which means the game is set against us from the start. We walk into the open maw of a deathcrawler lying in wait for us."

Actaeon grinned. "Then we bring what we need to kill it."

"If only I shared your sentiment that it will be so simple," said Aethelgard.

The rain began to fall harder then, as if to emphasize their dilemma.

There were no other clues on or around the Avenue of Glass. No footprints in the mud beside the road near where the disappearance occurred. No further information to be gleaned from the contents of the cloak.

And so, the investigation brought them to Canal Keep. Despite Aethelgard's numerous protests, the Paladin Arbiter sent a team of four additional Arbiters to protect them – two Knights and two Initiates.

The Knight Investigator ranted most of the short trip over about how such a big group would be impossible to keep unnoticed. He'd insisted that they all dress up as a crew of Thyrian sailors, replete with quadcorne hats and sabres instead of their normal arming swords.

"I really hate when we have to dress up for these cases," said Actaeon as they strolled down a narrow causeway between buildings on their way into the Thyrian Hold. Before they departed, he'd fashioned a shaft for his halberd that could be broken down into three pieces. The portions were in a crude scabbard that hung over his shoulder beside his arrows. He fingered the hilt of the sabre. "If I have to use this, we are out of luck. I may as well just throw it at Ruinlock."

Aethelgard shushed him and shot him a glare with his cobalt eyes. "Keep quiet with that name. There are ears everywhere in these places. And, if you believe for a lifebeat that I brought you here for your skill with weapons, Engineer, then you really do have much to learn."

Actaeon laughed at that. "Well, that much is obvious. If we are attacked though, I would do much better keeping a threat at bay with my halberd in one piece."

"If the intent was to attack us as such, it would've happened already," said the Knight Investigator, tipping his quadcorne hat dismissively. "Now," he said, looking at the other Arbiters behind them. "I want you all to scatter from here in teams of two. We're looking for supplies for our ship. Show the merchants the rubbing of the bit I gave you and see if any of them can tell you anything about it. If asked, you heard rumors about a sailmaker that uses that sigil. Watch their eyes when they first see it. If you see recognition, I want you to remember and tell me. We rendezvous again before the Dome when the sun is at its apex."

The great Pulsedome was a massive building of the Ancients at the bend of the canal. It was the main meeting hall of the Thyrian Captains when they were ashore, and also housed offices for the various trade guilds that supported the seafaring operations of the dominion. It was so named because of the flexible hemispherical roof that heaved up and down like the skin of a drum. Inside, the irregular movements generated gusts of wind like those at sea. There, the Thyrians had set up simulator pools where new sail and hull designs could be tested and iterated at smaller scales before being used in the ships of their fleet.

"The Paladin Arbiter gave us strict orders to protect you," said Jauvis sof Oriburt. The stocky Knight Arbiter lifted his own hat from his blond hair and narrowed his deep brown eyes upon Aethelgard.

"The Paladin Arbiter gave you instructions to assist me in the way I see fit for this investigation. Protection is just a part of that assignment," said Aethelgard. Over his lenses, he shot a challenging gaze at his fellow Arbiter.

Jauvis frowned and shrugged. "Have it your way."

Each Knight Arbiter then took an Initiate and went their separate ways to start the search.

"Come, my friend," said Aethelgard with a thin smile. "Now the hunt begins!"

Through the narrow streets of Canal Keep they weaved. Past fishmongers preparing and salting their fish and fishermen tending to their nets and crab pots. Past trade depots receiving goods from incoming vessels while porters raced to load departing ships with items destined for other ports. Past heralds crying out news from across Redemption and demanding bits from anyone paying them heed.

It was before one of these heralds, a portly woman with a booming voice who wielded a bell and a scroll, where Aethelgard first stopped. He handed her several bits, which disappeared beneath her heavy coat nearly as quickly as she snatched them from his hand.

Without so much as a word of gratitude, she rang her bell in the disguised Knight Investigator's face and continued rattling off details of a feud between two captains Actaeon had never heard of.

"There's more in it for you if you can point us in the right direction." Aethelgard held out the copper bit with the sword-pierced heart. Went the woman went to snatch it, he snapped his hand closed into a fist. "My my, is someone greedy today. Not this one. Just look and tell me about the symbol on it and you can have more where the previous ones came from."

When he uncurled his fingers, the herald gasped at what she saw and withdrew her hand as if she'd been bitten. She quickly furled her scroll and scurried off without looking back.

Aethelgard looked to Actaeon and the Prince Engineer raised a brow.

"The symbol struck fear into her heart. It appears to be recognizable enough," said Actaeon, lifting his quadcorne hat to scratch his head behind the goggles. "We should keep asking around about it."

"His spies are undoubtedly everywhere," said Aethelgard. "We must tread carefully from here. I suspect our herald friend is already off to inform of our presence."

"Should we stop her then?" asked Actaeon.

"Perhaps we should have," said Aethelgard. "Though, the scene would have drawn Ruinlock's attention even faster. I fear we are in over our heads on this one. We should not have come here."

"Do you suppose that the kidnapped person Lauryn witnessed may have just been part of a ruse to get us out here?" Actaeon's emerald eyes darted about, looking for anyone watching them in the nearby crowd.

"I'm certain of that," said the Knight Investigator. "But the question that remains is whether the victim was truly kidnapped or simply played along as part of Ruinlock's plan."

"An associate then," said Actaeon.

"Right," said Aethelgard. "Though Lauryn was correct about it being an Ajmani woman. So we know at least that much."

Actaeon's eyes widened. "We do? How do you figure that?"

"The telltale stain of gorankh root was on the cloak in two places. It was quite easy to discern, even despite the rain." Aethelgard traced a line across his palm. "Religious Ajmani women often use dyes created from the root to paint intricate patterns on their hands. Whether the struggle was legitimate or no, the gorankh dye rubbed off on the cloak. The scent and the color left no other possibilities. And, even though I observed the straining of threads on the right shoulder joint of the garment, which might indicate a struggle, there is no way to know for certain that it wasn't simply an act for Lauryn's eyes."

"All to draw us out," whispered Actaeon.

"Precisely," said Aethelgard. "We must tread carefully from hereon out. Our very lives depend upon it."

Actaeon nodded and the two men continued on, weaving through the crowd in search of the next person that might yield the right information to them.

"There is one detail I cannot decipher," said Aethelgard. "That of their complete disappearance from the Avenue of Glass."

"Excepting the cloak," said Actaeon.

"Excepting the cloak," echoed Aethelgard.

"There are no artifacts that I have yet encountered which could explain such a phenomenon." Actaeon scratched his right hand through his fingerless glove. "Which doesn't mean there is not a yet undiscovered artifact capable of such an effect. There just is not one we know about. I would estimate a very small percentage of the technology of the Ancients has been found. Many possibilities are still out there, both for us and for people like Ruinlock, who would use it for evil."

"Whatever it was, it caused them both to disappear without any sign of struggle or passage after that point. I thoroughly searched for clues off the side of the avenue and there were none." Aethelgard frowned. "It was as if they just... vanished."

"There must be an explanation for it," said Actaeon.

"There is always an explanation," Aethelgard agreed. "We both know that from our respective lines of work. It is just a matter of finding it."

"That is always the challenge," said Actaeon.

When they rendezvoused outside the Pulsedome, one of the teams was missing.

Jauvis and his Initiate, a young, talkative man named Schlefer sof Jauvis, were nowhere to be found.

Matine sof Fystra, a short Knight Arbiter with a shaved scalp and a deep scar that ran between her eyes and down through her nose into her lip, and her Initiate, a feminine-looking boy with Shieldian features named Bergum sof Matine, were the only ones present when Actaeon and Aethelgard arrived.

The Knight Arbiter and Initiate had better luck than they had. One porter had recognized the symbol on the rubbing they showed him as the same one emblazoned on a warehouse door not far from the Pulsedome itself.

"All the others we showed it to rushed right off," said Matine, wringing her hands nervously. "I didn't want to check it out until we had the chance to tell you."

"You did just the right thing," said Aethelgard, offering her a thin smile. "Once brother Jauvis arrives, we shall all investigate the location together. Nice work, sister."

Matine beamed. "Thank you, Knight Investigator."

After waiting for Jauvis for the better part of the afternoon, Aethelgard rose from the bench he'd been sitting on. "They've run into trouble, I'm certain of it. We each attracted much attention during this reconnaissance exercise. They must have been intercepted and ambushed."

Matine looked at him with wide eyes. "Someone here would attack an Arbiter?"

"Or worse," admitted Aethelgard, causing the Arbiter's face to blanch. "Come. There is no time to lose. We must investigate this warehouse. May we find our brothers within."

Behind them, the Pulsedome began to thrum with a deep, regular beat that resonated in their chests. It was a foreboding sound that followed them as they walked the cobblestone streets toward their destination.

Matine led the way toward the warehouse as they hurried onward past overly burdened porters, stumbling drunk sailors, and noisy street peddlers. She made a left down a narrow lane that led away from the canal, the drumming following after them like an omen of doom.

Finally, they stood before a door upon which was a carved relief of the pierced heart. It faced them like a silent threat.

As Matine reached out to open the door, Aethelgard's hand snapped out and caught her wrist.

"Allow me to lead," he said. Then, instead of opening the door, he knelt and brought out his illuminated magnifier. Slowly, methodically, he examined first the knob and the jamb near the latch, then the hinges, and finally the flush stone inset into the cobblestones at the bottom of the door.

After several minutes of this, he stood and frowned, shaking his head as he returned the magnifier to his vest pocket.

"What is it?" asked Actaeon.

Aethelgard clicked his tongue and pushed the lenses back up the bridge of his nose. "This door has never been used. It was installed several arcs of the moon ago, and was never once opened."

The Arbiter Initiate offered him an incredulous look. "How could you know that, sir?"

"Dust?" guessed Actaeon.

"Precisely." Aethelgard snapped his fingers. "Our engineer friend gets it. The dust is the key. An abundance of dust, grime, and particulates gather upon all these surfaces. A thin coat of salt residue lies upon most things as well – this near to the Great Sea as we are. The opening and closing of a door will leave telltale signs – swiping such residue aside. There is none of that here. And a latch will scratch the strike plate as it returns to the closed position. None of that is evident."

Actaeon leaned forward to peer at the latch himself. "Almost as if this door was just dropped into place and never used. I see it myself now. The stones are freshly cut at the edges of the frame as well."

"And why would a door never be used?" asked Aethelgard, looking between the three of them.

Matine threw her hands into the air. "Beats me."

"A trap," said Actaeon.

"Right," said Aethelgard. "It lies in wait for something. Whoever installed it hasn't used it once because they know what waits on the other side."

"So, should we open it remotely?" suggested Actaeon. "I could rig up a mechanism to pull the door handle from a distance."

"Perhaps," said the Knight Investigator. "But first, I ask that you humor me and follow." He led the way to the left until the corner of the building where he turned to the right and continued along the wall.

The alley on that side of the warehouse was overgrown with a tangle of tall weeds and vines that broke through dirt and disused cobbles. An old, vine-covered barn door was chained shut with rusted chains that were locked with an equally rusty padlock.

Aethelgard inspected the padlock and the vines along the door before dropping to his hands and knees with a wince. Down there, he scrutinized around the immediate vicinity of the door with painstaking slowness.

Once he was completely satisfied, the Knight Investigator reached out for Matine's hand. The Knight Arbiter reached out to help him to his feet and Aethelgard dusted off his trousers before pointing to the door. "This door is in regular use."

"How could that be?" asked Actaeon. "It is completely overgrown."

"Take a closer look at the tiny roots that the vines use to latch onto things. You'll find that none of them are attached to this door." Aethelgard pulled on one in demonstration. "Instead, they have been moved and replaced frequently to give this door the appearance of disuse. In fact, some sort of large apparatus has been dragged in this way not too long ago judging by the gouges in the soil and the dislodged plants. The rusty padlock too is just a ruse – there is no rust inside the mechanism or around the keyhole where the key scratched it away during many attempts to unlock it."

As Actaeon leaned forward to inspect the vines for himself, Aethelgard slid his writheblade just a finger's width from its ceramic scabbard and used it to cut through the closest link to the lock and then another.

The rusted chains fell away, dragging more than a few of the vines along with them.

"Shall we?" suggested Aethelgard with a thin smile.

"Better this way than the way this bastard expects us to go," said Matine.

"I agree," said Actaeon, as he assembled the three pieces of his halberd before leaning upon the shaft. "If a trap lies inside, we had best enter through the unexpected way."

At Aethelgard's direction, Matine and her Initiate stepped forward. Each grabbed one of the big doors and, together, they slid them aside.

Within lay darkness.

Actaeon withdrew his luminary and stuck it under the strap of his goggles before pulling back the baffle to cast light into the warehouse. With his halberd held defensively before him, he stepped inside, Aethelgard at his side.

Inside was a wide passage full of cobwebs and mold. Aethelgard shined his own luminary at the floor and read the signs of passage.

"To the left," he whispered.

Together, they advanced until they reached a dead end with a crude wooden door.

Aethelgard pushed it open to reveal a descending staircase. The light of the luminary was insufficient to see to the bottom. The deep stench of stale and moldy air wafted up to meet their noses.

"This is the type of place that you take people to so that you can kill them," said Actaeon in a low voice.

Aethelgard glanced back at him, fear evident in his cobalt eyes. "And I thought I was the expert on such places."

Actaeon lowered the point of his halberd and led the way forward down the stairs. Aethelgard followed closely behind while the other Arbiters took up the rear.

The stairway led down through stone walls of the warehouse, which then transitioned to sharply cut rock walls. Actaeon counted eighty steps before they reached the bottom, which looked like the start of an old mineshaft.

"This is discomfiting," said Actaeon. "It must be below the water level of the canal. Something like this should not be here."

"And yet it is," said Aethelgard. "Thankfully, it is not underwater."

"Yet," said Matine behind him. "Gonna be a very bad day for us if that changes."

"Um... Maybe we should report this back to Arbiter Pyramid Command," suggested Bergum, the Initiate's voice quavering with fear.

"Steel yourself, brother," instructed Aethelgard. "Two of our own are missing. We do what we must to find them now."

"Yessir," said Bergum.

Farther along, the shaft was broken up by Ancient doorways set into the very stone. A dull hum resonated through the stone as they advanced — signs of artifact machinery operating.

"Perhaps the hum we hear is actually –" Actaeon's thought was cut off as one of the doorways shrieked behind him. He spun to find it closed, with only Aethelgard left behind with him. The other two Arbiters were behind a metal door which now separated them.

Aethelgard pounded on the door with a fist. "Stand clear!" he shouted. "I will cut it open." He drew his writheblade, filling the tunnel with the poignant smell of ozone.

Before he could cut through anything, they were plunged into darkness.

"Shit," said Aethelgard.

"Darkest Hour," said Actaeon. "Bad timing."

The hum sound had disappeared, which made the darkness feel even more oppressive.

"Good timing for our adversary," said Aethelgard. "Suspiciously so."

"What are you suggesting?" Actaeon lowered himself to the floor, couching his halberd against anything that might attack them from the shaft ahead.

"I was about to cut my way through the door and the artifacts all power off?" Aethelgard shook his head in the darkness. "All too convenient – the timing, that is."

"The last Darkest Hour was not so long ago," said Actaeon, wondering. "I remember the luminaries flicking off just after I awoke this morning."

"How often do they occur, would you say?" asked the Knight Investigator, knowing the answer already – he wanted to hear it from the Engineer.

"A little more than a day. The exact time varies. Never this quick though. Not that I have witnessed." Actaeon felt a chill and the hairs raised on his neck as he considered the possibility. "The ability to turn off power to artifacts at will…"

"Puts us at a significant disadvantage." Aethelgard completed his sentence. He hammered a fist upon the door and then waited. Only silence answered him.

"Either the door is too thick to even conduct such sound, or something happened to them." Actaeon worked his way around Aethelgard's side and searched the door for any grippable seams or hidden levers.

"Let's hope for the former." Aethelgard struck a dagger to flint several times, sending showers of sparks to the floor. It offered them glimpses of the tunnel around them with its impenetrable door.

After many more such strikes, a candle was lit. Aethelgard handed it to Actaeon, who searched the perimeter of the door with it, looking for anything his fingers might not have detected. There was nothing but unbroken metal surface right up to the stone. Even where there had been a doorway protruding from the rock earlier, there was now no sign of it – just a solid sheet of metal.

The silence in the tunnel was deathly. The hum of whatever machines had been operating was a fading memory.

"Ideas?" asked Aethelgard.

"My blue fire is one possibility," mused Actaeon. "But there is nowhere to vent the smoke. We would have to deal with it building up here. And there is little chance that the concoction would melt through such thick metal like this."

"How about one of your famous grenados?" Aethelgard offered him an unseen smile that quickly faded.

"They are luminary dependent. In the Darkest Hour they cease to function." Actaeon turned to the darkness before them. "We could carry on, looking for another way out."

"Into the toothless maw of darkness?" Aethelgard frowned deeply. "Straight into the arms of death, courtesy of Ruinlock."

"I do not intend to die so easily," said Actaeon with a grin. "The only logical choice is to continue forward." He lowered his goggles over his eyes and did just that, probing the floor ahead of him as he proceeded.

Aethelgard grunted his assent and followed.

Their footsteps and breathing were the only sounds as they walked cautiously onward.

The addition of a splash to the limited sounds brought them both to a halt. Actaeon knelt and lowered the candle to find water on the tunnel floor. He handed the candle to Aethelgard and drew his dagger to place it, point down, into the water. As he waited, the water climbed upward to the next gradation mark etched into the back of the hooked blade. And it was not long before it worked its way up to the next.

"We need to move," said Actaeon, returning the blade to his belt. "The tunnels are flooding. If I were to hazard a guess, I would say that the humming sound we heard earlier was the sound of pumps running to keep the canal water from inundating this shaft." That said, he started forward at a slow jog, tapping the butt of his halberd on the floor ahead intermittently to verify it was still there.

The water rose steadily as they continued until it was up to their knees and then their thighs.

Through deepening chill water they slogged.

Aethelgard lit a second candle with the first before it burned down completely. "One half of an hour has passed."

By the time Aethelgard lit the third candle, they were up to their chests in chill water. Both of them had begun to shiver.

"We've been walking for a full hour now and this shaft just continues on with no end in sight," said the Knight Investigator.

"And power has yet to return to the luminaries," Actaeon noted. "Do you suppose Ruinlock intends to try and kill us this way?" He waded forward, careful to still check the floor ahead with his weapon. It wouldn't do to fall into some deep hole beneath the water.

"Drowned and frozen in a dark, narrow abyss?" Aethelgard pulled the lenses from his eyes and stashed them securely in a pocket of his vest. "I admit, my mind is not at its sharpest under these conditions. However, it doesn't add up. There is more going on here than meets the eye. The marks outside the warehouse of large things being dragged within indicate there is something more to be anticipated. The scratches and scuffs I noticed on this very tunnel floor before it became flooded are enough to make me suspect that we'll encounter whatever Ruinlock has prepared for us. The missing Ajmani woman is another factor. I suspect when we find her, we'll find whatever Ruinlock has prepared for us. Judging by the depths of the gouges and the number of times things have been hauled this way, I imagine it will be quite large."

Actaeon looked back at him for the first time in awhile and arched a brow over one goggle-clad eye. "Is there anything else you can tell me about what we might expect?"

"Whatever it is was heavy enough to require a wheeled cart to carry the components. Other than that, I can't tell you more. There was no residue or debris left behind to give me further information." Aethelgard used the candle to light his pipe, filling the narrow space remaining between the water and the top of the shaft with the pungent scent of guaraja root. He took some deep puffs and blew the smoke into the air around them. "Oh, and one thing that struck me as odd is that, even with all the passages bearing heavy loads through these tunnels, none of them ever left this way when they were done. All of the boot scuffs and drag marks from the wheels head in one direction: farther along."

"And you did not think to mention that earlier?" Actaeon gave his friend a flabbergasted look.

"My apologies, my dear engineer," said Aethelgard, puffing calmly on his pipe. "In my abject terror, I neglected to do so."

Actaeon laughed. "Rarely have I seen a man in abject terror act with such serenity as yourself in this moment."

Aethelgard spread his hands. "Would you have me rave like a lunatic? Perhaps foam at the mouth? What good would that accomplish? Carry on, my friend. I will follow as best I can. The good news is with the cold of the water my knee stopped hurting."

When they reached the door, it came as a shock to them both. For so long had they been walking down the tunnel that ran straight as an arrow without any other features or breaks that something so different was both welcome and frightening. A secondary tunnel sloped steeply up to one side, rising out of the water to a crude door made from wooden planks.

Hidden beneath the water were steps that they ascended until they were out of the chill. Actaeon swung open the door and they both pushed into the chamber beyond and fell to their knees. There was a whoosh and a metal panel slid across the doorway behind them, barring their access to the flooded tunnel they'd come from.

"Gods of old and gods of new..." Warm arms clad in soft silks wrapped around Actaeon. "Your Grace – is it really you? Have you come to rescue me? I am so glad to see you, but... You shouldn't have come." The voice was familiar and when Actaeon looked up, he recognized the captivating smile of an old friend. He offered her a weak grin.

She helped him to his feet and then reached out to help the Knight Investigator up.

The well-lit room in which they found themselves was nothing like the dank tunnel outside. The floor was covered in a neat grid of tiles and ornate carved pillars stood against the smooth stone walls at intervals, as if they were holding up the arched ceiling above. Luminaries were inset into a rib of stone that followed the top room of the ceiling and bathed the room in a faintly greenish light. Against one wall was a large wooden bed with an ornate mirror that hung above it. Opposite it was a fabric-covered divan that had a painting above it of two young girls holding hands and looking out over the Great Sea from the Blacksands Beach. A gentle trickling sound from one corner revealed a small privy with running water.

"It appears we've found our victim." Aethelgard leaned against the wall and massaged his bad knee through his trousers, trying to get the blood flowing again. "I am Knight Investigator Aethelgard. Maerdia Bazardjan, I presume?"

Mae took a step backward and cocked her head to the side. "Have we met?"

"We have not," said Aethelgard. "But your works have become renowned. I pass them most every day in my duties." When she still looked confused, he gestured to her hands. "It is a most simple deduction, my dear. Your hands are calloused from the work, as anyone can plainly see. There are other signs for those who would take their time to cast a discerning eye: the slight rasp at the intake of each breath from the stone dust in your lungs and the flecks of damaged skin around your eyes and, indeed, even on your cornea. Our friend here can surely fashion you a nice set of goggles and a filter to protect you during your work in the future. Not to mention the gray discoloration of the fine colors of your silks at the sleeve fringes from years of stone dust."

The sculptor nodded and traced an elegant curtsy, offering him a gentle smile. "I can appreciate one who sees the fine details of things. Which is the reason I don't obscure my senses. To see every detail of the stone, to feel it, to taste its givings on my tongue – there is no better way to know my medium. You must understand that."

Aethelgard offered her a thin smile in return, pushing his lenses up along the bridge of his nose. "I most certainly do. It is a boon to be able to read all those fine details – one which I've come to realize over the years that very few possess. And one that has me at this very moment in quite a state of terror."

"Terror?" echoed Actaeon. He had made his way into the room and was examining another metal panel like the one that had closed the way behind them, looking for a way to open it. There were several more such panels in the chamber.

"Your luminary," said Aethelgard, simply.

Actaeon raised his hand before the luminary in his goggle strap and the color drained from his face. "By the Fallen..."

"What is it?" asked Mae, fear in her eyes as she looked back and forth between the two men.

"Ruinlock found a means to selectively turn off the power to some artifacts and not others," said Actaeon.

Aethelgard slid his writheblade partially from its scabbard and it was also lifeless. He stepped past Mae until he was in the center of the room and raised an accusing finger up at a small black insect that clung to the ceiling there. "Show yourself, Ruinlock. Stop hiding behind your toys and face us directly."

A beam of light shimmered from the bug and cast a featureless green face upon the wall above the divan.

The lips curled into a smile that was half scowl and blank green orbs stared out at them, unblinking. The voice that came out when the face opened its lips to speak seemed to come from everywhere at once, the words crisp and well-spoken in an accentless tone that ended each syllable with a whizzing sound like the beat of an insect's wings.

"The pair of you could not have been more predictable in your quest to save this woman."

"Gloat and brag if it please you, Ruinlock," snapped Aethelgard, narrowing his cobalt eyes upon the projected face. "You clearly intend to kill us here. My only question is this: Why bring us all this way?"

The head on the wall tilted forward in acknowledgment. "Of course, you are right. I've brought you to this place because I have designed a contraption to rid the world of you both. You are clever enemies, and that I admire. So, what better way than to watch you apply your wits to try and escape your demise? A more fitting end, I think, to show you both, in your hubris, that there are things in this world not to be trifled with."

"You speak of hubris, and yet you are the one who killed a man inside the very Pyramid I'm sworn to protect." Aethelgard lifted his cane in both hands and twisted it within his fists. "Are you such a fool, that you expected me not to investigate?"

"Have you learned nothing from the end of Belidur sof Balur?" The face's eyes narrowed upon them. "A message given in vain, I have come to find out."

"That you murdered Belidur has naught to do with this, Ruinlock." Aethelgard spat the words beneath a barely contained roiling anger that grew within him. "How were we to know that you were behind the death of Baron Thrist before we'd completed our investigation? You're foolish if you think that the Order of Arbiters would not investigate any crime that takes place under our watch on the off chance that it might be connected to your unsavory dealings."

"Ah, but the fool here is you, poor, dear Aethel." The lips twisted into a cross between a grin and a snarl. "You found the glider that our friend the Baron let loose with my name upon it, and yet you continued the course. Perhaps you don't like your face much? Wanted to match that fool Belidur, did you?"

The cry of anger that Aethelgard let out caught Actaeon off guard. The Knight Investigator leapt forward and punched the green face straight between the eyes. His fist struck the stone wall with a dull thud.

The head reared back at the action and roaring laughter filled the chamber.

"Now now, foolhardy Aethel. You had best save your energy. Lady Bazardjan's gods of old *and* her gods of new both know you're about to need it." The face chuckled again. "And even if I had doubts about your knowledge that the Baron's murder was MY DOMAIN," the words boomed throughout the chamber, "I was utterly convinced that you brazenly failed to heed my warnings when you found my calling card when investigating Lady Bazardjan's abduction and yet I find you standing here before me now."

Aethelgard's face turned ashen.

"That's right, Aethel," spoke the green lips. "My eyes are everywhere. Be careful who and what you trust – not that you'll need that advice for too much longer." The face turned to Actaeon then. "And as for you... the Rellios that became a Caliburn. So disappointing that you followed him into this pit that will be your demise. Quite promising, you were. It pleased me to see your rise to power after I orchestrated your wife's ascension to the throne of Raedelle. There are so many good things you've done for my city. A shame you have to die now."

"What do you mean that you orchestrated her rise?" Actaeon's brow arched in curiosity.

"Do you really think that she would have been Yonniker's first choice?" The green lips smirked again. "No, he'd wanted Aedgar – that big, dumb idiot. An easy man to manipulate, that one. But I knew from the start that he'd be a disastrous choice. Another Thernaxis, at best. The Second

Invasion War would've been determined at Glass Spire with him in charge. So I had my agents dispose of him. That your scatterbrained wife might have a better chance at it."

Actaeon shook his head. "You lie. The Shieldians brought us the news of his death, while fighting the initial tribal incursions south of Rust."

"Careful of such accusations," warned the projection. "I believe in the power of truth as much as you do. I just put it to more effective use than you. If you think I don't have Shieldians working for me who could orchestrate such a coverup, then you're not as smart as I'd thought."

Actaeon narrowed his eyes. "Are you a Starborn then?"

Laughter filled the room. "No more than you are. But I *am* the best defense against them. And I keep my city safe from their corruption better than even you, Engineer who became a Prince. I thank you for your service to my city. I shall take it from here."

"Why do this?" asked Actaeon with a shake of his head.

The eyes narrowed in anger. "Because you dare threaten me. I'll not abide it." The face's expression softened then. "Of course, there is always a chance you will figure something out. That's part of the fun, isn't it? I'll be watching and recording your actions in your final moments for posterity. Don't disappoint me now!"

The face vanished and the bug fell from the ceiling to disappear in a small burst of flame and a cloud of smoke.

And then the three of them were inside a cage of light. Closely spaced beams of energy, like those from a light lance, emerged from the floor around the perimeter of the room. Each one scorched a mark in the stone ceiling above. The bed and divan burst into flame as the beams tore through them. The stench of ozone filled the room like a hundred writheblades like Aethelgard's had been drawn.

The Knight Investigator sank to his good knee and let out a sob.

Mae clasped her hands together and began to murmur a prayer.

"Now is not the time for despair, but for action," Actaeon said sternly. He grinned at them before approaching the nearest edge of the cage of beams that crackled all around. "A problem to be solved like any other. That is all this is. Now we do what we do best." As he watched, the beams slowly angled inward, etching scorched lines into the ceiling as they traced a path toward the center of the room. "If we can find a way to interrupt some of these beams near one of the metal panels, then we just need to defeat the panel to escape. Perhaps we can use the beams themselves to do that. Aeth, can you tell me which exit received the greatest traffic?"

The Knight Investigator snapped into action. The climb to his feet made him wince, but he started around the perimeter of the room, looking for the signs of heaviest use.

"How may I help?" asked Mae. Acrid, black smoke from the burning furniture poured upward toward the ceiling and began to bank down toward them.

His eyes darted around the room quickly and Actaeon took stock of everything in the diminishing space. "We need to get to that mirror," he said, gesturing to the frame hanging on the wall beyond the burning bed. "Do we have anything that could temporarily block the beams?"

"Could you use my magnifier lens?" suggested Aethelgard. He handed it to Actaeon before continuing his investigation.

"Here," said Actaeon, handing it to Mae. "Hold this in place against my halberd while I bind it." He withdrew a roll of thread from his jacket pocket and began to bind the handle of the magnifier to the base of his halberd shaft. Once it was adequately secured, he tied off a neat knot and cut the excess with his dagger.

"Is that good?" asked Mae.

"Let us find out." Actaeon pulled out a tinted lens attachment and affixed them over his goggles. "Stand clear. I cannot be certain how the beam will react."

Carefully, he extended the butt of his halberd, watching through the corners of his eyes. When the magnifier hit the beam, there was a flash, followed by a burst of heat on his face and then green-tinged darkness.

Actaeon cried out and dropped the halberd, falling to his knees and covering his eyes. "Shit, shit. Very stupid, Actaeon," he scolded himself.

"What happened?" came Mae's voice beside him, her hand on his shoulder.

"The magnifier lens converges light to a focal point and then it diverges. I just blasted myself with a portion of the beam's energy." Actaeon laughed at his stupidity as tears streamed down his face from his injured eyes. "I probably just blinded myself for the final moments of my life. By the Fallen, I should have known better."

Mae squeezed his shoulder. "We are all under duress here, brave Prince Engineer. Do not doubt yourself. You had a plan. Tell us what it is."

"We must retrieve that mirror without losing it to the beams," said Actaeon. "But I don't think we have anything else that could possibly block them. I really should have known better than to use a lens like that. In my haste, I did not consider the way in which such a lens deflects light."

Aethelgard came over to join them and began stripping his clothing off.

The Ajmani artist's eyes widened as he unbuttoned his vest and tossed it aside. "What are you doing, Sir Arbiter?" The beams were slanting substantially across the room now and between the angle of the beams and the banking smoke, they all ducked low to keep beneath the hazards, Mae guiding Actaeon in the process.

"I believe I have a way to block the beams." Aethelgard tossed his tabard aside and unbuttoned his trousers, yanking them down as well to reveal a shimmering set of shirt and long shorts.

"Brightweave!" exclaimed Mae.

Actaeon grinned, despite not being able to see what was going on. He opened his eyes to see a very blurry, half-naked Aethelgard before him. "You are truly wearing brightweave underwear?" Brightweave was a material of the Ancients that was virtually invulnerable to puncture and penetration. It was also highly resistant to fire and burning.

"Well, I can't readily wear it as my Arbiter uniform, can I?" Aethelgard pulled off his shirt and placed it into Mae's hands. "Avert your eyes, if you would, madam." When she did so, he slid off his shorts and quickly began to pull his trousers and other overclothes back on before anyone was scandalized.

"You have... most interesting friends, Your Grace," said Mae with a smile despite the circumstances.

"Yourself included," said Actaeon with a grin. He blinked multiple times, but his vision failed to clear. It felt like a giant dust mote was in each of his eyes and everything was a blurry blob of color and motion before him. He watched as Aethelgard changed from a skin tone blob back to the dull gray blob of his Arbiter uniform.

"Alright, Act," said Aethelgard. "Lady Bazardjan is right. You need to guide us as we carry out your plan. The beams are at about thirty degrees from vertical. A third of our time is now gone."

"Very well," said Actaeon, resolving to the fact that he'd need to walk them through each detail of the plan. He squeezed his eyes shut and felt a slight decrease in the pain as they were ensconced in darkness behind his tear-filled eyelids. "Drop the brightweave in a way that covers as many of the beams as you can to one side of the burning bed. Grab the mirror as quickly as you can and slip it out without letting it touch any light beams. Then pull the brightweave free. It will not last long under that level of energy intensity."

Mae readied the shirt while Aethelgard held his shorts. They shared a look and a nod before they tossed the garments forward to cover the bottom of five beams. Mae stood then and snaked her arms in behind the remaining beams. The flames from the bed licked her silken sleeves as she plucked the mirror frame from the wall and gingerly passed it back to the Arbiter. Aethelgard slid it aside and then reached out to guide the artist back safely to the other side of the beams.

Together they slipped the brightweave away and the beams shot back up to the ceiling, continuing their scorched paths after a brief interruption.

"Now what?" asked Aethelgard.

"Now break it," instructed Actaeon.

"After all that, we break it?" Mae looked at the mirror skeptically.

"Let us be safer about it. How much time is left?" asked Actaeon.

"Forty degrees now," said Aethelgard, eyeing the beams. "Perhaps forty-five."

"Pull the mirror from its frame," said Actaeon, holding out his dagger hilt-first. "Be quick about it."

Using Actaeon's hooked dagger, Mae pried the flat nails that held the mirror into its wooden, partially burnt frame. After they lifted the mirror from the frame and set it aside, she turned to the Prince Engineer. "What now?"

"Here," said Actaeon, feeling his way over to the mirror's edge. "Pass me the dagger." Once it was in his hand, he traced one side of the mirror with his finger and laid the shaft of his halberd across it, parallel to the edge and a splayed hand's width away. He placed the point of the dagger against the glass and used it to score along the length of the shaft to the opposite side. "There. Now, Mae – flip it over and stand on the thin section with your slippered feet. Aeth, you can lift the opposite side. It should snap neatly about the score mark I left."

They did so, and, with a crack, the mirror separated neatly into two sections.

Actaeon scored the thin section of mirror perpendicularly to the original score then and this time broke the smaller section himself. A hand-sized section of mirror was now freed. He placed a boot on the blade of his halberd and levered the shaft upward until the blade began to bend. "Help me," he instructed, and the others pushed the shaft of the weapon upward. The tip of the blade bent at a right angle.

"Sixty degrees, Act," said Aethelgard. "Fifty-five, maybe?"

Actaeon withdrew a bottle full of brown goo from his jacket. "Apply this to the non-mirrored side of the glass. It should be sufficient to hold it in place against the bent blade of my halberd, at least for the duration of this operation."

Mae took the bottle from him and did so. She placed the mirror against the blade and, sure enough, it stuck in place. "Ready."

"Now is the difficult part," said the Prince Engineer. "Aethelgard, did you find the most heavily trafficked door?"

"Over here." Aethelgard led them over to the metal plate set into the wall at the corner of the room farthest from the panel through which they had entered. "Careful, Act. The beams are quite low now. Keep to your hands and knees. I don't want you to lose your head here."

"What now?" asked Mae.

"Alright," said Actaeon. "Mae, you should be the one to do this. It requires the precise hands of a sculptor. Using the mirror on the end of the halberd, reflect one beam back toward the metal. With any luck, it should cut through the metal plate. You must steer it accordingly to cut a hole large enough for us to fit through. Be sure to steer the mirror in from the side. Mirrors are not perfect. Part of the beam will pass through and diffract through the glass. You will want to be away from that. So do not stand in the path beyond the mirror. Understand?"

"I think so," said Mae, sounding uncertain.

Act felt Aethelgard's hand on his head pushing him closer to the floor. "Seventy degrees. Stay low."

Allowing his friend to guide his head lower, Actaeon opened his eyes to regard the red blur of Mae's silken form and reached out to offer a touch of reassurance that happened to be at her waist. "You can do this. Just take it very slow and watch where the light is steering in both directions. Make sure you are well outside of the diffracted portion of the beam and that the reflected portion is where you want it to be. Take your time and do it right. We have one shot at this."

"Not too much time though," said Aethelgard, coughing a bit as the layers of smoke began to reach their level, fed by the smoldering remains of the furniture.

"I can do this," said Mae. She held the halberd like an artisan's tool and carefully guided the mirror forward until it intercepted her beam of choice.

The mirror sent the beam tearing through the metal plate. Excited, she steered it in a wide arc along the bottom of the panel. Then she remembered what Actaeon had said and slowed her approach. She deftly traced the beam up one side of the panel and then across the top.

Actaeon grinned as he smelled the burning metal. The plan was working! Then a clattering sound came, followed by the sound of glass breaking.

"Gods of old and gods of new," whispered Mae.

"What is it?" asked Actaeon.

"The mirror came loose," she said. "It broke."

With no time to waste, Actaeon opened his eyes to reveal the blurred room and crawled his way on his belly back to where the larger mirror lay. He found the thin sliver he'd broken off originally and quickly scored another line across it.

"Eighty or so, Act," called out Aethelgard, spreading out his brightweave garments in preparation for their exit. "Hurry up. Our time is running out!"

Ignoring the sensations of his hair beginning to burn as the beams closed in on his prone form, Actaeon cracked the new section free, feeling the other end of the glass in his hand shatter as it struck a beam when he levered it upward. With their lifeline mirror clutched in his fingers, he pulled himself forward on his elbows as quickly as he could manage, thankful for Mae's bright red silks that provided a faint contrast with the orange-yellow of the beams.

Mae had already slathered more of the sticky brown goo that was one third of Actaeon's blue fire concoction on the halberd's blade. When Actaeon arrived, she stuck the mirror fragment in place and wasted no time in completing the final slice down the other side of the metal plate, angling the beam expertly from her belly down position on the cold stone floor. She could barely see the top due to the thick smoke, but she wiggled the beam around there until the section of panel fell free with a loud smack against the floor. It landed atop the beams and glowed red before the energy lances bored their way through the thick metal to continue on their deadly downward angling.

Aethelgard threw the brightweave over the beams, one garment and then the other. He gritted his teeth in pain as he sprang forward and through the freshly cut hole. Turning, he grabbed Mae's arm and yanked her through, along with the Engineer's bent halberd.

"Roll to your right, Act," he instructed. "Quickly. And stay low." When Actaeon did so, Aethelgard and Mae stepped over the smoking brightweave and red hot panel to each grab an arm and pull him up and out.

Once Mae and Act were both safely in the corridor beyond the cut metal panel, Aethelgard reached in to snatch back his smoldering brightweave undergarments.

The three of them collapsed together in the corridor, breathing heavily.

"It appears your brightweave underwear saved us," said Actaeon with a grin.

"That's why I wear it – to save my ass," said Aethelgard with a sigh of relief.

Mae was the first to laugh, and the two men followed suit – the three of them joyful to be alive.

The dead Arbiter was at the end of the corridor.

A folded note was pinned to Jauvis sof Oriburt's chest with a dagger. A short loop of chain dangled from the hilt, at the bottom of which was a broken, hexagonal artifact lock.

Beside him was his Arbiter Initiate, bound and gagged. The young man squirmed and shifted, trying to free himself.

Aethelgard knelt before the slain Knight Arbiter and reached forward to close the man's staring eyes. "That monster let him bleed out here after pinning the note to him." His hand clenched into a fist before he yanked the dagger free and tossed it behind him down the hall. With fresh blood on his hands, he opened the note with shaking fingers.

A picture fell into the pool of blood on the floor. It showed the three of them as they struggled to escape the room – the deadly beams closing in on their heads.

Leaning forward, Actaeon peered at the note but couldn't make out the words.

Aethelgard read it aloud for him.

So you managed to escape.

Impressive...

Even so, let this Arbiter be your reminder that crossing me always comes with a cost. I warned you not to meddle in my affairs.

I know thee both, righteous Knight Investigator and prodigal Prince Engineer – and that means I know that neither of you give up so easily.

And so, next time it will be someone even more dear to you than the lovely artist from Ajman. Won't that be a surprise for you?

Your next challenge will not be such an easy one.

I delight in seeing that!

Your dear friend,

Ruinlock

Just as he finished reading, Mae pulled the gag from the Initiate's mouth and Schlefer sof Jauvis let out an ear-piercing wail, tears streaming down his face.

The Initiate's scream brought Matine and Bergum to them.

After some talk about Aethelgard tracking Ruinlock from the scene, the Knight Investigator looked from flash-blinded Actaeon to dead Jauvis and shook his head. "We're in no shape to do that. No. We return to Redemption and regroup. From there we can better prepare. Besides, our mission was to find Lady Bazardjan. We owe it to our fallen brother to bring her home."

The journey back to the Pyramid was uneventful. Aethelgard led the way while Mae guided Actaeon by the hand and the other three Arbiters carried their dead colleague on a litter.

Through his Thoughtlink Artifact, Actaeon shared the news with Eisandre about Aedgar. She immediately sent a missive to the Prince General of Shield and started her plans to travel to Rust to find out more about what really happened. With regret that he would not be able to accompany her, Actaeon explained about his own injury. His wife reassured him, but the anxiety she radiated at the fact that he wouldn't be there was palpable even through the artifact.

Once everyone was safely back at the Pyramid, Aethelgard wasted no time in visiting the site of Mae's abduction. There, he scoured every square inch of the area, in search of something he missed.

In that manner, he located an area of trampled grass off to the side of the Avenue of Glass, along with heavy bootprints that couldn't be traced to any immediate area nearby. Some fresh dirt was disturbed there and when he dug it away he found a plain brown box.

Inside was the same bloody hexagonal lock which he'd discarded from Jauvis' body and a new note. There was but a single sentence upon the page.

I told you that I knew you.

Aethelgard paled and made for the workshop.

When he burst in, Actaeon was at work at a workbench, talking Lauryn through the repairs to his halberd. They both looked up in surprise.

"Act, you must find a way to prevent him from shutting off the power to our artifacts," said the Knight Investigator.

"Not to worry, Aeth," said Actaeon with a grin. "Next time we shall be prepared."

The Shackled Heart

"I FAIL TO UNDERSTAND HOW YOU derive enjoyment from this." Actaeon pulled in his line, once again empty as the fifth one of the day escaped him.

The pair of them – Knight Investigator and Prince Engineer – sat in cramped quarters in a tiny rowboat off the shore of Blacksands Beach. Since Actaeon's eyes had been injured on their last case where they encountered Aethelgard's nemesis Ruinlock, the Arbiter had visited him in the workshop daily to check on him. When he'd found Actaeon fiddling in frustration repeatedly with parts he could only faintly make out, Aethelgard had insisted that he join him to go fishing.

Ever since, the pair had been out fishing often, taking the walk out to the fine sands of Blacksands Beach to launch a small rowboat that Aethelgard had hidden away in the brush there. The Arbiter had a knack for fishing, and for finding fish, that Actaeon lacked completely.

"I must be the worst fisherman who ever trawled these shores," said Actaeon, wincing as he pricked himself on one of the treble hooks that hung from the carved, wooden lure.

Beside him, the Arbiter smiled thinly and skillfully landed another fish at the back of the boat. "You're doing fine for a novice. It takes practice."

"Practice? It has been over a year since I started fishing with you." Actaeon nudged the newly arrived flopping fish that was the size of his forearm. "You have enough to feed the entire Outskirts. How much longer must we remain out here?"

Aethelgard laughed. "Until you catch one, of course."

With a frown at his friend, Actaeon cast his line out again toward the place the Arbiter told him the fish would be. Once again, it fell short. "So what is it?" He gestured to the water in the vague direction of his lure. "Why do you like this?"

"It's the hunt," said Aethelgard with a big grin. "It's not like the rush of a big game hunt on land, or the thrill of an arrow sent aloft to take down a bird. No, it is the understanding, the discernment of the motivations and stimulations of the most alien creatures we know – those that reside beneath the waves. It requires the utmost sharpening of one's skill to decode the behavior of these fish. They live in a universe quite outside of our understanding.

"To catch them we must understand what they feed on and when and where and why. Thus, we find them this morning hiding behind coral structures so they might burst up and surprise the smaller fish that are coming into shore. Why are the smaller fish coming in at this moment? Because the wind and the tide pounds the shore and churns up bloodworms and beetles that find their home in the dirt and sand there, just beneath the water. And let's not forget what they fear. The shadows of bigger fish – of apex predators that ply the seas. If we wish to catch them, we must position ourselves such that we don't induce them to flee. And we must emulate with our lures the behavior of the very prey they seek." The next cast of Aethelgard's lure landed perfectly in the spot he'd indicated to Actaeon earlier in their expedition. "It keeps one's mind sharp to deduce so much from so little available information. For me, it is an incredibly satisfactory mental exercise."

Actaeon tugged at his slackened line and wound a bit around his reel. "Incredibly dull, if you ask me."

Just then, Aethelgard's fishing rod jerked and he yanked it back to set the hook. The Investigator fought with it for some minutes, wrestling the line in and sometimes letting it out. Ultimately, he landed a fish twice as large as the largest he'd yet caught.

Actaeon grinned. "Damned show off."

Aethelgard arched a brow and shrugged. "Catch one and we go back in."

Something on shore caught Actaeon's attention. It was a blond woman in a bright yellow dress – that much he could see. She waved a handkerchief in the air over her head, trying to get their attention. With a grin, he motioned to the shore. "We had better head in to see what she wants."

"You haven't caught anything," grumbled Aethelgard.

"No, but she has caught my attention," said Actaeon with a genuine smile.

The woman continued to wave her handkerchief even as they dragged the fish-laden boat up onto the beach.

"We see you, madam," said Aethelgard, before glancing at his friend. The Knight Investigator paused to flex and unflex his leg, wincing at the effect the prolonged sit in the boat had on his bad knee.

"Are you the Knight Investigator?" she called out.

"Yes, I am," answered Aethelgard.

The woman came down the beach and threw herself at the two men's feet, clasping her hands together where she wrung the handkerchief. "Please, please. You must help me. They told me you might be here. I need your help. A dreadful crime has been committed."

Aethelgard reached out to touch the woman's shoulder. "Calm down, madam. Tell me your name and what happened."

She blinked and wiped the tears that were streaming down her cheeks away with the handkerchief before looking up with pleading eyes. "I am Faihlei Schossvark. I live in the Outskirts. My husband was taken from me."

"By what means was he taken, Madam Schossvark?" asked Aethelgard. "Was he killed, or kidnapped?"

"Gods no!" gasped Faihlei. "Nothing so benign. It was that slut, Emithy – she stole him from me."

Aethelgard and Actaeon turned to one another in disbelief.

When Aethelgard slowly spun back to face the woman, his mouth hung open. Once he managed to compose himself, he spoke. "Infidelity is not a crime recognized by the Order of Arbiters. You will need to take up your issues with your husband."

"Uh uh," said Faihlei, shaking her head adamantly. "No way. It's not by his choice! That harlot has him under some sort of spell. I need your help to find out why."

"I have quite heard enough." Aethelgard grabbed the rope tied to the bow of the boat and began to haul it farther up the beach.

"Hold on, Aeth," said Actaeon. "Let us hear her out. What makes you so certain that your husband has not simply decided to have an extramarital affair? That is a common occurrence, after all."

"My Jolepy would never do such a thing. He is the most devoted, the most faithful, the most loving husband in all Redemption. No way would he ever choose to cheat on me." Faihlei shuddered at the thought. "We are to start a family. He already has the names chosen. I'm the only woman for him. He's made that clear in every action and every word he's ever said."

"Oh?" said Aethelgard, losing his patience. "And that's why he's in the bed of another woman? Quit wasting our time." Rope over his shoulder, he continued to drag the boat up the beach.

Faihlei Schossvark fell to her knees and began to weep openly.

Unable to simply leave the woman there in such a state, Actaeon knelt before her and placed a hand on her shoulder. "Tell me what happened. As I said, people are often unfaithful and mislead one another. Why is your situation different?"

A sob racked the woman's chest. "I know my Jolepy. He's been nothing but dedicated and loving, even though I've failed to bear him a child. Emithy pursued him even before we'd met, and she continued to pursue him even after he declared his love for me. The harlot was just obsessed with him. If he'd been interested in her, he could've had her before he'd even met me, but he didn't – he wasn't interested, you see?"

"And what if the difficulties you both had in bearing a child caused him to reconsider? Might that be a possibility?" Actaeon frowned as the woman shuddered beneath his supporting hand.

"Never! My Jolepy proclaimed his eternal love for me at the deepest depths of our sorrow." She let out a sob. "Every morning he gathered me a bouquet of wildflowers and told me he loved me before going off to work for the day. Every night we made wild and passionate love. That is, until one evening when he didn't return home. After a desperate search, I found him in Emithy's little shack at the edge of the Outskirts. He ignored my every plea and Emithy told me he was hers now. That's when I knew it. He'd been bewitched by that whore of a woman!"

"Bewitched and not simply besotted?" asked Aethelgard, his voice dripping with skepticism as he returned from hiding the boat away. "Many a man has left his woman for another throughout history. Many a woman for that matter. What makes your case unique?"

Faihlei stood quickly, and glared at Aethelgard like he'd just struck her. "He's the love of my life, and I his. I'd have noticed some period of transition. I'm not some moron. One day, he gazed at me with eyes filled with affection. Then the next that look was gone. He didn't have it for the harlot either. No love in his eyes. No, he looked like some sort of shambling corpse – his eyes were dead, like... like..."

"A drug addict?" suggested Aethelgard, he glanced at Actaeon and raised a brow.

"Yes!" Faihlei nodded emphatically. "I've seen the like at the edges of the Warrens. Strung out and with their eyes empty, like the living dead."

Actaeon nodded and scratched the back of his right hand through his fingerless glove. "It *does* sound like something unusual happened here. It may merit investigation."

"Unprecedented, for the Arbiters to investigate a matter of marital infidelity," grumbled Aethelgard.

"Even if there are mind altering factors involved?" Actaeon retorted. "We should, at minimum, rule out that factor. If we find that her Jolepy truly has turned his back on her, then the investigation is over."

"Very well," said Aethelgard. "But I don't like it."

"Oh, thank you sirs!" Faihlei threw her arms around Aethelgard, eliciting a scowl from the Arbiter like none Actaeon had seen before.

The first person they brought into the Rainbow Room was Jolepy Schossvark himself. The conical chamber was nearly white with the lack of emotion even after the man had arrived. A handsome, middle-aged man with the worn, rugged clothing and coveralls of a carpenter, he cooperated fully as the Arbiters led him to the single chair in the center of the room and guided him to sit down.

"What is it?" asked Jolepy. "I should be workin'." The room remained mostly white, but variegated between light red and a light forest green. The look in the man's eyes was distant and vague at best.

Aethelgard glanced at Actaeon and the Prince Engineer raised a brow. The room briefly flashed orange. The Knight Investigator shook his head and commenced his interrogation with the usual set of baseline questions intended to establish the emotional color state of the individual.

Jolepy answered the questions with patient disinterest interspersed with complaints that he should be working.

"What are you working on today, that your need to be there supersedes an investigation of a crime?" Aethelgard cocked his head. "Somewhere in the open markets, no doubt."

The room turned a mild shade of orange. "How could ya know that?" asked Jolepy, looking around suspiciously.

With a gesture to the man's feet, Aethelgard offered a thin smile. "The dark red clay on your right shoe and pantleg is a giveaway. As far as I'm aware, the only place it exists in the city is in one of the same cliff walls that houses the openings to the Warrens. Now what, may I ask, is more than a story tall there? Not much that I'm aware of. Something new then?"

Jolepy shook his head in incredulity. "How could ya figure somethin' like that? This some sorta trick?" As the room turned a shade of dull green, he leaned forward and peered at the Knight. "You been watchin' me?"

"Oh, nothing of the sort," said Aethelgard, leaning heavily on his cane. "Care to answer my question?"

The man's eyes narrowed. "You tell first. How'd ya know that?"

Aethelgard sighed and rolled his eyes at Actaeon before he began to point in quick succession as he rattled off the reasoning. "It's quite obvious to anyone who regularly employs their senses. Those fresh scuff marks on the inside of your soles are from repeated, recent slides down a wooden ladder. There is even a fresh splinter or two there, which would have fallen away if the action weren't so recent."

The carpenter reached down to brush some of the splinters away from his shoes and winced as one lodged itself behind the side of a fingernail.

"Then you have the crease in your coverall over your breastbone. You must have gotten it by leaning for a good portion of the day against the rung of a ladder. Working off of it, I'd say. The crease is quite set into the material since you haven't laundered it recently. I suppose you need to return today to finish up the western side of the building?"

"Now how could ya possibly know that?" sputtered Jolepy. The room flickered a sky blue color that quickly faded back to white.

"I will second that question," said Actaeon, working to keep his feeling of curiosity in check to minimize the Rainbow Room's reaction to him.

"A rudimentary observation." Aethelgard pushed his lenses up the bridge of his nose. "The clay I spoke of earlier flows from the cliff face on the northern side of the marketplace. When the rains fall, it makes the clay run along the low point at the base of the cliff before disappearing into the ruins or the openings to the Warrens. The right leg of your ladder was, at times in the remnant of the clay runoff, and you splashed down into it when sliding down the ladder – which is clear from the dried red splatter on that leg of your trousers." He smiled thinly. "I do hope you aren't building that structure right up against the cliff face. My engineer friend here will tell you that any structure built there is bound to have flooding issues."

Jolepy's eyes widened and when he glanced at Actaeon, the Prince Engineer nodded. He stammered a bit, trying to spit out a reply, but at the end he was at a loss of words.

"Are you ready to answer my questions now, or do you have more inquiries into my investigative process?" asked Aethelgard, guiding him back on track.

Jolepy shook his head as if he were snapping out of a trance. "That artifact dealer... Myridia's her name. She hired me to work on her shop – upgrade it from a little shack to the finest storefront in the open markets."

Aethelgard glanced at Actaeon and lit some guaraja root to smoke it in his pipe before asking the next question. "And how does your wife, Faihlei, feel about your working there?"

At the mention of the carpenter's wife, the room briefly shifted to a bright shade of green. It dulled to a white a short moment later.

"I wouldn't know," came his answer.

"How about Emithy?" asked the Knight Investigator next. He leaned forward and rudely blew guaraja smoke into the man's face.

Jolepy recoiled at the smoke and waved it away. The room flared a bright yellowish-green and remained there. "Emithy..." he said dreamily, his eyes drifting off in a happy haze at the thought.

"She's just outside," said Aethelgard.

Jolepy's entire face lit up. "She is? May I see her?"

Aethelgard shrugged. "Can you bring her in, Act?"

Actaeon nodded and left to get her. When he brought the woman in, the room shifted to a purplish color. She rushed Aethelgard and immediately began battering him with her open hands.

"Let us go!" she shrieked in his face. "You can't keep him here. Let us go, you monster!"

Aethelgard ignored Emithy's multitude of strikes and, instead, kept his eyes on the carpenter. The moment recognition dawned on the man's face, the entire room returned to the yellowish-green color from earlier.

"Thank you for your cooperation, both of you." Aethelgard snatched the woman's hand out of the air before she could smack the lenses from his face. "Now, kindly make your exit before I have you arrested for assaulting an Arbiter."

The woman looked at him in disbelief before rushing to the carpenter. She grabbed his hand and ran from the room, the smitten man in tow.

"Did you observe the manner in which Jolepy's emotions cleared so quickly? All except his lust for Emithy – my, that woman was a banshee!" Aethelgard brushed off the shoulders of his tunic.

"I most certainly did," said Actaeon. "And I suspect an artifact is behind it."

"We are in utter agreement on that fact," said Aethelgard. "I've no doubt in my mind. And, more importantly, I have solved the crime."

"You have?" Actaeon arched a brow.

"Indeed, I have." Aethelgard offered him one of his thin smiles and gestured up at the cone before taking another puff from his pipe. "A marvelous room, is it not?"

"I suppose then, that you do not plan on telling me the details yet?" Actaeon shook his head in fond annoyance.

The Knight Investigator snapped his fingers and pointed to Actaeon with his pipe. "Patience, my good engineer. I have but to confirm my conclusion with a single trip. I will visit you in your workshop tomorrow morning with the complete story."

"You do not require my further aid then?" Actaeon leaned heavily against the shaft of his halberd.

"Not now that I fully understand the artifact's mechanism. I promise that I'll bring one to you on the morrow to study. Perhaps you'll find a less nefarious use for it." The Knight took a deep drag on the guaraja root. "I'd best not delay though. I must act quickly before someone else falls under the spell that poor Jolepy did."

The next morning yielded no sign of Aethelgard, nor did the following morning.

On the third day, the Knight Investigator's absence was suspicious. And so, Actaeon took the short trip to Pyramid to see his friend. In the halls of the Arbiter Pyramid Command, Aethelgard's office lacked its occupant. That, in itself, was not unusual, but the fact that all of the luminaries were covered in shrouds was quite strange. It was as though he wanted to leave the impression that the office was closed.

Actaeon frowned and poked around to make sure his friend wasn't napping off in some corner – strange as though that might be. The search turned up nothing. There was no sign of his Knight Investigator friend. In an effort to emulate him, Actaeon stood before the desk and searched for those tiny details that Aethelgard was always going on about – the details that would ascribe the reasoning, the motivations, and the current whereabouts of his friend. In the end, only one thing stood out. The large hand lens magnifier that the Knight Investigator always used had been left inside his desk drawer – it was the one inset with luminaries that Actaeon had engineered for him. The Prince Engineer picked it up with a frown and dropped it into the inside pocket of his jacket.

Just outside, Knight Arbiters paced to and fro, returning or departing for patrols or guard duty. Nobody appeared particularly concerned with the absence of their expert detective.

One of the Arbiters that passed by backpedaled and peeked in with a confused expression. It was Sentinel Arbiter Corvin sof Haringar, an old friend. "Your Grace? What brings you here?"

Actaeon rapped his knuckled on the desk and cocked his head to the side. "Cannot a man visit his friend?"

"Then you haven't heard?" Corvin let out a long sigh. "Aethelgard resigned his post."

"He what?!" Actaeon nearly tripped over the corner of the desk as he rounded it to approach the Sentinel Arbiter. He couldn't believe his ears. "He resigned, you say?"

The Sentinel ran a hand through his short hair, lingering on small bare patch caused by a scar there. "He did. The Paladin Arbiter refused him, but he just removed his cloak and armband and walked out. He said, 'Since you refuse to hear me, I am forced to take action.'"

"Was he... angry? Or otherwise emotional?" Actaeon's mind raced as he wondered at whether something that happened in the investigation could've upset him enough to cause him to quit the Order.

With a shrug, Corvin said, "If anything, he was as calm and logical as always. Seemed he'd already made up his mind though. And there was no way that any of his brothers or sisters could change it."

Actaeon shook his head, looking at the floor. "It makes no sense. Do you know where I might find him?"

"I don't." Corvin shook his head. He reached out to touch Actaeon's arm. "Look, Your Grace... I hate to say it, but I've seen a lot of Arbiters throw in the towel these last few years. The Siege of Pyramid was a terrible thing to live through. And most of our leadership perished that cycle. There were a number of new recruits too – inspired by what we managed to do here. But we lost a lot of good brothers and sisters in the arcs of the moon that followed. The Knight Investigator has seen a lot of things in the course of his duties. More than most of us. And while looking in painstaking detail at the most horrid of horrors. I... wouldn't be surprised if it just became too much for him. If I'm being honest, my mind has strayed there too at times, particularly after the loss of Sentinel Kylor and Paladin Cignith, but my vows have always kept me on track."

"That is not it," said Actaeon, certain of it.

The Sentinel arched a brow. "No?"

"As Aeth would say, something is afoot. And if he were here, he would undoubtedly know the answer as to what." Actaeon grinned. "I am not so certain, but my intuition tells me that there is something more to the matter."

Corvin smiled. "Well then... if there's anything the Arbiters can provide, you have but to say the word."

"I shall keep that in mind, Sentinel, but the Arbiters would attract too much attention for what I have in mind." Actaeon reached out to grasp the man's shoulder.

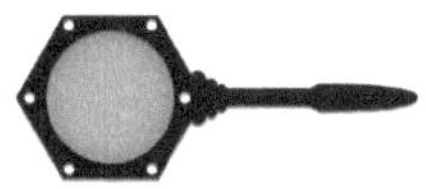

At the entrance to the Pyramid, he stopped to speak with one of the Arbiters stationed there. "Good afternoon, Knight Arbiter Elmerth. Do you happen to know where Aethelgard went when he left Pyramid?"

Elmerth's face lit up in surprise when he realized who it was. "Oh! Ah, Your Grace! Good afternoon to you too. Yes, I was... I mean, I wasn't on duty, but... well, the brothers and sisters have been talking. Knight Arbiter Matine told us he didn't even say goodbye. Just turned and headed to the east along the Avenue of Glass. We guarding here haven't seen him since."

"Thank you, good Knight," said Actaeon with a grin. He started on his way.

"Um, you're going to find him, right?" asked Elmerth, taking a few steps after. "Can I help you?"

Actaeon turned to look the young man in the eye. "If I need help, I will be sure to ask. I must do this alone for now."

"Very well. Good luck, Your Grace!" Elmerth called out after him as he strode away.

At the Open Markets, Actaeon purchased a cloak with a hood. He removed the goggles from his head and tucked them into a pocket of his jacket. A visit with Grameera the blacksmith gave him a place to store his recurve bow after removing the scope.

"Here. Ya'd best eat these sausages." Grameera put a plate beside him, heaped high with meat. "And drink up yer ale. Can't be havin' ya run outta energy. Best leave that halberd here too – anyone'll pick ya out of a crowd with that big pointy thing."

Actaeon nibbled on one of the sausages and grinned at her. "Did you forget I am not Trench?" He laid the halberd across his lap and regarded the blade. "Perhaps I can cover the blade with something? Do you have an extra sack? It might make it look more like a staff or a shepherd's hook."

"A shepherd with a sack on their hook?" Grameera slapped him in the arm. "Ya'd best stick ta what yer good at an' let that Arbiter feller yer friends with do the sneakin' 'bout." She pulled out a small coal sack that had been emptied and shoved it over the tip of the halberd. "There. Now ya look like a right weirdo."

Actaeon pulled the hood up over his head and smiled at her. He finished the sausage and took a final sip of his ale. "You are the best, Grameera. I must be off now."

"Better not leave all that sausage!" Grameera was back at the forge, hammering away at a workpiece. "Take it with you."

"After I return for my bow, I will be sure to take the rest," he assured her. He left a handful of copper bits on the table next to the plate despite her loud protests about it.

With his new disguise in effect, Actaeon headed deeper into the Open Markets. In one of the busiest locations, he found an open air cafe, ordered something, and sat down, nursing a tea and nibbling some cheese.

The work was boring. Just sitting, and waiting, and watching, and waiting. His mind kept wandering to various projects back at the workshop. During those periods, he noticed that too many people would pass by without him realizing, and so, he made an effort to force those thoughts from his mind. He needed to find Aethelgard. Whatever had caused the Arbiter's sudden change of attitude had to have an explanation. It must be tied together with the Schossvark mystery. That's why he needed to be patient and vigilant.

The sun settled behind the pinnacle of Pyramid before the Knight Investigator showed up. It cast the marketplace into shadow and made everything more difficult to see.

Actaeon would've missed him but for Aethelgard's signature cane and limp. A large bundle was over one shoulder as he puttered along through the now dwindling crowds.

Leaving a few bits on the table, Actaeon waited until he passed by and then stood to pursue him.

The way led toward the Warrens, and sure enough, there was a new building that had been freshly constructed in a dead end path between the stalls that terminated at the face of the big cliff. One of the big tunnel openings was right nearby. An Arbiter was stationed there.

Actaeon took an adjacent path that branched off toward a small chicken farm. He paused near a wire fence post and took out his scope. From here, he could make out the structure clearly.

When he lifted the scope to his eye, he caught a glimpse of Aethelgard pushing the door open to head inside.

A woman with a gray bonnet that framed her curls of blond hair was there to greet him. She wore a verdant green dress that she hiked up to reveal sturdy black boots that laced up to her knees. The next action nearly made Actaeon drop the scope. He watched as she pulled Aethelgard to herself for what he could only describe at his distance as a passionate kiss.

Once they disengaged, they smiled at one another and she gave him a gentle pat on the behind before he carried the bundle inside. The woman then proceeded to stride around the building, inspecting the structure in detail before walking around back.

"Watcha lookin' at, Mister?"

Actaeon opened his other eye to find a little freckled girl just on the other side of the chicken wire. He smiled at her and closed the eye again to keep better watch. "Just that shop over yonder. Do you know what the woman sells there?"

"Well, you're in the wrong lane. It's the next one over," said the girl, trying to be helpful. "Papa says she sells love potions. Gets people to fall in love with you. He went over there yesserday and Mama ain't been talkin' to him since. I went over today and that witch chased me off. It ain't fair. How else am I gonna get Tressy to kiss me?"

While she spoke, Actaeon watched Jolepy, carrying a ladder and a satchel of tools, come around the far side with the woman, whom he guessed must be Myridia. She spoke with the carpenter at length, gesturing to the new building, and he nodded emphatically before she handed him a small bag of coin.

"Does a young lady like yourself not have better things to do than trying to get people to kiss you?" asked Actaeon, narrowing his eye against the scope.

As Jolepy headed off with his ladder, he passed an Arbiter, enroute to relieve the one at the tunnel, more than likely.

"Better ta do? In this hole fulla chickens?" The little girl stomped a foot to emphasize her point. "Plus, you ain't seen Tressy. Sooo handsome. He's the butcher's boy. When we're big, I'm gonna have 'im take me to a Niwian ball so we can dance!"

Myridia went back inside and closed the door behind her. It was starting to make sense now – Aethelgard was undoubtedly undercover trying to unearth some new clue.

Actaeon lowered his scope and stowed it back in his pocket. Before him, the little girl stood looking at him with a big, toothy grin.

"Well, thank you for the conversation," Actaeon said to her. "One day, if you work hard at it, your dream might come true. What is your name. I am Actaeon."

The girl's eyes went wide and she dashed away. At first Actaeon thought that she recognized his name, but then he realized she was looking at something behind him.

He spun on his heel in time to catch a boot in the center of his chest. Crashing through the wire, he landed in the dirt of the chicken run behind him to a cacophony of clucking protests.

Over him stood Aethelgard, and his friend did not look happy. "Stay out of my business, Actaeon!"

Actaeon gasped as he caught his breath. "By the Fallen, man! What are you doing? You resigned?"

"It's my turn now to live a life free of endless death and investigation," said Aethelgard. "I found love – a new life. Be happy for me and leave me alone. Did you really think I wouldn't recognize a halberd because you stuck a coal sack on top?"

"One day you are off on an investigation of our case and a few days later you are in love with the very woman you went off to investigate?" Actaeon threw back the hood of his cloak and sat up in the dirt. "Nonsense! You must have had the same effect used against you that was used against the Schossvarks. Come back with me to the work-"

Aethelgard balled his fists up in Actaeon's cloak, lifted him up from the ground and punched him in the face.

Actaeon staggered backward and cast off his cloak. It landed atop a cadre of clucking chickens, much to their consternation. Voices began to shout now at the two men fighting.

"I told you to leave me be," said Aethelgard.

"I will not leave here without you," said Actaeon.

Aethelgard frowned and drew his crackling writheblade.

Actaeon's eyes widened. "What the…"

He was interrupted as his friend swung the artifact blade at him wildly. He dodged out of the way and a section of fence was cleaved in two.

Reaching up to rip the coal sack free, he brought his halberd to bear before him. "Stay back, Aeth. What, are you crazy?"

Aethelgard continued to slice the writheblade to and fro, pursuing Actaeon into the chicken run. Actaeon backed up and managed to scramble backward and just out of the way of the deadly weapon. More of the fence fell, and chickens were cauterized in the melee. Feathers floated between them and poultry cried out in terror at the deaths of their kin.

Actaeon scrambled back farther and felt his back hit the solid wall of a chicken coop. The next slash was coming straight at him and he lifted the halberd's shaft to block it. The writheblade cleaved it in two and the next slash came right at his head. He ducked to one side as the artifact tore through the chicken coop, leaving behind a flaming gash in the wood.

"Shit, Aeth. Stop it!" he cried out.

Before Aethelgard could make another move, the two Arbiters interposed themselves between them, swords out.

"Weapons down, both of you," said the elder of the Knights. "I don't care *who* you are."

Aethelgard pointed at Actaeon with a scowl. "This man is harassing me. I asked him to leave and he refused. I will gladly pay for the damage to my neighbor's coop, but please, by the Fallen, make him leave me be." Reluctantly, he returned the writheblade back to its ceramic scabbard.

The Arbiters turned to Actaeon who still held both separated halves of his halberd. "You heard the man, Your Grace. He wants to be left alone."

"Very well," said Actaeon, placing both halves into one hand. "But you know this is wrong."

That said, he started off back toward Grameera's shop.

He really could use the rest of that sausage now.

And the tankard of ale.

"You want me to do what?" asked Voice Ithelie. The Raedellean religious leader had been out visiting the Caliburns at Actaeon's workshop when he'd arrived looking like he'd just rolled around in a chicken coop.

"To go undercover," Actaeon said.

In the years since the war, Ithelie's light blond hair had turned completely white, adding to her appearance as a religious figurehead – though Actaeon didn't think she needed any help with that after everything he had seen her do. She had carried herself as bravely as any soldier during the Second Invasion War, and her moral support had arguably ultimately guided his troops to victory in the face of hopelessness.

Though he didn't practice religion himself, he found the Voice's wisdom to be insightful and far beyond her years. Her company was always welcome in the workshop, where they would talk for hours about spirituality and philosophy over cups of tea while she watched Actaeon fiddle with his various inventions.

Ithelie actually laughed at that. "Very funny, Your Grace. Don't you think that I stand out a bit too much for that?"

"True." Actaeon nodded. He poured them both cups of tea with water from the kettle. "An excellent point," he said between sips. "Which is why you could go as yourself. Neither of them know who you are."

"Didn't you say it was a shop that sells love potions?" Ithelie took a sip of her tea.

"Love artifacts, I suspect," he clarified. "And correct – you can tell them you are a victim of unrequited love."

Ithelie spit out her tea and began to cough. Once she managed to contain herself, she offered her friend an incredulous look. "You do realize I've taken vows? I'm committed to my order – it is not in my nature to long for a deeper human connection."

"They need not know that," countered Actaeon.

Ithelie wagged her finger in the air. "Also not in my nature to lie."

Actaeon spread his hands and grinned. "I never said anything about lying. Just to stretch the truth a bit. You yourself have said that you love all of your flock. Well, one of your flock is in trouble now. There are people being manipulated against their free will and I need your assistance in helping them."

The argument gave the Voice pause and she ruminated over her cup of tea, as though trying to divine the answer from the leaves. After a time, she shook her head from side to side. "What you say *does* make sense. You know I cannot turn a blind eye to those in need. But unrequited love... How can I make sense of that?"

Actaeon shrugged. "Not all your followers share your faith, correct? Certainly, there are those who spurn your blessings at every turn."

Ithelie's mouth spread into a little smile and she lifted the cup to take a sip. "I do believe I know just the one."

And that was how the Voice of Raedelle came to brazenly stride into Myridia's shop garbed in the green robes of her order.

A gentleman working outside up on a ladder slid down to get the door for her, tipping his head politely.

A bell rang as Ithelie made her way inside the small shop. She was surprised to find it filled with a broad variety of flowers. She leaned forward to smell one of her favorites: the sun-laced bonhomie. It always reminded her of the pleasant smell of one of her father's woodworking oils. She smiled upon inhaling the welcome scent.

"Welcome!" The woman with the gray bonnet full of blond curls that Actaeon had described appeared in the doorway behind the freshly hewn counter. She was wearing a cerulean blue dress today, instead of the verdant green. "The name is Myridia. How may I be of service?" The shopkeeper had kind eyes. Ithelie had trouble believing that she'd harm people in the way Act had explained to her.

"I was told that you might help me," said Ithelie.

The woman placed her palms on the counter and cocked her head to the side to regard the Voice. After a moment, she arched a brow. "Well now. It isn't everyday a Voice comes calling for *my* help."

Aethelgard chose that moment to enter the room. He took a seat in the corner and folded his hands in his lap, holding the cane between his knees.

Myridia followed Ithelie's glance and smiled. "Don't mind him. That's my associate, Aethelgard. Aethelgard, this is..." She paused. "Why, you didn't mention your name, did you?"

"Ithelie," she said. "Ithelie Faris."

Aethelgard inclined his head toward her in greeting.

"And what, exactly, did you come seeking help with?" Myridia leaned forward and steepled her fingers.

Ithelie blinked. "I'd heard that you were the expert in matters of... love."

"Allow me to guess, you need help with a pair in your flock?" Myridia flashed her a well-crafted smile.

"Be careful," said Aethelgard. "This one hides something."

"Everyone hides something, my dear," said Myridia, shooting the former Arbiter a look and a wink.

Ithelie glanced nervously at Aethelgard and shook her head. "Not exactly. I have... my own needs." She looked down at her toes abashedly.

"Oooo," murmured Myridia, bringing her lips together in a tight circle.

"And if I helped you, you'd be willing to abandon your spiritual role for Raedelle?"

Ithelie's striking brown eyes shot up to meet Myridia's violet ones. "That is my business and no concern of yours. I'm here to see what you can do for me."

The sternness of the Voice's tone caused Myridia to take a step back from the counter. She held up a hand. "Okay, okay. Your point is taken. What I can do for you depends on the nature of your request. Are you willing to share your story? At least the pertinent details?" She came around the counter and gestured to a little table off to the side with a pair of chairs beside it. A look sent Aethelgard into the back rooms.

Ithelie offered her a shy nod and took a seat at the table.

Myridia sat across from her and waited silently for the Voice to begin.

The Voice pushed the cowl of her hood back, revealing her shock of white hair that fell to her shoulders over her ears. She opened her mouth like she was about to speak, but then closed it again as Aethelgard arrived bearing two cups of tea. He set the cups down, offered her a thin smile, and left the room.

After clearing her throat and taking a sip of the tea, Ithelie spoke. "One of my flock, as you call it." When Myridia nodded, causing her curls to bounce, she continued. "I love her, but the feeling isn't reciprocal. It... bothers me. I... no longer wish to deal with it. I want her to love me back too, in the same way I love her."

Myridia tilted her head as she cradled the teacup against her lips and sipped. She smiled and put the cup down. "Desire has its way of pulling us to and fro like that."

"If you say so," said Ithelie, gazing down into her tea as though it might save her from the embarrassment of the situation.

"I do," insisted Myridia with a sly smile. She reached out with both hands to take Ithelie's in her own. "And you've come to the right place. I have the solution you yearn for. Your love will be returned... for a price, of course. But before we talk payment, may I ask how you heard about my services?"

"The poultry farmer across the way made mention of it to another customer when I was making a purchase. Your new shop here drew their attention. It was Ancestor's guidance that led me to be there at such a fortuitous time." Ithelie smiled and hoped that Myridia would buy the story.

The woman's lips curled into smile and she nodded. "Ah, yes." She proudly gestured to the new shop floor about them which still smelled like the fresh sawdust of new wood frame construction. "As you can see, my successes have brought me the greater wealth I needed to expand my operation."

The Voice placed a hefty sack of copper bits that Actaeon had given her on the table between them. "This should be enough to cover your services, I'd expect. When the job is done, I can provide more."

Myridia snatched up the coin purse and hefted it in her hand before opening it to withdraw a few bits to inspect them. "You've no questions about my methods?" She arched a brow.

Ithelie sipped the tea and shrugged. "So long as they are effective."

"Very well." The coin purse was secreted away into the folds of Myridia's dress. "Tell me of this woman whose love you yearn for."

The Voice blushed. "Jezail Vren is her name. The Captain of the Wall Breakers warband. I've shown her much love over the years and... it has not been returned. I wish..."

As she trailed off, Myridia spoke up. "Jezail the bard? She plays in The End from time to time, no?"

Ithelie gave a small nod.

"Perhaps she isn't interested in women?" Myridia spread her hands. "Not that it matters. My methods will work their magic regardless."

The Voice shrugged. "Whatever it be, I do love her."

"And you wish that she loved you back in return." Myridia completed the thought for her. "I can make that happen for you. It is my expertise."

Myridia mused, clicking her tongue against the roof of her mouth. "The redheaded bard, eh? I can make that happen. Where can I send for you when I'm ready?"

Three days later, Ithelie was summoned to Myridia's shop in the early evening hours. A small gathering was present, including Aethelgard and an eclectic collection of merchants and shopkeepers from the area.

Instead of the normal robe of her order, Ithelie wore a simple cotton jerkin and skirts. Her white hair hung loose to fall about her shoulders, framing her face.

In the corner closest to the entrance sat Jezail, playing a simple tune on her fiddle. When Ithelie walked in, she looked up with surprise that was enhanced by the scarred and stretched skin around her right eye. She offered the Voice a smile of recognition without missing a note of her song.

At the center of the shop floor, Myridia took Aethelgard's hand and kissed him on the lips. She wore a yellow dress and her usual bonnet. He took the opportunity to put his arms around her and kiss her more deeply before she patted his arm and then guided him to her side. She turned to those gathered and Jezail paused her playing. "Thank you all for coming to the grand opening celebration of Myridia's Matchmakers. It is a place where love blossoms and grows into something beautiful."

She took Aethelgard's hand in hers and he smiled down at her, smitten. "Even I have found my special someone here. Isn't that right, Aethelgard, my dear?"

"So right, my dearest." Aethelgard put his arm around her waist and pulled her close to him. "After a life alone, I've found my soulmate."

"And now we will help others find theirs." Myridia turned to a couple behind her. "Isn't that right, Jolepy? Emithy?"

The carpenter pulled a frail woman with haggard features against him and beamed. "I'd a' never realized what I'd been missin' all my life without yer help, Mrida..."

"Myridia," she corrected him.

Jolepy nodded and continued. "Emithy been afer me all my years and I never saw her there 'til you worked yer magic."

Ithelie hazarded a glance at Jezail and the warbander rolled her eyes and offered a little shrug.

"That's because at Myridia's Matchmakers, there is love and magic in the air," said the shopkeeper with a sweep of her fingers above her head. "Tell your friends and colleagues. Spread the word. Myridia will help you realize true love." She snapped her fingers then and when Jezail didn't notice, she snapped them again twice.

Jezail offered Myridia a glare and a lopsided smile before shaking her head and commencing a new song that reminded Ithelie of stories of fairies playing in the jungle she'd heard as a child.

"Everyone help yourselves," said Myridia, gesturing to the counter full of assorted snacks and drinks.

As the small crowd was distracted with the food, she sidled up alongside Ithelie and whispered in her ear. "Just wait here and don't take your eyes off of her."

Myridia sauntered over to Jezail and smiled. She slid her hand along the musician's shoulder to her back, drawing a sidelong glare from her. She smirked and leaned down to whisper something into the bard's ear, her hand continuing across Jezail's back to her other shoulder beneath her tunic.

Jezail looked up and her eyes locked with Ithelie's.

As the Voice watched, the redhead bard's eyes dilated and her jaw dropped open in wonder, as though she were seeing Ithelie for the first time. The music ended abruptly as Jezail lowered her fiddle and stood. She strode with purpose up to the Voice and wrapped her arms around her, gazing intensely into her eyes before she leaned forward to kiss her hard on the lips.

Ithelie felt the bard's tongue against her lips and turned to the side. She smirked and caught a glimpse of Myridia's eyes narrowing upon her. "Sorry, Jezail, but I am already committed to my service to the Ancestors."

The hurt in Jezail's eyes was palpable, and Ithelie felt bad for her. She hadn't considered how this might affect the bard and that was not fair. Reaching up, she brushed Jezail's cheek with her fingers.

Jezail leaned into her hand and regarded her with pleading eyes. "Is there no way?"

The Voice leaned forward to kiss her other cheek and slid her hand down and along Jezail's shoulder beneath her tunic until she found it.

The instant Ithelie pulled the disc from her shoulder, Jezail's expression changed, shifting to confusion, then anger, then embarrassment. "I'm so sorry, Ithelie." She shook her head and squeezed her eyes shut before opening them to regard her once more. "I don't know what came over me."

Now, Your Grace. I have it! thought Ithelie over the Thoughtlink Artifact hidden beneath her hair where Actaeon had clipped it to her ear. She knew that both the Prince Engineer and Princess of Raedelle could hear her thoughts through it. "I do," she replied to Jezail.

Before she could say another word, Myridia grabbed her elbow roughly and yanked her aside. "Just what do you think you are doing?" The shopkeeper ripped open one of the pockets on her jerkin, looking for the artifact. "Are you mad? Where is it?"

Just before Myridia could rip off another of Ithelie's pockets, Jezail slapped her hand out of the way and punched her right in the nose. A crack resounded through the room and Myridia fell back and landed right on her behind, bright red blood pouring out onto her yellow dress from where she held her hand over her nose.

Those gathered let out a collective gasp and Aethelgard rushed forward to kneel at Myridia's side, taking her in his arms.

"Forget about me," gurgled Myridia. She pointed at Ithelie. "She has one of my artifacts. Get it back."

Aethelgard stood and Jezail stepped between him and the Voice, narrowing her eyes and daring him to try.

Just then, the door splintered into a dozen pieces and Arbiters charged in, weapons drawn. They were led by Sentinel Arbiter Corvin and Actaeon.

The Prince Engineer pointed his halberd at Myridia, who still sat on the floor trying to stanch the flow of blood onto her bright yellow dress. "Arrest her!"

Before the Arbiters could reach her, Aethelgard interposed himself and drew his writheblade. The pair of Arbiters took a half step back and looked to one another with worry, but readied themselves to battle the former Knight Investigator with his powerful artifact weapon.

Instead of fighting them, he held up a hand. "Hold." Aethelgard's shrewd cobalt gaze returned and he turned his attention to Myridia on the floor behind him. "What have you done to me, enchantress?"

"Why, I've done nothing but love you," said Myridia, drawing to her feet and lowering her hand from her broken nose. The blood, running freely now, ran down across her lip and chin.

"Check your shoulder," advised Ithelie.

Aethelgard slid his off hand under his tunic to dig around on both shoulders until he found it, a skin-colored disc that shimmered with iridescence.

"My Aethel, please..." Tears fell down Myridia's face as she pleaded with him.

The Knight Investigator narrowed his eyes upon her and carefully ground the disc against the edge of his artifact blade until it burst into smoke and flame and he dropped it to the floor. The rest of it he crushed with the heel of his boot.

"You're one damned good actress," he said to her, voice dripping with vitriol. "Too bad you won't be able to put it to use where you're going to end up." He turned to the Arbiters and nodded. "Arrest her."

There was a commotion just then back near the counter, and the carpenter, Jolepy, ripped his arm away from Emithy and walked up to Aethelgard. "What's happened? Why am I here?" He looked like someone who had just woken out of a very long dream.

Actaeon stepped forward and pulled open Jolepy's shirt at the shoulder to reveal another of the shimmering discs. He pulled it free and slid it carefully into a small metal container that he then placed back inside his jacket. "I am afraid you have been duped. Your wife, the Lady Schossvark is waiting for you at home. She never doubted you."

Jolepy glanced back at Emithy and scowled. "Ya horrid, little thing." Then he was off and running past the splintered door on his way home.

Emithy sobbed and fell to her knees.

"Take that one into custody as well," said Aethelgard. Corvin nodded and had his Arbiters shackle her.

"Everyone is to be searched before leaving this place," Aethelgard instructed. "We must ensure no others have been manipulated by these things.

"Oh, and..." Aethelgard paused and turned to the Sentinel Arbiter, arching a brow. "I shall need my position back."

Corvin smiled. "You never lost it, Knight Investigator." He slapped him on the shoulder. "Glad to have you back."

"Aye," said Aethelgard with a thin smile. He returned his writheblade to its ceramic scabbard and gestured for Actaeon to follow before leading the way past the counter and into the back room.

Actaeon, Corvin, Ithelie, and Jezail followed.

The Knight Investigator paused before a blank spot on the wall. He touched it gently on one side. It clicked and a hidden door swung out from the wall to reveal a small closet within. Inside lay a chest. He drew his writheblade again and neatly sliced the padlock off.

When he kicked it open, discs scattered onto the floor. The chest was piled with hundreds of the thin artifact discs.

"Ancestors..." breathed Ithelie. "Was she to steal the hearts of so many?"

"And shackle them to those who would never be deserving of their love without it," said Aethelgard, his voice dripping with disgust.

"Unbelievable," said Aethelgard as he burst into the workshop. "She escaped!"

"Who escaped?" asked Actaeon from where he stood by the forge. "Myridia?"

The Knight Investigator leaned heavily on the nearest workbench and sighed. "Myridia... That witch... She used a smoke bomb somehow and disappeared as they marched her and Emithy back to the Pyramid for sentencing. She's out there now, Act. Out there and able to manipulate and possess more people."

Actaeon grinned and kicked the chest at his feet. "Not if I have anything to say about it. Do not despair. I am confident that the Arbiters will catch her. What became of Emithy then?"

"Sentenced to three years of labor in the Garden Terrace." Aethelgard smiled thinly.

"Toiling under Shard," said Actaeon, considering. "It seems fitting."

"Agreed," said Aethelgard. "And all thanks to you, Investigator."

"Investigator?" Actaeon's eyes widened in surprise.

Aethelgard shrugged and lit his pipe. "I couldn't have done it without you. Would have been trapped there for the gods know how long, in fact. Yes, I daresay we have something special here, my engineer friend."

"Partners in investigation, then?" Actaeon grinned.

"Best partner I've ever had," Aethelgard agreed, extending his hand.

Actaeon accepted it and they shook. "It calls for a drink, I would say."

He poured them both a tankard of ale from the tapped barrel in the corner of the workshop and brought them back to the workbench.

Aethelgard lifted his. "Whenever I'm in dire need, there's none other I'd rather have at my side to solve the damnedest difficult puzzles."

Actaeon tapped his tankard against his friend's and they both sipped. "I am glad to be a part of your problem-solving team."

"An essential part," said Aethelgard, and when Actaeon didn't reply, he changed the subject. "What will you do with those?" He pointed to the chest full of heart shackling discs.

Swallowing another gulp of ale, Actaeon put up a finger before setting his tankard down and returning to the forge. There he pumped the bellows several dozen times until the fires of the forge were roaring hot. Smiling at the Knight, he hefted the chest and poured the contents into the fire. "Nothing good can come from the manipulation of people's minds."

Aethelgard watched as the waterfall of shimmering discs fell into the flames to be consumed. After the job was done, he gave a thin smile. "I'm surprised you didn't keep some to study."

Actaeon grinned. "Who says I did not?"

Emergence Day

94 A.R., THE 55TH DAY OF ARRIVAL

"SHE IS A ROGUE, A cheat, a manipulator, a harpy. The sort of person I've spent my entire life thwarting in the name of justice. So, why then, can I not rid her from my mind?"

Aethelgard had no sooner arrived in Actaeon's workshop than he began to rant about the woman from their last case.

Offering his friend a grin, Actaeon shrugged. "Perhaps Myridia has stolen something from you?"

"Stolen something?" Aethelgard arched a brow. "What?" he practically snapped.

"Your heart," said Actaeon with a chuckle.

"My... you..." Aethelgard sputtered and shook his head. "No! Absurd. I'm free of her ensorcellment – you saw to that."

Actaeon spread his hands. "I am simply suggesting that there are other, less nefarious means." He shrugged again. "She *was* a clever one."

The Knight Investigator narrowed his eyes. "Are you suggesting that she has some sort of hold on me beyond that of the artifact?"

"You tell me," said Actaeon with the wave of a hand and a smirk. "After all, you are the one who barely removed your cloak before you began speaking of her."

Aethelgard returned Actaeon's amused look with a challenging glare.

The Prince Engineer met the glare with a look of amusement, his grin growing as they locked eyes.

Finally, both of them burst out laughing.

"Quite the silly thought," said Aethelgard as their laughter wound down.

"Aye," agreed Actaeon. "As if you would ever settle down and help a con artist manage her manipulation of innocents for profit. I mean, aside from that time you settled down to help a con artist manage her manipulation of innocents for profit."

They laughed again at that.

"I have a feeling we haven't seen the last of her," said Aethelgard.

"And next time, we shall make sure she does not escape," added Actaeon.

"Just so," said the Knight. "Enough of that, then. Tell me why you summoned me here."

The missive that made Actaeon request Aethelgard's presence in the workshop carried with it a request of the utmost urgency.

'The Prince General of Shield requests the presence of Prince Engineer Actaeon Rellios Caliburn and Knight Investigator Aethelgard sof Leaf at the Iridescent Palace. A grave crime has been committed that threatens the very stability of the Interdominional Alliance. Your investigative skills are required.'

At the bottom of the scroll was a stamped shield with a diamond upon it – the sigil of Shield.

Aethelgard leaned forward to scrutinize the document for a time. When he finally straightened, he lit his pipe and sent a puff of smoke drifting toward the roof of the workshop.

"Trying to solve the crime already?" Amused at his friend's thoughtfulness, Actaeon got them both tankards of ale from the tapped barrel in the corner near the cellar entrance.

When he set them down on the workbench, the Knight Investigator toyed with his as though considering it like another piece of evidence before lifting it to his lips for a sip. He wiped a stray drop from his narrow beard before pushing the lens frame back up along the bridge of his nose.

"Quite unusual for anyone to summon the assistance of the Arbiters so far from the Pyramid."

"Not the first time though," said Actaeon, taking a sip from his tankard.

"Not the first time," Aethelgard agreed. "But the first time Shield has. They don't like any outsiders snooping into their business."

"And why summon me as well?" mused Actaeon. "Do you suppose an artifact is involved?"

"Or they know that we're associates and they trust you more than they trust me," suggested Aethelgard.

Actaeon grinned. "Only one way to find out."

The journey to Rust was cut in half by the underground passage between Pyramid and the Arbiter fortress of Redoubt. Actaeon had never seen it before. It was off limits to anyone outside the Order of Arbiters. Now he was working with a Knight Investigator though, and Aethelgard brushed aside any questioning from the Arbiters guarding the broken corridor in the sub-levels of the Pyramid.

The passage itself was hexagonal. It reminded Actaeon of the corridors that had been in Travail, the Loresworn's old – now destroyed – headquarters.

That wasn't the impressive part though.

No, the impressive part was the floating sled that approached them when Aethelgard placed his hand against the wall. It slid to a stop before them by some unseen mechanism.

Actaeon knelt down in fascination to peer beneath it. He shined his luminary underneath and found nothing at all there. A sweep of his halberd confirmed his visual observations.

"Fascinating," he said. "It floats like Kryo's dronespheres." The Loresworn leader often showed up via a projection from a sphere that floated in a similar manner. At a time when death had seemed all but certain, the Loresworn had told him that the dronesphere floated using particles excited enough to emit something called electromagnetic radiation, forcing it upward like the jerk of a crossbow. "May I return to study this further?"

Aethelgard shook his head and tapped a surface on the artifact that caused an elderglass bubble on the top to slide open. "I'm afraid not. Feel free to glean whatever you may as we ride though. Go ahead... step within and have a seat."

Once both of them were seated in the artifact craft, Aethelgard touched another panel and the bubble slide shut around them.

A sudden jerk of acceleration caused Actaeon's stomach to lurch and they were zipping along the hexagonal passage at tremendous speeds. The glow of inset luminaries zipped by quickly, making Actaeon wish he had estimated the distance between them before they had departed. Instead, he tried to count how many passed in a hundred lifebeats. It was fast, but he thought it was about five hundred for every hundred lifebeats.

At one point another artifact craft appeared in the corridor ahead. Instinctively, Actaeon threw himself to the side, but the other floating pod leapt over theirs in a neat little arc to continue along behind them. Aethelgard didn't seem bothered by it at all, and he glanced over at Actaeon with a thin smile of amusement.

It wasn't very long before they slowed to a stop. Aethelgard pressed the panel and the elderglass dome slid open to let them out.

As Aethelgard led the way onward, Actaeon counted his steps to measure the distance between two of the inset luminaries. A quick calculation in his head made him gasp.

"What is it, Engineer?" asked Aethelgard with a smirk.

"That artifact craft can move a hundred times faster than a person walks," explained Actaeon. "It's incredible. Imagine the possibilities if such technology could be harnessed for all travel."

"That's precisely why we use it," said Aethelgard with a chuckle. He led the way up into Redoubt.

Once outside of the elderstone fortress, the going was difficult. Actaeon led the way, picking the best route through the unstable ruin pile that bounded the northern edge of the Underforest. Behind him, Aethelgard struggled to keep up, pausing periodically to massage his right knee.

"If you allowed me to study those artifact craft, there exists a possibility that you would never again need to make this journey on foot," said Actaeon over his shoulder.

"You're lucky I was even allowed to bring you through that route," said Aethelgard with a grimace. "Keep asking questions and I guarantee next time we'll be denied."

"Your loss," said Actaeon with a grin. When his friend caught up, he handed him a vial of his custom-made pain medication. Anticipating this difficulty, he'd made a few for the Knight Investigator before their departure. Aethelgard accepted it gratefully and quaffed it immediately.

"Your Grace! Your Grace!" a distant voice shouted.

Behind them was a squad of soldiers garbed in brightly striped red and gold pantaloons that puffed out from beneath gold-plated cuirasses. The lead soldier held aloft a banner with the golden starfield of Ajman.

Actaeon grinned. "The Raja's Portent."

Indeed, beside the bannerman, a tiny man wearing similar pantaloons that threatened to swallow him leapt and waved his arms at them.

When the Ajman delegation caught up, Gaemri Ip Monjata traced a flourishing bow to Actaeon and eyed Aethelgard skeptically before straightening to adjust his lavish, oiled pompadour. "Your Grace, it is indeed a surprise and a pleasure to meet you all the way out here."

"Indeed, it is," said Actaeon. "What brings you this way?"

"We were summoned by the Prince General," said Gaemri, interlacing his fingers to crack the knuckles of one hand.

"Might I ask as to the nature of the summons?" Aethelgard's eyes narrowed upon the smaller man.

Gaemri unlaced his fingers and spread his hands. "Official business, on behalf of the Raja."

A powerful woman in leather armor and a tight queue of dark hair emerged from behind the soldiers and approached them. Looking completely out of place among them – Calisse' garb conveyed a practiced lethality that the soldiers' uniforms lacked.

"I apologize for the Portent's minced words, Your Grace," said Calisse, casting a stern look at the small Portent. "The Prince General has an important trade proposal for us which we are journeying out to hear."

Actaeon smiled at the sight of the warrioress and extended his hand. "Glad to see you, Calisse." He glanced at Aethelgard, but the Knight Investigator shook his head. "I appreciate your straightforward candor with us. We have also been summoned by Indros. However, I believe the Prince General expects us to maintain confidentiality as to our reason for visiting. I can assure you though, it has nothing to do with any trade proposal."

The Raja's Warrioress clasped her forearm to his and offered him a slight smile. "Oh no? Hmm." She made a show of looking around. "Where's your Companion?"

Actaeon smiled knowingly. "Yanelle is with my wife. Just the pair of us for this particular journey."

Calisse nodded in disappointment and turned to Gaemri. The little man was busy slathering lotion on his hands and forearms under his sleeve. When the Portent didn't take the hint, she inclined her head and kicked his shin.

"Ouch!" Gaemri offered her a blank look before realization finally dawned on his features. "Oh! Right. Care to join us for the remainder of the journey, Your Grace? Power in numbers and all that. Nothing less for a friend of the Raja and, indeed, of Ajman itself. Please do accept."

"Thank you, Portent Gaemri," said Actaeon with a grin. "I graciously accept your company for the rest of our travels."

The remainder of the journey couldn't pass by quickly enough for Aethelgard. The Raja's Portent had taken to the Knight Investigator and worked incessantly to talk both of his ears off. When the shimmering spires of the Iridescent Palace – the seat of power in Shield – finally came into sight, he let out a sigh of relief.

"Are you quite alright, Knight Investigator?" asked Gaemri. "I heard your gasp for air. I'm also similarly at odds with such extended travels. People such as us aren't inclined to such exertions, though we do as we must for those we serve, of course."

"It is the exertions of my ears that I am most concerned about," muttered Aethelgard under his breath.

"What is that now?" Gaemri asked. "Oh yes, these exertions are concerning. Too much walking is never good for one's heart, you know. It's alright though. We are nearly there."

"Thank the Fallen," said Aethelgard, rolling his eyes.

"The gods of old and the gods of new are kind to us, yes," agreed Gaemri.

As they approached the palace entrance, a young, slender Shieldian soldier stepped forward. His eyes widened when he saw Actaeon. "Welcome. Are you, by chance, the Prince Engineer?"

Actaeon nodded. "Indeed, I am."

The color left the soldier's face. "You knew my sister before she died."

"Did I?" Actaeon arched a brow and regarded the young man with his sharp emerald eyes. "What was her name?"

"Shar Minovo... she was the –"

"Adjutant to the Prince General," said Actaeon. "Yes, I know. Your sister was a brave and formidable woman. What is your name?"

"Thank you, sir... er... Your Grace," said the young soldier. "I am Mak. Mak Minovo."

Actaeon put a hand on Mak's shoulder briefly. "If you are anything like your sister, Mak, then you have a bright future ahead of you."

Minovo dipped his head in respect. "My thanks, Your Grace." When he raised his head again, he glanced at the other soldiers near the gate before returning his gaze to Actaeon. "May I ask your business?"

"My business?" It was Actaeon's turned to glance at Aethelgard. The Knight shook his head and shrugged. "We were summoned here by the Prince General. On a matter of confidence and urgency. Our Ajmani friends were also summoned for a trade proposal as I understand it."

Gaemri nodded. "Yes, that's right. We are quite eager to speak with the Prince General on the matter."

Mak Minovo nodded to the other guards, and they opened the gates to allow them in.

Servants guided Aethelgard and Actaeon to a suite on the first floor of the palatial structure.

"Something is afoot here," said Aethelgard as he paced the room and struck some flint on the blade of his dagger to light the guaraja root in his pipe.

"It really does seem odd." Actaeon reclined in a cushioned chair, laying his halberd across his knees. "If I had to guess, I would say they had no idea what we were talking about."

"They didn't," said Aethelgard. "Which means one of two things that I can surmise: either Indros Zar cannot trust even his own people, or –"

"He did not write that letter to us," said Actaeon, completing the thought.

There came a rap at the door, interrupting their thoughts. It swung open and Mak Minovo stood there. "Excuse me, Your Grace, but His Most Venerable Grace would like to extend his invitation to you both for dinner this evening. He asks that you be there at sundown."

Aethelgard nodded. "We will be there."

Minovo bowed his head. "Thank you. If you need anything, I have an attendant posted just outside." The soldier spun on his heel and was gone, the door closing behind him.

A moment later, the room plunged into darkness as the luminaries all shut off during the Darkest Hour. When their eyes adjusted, only the dim glow of Aethelgard's pipe lit the room. It floated to and fro as the Knight Investigator continued to pace.

"Something is wrong here," said Aethelgard in the darkness. "I can't put my finger on it just yet, but something is not right."

Dinner took place in a majestic, vaulted chamber decorated with many crystal chandeliers fitted with luminaries that cast dazzling rainbows throughout the room.

Aethelgard nudged Actaeon where they stood before a pair of chairs at the long metal table ornamented with gold and chrome-plated elements that framed colored elderglass insets. "I thought we were summoned to investigate a crime, not attend a banquet of nobility," he whispered.

"It really does appear to be the latter," said Actaeon, scanning the others present with his piercing emerald eyes.

On the opposite side of the table sat the short, bald Loresworn leader, Kryo, wearing a shimmering brightweave outfit. Beside him was a young Loresworn woman Actaeon didn't recognize. The woman had pale skin and short black hair that was shaved into distinct rows that ran to the back of her head. She wore a constant smirk as she looked around and, when she met Actaeon's eyes, she actually chuckled aloud before continuing to sweep the room with her gaze.

Next to them were the two Thyrians: Supreme Captain Amodeus Jarval was wearing his finest white dress uniform. He tugged at his red mustache as he waited for the Shieldians to arrive. Captain Harvand Xula stood beside him, beads of sweat on the dark skin of his bare scalp. His quadcorne hat sat on the table before him.

Earlier, Captain Xula had spotted Actaeon in the hallway where their rooms were and the muscular sailor had grinned and embraced him fondly. Now, he looked about suspiciously at the others in the room.

The Raja's Portent and Warrioress, Gaemri and Calisse were beside

Aethelgard. To Actaeon's side was the Althean Matron Seraeta with her severe nose and bun of gray hair. Her white robe was ratty and stained in places with faded blood, a fact that seemed not to bother her at all. Beside her, and seated closest to the head of the large table, was Fallis, the Althean Attaché to Shield. She was an intense-looking woman with graying wisps of hair and narrow eyes.

The next person who walked into the room brought a smile to both Actaeon and Aethelgard.

Captain Jurlan ris Minovec wore the red plate of the Niwian Reds and carried her helmet tucked under her arm. A brown plume of hair stood straight up from her head, held by a silver and red clasp. She paused to regard the room and her face lit up when she saw the pair of investigators. "Uh oh," she said with a smirk that twisted the scar that ran down her left cheek and through her lips. "If you two are here, that can't mean anything good."

"We could say much the same of you," said Aethelgard, with a thin smile.

Behind Minovec arrived a figure that wiped the smiles from Actaeon and Aethelgard's faces. Keeper Knight Nathis Carrillum fit right in at the opulent Iridescent Palace with her ornamented armor of silver and gold inlaid with colored facets that shone in the luminary light. The Knight bumped Captain Minovec's shoulder with her own as she moved past, offered them a scowl, and found a place at the table.

The last of the non-Shieldians to arrive was Dek, a former Czeryn warrior with a mad look in his eyes who now served House Voitek in the Raedelle Dominion. The man saluted Actaeon, fist to chest. "Your Grace," he said, before finding a spot at the far end of the table.

Mak Minovo entered next and clapped his hands twice. "All rise for the children and grandchild of the Prince General of Shield."

Since everyone was already standing, nobody moved.

On the upper tiers to either side of the chamber, two columns of three soldiers each marched into position and snapped to sharp attention before pivoting on their heels to face the hall.

From the door behind the head of the table, arrived the Zars.

Enrion Zar, the Prince General's son, arrived first, carrying his little daughter Indovo in his left arm – his right was missing from above the elbow. The little girl clung to her father's neck and looked out over those gathered with fascination. With him was his wife Kiroko with her wise eyes – a star of metallic sticks protruding from the rear of her head held a neat bun in place. Enrion offered a smile and a slight nod to Actaeon before standing to one side of the head of the table.

Next came the Steel Rose, Endira Zar, the Prince General's daughter. The short, black and silver-lined dress she wore was a strange mixture of seduction and lethality. It was tightly fitted about her chest and hips to show off her body. An array of armor plates that left more than one critical location exposed were fastened to the dress in various spots about her torso and arms. Throwing daggers were attached to more of the plates than not, and a pair of sword hilts was visible over her left shoulder. She wore open toed sandals that laced with thick leather thongs all the way up the bare skin of her legs to disappear under the hem of her dress.

Actaeon couldn't help but grin, but he bit back any comments on the comical impracticality of the outfit as Endira turned sideways and actually struck a pose at the opposite side of the head of the table, eyes glittering.

Trailing behind her was the youngest of the Prince General's children. Vindra Zar was a stark contrast with her sister. Her hair was cut short, trimmed just above her ears and she would've passed as a man if not for some of the slight, feminine features of her face. Unlike her sister, the garb she wore was practical – full scale mail armor that gleamed with golden inlays. She surveyed the room with a commanding gaze, her hand resting easily on the hilt of her sword.

"Attention!" barked Vindra, and all of the soldiers snapped to an even sharper attention. "His Most Venerable Grace, Indros Zar, the Prince General of Shield!"

The Prince General almost looked as though he were gliding into the room with his legs hidden beneath a red and black robe that brushed the floor as he walked. With jet black eyes, he peered at those present from beneath the tall mitre that perched atop his head. In his withered hand, he clutched an iron shod staff that terminated in an arc with the sun on one side and the moon on the other.

Before his own chair at the head of the table, Indros Zar paused and stroked his long beard thoughtfully. The Shieldian leader took the time to examine each attendee closely as they all waited for him to sit before taking their own seats.

Only, he didn't sit. Instead, the Prince General cleared his throat and began to talk. "I am truly glad for this outstanding show of company on my emergence day. But it does lead me to wonder who arranged this, because I certainly didn't invite you here."

Everyone present began to look at one another in confusion before their eyes finally settled back upon Indros.

Aethelgard grunted and raised a finger. "If –"

But Indros rapped his staff on the table, bidding everyone to be silent.

"It begs the question: Why, in cracked Redemption, are you all here?"

"You sent us an invitation," protested Captain Xula.

Indros slammed his crozier against the table, shattering one of the elderglass inlays.

Xula jumped and shut his mouth.

"I'm not finished speaking," said Indros. "Because another question remains. Why shouldn't I have you all killed? Your very presence reeks of treachery."

The Prince General snapped his fingers, and the soldiers all unslung their loaded crossbows and aimed them at the guests.

Enrion ushered his family backward toward the walls while his sisters moved to flank their father.

"Now, now," said Gaemri. "Let's not do anything rash."

Indros' lips slowly curled into a smile. "It is the wise man who strikes first. I admit, I will miss some of you dearly."

At that moment, the luminaries went out and plunged the chamber into darkness. A cacophony of cries and shouts followed. Crossbows twanged and there was a horrible, blood-curdling yell that ended in a gurgling choke.

Actaeon felt a warm droplet strike his cheek – blood.

"Protect my father!" shouted Enrion.

"Candles! By the Fallen, light the candles, you idiots!" shrieked Endira.

Before most people in the room could even react, the luminaries snapped back on, filling the room with light and rainbows.

One of the rainbows reflected off of the blade of a straight, single-edged sword that protruded from Indros' sternum. Rivulets of blood streamed out from the Prince General's chest along the blade, to drip down and splatter on the already blood-drenched tabletop.

Indros opened his mouth to speak and blood poured out. Realization dawned on his face and his staff fell and clattered against the table and then the floor below. In a last move of desperation, he reached out a pleading hand toward Aethelgard and Actaeon, before falling backward, the tall mitre toppling from his head.

Endira caught him, and cried out in a wounded rage.

"Nobody leaves!" shouted Enrion, his voice cracking. "Nobody leaves!"

At his order, the doors all slammed shut and were barred.

On the upper tier, one of the guards lay dead – his throat opened by a bolt.

The Loresworn woman across from Actaeon staggered forward against the table. Blood streamed down her arm where a crossbow bolt was lodged in her bicep.

Actaeon left his halberd and leapt across the table to help the Loresworn woman. He pulled a bandage roll from his leather jacket and unrolled it to spin it into a tight band. That done, he grasped the woman's forearm to tie the bandage tightly around her arm. With his hooked dagger, he poked two holes in the material and slid one of the charcoal sticks he used for writing through them. With the stick in position, he spun it until the bleeding from her arm stopped and tucked the point of the charcoal stick under an edge of the bandage.

Matron Seraeta of the Altheans was at his side by then. "Well done," she complimented, before leading the woman to the side of the room to sit her down against the wall.

"Nobody is to leave until we figure out who murdered my father!" shouted Enrion, his daughter in his arms still, now crying. He passed Indovo to his wife and ushered her out of the room. Vindra drew her sword and escorted her sister-in-law out. Once his family was safe, Enrion turned back to face the room. "Which of you did this?"

"Who did this?" shrieked Endira. "Who? I'll kill you!"

"Enough of this," said the Keeper Knight. "It's your own sword in him, girl. Stop trying to trick us."

"She's right," said Calisse. "Did you kill him to take his throne? Let us out of here. The deed is already done. I'm sure you'll get your wish."

"I..." Endira reached up over her shoulder and found only one of the two hilts that was supposed to be there. The color left her face. "I didn't... No... I didn't. Someone took my sword out. Someone killed father with my own sword! Who did it?" There was rage in her tone still, but now it was weak with doubt.

"He pointed at these two right before he died. I saw it – he reached out right toward them. Why else would he do that?" said Fallis, The Shieldian Attaché, pointing at Aethelgard and Actaeon. "They killed him."

The Knight Investigator rolled his eyes. "Of course, because Arbiters always ensure they're far away from the Pyramid before we murder someone."

"I'd be hard-pressed to believe anything other than the Lady Zar killed her father given it's her blade in his back," said Supreme Captain Jarval.

"It *is* a tough bit of evidence to dispute," said Captain Minovec, who had backed away from the table, her own sword in her hand as she eyed everyone around her mistrustfully.

Enrion stepped forward and raised his remaining arm into the air. "We are in Shield. Under our jurisdiction. I ask that the Knight Investigator and Prince Engineer help figure this out. You've both solved a number of crimes, haven't you? Until then, everyone stays in place."

Aethelgard spread his hands. "There's nothing to figure out. It's crystal clear who committed this act."

"That's right," said Nathis. "The one whose sword is in the Prince General's back."

"Incorrect." Aethelgard shook his head and pushed his lens frame back up along his nose. "The Lady Zar did not kill her father."

Everyone looked at the Knight Investigator in shock and confusion.

"Thank you," said Endira in exasperation.

"Then who did?" asked Enrion.

"Will you allow us, myself and my esteemed engineer colleague, full control over this investigation so that we can confirm my suspicions?" Aethelgard leaned forward on his cane and cocked his head at Enrion.

Enrion looked to his sister and she nodded. "Yes," he said. "Do it."

"Very well," said Aethelgard. "Firstly, I will need the chance to examine the Prince General. Secondly, guards from outside this chamber will escort everyone present, including the guards in the room, to quarters. There, they will all remain under guard until I have a chance to question everyone. Thirdly, I must ask that everyone place their weapons down on the floor. I will not be fighting any battles today over this."

Enrion nodded and motioned to Mak, who opened the door behind the head of the table and shouted some commands.

Endira gently lowered her father down upon the table, so that he was face down.

An object slid along the blade sticking out of Indros and struck the Prince General's body in the back with a soft thud.

"By the Fallen," said Aethelgard, leaning forward to peer at it.

Actaeon moved closer to get a better look as well.

It was a broken artifact lock, its shackle of metal hooked around the blade of the sword between the hilt and the body.

"Well then," said Aethelgard, his face growing pale. "Things just got more interesting."

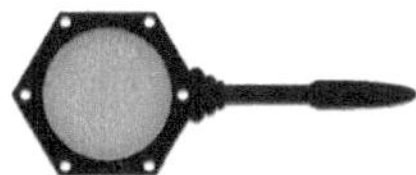

After a number of lengthy arguments about being detained and losing access to their weapons, the guests were all escorted to their rooms and confined there. Enrion finally assuaged their concerns by relinquishing his weapons and convincing his sister to do the same. He also ordered the remaining guards, including Mak Minovo, to take orders directly from Aethelgard until the murder was solved.

"That was no Darkest Hour," said Actaeon.

They were now alone in the chamber with Indros' body with only Mak Minovo and the Niwian Captain, Jurlan ris Minovec, who Aethelgard had asked to stay and assist. At first, Enrion Zar had insisted upon staying, but the bloody scene proved too much for him to handle and he quickly left to check on his wife and daughter.

Aethelgard didn't respond. The Knight Investigator lit some dried guaraja root in his pipe and puffed at it as he considered the scene before him.

Indros Zar lay facedown, but nearly sideways upon the table, his body propped at the odd angle by the blade of his daughter's sword that stuck out from his chest. His jet black eyes stared blankly at the darkening pool of blood on the table beside him – they were already beginning to cloud over.

It was a shame, Actaeon thought, that he'd never be able to converse with the man again. The Prince General had such a philosophical mind. Though rare, their conversations had never failed to be enjoyable.

"Fine. I'll bite," said Captain Minovec. "Why wasn't it a Darkest Hour?"

The question brought Actaeon out of his brief reverie and he turned to her. "Another Darkest Hour happened directly before the dinner. It is extremely unlikely for two Darkest Hours to occur in such close proximity.

There are only a few mentions of it in history, and even those are unreliable accounts at best. I have never experienced such an event in my lifetime. Have you?"

Minovec shook her head, the vertical braid bobbing left and right like that of a jungle bird's plume.

"Right," continued Actaeon. "And the duration was another giveaway. The Darkest Hour is named precisely for its length." He turned to Mak. "Could you send out a few soldiers to check if others in Rust experienced a second, briefer Darkest Hour? I would be willing to bet that this was a local occurrence, especially given what we know about the person who hung the lock on that blade."

Mak nodded. "Excuse me one moment." He stepped out from the hall to give the orders.

Actaeon circled the table and leaned forward to scrutinize the lock.

"So, who's the culprit, Arbiter?" The Niwian Red turned her attention to Aethelgard. "And how'd you figure it out?"

Aethelgard let out a puff of smoke. "Until I have all the details sorted, I won't make any accusations. Only one person in the room could've done it, but there is one detail that eludes me. Until then, best I did not bias your own perceptions on the matter."

Jurlan ris Minovec laughed so hard that her plate armor clattered. "Bias my perceptions? Really? You'd have to be a sorcerer to convince me anything other than Endira Zar killed her father. There was barely time enough to even draw a sword, let alone sneak around the table, kill someone, and get back into place before the lights went on."

Steepling his fingers above the pipe, Aethelgard offered her a thin smile. "One must look at all the elements to ensure they are consistent with a given theory. Once you do that, you'll see that Endira Zar must be ruled out as a possibility."

"I'll believe it when I see it," said Minovec, skepticism in her voice.

"You'll see it soon enough," said Aethelgard. He turned to what Actaeon was doing and pushed his lenses up along his nose. "What details have you found, Act?"

"It is consistent with locks I have encountered beneath the ruins – typically used as a shackle to lock away various glass rope junctions. They can usually be unlocked by tapping a corresponding key artifact against it. This one is broken, of course. Consistent with our friend's modus operandi."

Actaeon pointed to the center of the lock. "The main body is cracked and scorched as though the inside overheated and burned."

"You've had a run in with the person who left that there before?" asked Minovec, blinking rapidly as she took everything in.

"A few times," said Actaeon, giving a questioning look to Aethelgard.

"Oh? Who is it then?" When both men didn't answer, the Captain folded her arms over her chest. "Look – if you want me to help you with this, you'd better come clean about what you know."

Aethelgard sighed and dashed the ashes of his spent pipe to the floor nearby before returning it to his pocket. "An old nemesis of mine," he explained. "One that I've thus far failed to apprehend."

"And that nemesis was one of the people in the room with us?" Jurlan ris Minovec's eyes widened. "Was the person who killed the Prince General?"

"Believe me," said the Knight Investigator. "I'm as baffled by it as you are. But it does appear to be the case." He sighed and pulled the lighted magnifier from his pocket to hand to Actaeon. "Here. Take a closer look at it. You're missing a critical detail."

Actaeon took the magnifier lens and slid aside the baffle before lowering it to the lock. He grinned as he spotted what his friend was referring to. Pulling the red thread free, he lifted it and the magnifier up to his eye. His grin faded as he looked from the string to the red sleeve that protruded beneath the plate on Captain Minovec's arm.

Aethelgard followed his gaze and smiled.

Enrion Zar chose that moment to walk back in with Mak Minovo. He followed their gazes from the string to the Niwian Captain. "What's going on now?"

Minovec blinked and held up her hands. "Oh no, don't you all be looking at me like that. I had nothing to do with this."

"I know that," said Aethelgard. "But everyone else doesn't. Perhaps it's best if you confined yourself to your quarters for the meantime."

Mak Minovo moved to stand behind her.

Jurlan ris Minovec sighed and lowered her hands. "Fine, fine. I'll go. Darkest Hour take you! Figure this out soon though – it's gonna be a snooze to sit in my room the rest of the time."

"Shouldn't be long, Captain," Aethelgard reassured.

Mak escorted the Niwian Red out and The Knight Investigator took the magnifier from Actaeon and lowered himself down to examine the floor behind Indros' chair. "Most curious."

"What is it?" asked Actaeon, moving to stand near his friend, but not close enough to accidentally trod upon any evidence.

"The entry of the sword into Indros' back should have caused a back splatter of droplets that would have ended up on the floor or on the killer. The person who did this must have used something to block it, then pocketing the object of incrimination. Whoever the killer is must have it on them, or in their quarters." He stood and pocketed the magnifier.

"Right. So, what is this other missing element that you are struggling to figure out?" asked Actaeon.

"I know who killed him. There's no doubt in my mind that I'm correct," said Aethelgard. "I can't believe it – that the killer is Ruinlock and that they were right under our nose in this. But I cannot, for the life of me, figure out how they might've drawn Endira's sword as it was, without alerting her to the act."

"Ruinlock?" asked Enrion, the color draining from his face. "They... He..." He turned to Actaeon. "Did your wife tell you what happened here?"

"The execution of Ruinlock's minions?" asked Actaeon. "Aye. She told me about that."

"Then he..." Enrion shook his head, his remaining hand shaking in fear. "Impossible though. How could he? It..." He turned to Aethelgard then. "Don't speak his name again! To speak his name invites death. The traitors said that. They promised this day would come. By the Fallen... Father..." Raising his hand to his face, he sobbed.

"I am sorry for the loss of your father, my friend," said Actaeon. "He was a good man, and I will miss him. We will catch his killer though and bring them to justice, right Aeth?" Arching a brow, he looked to his partner.

"To the best of our ability, we will stop him for good on this very night," said Aethelgard. "There are a few people we must speak with first, however."

Enrion stifled another sob and nodded.

"Tell me something first though," said the Knight Investigator, pulling the missive from his pocket before passing it to the Lord. "Do you recognize the handwriting on this invite?"

After looking at it briefly, Enrion passed it back. "Of course. It's in my father's own hand. I'd recognize it anywhere. Only..." The Lord Zar trailed off.

"Tell me," urged Aethelgard.

"My father wouldn't have sent you such a note by his own hand," said Enrion with a frown. "He'd have dictated to a scribe."

"Hmm," mused Aethelgard. "Then he was able to somehow find the Prince General's handwriting and create a perfect copy. Thereby enabling him to invite all the people we saw and sow confusion while he committed the murder."

"If this really is who we suspect it is –"

"It is," said Aethelgard, interrupting Actaeon.

"Well..." Actaeon continued. "Then that fact lends itself to the strong likelihood that an artifact was used to draw Endira's sword."

"Right," said the Arbiter. "And Endira's exactly who I'd like to speak with next."

"Follow me." Enrion led the way from the room.

Endira had already changed from her blood-spattered outfit into another, less revealing, one. A loose-fitting formal robe of black with floral patterns sewn into it with silver thread now adorned her slender form. Two hilts protruded over one shoulder – she had already replaced the sword that was now lodged in the body of her father.

Anger was in her eyes as she opened the door for her brother, but they softened as she saw who was there. She clasped her hands before her and nodded to them. "Thank you for your confidence in me. I trust you can prove to all those present it was not I who did this?"

"That depends..." said Aethelgard. He reached out to take one of her hands and caressed her palm gently.

The Lady Zar's eyes narrowed and she yanked her hand away. "Depends on what, exactly?"

"Well..." said Aethelgard, trailing off. Then he snatched Actaeon's halberd from his hand and swung it at Endira's head.

In a flash, one of her swords was in hand. A clang resounded as she easily parried the blow.

"What is the meaning of this?" she shouted.

Aethelgard offered her his thin smile and passed the halberd back to Actaeon. "I had to know for certain."

"Know *what* for certain?" Endira rasped.

"You'll see soon enough," said Aethelgard. "For now though, I have no further questions for you."

"See this!" The Lady Zar's fist snapped out and caught Aethelgard in the nose. The Knight Investigator stumbled back and was caught by Actaeon, who held up a hand to prevent her from striking again.

"Trust me," said Actaeon. "He always has a plan. Where there seems to be madness, there is a method."

"Get out of here before I bloody your nose too! Gods as my witness!"

Actaeon yanked Aethelgard back out into the hallway, bumping into Enrion as they rushed to retreat. Enrion's eyes widened as he saw the stream of blood that ran from the Arbiter's nose. He leapt out of the way to avoid getting any on him.

"Are you crazy, man?" asked Enrion, astounded. "Nobody toys with my sister like that."

Aethelgard offered him a thin smile and removed the lenses from his nose to twist their copper wire back into shape. "Some of the most important answers carry with them intrinsic risk." He replaced the lenses on his face.

"Also, he is fairly crazy," said Actaeon, with a laugh.

The Knight Investigator lifted a kerchief to his nose and chuckled as well.

Endira's angry shouts followed them all the way down the long hall.

Once Aethelgard stanched the flow of blood from his nose, their next visit was to the Loresworn.

Kryo frowned upon their arrival. "I trust we'll be released soon?"

"Indeed you will," came Aethelgard's nasally response as he spoke through the cloth pressed to his pinched nostrils. "Thank you for your patience."

Actaeon brushed past Kryo to join Seraeta beside the injured Loresworn woman.

The Althean was busy at stitching the wound from the recently removed bolt. She looked up at the Engineer and Arbiter before offering them a cursory nod and returning to her work. "I suppose you want me to look at your friend's nose. Well, he'll have to get in line. Must get this closed up to release your tourniquet. Else the tissue dies."

"Don't let the tissue die," pleaded the Loresworn woman.

"Manners, please!" said Seraeta as she slid needle into flesh again.

The Loresworn yelped. "*Please* don't let the tissue die?"

"A pleasure to meet you, Lady Loresworn," said Actaeon. "I am Actaeon Rellios Caliburn, of Shore."

"I know who you are, Your Grace," said the woman. "I wasn't born under a rock. Merivek Qi. That's my name. Pleased to meet you as well. And thankful to boot for your quick action with my injury here."

"Not a problem," said Actaeon. "You are in good hands now."

"Thank you," she said. "It is a great honor to be in your presence after all that you've done for Redemption."

"Come now," said Kryo. "The Prince Engineer is but a man. A stubborn one at that."

Actaeon grinned. "More stubborn than you, you old Loresworn fool? Determined as ever to keep the world's secrets to yourself..."

Kryo chuckled. "Better than your foolhardy insistence on sharing the deadliest secrets with the masses."

Actaeon spread his hands. "What better way to protect the masses than the masses themselves?"

Kryo shrugged and shook his head in displeasure. "I don't know. Perhaps by vetting those who will handle such secrets to ensure they will handle them responsibly?" He glanced to Qi and rolled his eyes. She smiled in return.

"Once you have an effective vetting process that can extend beyond my workshop to all in Redemption who handle artifact technology, do let me know," said Actaeon with a grin. "Until then, I shall continue to be skeptical as long as I continue to meet Loresworn who suck themselves through tiny apertures and destroy perfectly good artifact arms due to a lack of caution."

Kryo smirked and sighed. "Comeris was an exception."

"It sounds as though you need better governing rules for your organization – ones that do not produce exceptions." Actaeon arched his brow and cocked his head at the short Loresworn leader.

Kryo frowned and interlaced his fingers. "I trust you have another reason to be here aside from poking fun at a scientific organization that predates you by more than half a century?"

"You could have had me as a part of your organization," Actaeon reminded him.

"I'd never have taken such a brazen risk," countered Kryo with a smile.

"And yet, when all of Redemption was about to be destroyed, you still did call me for help." Actaeon grinned in return.

"Enough of this!" snapped Aethelgard, raising his tone. "A man has been killed. Save your bickering for another time. We are indeed here for a good reason. My esteemed colleague has a theory that what we witnessed wasn't really a Darkest Hour." He looked between Kryo and Qi. "Can you confirm or deny that?"

Qi was the first to answer. "It –" She yelped as Seraeta hit another nerve in the mending. "– was definitely not a Darkest Hour. Something else happened."

Aethelgard turned his shrewd cobalt gaze upon Kryo then, arching a brow.

"The young lady speaks the truth," said the Loresworn master. "It couldn't have been a Darkest Hour. The Prince Engineer was correct. Neither was it long enough, nor was there ample time since the previous one. Naught in all of our knowledge of how the Fount operates would explain such an unprecedented hiccup. Which could only mean..." He trailed off.

"Someone exercised active control over it, and disrupted all artifact power – most likely in our localized region." Actaeon scratched his right hand through his fingerless glove.

"Well," said Kryo. "That isn't entirely true. It didn't interrupt *all* artifact power." He pulled a small, transparent disc with a copper ring around it from one of his brightweave pockets. "This device detects the presence of artifact power. Fortunately, it does not use any power to function. It buzzed in my pocket just after the false Darkest Hour event began. Near what I'd presume to be the moment Indros Zar was murdered."

Kryo smiled in amusement as Actaeon's eyes widened at the artifact. He flipped it in the Prince Engineer's direction like a coin.

Actaeon caught it in one palm and stared at it in fascination, thinking about all the things he could do with such a device. He looked back up at

Kryo and the Loresworn smiled. "Keep it. You may well need it for your investigation."

"Thank you," said Actaeon with genuine appreciation. He tucked the invaluable device into his jacket pocket. "Tell me one thing."

Kryo spread his hands. "If I can."

"Old Sollemnis used a device years ago. It mended a wooden bowl that was smashed. Could such an artifact be used to manipulate matter?" Actaeon leaned heavily on his halberd, looking forward to the explanation.

The small Loresworn smiled. "Your deductive leaps never cease to amaze me. Sol's device was merely a particle state repositor. It just found the likely states of the particles on an atomic level and restored them, thus reassembling the object you described. Matter manipulation, on the other hand, is something we only once achieved within the confines of Travail. It took a marvelous amount of processing power and it was extensively difficult to accomplish. We were never able to achieve the same outcome twice. However, our experiments served to prove that the Ancients must have been capable of such things."

"Your help in this is appreciated," said Actaeon.

"Of course," said Kryo. "We cannot have people wandering about and murdering the leaders of our civilization, can we? Anything else you need, you have but to ask."

Once they were back outside of the Loresworn room, Aethelgard turned to face Actaeon. "What is it, Act? I can see the gears turning in there."

"It strikes me that the burst of power that Kryo detected could have been a sort of matter manipulator that pulled the sword from Endira's sheath and delivered it into the hands of the killer. Perhaps it even bypassed that step and just plunged it straight through the Prince General on its own." Actaeon frowned as he considered the possibility.

"It is sorcery you speak of," said Enrion, who had waited outside in the hallway. "Surely, you must have a better explanation for what killed my father."

"I am relieved that Kryo provided all these explanations," admitted Aethelgard, ignoring Enrion. "It allows me to rule him out as the killer. Aside from the person I am increasingly certain committed the act, he was the only other one who might have fit the profile of the killer due to all of the evidence I observed."

"You've said you know the killer already," whined Enrion. "Will you now tell me who it is?"

Aethelgard raised a hand. "Patience, now. There are other factors I must prove out."

Enrion balled up his hand into a fist. "If you insist! But be quick about it. My patience is wearing thin with you." That said, he stormed off, leaving them alone in the hallway.

"If the killer had a remote matter manipulator that communicated with a distant device that could run the advanced calculations necessary to perform such a task, it could explain your missing element," said Actaeon.

"A fascinating possibility," agreed Aethelgard. "And it wouldn't have to be too complex, because the killer had their hands on the sword. There were fresh hand oils in the wrong locations on the hilt, including the pommel, as if the killer didn't know how to use such a weapon. I was able to differentiate them from Endira Zar's hand oils after I felt her palm – the killer has much greasier palms, and a lotion to boot."

Just then, Mak Minovo arrived. "The runners have returned."

"Let's hear it then," Aethelgard said. He experimented with removing the bloody kerchief from his nose, but a trickle of blood convinced him to replace it for longer.

"They confirm your suspicions," said the Shieldian soldier. "Just outside the palace, nobody experienced any sort of Darkest Hour at the same time that His Most Venerable Grace was slain." There was anger in Mak's tone when he said that, but he continued on. "On a whim, I also sent runners to the top of the palace and down into the subfloors below to check. No Darkest Hour there either."

"A radial area of effect then," said Actaeon. "I suspect it would show that the point of origin was the banquet hall where we prepared to dine with the Prince General."

"Yes," confirmed Mak Minovo. "I thought the same might be true and the soldiers noted the positions of the first people who said they hadn't experienced it. Based on what they returned with, it's like a big sphere."

"Fine work there, Mak," said Actaeon with a grin. He turned to Aethelgard.

Aethelgard tucked some guaraja root into his pipe and lit it, taking a puff that made the Shieldian guard scowl and step back, waving his hands to clear the smoke between them. "I have everything I need now to announce my findings. Please summon everyone to the banquet hall where Indros Zar was murdered. There I will announce the killer to all."

Minovo nodded and started off, looking pleased to exit the cloud of guaraja root smoke that the Knight Investigator was producing.

"Oh, and guard?" Aethelgard pulled the pipe from his lips.

"Aye, sir?" Minovo turned about.

"There's one room which you are to search after everyone is in the hall. I'll tell you just what to look for." The Knight Investigator's lips curled into a thin smile and when he pulled the kerchief from his nose, the bleeding had finally stopped.

"Is something wrong?" whispered Actaeon. "You still look perturbed."

They stood before the head of the table in the grand banquet hall of the Iridescent Palace, flanked by an angry Endira Zar and a revolted Enrion Zar. Actaeon had kept between the Shieldian Lady and the latest object of her ire, which left Enrion to stand nearer to the blood-soaked Knight Investigator. All the others were present, save Indros and the dead guard. Both bodies had been removed, though the dried pool of blood was still present — a reminder to all of the atrocity that had been committed in that very chamber. Atop the bloody surface was Endira's single-edged sword that had been used to end Indros' life.

Aethelgard wobbled his head from side to side and whispered back. "It's just that it was all too easy for..." He frowned at Actaeon and trailed off.

"For Ruinlock..." replied Actaeon as quietly as he could.

The Arbiter didn't answer. Instead, he pulled the bloody artifact lock from his pocket and tossed it onto the table in the center of the dead man's blood which had bloomed and darkened like a flower of death.

"Some of you have undoubtedly heard whispers in the shadows of the man called Ruinlock," he began.

There was a gasp, and several people took a step back from the table, including Enrion Zar, Gaemri Ip Monjata, Merivek Qi, Amodeus Jarval, Nathis Carrillum, and Jurlan ris Minovec.

"I find it curious," spat Aethelgard. "It does appear that many here recognize the name readily. And yet, upon seeing Ruinlock's calling card, all of you failed to mention it when accusations were being cast upon the belated Prince General's daughter." He gestured toward Endira. "Instead, she was forced to endure allegations that she murdered her own dear father. So, why didn't anyone mention it? After all, such a realization might have eased her devastation and allowed her to mourn instead of defend."

Steepling his fingers, Aethelgard looked at Gaemri. "Perhaps you were afraid?"

His cobalt gaze drifted to Jurlan ris Minovec. "Or complicit?"

"Or, maybe, you were glad the Prince General was dead?" His eyes drifted from Supreme Captain Jarval, to Keeper Knight Carrillum, and then to Merivek Qi, the Loresworn.

"Absurd!" shouted Jarval, pounding a fist against the table's surface.

"Whatever the reason," said Aethelgard, spreading his hands, "you were quiet then, and so I'll bid you remain quiet now."

"How dare you?" snapped the Supreme Captain.

"I dare because this is *my* jurisdiction," said Aethelgard. "Investigation is my purview. Once that is done, you may resume your pontification. Perhaps your subjects might lend their ears to such dithering, but, let me assure you, there is no place for it in my investigations. So, kindly keep your mouth shut until I am done."

The Thyrian leader looked like he was about to leap across the table, but for Harvand Xula, who placed his hands on his superior's shoulders and guided him back.

Aethelgard looked up at the crystal chandelier and smiled his thin smile. "As it turns out, Ruinlock is here, in this very room. And I know exactly which of you it is." He lowered his eyes to those present and scanned the room. "That's right. And do not think to eliminate me, for by this point most of the Shieldian guards also know your identity. You will not escape justice this time."

"Enough already!" demanded Enrion. "Tell us who it is. Who murdered my father?"

"Very well," said Aethelgard. "There is only one of you who could have killed Indros Zar. The angle that the sword was thrust into the Prince General was consistent with a specific height and stance that was needed to generate enough force to shatter the man's sternum." Behind him, Mak Minovo entered the room and cleared his throat, but the Arbiter held up his hand to stall him. "The height required was substantially less than Endira, and the sword used was not her preferred sword."

The sudden realization and relief on Endira's face would have been almost comical, if one failed to consider the loss of her father.

Aethelgard continued. "The evidence points to a short person. I might have taken the additional finding of a red thread upon the lock to be a plant, if not for the heavy hand oils that I found on the sword hilt, and the smell of lotion that I'd only witnessed one person here using before the crime was committed."

At a gesture, Mak Minovo stepped forth and unfurled a bloody shirt front. The fabric was crimson red, with gold thread around the fringes. The middle had a dark red stain of dried blood.

"When the Prince General was stabbed from behind, the blood spatter covered your shirt front, did it not, Gaemri Ip Monjata?" Aethelgard's shrewd gaze landed upon the Raja's Portent. "You came prepared for a killing though, didn't you? You had a section that you pulled up in front of your face and down to cover your ridiculous pantaloons. Then you rolled the entire business up and tucked it away so that none of us would suspect it was you. But you forgot that you were right beside me, and, even in the darkness, I felt the rush of air when you disappeared to commit your murderous act."

Calisse gasped from her spot beside Gaemri, and she took a step back from the Portent. "Is what he says true?"

"Ridiculous!" cried Gaemri, his voice cracking. "I am but the Raja's Portent. Me a murderer? As if I could achieve such a thing! Ha! Like I would even have the strength."

Despite Gaemri's protests, Aethelgard circled the table until he stood before the Portent. "My thoughts as well, Gaemri. Or should I call you Ruinlock? Such a thrust would've required much more force than your gnomish form is capable of. That is, if you were to grasp the hilt normally. But you didn't do that, did you? No, you pushed up against the pommel with all your might, thrusting Endira's sword upward with enough force to shatter Indros' sternum."

Gaemri let out a loud guffaw. "Oh, sure. As if that would even be possible for me."

"But not without consequence, Ruinlock," stated the Knight Investigator. "For such force was required that you bruised your palm in the process, didn't you?" Before the Portent could protest, he snatched the man's right hand and unfurled his fist with both hands, revealing an ugly black bruise.

Everyone present gasped at the realization.

Gaemri recoiled, as if struck, and yanked his hand out of Aethelgard's grasp. Then his lips curled into a broad grin. "Always so sure of yourself, Aethel." He reached his other hand into a pocket in his pantaloons to touch something.

Suddenly, the sword that was used to kill Indros lifted from the table and flew into Gaemri's bruised hand.

Aethelgard was ready though. As Gaemri swung the murder weapon at his head, he drew his writheblade from its ceramic scabbard. With the artifact weapon, he blocked the blow. There was a crack, and the sword was sliced neatly into two pieces. The end of it twirled through the air in a lethal dance and sliced into the Knight Investigator's cheekbone under his eye before lopping off the top of his right ear.

The Arbiter cried out as fresh blood spilled down his neck for the second time that day.

Gaemri took the opportunity to duck down and race past Aethelgard before the Knight Investigator could react. He rounded the table toward the door at the back of the room, but Mak Minovo was faster. The Shieldian guard drew his own blade and interposed himself between the killer and the way out.

The Raja's Portent shrieked. "You'll never stop me!" He reached into his pantaloons once more and all the luminaries in the room flickered off as another false Darkest Hour descended upon them all.

And just like that, Ruinlock had escaped.

But Aethelgard wasn't ready to let that happen.

But before he could move, Actaeon reached out to grab the Knight Investigator's writheblade.

"What are you doing?" asked Aethelgard, tugging the artifact weapon away.

"Trust me," said Actaeon, in the darkness. He pulled at the writheblade once more.

It was useless anyway with Ruinlock's Darkest Hour artifact. Aethelgard released it to his friend and yanked the boltcaster free from Actaeon's thigh holster. "Fine. We trade then."

Armed with the Engineer's weapon, Aethelgard ran after Ruinlock, wincing at each heavy step upon his bad leg. He barreled straight into a Shieldian guard. There was a twang and a spark lit the room as a bolt from the guard's crossbow struck the ceiling. In the brief light, he saw Ruinlock disappear at an intersection of corridors, headed to the right.

The impact caused him to stumble backward though, and into Endira Zar's arms. She levered him to his feet and snatched his wrist in her free hand – her sword was in the other. "Let's go," rasped the Steel Rose of Shield. She yanked him after her, past the guard, in pursuit of her father's killer.

"He went right at the next bend," Aethelgard managed.

"I know that," she snapped. Without missing a step, she pulled him around the corner to the right. Both of them could hear the Portent's heavy breathing ahead. "You'll not escape my blade!" Endira shouted.

The Lady Zar knew these halls like the back of her hand, having grown up in the palace. She pulled Aethelgard along at a run, following the heavy breathing and the sound of footfalls. They made several turns until the Knight Investigator was thoroughly lost.

Then the sounds of their quarry disappeared.

Endira stopped so suddenly at the next intersection that she nearly yanked Aethelgard's arm from its socket as he continued past. "He's hiding."

"I know that." It was Aethelgard's turn to snap back at her.

The luminaries flashed back to blinding life then and they both reflexively squeezed shut their eyes.

The Raja's Portent leapt from the shadow of a doorway and stabbed Endira in the back with the remaining shard of her stolen sword. "No, dear – you'll not escape your own blade!"

The Lady Zar shrieked in pain and rage.

Aethelgard spun to aim the boltcaster, but they plunged once more into darkness and he didn't pull the trigger.

Off to their left, the heavy, padded footfalls and rustling of pantaloons resumed as Ruinlock fled once more.

This time it was Aethelgard who grabbed Endira's wrist and tugged her along after him in pursuit. It didn't take long before the woman began to flag. She pried her wrist from his grasp. "Go on then. The prisoner-kin bastard got me good. Catch him for me, will you? Kill him!" The last words were a hiss, and before he could respond, she crumpled to the floor.

"Ancestors' tears," he cursed. Before the sounds of Ruinlock fleeing could fade, he turned to pursue, leaving behind the dead Prince General's dying daughter. Struggling to maintain the pace with the pain lancing through his bad leg, he loped ahead into the darkness after the killer, his left hand brushing the wall to keep him on track. In that way, he followed, turning twice to the left and traveling down three sets of stairs before passing another corridor without noticing.

He nearly missed it, except that he heard Ruinlock mutter something. "Gods-damned maze," he thought he heard. Retracing his steps, he could barely hear the sounds of the fleeing man over the other shouts that were beginning to echo in the halls of the palace as all the guards went into high alert. Expecting his knee to give out at any moment, he took off after the killer at a sprint, the pain flaring up so much that red flashes blazed across his vision.

"Ruinlock!" Aethelgard shouted, warm blood still trickling down his neck from his injured ear. "Turn and face me, you coward!"

Light returned to the corridor in answer to the demand. It flickered in a steady period of intermittent flashes.

Far ahead stood Ruinlock, illuminated in each flash. The little man gripped the fractured remnant of sword in one hand. The ridiculous pompadour had unraveled and clung, matted against the side of his bloody face. At some point during the chase, he must've fallen or run smack into a wall. He dug around one of the pockets of his pantaloons in a panic, confusion writ upon his features.

As the flashes continued, Actaeon emerged from another corridor behind Ruinlock. With a grin, he held up a device that resembled a writheblade with coils of glass rope around it that flashed bright purple in sync with when the lights shut off.

"What is the matter, Ruinlock?" asked Actaeon. "You look confused."

"Aethel and the Engineer," rasped the man they'd known as Gaemri. "You both think yourselves so clever. And yet, you failed to realize the impudent Indros Zar would die right under your very noses." He laughed, pointing toward Aethelgard with the sword half. "I knew you'd fail to prevent that one – it was just my way of showing you how truly powerless you are against me. But then... Ha!" The laughter brought chills to Engineer and Investigator alike. "But then, you deliver the Zar girl right into my hands, thus achieving for me two thirds of my goal. I've but to finish the Zar boy now for the count to be complete." He cocked his head at Aethelgard.

"Care to deliver him too before I depart?" The statement was followed by another bout of laughter.

"Why do this, Ruinlock?" asked Aethelgard. "All this death – this horror. What's the purpose?"

Gaemri smirked at him and spread his hands. "Suffice it to say that if I didn't do these things, the people of Redemption would follow right along after the Ancients. You wouldn't have survived a decade without me. Thus, you'll learn not to question my methods or my decisions. You'll learn or you'll die. With the pair of you, I can see you're yearning for the latter. But don't worry – I'll help you along with that. It'll be my pleasure."

The little man's twisted, half-bloody smile illuminated by the flashing light made Aethelgard shudder. With a scowl, the Arbiter raised the boltcaster at him. "You're in no place to make threats, Ruinlock. Not when you're trapped in the middle of the two people most determined to catch you."

"Trapped... right," said Ruinlock. "And I suppose you believe you'll bring me to justice on this day? That's a thought! Oh, but you've no idea that this has just begun. And how will it end, you wonder? With your blood on my broken locks, of course. Can't wait to see it."

The next actions took place so quickly that Actaeon had trouble following it.

Ruinlock jerked to the side and there was a crack as Aethelgard pulled the trigger of the boltcaster. The bolt lodged in the side of the killer's belly and he cried out in anger. But he was already moving to the side, directly toward the elderstone wall. Into it he disappeared – there one flash of the luminaries and gone the next. But where Ruinlock had been, a spray of blood covered the wall and a severed foot lay on the floor, framed in its pool of blood by the bloom of a colorful pantaloon bottom.

Aethelgard cried out in anger as he arrived at the spot where Ruinlock disappeared into the wall. In a rage, he threw the spent boltcaster against the solid stone. The weapon broke and its spring punched free and bounced back and forth off the walls to skitter down the hall. The Knight Investigator pounded a fist against it repeatedly.

Actaeon's hand on his stopped him. "Hurting yourself will not put us closer to catching him."

"You're right, my friend," said Aethelgard with a sigh. "We were so close to having him within our grasp."

"We were," Actaeon agreed. "And so, we shall keep refining our approach until we do."

Aethelgard pushed his lens frame up his swollen nose, wincing. "How'd you do it then? Interrupt his Darkest Hour?"

"It was simple once I understood it," explained Actaeon. "I saw that the artifact which Kryo gave me activated when Ruinlock triggered the Darkest Hour artifact and caused the local power interruption. But it pulsed rapidly instead of just buzzing steadily while it was active. That realization helped me understand that the signal being sent out from Gaem... er, Ruinlock's artifact must be cyclical in nature, as opposed to a steady single pulse. So, with that in mind along with my prior knowledge of the disruptive nature of the writheblade, I borrowed yours. With that, and a few glass ropes I had on hand, I was able to connect the writheblade's power receiver to Kryo's artifact detector in such a manner that the detector's pulses would power up the writheblade at a frequency that matched the detected artifact cycle. In that way, when I got close enough, Ruinlock's artifact failed, at least partially, as the modified writheblade created a disruptive signal pulse for his power interrupter. An interference cancellation resonator, if you will, using the detected signal from the very thing it is aiming to disrupt."

Aethelgard's eyes widened and he nodded. "Well, color me impressed, Act. I'd not have thought you could rig up such a thing so quickly."

"Not until recently," said Actaeon. "But I have been practicing wiring artifacts with the glass ropes. It is not really all too difficult. Though, I had to act fast to make it happen. Enrion and Mak helped me set off down a service corridor in the same direction you had taken off toward. From there, the buzzes of the artifact detector kept me on track. The stronger they were, the closer I was to you."

Aethelgard knelt to examine the severed foot.

"The artifact he used to pass through the wall must have suffered from similar interference just as he used it," Actaeon explained. "Its thickness is not insignificant. I imagine he lost a large portion of his leg within it."

"That means Ruinlock cannot be far," said Aethelgard, still determined. "Are they with you? Lord Zar and Mak Minovo? We should scour the area."

A prolonged search of the Iridescent Palace yielded nothing except a smattering of blood stains in random rooms and corridors throughout.

Somehow, against all odds, Ruinlock had disappeared without a trace. Endira Zar declared martial law over all of Rust and massed Shieldian troops at the border, but there was no sign of Gaemri Ip Monjata. Even a search far beneath the palace in the depths of the Rust ruins yielded no sign of the man.

Fortunately, what Aethelgard thought was a fatal blow for Endira Zar turned out to be not so bad. The broken sword had caught on her shoulder blade and left her with a nasty scar, but a quick recovery. While her brother Enrion, in fear of further retaliation from Ruinlock, went into hiding, Endira Zar took over command of Shield and set its armies on a years-long search for her father's killer. Her sister, Vindra, led the hunt.

In the years that followed, the events surrounding Indros Zar's death and the elevation of his daughter to Princess General became a thing of legends. Ruinlock became a bogeyman to all the children of Redemption. Stories spoken in hushed tones told of the one-legged man who could pass through walls and kill misbehaving kids.

Months after the incident, Knight Investigator and Prince Engineer sat in the workshop while one played the fluted pipe and the other tinkered with the artifact power detector, trying to boost its range by connecting it to various shapes made from copper wires.

"Do you think we will ever find him?" asked Actaeon.

Aethelgard paused his song and smiled his thin smile. "Part of me likes to think that he died deep down in the bowels of Rust, bleeding out from his leg as he lay alone to be entombed down there forevermore."

Actaeon grinned, raising his goggles to his forehead to regard his friend. "And the other part of you?"

Aethelgard let out a deep sigh and wriggled his nose. One of the benefits of having broken it was that it healed crookedly and prevented the lens frame from sliding down his nose anymore. "The other part of me knows without a doubt that Ruinlock is still out there, rebuilding his strength and planning for the day where he will find us both to try and kill us."

As Actaeon hooked up the next antenna, the artifact detector began to buzz so aggressively that it walked a short distance across the workbench.

"Let him try," said the Prince Engineer. "We will be ready."

Thieves Among Us

SAINT TORIN'S HOLD WAS ABUSTLE with activity. The Lords and Ladies of the Raedellean Conclave were all in attendance for a rare meeting outside Raedelle itself.

It was an unusual occasion, for the Prince Engineer, who usually took a back seat to the politics of the Dominion, had a meritorious announcement to make and had summoned them all there to hear it.

Actaeon sat beside Princess Eisandre at the head of the massive table where the two Rellios Caliburns typically installed themselves as protocol dictated. In an exception to that protocol though, Lauryn sat near Actaeon next to the head of the table. It was an especially unusual thing for the woodcarver turned engineer to sit in such a position of honor with all the Lords and Ladies present.

Actaeon stood and lifted his tankard of ale. Everyone present lifted theirs in turn.

"To our Great Raedelle. Together, may we make an impact on this world that surpasses even that which the Ancients once accomplished," he said, before taking a deep sip from the tankard.

A few there gasped at the implications of what he suggested, and others scoffed at it. But when, first the Princess and Lauryn, then Voice Ithelie, and then all the collective Companions lifted their tankards to drink to the toast, the others did as well. There were even a few loud exclamations of "Hear! Hear!"

The Prince Engineer grinned and set down his tankard before continuing. "I thank you, my brothers and sisters, for sharing this sentiment with me, even though most of you probably thought it preposterous." When several people laughed at that, he joined them before continuing. "But, let me assure you that the announcement I have summoned you all here for may well morph that word preposterous into something else: possible."

Letting that word sink in, he turned to Lauryn and motioned for her to stand up with him. Her face reddened and she shook her head, but then relented and stood up beside her mentor and now colleague.

"Yes, Engineer Lauryn – I want you standing beside me for this, because it is as much your dream as it is mine." He smiled at her and touched her shoulder before returning his attention to those present. "For the last century, our fellow Dominions have considered Raedelle to be little but a near-tribal, backward people." There were murmurs of disapproval to that. "Yes, they recognized our strength and prowess in battle, but they never considered Raedelle to be more than a fringe portion of their 'civilized' society. That is, until a decade ago, when we Raedelleans led the effort to first save Redemption from a tribal invasion, then lead the creation of the first Interdominional Alliance to ensure a secure future for humanity, and, finally, to spearhead the defeat of not one, but two dangerous entities called the Starborn, who threatened to destroy us all."

A cheer resounded through the Hold at that, and everyone was suddenly on their feet.

"We'll all drink to that!" shouted Lord Ackart of Southward. He stood and gulped from his tankard and everyone present followed suit before returning to their seats.

"Raedelle has," continued Actaeon after the people settled again, "shown that we are not only the strongest, but also the most compassionate, the most resourceful, and the smartest people of Redemption. And that is why I am proud to announce the creation of an institution that will act as yet another great leap forward for Raedelle and Redemption as a whole. Lauryn, will you tell them what that is?"

The younger woman stepped forward and pushed a lock of brown hair behind her ear before smiling shyly at the crowd. She put her fist into the air. "It's the Raedellean Academy of Engineering!" That said, she took a half-step back and looked to Actaeon to continue. When he just grinned at her, she giggled and nudged him in the ribs. "Go ahead, Act, er... Your Grace. Tell them what that means."

"That means that the brightest and most creative problem solvers in and out of Raedelle will have a place to learn, study, and expand the fields of engineering and science. Together, we will lead the effort to discover new technologies for the benefit of our people and, in certain cases, all of Redemption. We will spearhead the research into the artifacts of the Ancients and build a special branch of the Academy which will recruit and train Lost citizens who are interested in using their special abilities to decipher and translate the language of the Ancients. This effort will put our Dominion at the forefront of a technological golden age that will accelerate our people into the future.

"And, as is quite fitting," Actaeon continued, beaming, "the Academy will be built across the River of Arches from where Travail once stood, in the Hold of Wither. It will start using construction techniques we are all familiar with, but as we learn more, future Academy buildings will be constructed using the techniques of the Ancients, as much as we can manage."

Actaeon's speech was followed by brief words from Princess Eisandre extolling the virtues of the Academy and expressing how much it would benefit Raedelle in the decades to come. Voice Ithelie then led then in a blessing, asking for the Ancestors to guide them forward in the effort. Lastly, the Princess' sister and Lady of Wither, Eshelle Caliburn, spoke about how excited the Witherians were to host the location of the Academy.

It was after all this, and past the celebratory meal that had been enjoyed, when the Knight Investigator found Actaeon.

"Congratulations, my friend," said Aethelgard, patting the Prince Engineer on the back. "It all looks to have gone well."

"Better than I expected, even," said Actaeon with a smile. "Never could I have dreamt that my dream of creating and solving problems in a little workshop would grow to such a scale."

"Well, then," said Aethelgard with a thin smile. "You wouldn't mind helping me out with another problem then?"

"Of course," said Actaeon. "Come seek me out in the morning."

Aethelgard adjusted his lenses and shook his head. "Oh, no. This problem requires your immediate intervention. I'm afraid the consequences of not solving this mystery are beginning to expand exponentially in ways that might even impact the future of your Academy."

"What?" asked Actaeon. "What could possibly have happened?"

"Someone stole a box..." said Aethelgard.

"A box?"

"I thought the same. They're pretty upset about it, though." Aethelgard took his arm and began to guide him out into the Mirrorholds. "Now come, before a war breaks out. This is a strange one. You'll be intrigued. It's only a short walk down the hall. With any luck, I'll have you back before your friends have retired for the evening."

In contrast to the celebrations in the Raedellean embassy, the atmosphere in the Niwian Hold looked more like a funeral. The gathering was just as large, with visiting delegations from the Ajman Dominion, the Keepers, and the Loresworn.

A large circular table sat at the center of the room and, notably, everyone stood away from it, off to the sides.

Unlike Saint Torin's Hold, where the Raedelleans had covered the mirrored walls with various tapestries, the Niwian walls were left unadorned, which made the chamber appear vast. Strings of colorful flags crisscrossed the room just over everyone's heads.

A gentle murmur of conversation faded to silence when Aethelgard and Actaeon entered.

"Don't look so glum!" Aethelgard cast his hand into the air. "As I've said, I'll find your box. In fact, I have with me an expert in such mysteries. Many of you know him, I'm –"

The Elocutor of the Keepers actually spat on the floor before interrupting him. "Of course, we know this heathen who goes by Prince Engineer." The last words were a snarl. "And why should we listen to anything a blasphemer of the Allfather says?" Fatuan Molvich lifted his stained, wooden cudgel from the table beside him and pointed it at Actaeon. The frail old man glowered in his direction with smoldering eyes.

"Please, Fatuan," said the Lord Protector of Niwian, looking at his Keeper ally with pleading eyes. "It's critical the Knight Investigator find who stole my box."

To Actaeon, Faschin vor Steubick looked like a fool at a children's party, such was the manner of puffy dress he wore. It was consistent with flamboyant Niwian fashion, but multiplied tenfold. The topper was, quite literally, the fact that the man's hair had somehow been formed into two big loops that arced from the top of his head down to his shoulders, where they were fastened to the epaulets of his wide dress of blue and silver cloth.

The Elocutor was undeterred. "You shouldn't have brought that abom-"

It was Aethelgard's turn to interrupt. "Last I checked, Elocutor, the Niwian Dominion claims ownership of this Hold. An official investigation into this incident has been requested of the Arbiters, and I intend to fulfill that obligation. Now, if you will kindly keep your thoughts to yourself, I will explain to everyone present how we shall proceed." He held the Keeper's smoldering gaze with his shrewd cobalt eyes and when the man said nothing, he continued. "From my initial conversations with this group, I have gleaned that the artifact box in question was stolen in the midst of a celebration you were having regarding a new trade agreement, the details of which you were not yet willing to share. The Lord Protector described the missing artifact as a shimmering, metal box with glowing orange lines that slowly shifted across its surfaces." He made a point to look at Actaeon, but the Prince Engineer just shrugged. "The box in question stood upon the center of the pedestal until such time as the Lord Protector gave a toast, after which it had vanished. Have I missed any critical facts pertaining to the timing of events that were witnessed?" He stroked his short beard and swept the crowd with his gaze.

"Only that the Ajmani stole it," spat Fatuan Molvich, pointing his club at the Raja's Consort on the other side of the room.

"Absurd!" shouted Selnij sil'Mujarba Tri'akala. The Raja's Consort was the leader of the Ajmani delegation. His long, oil-slicked hair hung down upon a sparkling red robe that hugged his figure. Narrowing his eyes upon the Elocutor, he cocked his head. "You invite us here only to insult us? The Raja will not be pleased."

"I've enough of your attempts to ruin this trade agreement, Molvich," the Lord Protector snarled uncharacteristically. "You know I've been working on this for years, but no, you cannot see me have a diplomatic success, can you? No, I bet that you stole my artifact box in an effort to disrupt everything I have been working toward."

Fatuan Molvich actually slammed his cudgel into the small table beside him, sending up a shower of splinters. "We've abided your artifact indulgences for years, and now you accuse me of stealing it? Had I wanted your sinful box gone, I'd have smashed it right before your very eyes, not secreted it away like a thief. Keepers are warriors, not thieves!"

"You make a good point, Keeper," said Selnij with a smirk. "If only you used that pea-sized brain of yours, then you might have concluded that it makes more sense for the Loresworn to steal an artifact. Why, after all, would we ruin a beneficial trade agreement to steal a simple artifact?"

All eyes turned to the leader of the small Loresworn delegation.

Merivek Qi was the Adept Loresworn's name. The familiar, young woman had short hair that was shaved into neat rows that ran to the back of her head. She met Actaeon's gaze and waggled her eyebrows at him, her lips twisting into a tight smile before she turned to address the accusation. "Please... We have plenty of artifacts to study. The Loresworn need not steal them. How do you know the Lord Protector himself didn't have it taken to enhance his negotiating position here?"

"Oh, come now!" cried Faschin. The Lord Protector's loops of hair jiggled with indignation. "You accuse me of deception now?"

The Hold erupted into shouting from all the parties involved.

The shrill pierce of the Arbiter's whistle that Aethelgard brought to his lips brought back silence. It also brought four Arbiters from without, who rushed into the Niwian Hold, only to be stalled by Aethelgard's fist in the air. "Hold your accusations and conjecture. I will be the judge of guilt in this. And once my associate and I decipher this mystery, the evidence we place before you will be irrefutable.

"Now," he continued before the room could grow loud again. "I will have you all separate into groups, each to go with one of the Arbiters to a spare chamber, where you may stay for the duration of this investigation. The Lord Protector will, I'm sure, cover the costs of your quartering, correct?" He arched a brow at Faschin, who nodded quickly in agreement. "I ask that you give me at least this evening and night. If, by morning, I haven't solved this crime, you may leave. But until then, I need everyone present to remain for interviews. Is everyone in agreement?"

"Interviews?" The Elocutor was shaking his head. "We've heard about your Rainbow Room. The Keepers will not partake in your profane sorcery. Interview us without your artifacts, and we will agree to remain."

"If the Keepers won't be interviewed that way, then neither will we," Selnij asserted.

"Then neither will any Niwian," said Faschin.

"Very well," said Aethelgard. "I won't utilize my Rainbow Room. If that is all, then your cooperation is appreciated. Now, please follow my fellow Knight Arbiters who will show you to comfortable accommodations in the meantime."

Once the Hold was vacated with the exception of a handful of Niwian guards, the pair of investigators set to work.

They started with the center table, where the stolen artifact box had been set atop a carved stone pedestal half the height of a man. The pedestal was empty, although there was some blue powder on one side of it that was also all over the table beneath it. There were no signs of footprints upon the table or anything out of the ordinary on the pedestal itself.

A scattering of tiny elderglass fragments on the table cast little rainbows everywhere across the white tablecloth.

"Notice anything about these glass shavings?" asked Aethelgard, lifting one up to his magnifier for a better look.

"Only that it is incredible that the Niwians would risk accidentally ingesting such a thing, simply for aesthetic enjoyment," said Actaeon. "These would cut quite a bit on the way down."

"And on the way out, I'd suspect," added Aethelgard with a thin smile. "Only, that isn't what I was looking for. Do you notice anything else about them?"

"They are spread fairly homogenously across the tables?" Actaeon guessed, arching a brow at his friend. "What are you getting at?"

"Right," said Aethelgard. "Spread evenly. And, if I were to move one of the centerpieces on a different table..." He did just that, and found no tiny glass shards underneath it. "Look at that. There are none beneath. So, what does that tell us?"

Actaeon leaned forward to peer at the surface of the center table. "That the pedestal has not been moved?"

"Precisely!" said Aethelgard, looking pleased. "So, with no indications of a disturbed pedestal, and no signs that the table was trodden upon, how did our thief manage to steal our artifact box?" The Knight Investigator pocketed his magnifier and leaned forward to observe the pedestal from a different angle, before bending to scrutinize the base again. "Could an artifact have been used to warp the box to a different location? Or, perhaps an artifact drone swooped in to grab it and floated away with it? Any thoughts?"

After a long moment of silence, where the pair just stared at the scene before them, Actaeon shook his head. "I just do not see it." He extended his halberd up to lift a string of flags. "Dozens of these flag strands crisscross right above the pedestal. Were a flying artifact to swoop over, these flags would have certainly been disturbed. Someone would have noticed that, and I am quite sure the rush of air would have flipped at least some of the flags back over their strings. Yet, I see no evidence of such. All the flags hang perfectly, as though meticulously arranged by the decorator. Similarly, anything that could alter gravity, or 'warp' the artifact box away, as you say, would likely have created an effect that would have been noticed by those gathered. We can ask them again, but I would be surprised that none mentioned a disturbance among the flags originally. It would have been quite noticeable."

Aethelgard smiled. "Excellent observations there, Act. Any other thoughts on what it could be?"

"Well..." Actaeon began, but then he shook his head.

"Spit it out, man," Aethelgard encouraged. "No idea is too wild with our business."

Actaeon shrugged. "I was just thinking that the box disappeared during the Lord Protector's toast. Well, perhaps he did or said something to draw everyone's attention away for a moment. A simple device extended to the pedestal could have snatched it away." In demonstration, he touched the blade of his halberd against the top of the pedestal. "Something with a grabber mechanism. Or something magnetic, perhaps."

"Then, you suspect it was the Niwians who stole it after all?" asked Aethelgard.

"I would not presume to determine that until we have proof," said Actaeon.

Aethelgard smiled broadly at his friend. "That's right. You've come a long way, Act."

"Thanks, Aeth," said Actaeon with a blush. "So, what is next?"

"Well," said Aethelgard. "Now we go ask some questions."

It turned out that there was nothing in the Lord Protector's speech that drew anyone's attention away from the Niwian leader himself. On the contrary, most people they spoke with described a morbid fascination with his strange hairstyle – even some of the Niwians.

Nor did anyone witness a fluttering or other disturbance of the flags at any time during Faschin vor Steubick's speech.

In fact, all of the esteemed delegates at the table hadn't noticed anything at all out of the ordinary. And, collectively, they had been facing the Lord Protector from all angles across the center table. It was not fathomable that someone could have reached out with anything to snatch the artifact without at least ten other people easily seeing it.

"Could an artifact have frozen time?" asked Aethelgard, lighting some guaraja root in his pipe and crossing his arms to smoke it.

"Doubtful," said Actaeon. "With so many people in and around the Mirrorholds, someone at the edge of the affected zone would have been bound to notice."

"Teleportation to a different location?" The Knight Investigator was grasping at straws now, and he knew it.

"We have only encountered artifacts that may have accomplished such a feat a handful of times," Actaeon explained, "and each time it was a substantial machine. Also, the object being transferred was placed within the artifact. Targeted item teleportation is unlikely – though it could be possible, I suppose. It would likely require someone to aim an artifact though, which would have been noticed."

"Perhaps they were hidden from sight?" suggested Aethelgard, as he paced the room, chasing rings of smoke that he blew from his pipe.

"A collection of artifacts including an invisibility cloak?" Actaeon grinned and arched a brow. "As you have said before, every interaction leaves a trace. Even an individual shrouded from sight would need to be there to target the item. There will have been some evidence left behind."

"Or they used an invisible artifact drone to do the targeting..." mused Aethelgard.

"Let us continue the interviews. Something might come up that will point us in one direction or another," said Actaeon.

Aethelgard nodded and extinguished his pipe.

The Lord Protector himself was the next to be interviewed. The man still had his big loops of hair, and they jiggled as he sat down at a small table in the corner of the Niwian storage room that Aethelgard had commandeered. "Have you found the culprit yet?" he demanded. He wrinkled his nose at the smell left behind by the smoked pipe and looked at a crate of vegetables in the corner with a scowl.

"You will know as soon as I have reached a conclusion," Aethelgard assured him.

"I expect quicker results than this!" Faschin practically whined. "Someone could be leaving the Pyramid with my artifact box at this point."

"Certainly," said Aethelgard with a thin smile. "If you're unhappy with the way I conduct my investigations, I shall gladly turn the case over to your security personnel. I'm sure you have people with more experience than my decades of crime solving." The Arbiter turned to walk out of the room.

"Wait!" The Lord Protector stood up and raised his hand. When Aethelgard turned around and stroked his short beard, Faschin frowned. "Okay. Continue on with it. I want your help in this."

"Very well. Let's begin." Aethelgard sat down across from the Lord Protector and drew out his pipe to relight it. The Niwian leader's nose wrinkled again and he looked thoroughly displeased, but kept his thoughts to himself.

The details that Faschin gave were incredibly in-depth, even including, verbatim, every word from his speech. The trade agreement included shared access between the Ajman and Niwian colonies to the south, both of which had valuable farmlands and mines. The Loresworn were also to provide them with useful artifacts to help facilitate the mineral extraction in exchange for valuable minerals for their own needs.

During the colony part of the speech, Actaeon touched his ear and arched a brow. "What was the name of the Ajmani colony, did you say?"

"Kowakali's Stretch?" The Lord Protector shrugged. "I suppose it was named after the person who found it. I didn't ask. Why?" He looked at Actaeon expectantly.

Actaeon shook his head and waved him on. "Perhaps nothing. Continue, please."

After the pair of investigators struggled through the remainder of Faschin's speech, they couldn't get him out fast enough.

"And I thought *you* liked to talk..." Aethelgard rolled his eyes and made a show of grimacing at his friend.

Actaeon grinned. "Point taken. I shall try to be more like our Niwian friend."

Aethelgard grasped his shoulder. "Please, do not!"

The next person brought in was Fatuan Molvich, the Elocutor of the Allfather. The leader of the Keepers shot daggers at Actaeon with his smoldering eyes. He sat down heavily on the wooden chair and let his cudgel drop with a thud to the tabletop, glaring at the Prince Engineer as he did so. When he finally tore his gaze away, he turned it to Aethelgard. "I talk to you, and you alone. I'll not answer the questions of this blasphemer."

"Not a question then, friend," said Actaeon with a grin. "Just wanted to point out that you have dust all over your shoulder and chest plate."

Molvich actually growled at Actaeon, but his chin dropped and he looked down at the blue powder that clung to the shoulder of his black tunic and was sprinkled down one side of the blue chest plate. He frowned and stood to brush it off onto the floor. Once he was satisfied, he sat back down.

"That same powder was on the table next to the pedestal that held the missing artifact box," said Aethelgard. "How did it come to end up on you?"

The Elocutor balled up his fists. "Are you accusing me of something? If so, you'd better say what's on your mind!"

"I'm asking a question," said Aethelgard, patiently. "If I accuse anyone of something, I will do so with all evidence in hand and in the presence of all parties concerned. Now, I'll repeat myself for clarity: how did the blue powder end up on you?"

"One of the Ajmani sluts threw her eye makeup at me when I said something she didn't like," said Fatuan, narrowing his eyes at the remembrance.

"Was it before or after the Lord Protector's speech?" asked Actaeon.

The Elocutor stabbed a finger in his direction. "I thought I said I wasn't answering questions from this one."

"What was it?" asked Aethelgard, ignoring the inflammatory comment. "Before or after the speech?"

"After," spat Fatuan. "The vor Steubick was all upset about his box, and the Raja's Consort's little whore wasn't happy that I accused him. She's lucky it didn't get in my eyes – I'd have smashed her pretty head in right before him."

"Wait here. I need to check something," said Actaeon, excited. He snatched up his halberd and rushed out of the room.

Fatuan cast a thumb over his shoulder. "What's the Ruinthrall on about?"

Aethelgard shrugged. "You shouldn't concern yourself. After all, you didn't wish to interact with him, right?"

The Keeper just growled and kept silent.

After a few long moments, Actaeon burst back in with a huge grin upon his face. "You can cease this interview, Aeth. I have solved the case."

It was Aethelgard's turn to arch a brow in confusion. "You what?"

Fatuan's heavy cudgel was in his hand then. The old man stood and swung it down to smash the small table in half. He pulled it free of the splintered mess and pointed the stained head of the club toward Actaeon. "It wasn't me. This damned powder means nothing. I'll kill you if you dare accuse me!"

"I shall keep that in mind," said Actaeon. "As the Knight Investigator said: if we accuse anyone of something, we shall do so with all evidence in hand and in the presence of all parties concerned. Now, get out of here before we have the full force of the Order of Arbiters come in and drag you out by your feet."

The look in Fatuan Molvich' eyes could only be described as murderous. "This isn't over. You are a blight upon the world. Worse even, than the Loresworn. One day, I shall spill your brains myself."

The was a crackle as Aethelgard drew his writheblade and the small confines of the room suddenly filled with the smell of ozone, wiping away any olfactory remnants of guaraja root. "You'll have a tough time doing that if I split you in two first." The Knight Investigator winked at the Keeper.

"Allfather help me," muttered the old man. "You'll both be damned." He backed away from them and pushed his way through the door. In the process, he tripped over his own feet and landed hard on his backside before scrabbling out of the room, never taking his eyes off the artifact weapon.

When the door swung shut, Actaeon and Aethelgard looked at one another, and burst out laughing.

"I really enjoyed how you winked at him after you drew the writheblade," said Actaeon, holding his belly. "That moment will be seared into my mind forever."

Aethelgard restored the artifact weapon to its ceramic scabbard. "For me, it was how he tripped over himself and landed on his bottom on the way out."

"Yes," laughed Actaeon, leaning back against a barrel. "We do see some interesting things during your investigations."

"One of the perks of the job," said Aethelgard with a thin smile. "Now, you said you solved the case. How?"

"In due time, my friend," said Actaeon with a smirk. "In due time. Let us bring everyone back together in the Niwian Hold and everything shall come together for you."

"Are you making fun of me?" asked Aethelgard, amused.

"Of course I am!" Actaeon led the way out.

It was not hard to find all the parties involved. The screams and shouts were a clear giveaway. The full force of the Arbiters was on the scene in the Mirrorholds, standing between shouting Niwians that were brandishing swords while they helped one another strap on their brightly colored plate armor and taunting Ajmani who lifted curved falchions into the air while crying out their indignation.

A war was about to break out right there, if they couldn't calm everyone down. A conflict between Ajman and Niwian would fracture the peace of the Interdominional Alliance completely. Other Dominions would likely join or be dragged in as a close quarters war in the city erupted.

"We have to stop this," said Actaeon.

"I know," said Aethelgard.

"You have on your brightweave underwear under your clothes, right?" Actaeon asked, looking his friend up and down.

"I do..." said the Arbiter. "What are you thinking?"

"No time to explain," said Actaeon. "Quick, give me the pants. They will be easier to manage. Trust me."

Aethelgard's eyes widened. "You're truly serious, aren't you?"

"Deadly serious. All Redemption may depend on it," he responded.

"Shattered Redemption depends on my pants," muttered Aethelgard, shaking his head. He retreated out of the chaos of the Mirrorholds and into the empty Niwian Hold, where he sat down in the nearest chair, set his cane aside, and tugged off his boots. He loosened his swordbelt and shucked off his gray trousers to toss them aside. Then he stood, his lower half garbed in shimmering artifact fabric. "Whatever you've got planned better work, Act," he said, hands ready on the waist of the brightweave pants.

"Oh, it will work either way," said Actaeon. "This way has the best chance of not killing someone."

With a sigh, Aethelgard tugged off the brightweave bottoms and handed them to his friend, revealing his lower half in all its splendor.

Actaeon laughed. "I did not expect that they were really your undergarments. I figured you would have *something* on beneath them." He wasted no time in getting to work though and knelt to tie a tight knot at the bottom of one of the pant legs.

Aethelgard tugged at his beard and sat down on the chair to pull his trousers back on. "Only the best for the family jewels," he said with a smirk.

"Well, we are about to witness how well they are typically protected." Actaeon unclipped the grenado from his jacket and tossed it into the knotted pantleg. Then he tied the other end of the garment into a similar knot before standing. "Okay. Let us go."

Aethelgard stood and hopped on one leg, trying to get his trousers back on. "At least let me get dressed."

"No time," said Actaeon. "We have a war to prevent."

The Prince Engineer pulled down his goggles and rushed out with the brightweave package. Once outside, he felt for the pin of the grenado through the fabric. After finding it in his fingers, he twisted and pulled it out. "Everyone, out of the way!" he cried out as loudly as he could manage. He lifted the bundle over his head and ran forward like a maniac to throw it against the far wall. Arbiters and people from both Dominions dashed out of the way and Actaeon threw himself to the ground in the opposite direction before hazarding a peek back between the crook of his elbow at the hastily assembled apparatus. It wouldn't do to miss what happened.

The deafening crack that resounded through the Mirrorholds made him wince. But still, he managed to witness it. The pantleg ballooned up to five times its normal size temporarily and let out a puff of smoke from both sides before returning to its original shape. Smoke continued to seep through the two knots at either end.

Actaeon climbed to his feet to look around sheepishly at the crowd that was now staring at him. As the ringing in his ears began to reduce, he realized that everyone had drawn silent, waiting for him to speak.

Behind him, Aethelgard staggered out from the Hold, still trying to pull on one of his boots as he hopped over with the support of his cane.

The Prince Engineer spread his hands. "If everyone will return to the Niwian Hold in an orderly fashion. I am pleased to announce that I have solved the crime. I will reveal exactly who the culprit is once you are all inside, quiet, and seated with no weapons drawn."

The brightweave pants sputtered and then burst into flame as if to punctuate his words.

"Well then, I suppose there *is* a limit to their flame tolerance," said Actaeon, fascinated.

People from both sides exchanged looks before returning weapons to their sheaths and funneling back inside under the guidance of the Arbiters.

"You certainly have a way of getting things done, my friend," muttered Aethelgard, leaning in close.

"There is always a method to solve a problem, if one has enough imagination," replied Actaeon with a grin. Then, as they watched everyone file back inside, he added, "I am truly sorry about your underpants."

Inside, there was a tenuous truce after the close call that had happened out in the Mirrorholds.

"Thank you all for coming here," said Actaeon, spreading his hands where he stood beside the table at the center of the room. "I believe that you will all find you have been arguing over nothing once I show you who the true thief was."

The Keeper leader cracked his heavy cudgel against the floor. "Spill it already! We all know that the Ajmani did it – likely with the help of that

Loresworn scum." He narrowed his eyes upon Merivek Qi who frowned at him from across the room.

"Enough, Fatuan," said the Lord Protector. He was losing patience with his Keeper ally. "We will hear what the Prince Engineer has to say."

"Nothing that heathen says can –" began Fatuan.

"Shut up!" The Lord Protector's shout drew silence down upon the chamber like a curtain falling. "One more word out of you and my guards will drag you out of this Hold. I am the Lord Protector of Niwian, not you."

Fatuan's eyes were twin flames of barely constrained rage, but somehow he kept his composure and his silence. His right eye twitched as he resumed his seat and shrugged his shoulders.

"Continue, please, Your Grace," said Faschin.

"Thank you, Lord Protector." Actaeon pointed his halberd toward the empty pedestal. "Before I identify the culprit, I shall show you undeniable evidence so that all of you might see what I have seen." He grinned at Aethelgard, who offered him a thin smile. "May I ask my Knight Arbiter friends to please cover all the luminaries? I will uncover just this one." He leaned forward and pulled a cloth from a luminary that he'd placed upon another raised pedestal on one side of the table.

As the Knights covered the other luminaries in the Hold, eventually only the dim light of the single luminary in the center kept the darkness at bay.

"Now, observe what I did." Actaeon rounded the table to its far side and unfurled a white tablecloth that he had fastened to one of the banner ropes that spanned the room.

Gasps went up as the shadow of the pedestal was projected upon the sheet, cast by the single luminary across from it. Atop its shadow was the undeniable shape of a square.

Merivek Qi clapped her hands together and let out a sound of joy. "Oh, fantastic!"

"What is this sorcery you're showing us?" asked the Raja's Consort, looking on in confusion.

"There is no sorcery here," said Actaeon, gesturing to the shadow. "Only science. When we spoke with the Elocutor, he mentioned that one of your Ajmani entourage threw their eye makeup at him. It covered much of the table and the dust even went so far as to cover the top of the pedestal. I had not realized it at first, but after our Keeper friend told us that the powder was thrown at him *after* the box was stolen, it became clear. You see, there is a sharp cutoff where the powder ends and there is no powder at all beyond that – not even a single speck. And that cutoff is curiously shaped exactly like that of a box's corner. Now, what does that tell you?"

The Keeper was the first to answer. "Why should we believe anything you say about that? All I see before me is illusion. You could be working with the Loresworn girl to steal it, for all we know." The old man glanced sidelong at the Lord Protector and his eye twitched again.

The Lord Protector gave the Elocutor a hard look, but then turned to Actaeon. "Fatuan is right. How do we know this isn't just some clever trick you're showing us? And how does this trick of yours explain who stole my artifact?"

"It does not explain who stole it," said Actaeon. When grumblings of indignation began to sound, he continued with a raised tone. "The guilty party is none of you. And that is because nobody stole the box. In fact, the artifact box is still there. It remains exactly as it was before the accusations were made."

"How could that be?" asked Faschin, in genuine bewilderment.

"As I was saying," continued Actaeon. "The lack of blue powder in the area that the box occupied upon the pedestal led me to the realization that the box was, in actuality, exactly where it was left. Once I confirmed that the box was still there, I summoned all of you back here."

"Then what happened to it?" asked the Raja's Consort. "Why can't we see it? And how do you make it come back?"

"Yes," said Aethelgard with a thin smile. "Explain that for us, my Engineer friend." The Knight Investigator stood off to the side with his arms folded as he looked on in amusement.

Actaeon laughed. "Clearly, it is invisible. A perfect camouflage created by the artifact's surface. And yet, it still blocks visible light, as we can see by the shadow projected onto the sheet there. Still, even though it is an artifact effect, I have not explained why the effect activated in the first place. For this, you can thank the Lost translators of Raedelle, one of whom identified the mechanism." He gestured to the Knight Arbiters again. "Uncover the luminaries, if you please."

The Hold was once more filled with light and Actaeon pulled the sheet down and cast it aside.

"The Lord Protector was kind enough to repeat for us the speech he made to all of you. If you excuse me now, I will repeat a part of it.

Paraphrased, of course." Snatching up an empty glass from the table, he poured some Niwian berry wine into it from a carafe before lifting it into the air. Faschin shot him a look of annoyance and opened his mouth to say something, but Actaeon raised his hand to stay him. "Thank you all for being here. Tonight we celebrate a partnership between the Serene Dominion and our friends from Ajman.

"A trade agreement to the benefit of both our peoples," he continued, grinning as everyone's eyes fell upon him. "With our cooperation, and with help from the Loresworn, we will all obtain shared access to our colonies. Farmlands enough to feed both Dominions during even the worst of crop years, and deep mines filled with all the ore that we both need to manufacture weapons and armor to keep our lands protected. With the shared resources of Thernaxia and Kowakali's Stretch, we will find ourselves at the forefront of the Interdominional Alliance. Other Dominions will seek us out for the great wealth of resources we possess. All except for Raedelle, because, really, they have troves of resources already and will have no need for any from us. In fact, it is Raedelle's image that we hope to emulate in making this agreement."

Faschin cleared his throat, horrified. "That's not what I said!"

"Oh, right." Actaeon grinned. "I got a bit carried away, I suppose. But all that mattered was the part where you mentioned the colonies. And have a look – the box is back."

The artifact box was indeed atop the pedestal once more. There was another collective gasp at the realization. It stood there, shimmering in the luminary light, as though it never left.

"How?" managed Faschin, his eyes lit up at the sight of his artifact.

"Two of the words which were said in your speech," Actaeon explained. "When uttered, they combined to make a word of the Ancients, which caused the box to disappear and now reappear. The artifact box must have been designed to listen to commands. Once the appropriate word was said, it vanished before your eyes."

"What was it?" asked Merivek Qi, her eyes sparkling with curiosity. "The word..."

Actaeon nodded and offered her a grin. "The name of the Ajman colony – Kowakali's Stretch." The box shimmered and was gone.

"What?" shouted Faschin, reaching out for it. "Bring it back, at once!"

"Leestreks..." said Actaeon. The box reappeared again on the pedestal and the Lord Protector actually leapt up onto the table to snatch it away before it could disappear once more. "It is the Ancient word that means 'change state', or so I am told by our Lost translators. An approximation, they think. But the meaning is effectively that. And, once heard, the box did as it was commanded. By design, it vanished."

"Wow," said the Loresworn.

"That accursed thing nearly brought us to the brink of war," shouted Fatuan Molvich. "It must be destroyed." He pointed the head of his cudgel at the Lord Protector.

"I've had enough of your nonsense," snapped Faschin, his voice cracking. "You will not speak to me that way. I am the Lord Protector! The box will not be destroyed. Instead, I gift it to the man who found it and understands it better than any of us. It is yours, Prince Engineer. My thanks, for solving this mystery." The Lord Protector opened the box and dumped something into his hand before quickly stowing whatever it was in a pocket hidden within his over-the-top dress.

Actaeon's eyes widened in surprise, but he gladly accepted the gift. "Thank you, Lord Protector."

"Have it your way, Faschin," growled the Keeper, balling his fist. "We put you in power in Niwian and we can have you removed from it. Our relationship with the Niwian Dominion is at an end!" He cocked his head and led the other Keepers out of the room.

The room was silent for a long moment until the Lord Protector turned back to Actaeon and spoke. "I do believe the Serene Dominion will need the friendship of Raedelle in the years to come. We must talk more. There may be things you are interested in."

"Indeed, there may be," said Actaeon, thinking about the knowledge hidden within Memory Keep. "They are not at all beloved by me, but, nevertheless, I am sorry that your partnership with the Keepers fell through this way."

"It's been a long time coming," said the Niwian leader, carefully adjusting one of the loops of his hair. "I believe this just hastened along the inevitable. In either case, you averted a disaster here today. You have my thanks."

"And mine," added the Raja's Consort.

"Well done," said Aethelgard, as he walked Actaeon back through the Mirrorholds toward Saint Torin's Hold. "We should be able to get you back in time before the end of your own celebration."

"Aye," said Actaeon. "I am overdue to rescue Eisandre from the social obligations there. And thank you for saying so – I learned much from you over the years."

The Knight Investigator smiled and patted his friend on the back. "That you have. I admit that I was quite proud to watch you solve a case like that where even I hadn't yet deciphered the puzzle. I knew nobody there really stole it – just not how to prove it."

"Sure, you did," said Actaeon with a laugh.

Aethelgard laughed with him and lit some fresh guaraja root in his pipe. "Believe what you may about that, but do not doubt that I am impressed by your work."

"I shall not." Actaeon lifted the artifact box with a grin. "And I even got a new artifact to study!"

"I wonder what he had hidden in there." Aethelgard came to a halt before the Raedellean embassy.

"Oh, I peeked before the grand reveal," said the Prince Engineer with a smirk. "It was a projection disc that showed the locations of all the ore veins in the region of the colonies."

Aethelgard chuckled. "I'm sure you won't use those to Raedelle's benefit."

"Of course not," said Actaeon. "Just an iron vein. Or perhaps two."

The Knight Investigator smirked. "Enjoy the rest of your celebration."

"Why not join us for a while?" asked Actaeon.

Aethelgard blew a ring of smoke and held up his pipe. "A Knight Investigator's work is never done. Go and enjoy yourself. You deserve it." He turned to start off, his cane clicking on the glass floor.

"Have a good night, my friend," said Actaeon.

Without turning back, the Knight Investigator raised his hand in goodbye.

The Tubeway Murder

SPARKS CASCADED DOWN FROM THE walls, accompanied by the scream of metal scraping on metal.

"Full stop!" shouted Actaeon, gritting his teeth as the deck shuddered violently beneath his feet.

The shriek of the tearing metal ceased and everyone was thrown forward – the straps that they had installed were the only things that kept them from slamming hard into the consoles in front of them.

"Stopped," confirmed Lauryn from her console as she punched at several symbols. "Sorry, Act." Her cheeks glowed red with embarrassment in the dim light of the luminaries that lit the control room of the craft.

It had been an incredible discovery last cycle. An artifact hunter named Silgish showed up in Actaeon's workshop one day with the news of finding a working artifact room in the tunnels beneath Pyramid. The Prince Engineer went at once to investigate, bringing his colleague, Lauryn, with him. There he found something that was immediately clear to him was not, in fact, just a room.

It fit the tunnel it was found in rather precisely, as though it was designed just for it. The "room" was cylindrical in shape, extending along the tunnel. The front was a curved elderglass structure. However, the light of a luminary yielded no information about what was inside – the ancient glass kept it somehow hidden from them. After Silgish led them through the narrow gap to one side, they found a hatch in the surface of another curved elderglass wall that allowed entry. Inside were several rooms in succession. The first was an entry room. The next was filled with a large, cabled cylinder mounted on a shaft that ran the axis of what Actaeon quickly understood to be a transport craft. After that, and confirming his suspicion, came a large room with forty-eight seats and additional hatches on the sides. "A giant metal slug to move people," Actaeon had said with a grin. Another hatch in the front led to a room with several ancient consoles on the sides that flashed various symbols and projected images above them. There was an open hatchway there which led to the final room that was hidden behind the bubble-like elderglass. It had three distinct consoles which were all facing forward toward the bubble window and the open tunnel ahead. The centermost console was the most intricate of them all.

It was that one which Lauryn sat before now, replaying the past few moments in her mind and wondering how she had missed the debris that had jutted into the tunnel.

"Stupid mistake," spat Japhus, the blacksmith and metalworker who was part of the team Actaeon had appointed from the Raedellean Academy of Engineering to get the "giant metal slug" working again. "Let someone else pilot it next time, eh? I fancy my neck remaining in one piece."

"You'll keep your mouth shut if you know what's good for you," snapped Lauryn, glancing over her shoulder at the blacksmith.

Japhus smirked at her and stepped away from the console. "No worries. I'll be outside, checking the damage you just caused, lass." He left toward the rear of the craft and the hatch light on Lauryn's console lit up to show that he'd exited.

A glance to her right showed her a real-time projection of the blacksmith stepping down from the rear of the slug. "I hate that arrogant arse. Why do we need him on this, Act?"

The two apprentice engineers at the other front consoles, Valissa and Naimeth, shot sidelong glances at one another.

"Because he is one of the most talented metalworkers I have seen. There are few others in Redemption who could repair some of the damage we've seen in the Tubeways," Actaeon said, using the term he had coined for the tunnels that were designed to carry the metal slug. "Without him, I fear this project would take much longer."

"And without me?" asked Lauryn, half-serious.

Actaeon grinned. "Who are you kidding? You would not miss this for anything, Lauryn. I will have a talk with him about his attitude."

"And you think that'll change that chauvinist sop? He thinks he's better than me because he's got dangly bits between his legs? I've done more for Redemption on a lazy day in bed than he has in a lifetime." Lauryn fumed as she tapped furiously at her console to check the status of various systems.

Behind her, the apprentice, Valissa, laughed out loud at her comments. Naimeth hid his smirk behind a sleeve.

"Why not the pair of you go outside to see if Japhus needs a hand with any debris removal or repairs?" suggested Actaeon with a grin.

Valissa cut her laughter short and nodded. "Aye, Your Grace." Naimeth echoed her and they both scrambled from the room to help.

When they were gone, Actaeon joined Lauryn at the console and leaned forward to whisper to her. "It is not a good look in front of the apprentices, Lauryn. I would recommend you reserve your more virulent complaints for my ears alone."

"And let him step all over me?" said Lauryn. "No, I'd rather stomp on him in return. If there's one lesson we should be teaching them it's to stand up for ourselves. After all, we're the ones who are making a *real* difference in Redemption. The engineers will be the ones who bring our people into the future – not some nullwit blacksmith nor anyone else!"

"Engineers will do just that, I believe," agreed Actaeon. "They will change the very face of this world. But only with humility, openness, and objectivity. You are correct in asserting that Japhus is an imbecile, but do not let him bring you down to his level. The Lauryn I know is better than that."

"Down to his level?" snapped Lauryn. "Are you kidding me, Act? That jerk's been questioning my abilities since he first arrived here. I've absolutely had it with him. Go ahead and talk with him if you want, but if he's still on this slug after we get back to the Pyramid, then I'm out. Redemption would be better off with his guts lubricating the inside of the Tubeway."

Actaeon narrowed his eyes at his protégé. "You are completely out of line, Lauryn. The Redemption that we fought for – that so many of our friends died protecting – is not one where even the most rude men would be dealt with in such a way. I ask as your friend that you take back what you said."

Lauryn blushed furiously and shook her head. "I'll not do it, Act."

"Then I shall have you off the project instead of Japhus," he said. "You know I would side with you otherwise. But I will not have you speaking of people on our team in such a manner – even if their behavior is abhorrent."

"Is everything okay in here?" Companion Yanelle walked in with her hand resting easily on the hilt of her arming sword. She brushed a lock of red hair from her eyes and looked between the two engineers with concern.

Lauryn remained silent and looked down at her console.

"It is," said Actaeon, casting a disappointed look at Lauryn. "Thank you for checking in, Companion Yanelle."

"Of course, Y- ... Act," she said.

A speaker crackled and a voice came over from the external feed. "We're finishing up now. Coming back aboard. Japhus says the Tubeway's clear of obstacles now." It was Valissa's voice.

"Are all systems operational, Lauryn?" asked Actaeon.

She nodded. "Aye, Your Grace. Everything checks out."

Actaeon nodded and touched the symbol for the control room pickup. "Good work. Come back aboard and we will carry on."

The controls of the Ancients had always been a difficult thing to learn. Even the attempt to learn the meaning of the symbols left most with debilitating headaches. The effort was nearly impossible. It had been Actaeon and Princess Eisandre, using the Thoughtlink Artifact that bound their thoughts together as one, who had discovered that the Lost, of which the Princess was one, could learn the language of the Ancients without consequence. The Lost had always been considered broken, useless, a burden on society. Many were killed or abandoned to the wilds. But Eisandre was Lost and knew that all such children had potential. It was thus, starting with the Lost children of Raedelle, that Eisandre had established, as a part of the TriForge, a division of Lost whose purpose was to translate and interpret the symbols and writings of the Ancients for the non-Lost of Redemption. Some of them also came to learn at the Raedellean Academy of Engineering. This was how a young Lost man named Darbin ended up on the crew.

"Will do, Your Grace," sounded the voice of Valissa in answer.

Lauryn tapped a few symbols on the console to bring up the projection showing the slug's entry room. She watched carefully as, first Valissa who paused to check the console, then Japhus, and finally Naimeth climbed up through the hatch and entered the transport craft. When Naimeth boarded, the open hatch alert symbol disappeared, which, according to Darbin, indicated it was closed. Lauryn thought of the symbols in just those simple terms that the Lost man had explained to her. Any deeper thought about them would start her head pounding with pain.

"All confirmed aboard and ready to depart," she reported.

"Very good," said Actaeon. "Take us forward. The map projection shows a roundabout just ahead. If we can make it, let us turn about in it."

The metal slug advanced cautiously as Lauryn urged it forward. She didn't need to make the same mistake of striking debris again. With one eye on the proximity sensors, she kept the craft moving forward at a crawl. While she directed it, Valissa and Naimeth returned to their consoles behind her.

"Everything looks clear ahead," confirmed Valissa after surveying the projection above her console.

"All systems operating within acceptable parameters," added Naimeth as he scrutinized the information coming from his.

They continued forward at a crawl until they reached the roundabout. Lauryn directed the slug into it and made the quick loop around until they were in the main Tubeway again and facing back toward the Pyramid.

Now the way ahead was known. She tapped the symbol for speed and nudged it forward. The Tubeway began to zoom past around the perimeter of the bubble window. The speed increased until all the imperfections of the tunnel were but a blur to their vision. The luminaries affixed to the front of the craft lit up a space just in front of them as they zipped along, the spinning mechanism in the drive room somehow keeping the slug floating in the center of the Tubeway.

"Coming up on the hazard we just repaired," said Naimeth. "In four... three... two..."

He never got the chance to reach one.

The proximity alarm blared.

Ahead in the beam of the luminaries, a running figure came into view. At the last moment they all recognized Japhus running right toward them. The blacksmith slid to a stop and his jaw dropped open as the metal slug slammed into him and obliterated his body in a spray of red that splattered across the elderglass bubble.

Lauryn slammed her fist on the emergency brake symbol and the engine screamed behind them as it tried to stop the vehicle as quickly as possible.

But it was too late. Japhus was gone.

The realization dawned on them all.

Lauryn let out a horrified scream. "By the Fallen... I've killed him..." She fell to her knees beside the console and vomited.

Valissa rushed forward to take her place at the main console and made sure everything was shut down.

Lauryn slapped both hands against her forehead. "Gods... What have I done?"

"He had it coming," said Darbin. He was normally in some sort of mental fugue himself, but this time he broke them all out of their shock with his unexpected words.

Actaeon blinked as his senses returned after seeing the man explode on the front of the transport craft. "Yanelle, I need you to go to Pyramid on foot. Find Knight Investigator Aethelgard and tell him what happened here."

"Aye aye, Your Grace," said Yanelle. "But what exactly should I tell him?"

"There has been a murder," said Actaeon. "And we need him to determine who is the killer."

Lauryn looked at him and her face blanched as she realized the implications of what he was saying.

"It shall be done," said Yanelle. And she was off.

She squeezed past the bulk of the Tubeway vessel and they all watched her run forward in the luminary light, leaving bloody bootprints in her wake.

It was nighttime, Actaeon guessed, by the time Aethelgard arrived. It was impossible to tell in the darkness of the Tubeways, but so much time had passed that it couldn't be otherwise. Actaeon had kept everyone in place on the craft and away from the consoles while they waited. Silgish and Darbin had threatened to mutiny if the Knight Investigator didn't show up soon, so Actaeon was quite thankful when he finally did.

Into the lights of the metal slug limped Aethelgard, leaning heavily on his cane. Yanelle was just behind him. The Knight Investigator leaned forward and rubbed his bad knee which was throbbing after the long walk. He snapped his cane up in front of Yanelle before she could proceed farther forward. "Do not further sully the scene of the crime. Your bootprints are evident in the bloodstains already. I implore you not to disturb things more. Thankfully, your Prince Engineer has learned enough from his work with me to ensure there are no further blemishes upon the evidence. Now, carefully retrace your steps exactly to return to the artifact craft. See them right there? Yes, you have it." He nodded his approval as Yanelle gingerly picked her way back along her own footprints amid the dried pools of blood and spatter. "And tell Actaeon to keep everyone aboard and in eyesight. If there is a killer there, we will find them."

Once the Companion was out of sight and back aboard the metal slug, Aethelgard stretched his back and arms before pulling out his large, illuminated lens and squatting to examine the elements of the scene.

"What in cracked Redemption's he doing out there scurrying about like that?" asked Silgish in a buzz that ended with a squeak. The artifact hunter's face was completely hidden behind a fabric wrap and reflective goggles. Their voice was significantly modified by some artifact and it was impossible to tell their gender or origin. The goggles tilted to scrutinize Actaeon and the buzzy voice sounded again. "Why are we still here? It's time we end this charade. We all know she's the culprit. Why should we all be held here against our will?" Silgish pointed a gloved finger at Lauryn in accusation.

Yanelle folded her arms and stood between everyone and the exit.

"I swear by the Fallen that I didn't mean to kill Japhus," sobbed Lauryn. She sat heavily in one of the many chairs, wringing her reddish-brown hair in her hands.

"Not that we'd blame you," interjected Darbin. The Lost man blinked and then looked down at his hands. "Blood everywhere. Your blood, my blood. Same blood, no? Pumped through the veins to feed our tiny brains."

He balled up his fists and began to tap out a pattern against his head, drawing silent once more.

"My family will be worried by now that I've not returned," complained Valissa. "I need to at least send word somehow."

"And what about Japhus' family?" asked Actaeon. "He will not return ever. Should we not ensure that justice is done in his murder?"

"Oh, please," buzzed Silgish. "Dispense with the nonsense. We all know your friend there did it. Don't act so innocent. 'Redemption would be better off with his guts lubricating the inside of the Tubeway.' That's what you said, is it not?"

Lauryn's face blanched. "I... I didn't mean th-"

"Didn't mean to kill him?" suggested Valissa. "Well you did a pretty good job of it, Lauryn."

Lauryn narrowed her blue eyes at the apprentice. "Watch yourself."

"Or what? You'll arrange to kill me, just like you did Japhus?" Valissa stood from her chair and folded her arms across her chest.

"Calm down, everyone," said Actaeon. "We do not have enough information yet, so let us not jump to conclusions.

Silgish stood. "This is a waste of our time. It's clear what is happening here. You called an ally to help pretend to exonerate your friend here, but you haven't a leg to stand on with this story of yours." The artifact hunter started for the door. "Out of the way, Companion."

Yanelle's hand dropped to the hilt of her sword and she stood her ground.

"Excuse me, Companion Yanelle." Aethelgard, done with his investigative efforts outside, pushed past and entered the cabin. "This is now a crime scene under the authority of the Arbiter Pyramid Command, of which I, Knight Investigator Aethelgard, represent presently. And, as all of you are witnesses to what I understand to be very likely a crime and not an accident, you shall not be permitted to leave until you have availed yourselves to me for questioning."

"This isn't anywhere near Pyramid. I'm sure of it," said Silgish. "You've no authority here."

"It is my understanding that this artifact was discovered beneath the Pyramid," said Aethelgard, leaning forward to better inspect the artifact hunter. "Thus, the Arbiters claim right of property over it, and it falls under my jurisdiction."

"But I discovered it! You cannot just claim it as your own," argued Silgish. "It was my hard work that led to the finding."

"And I assure you that my Order's willingness to entertain your claim on the matter will quite depend on your cooperation as I investigate this breach of Pyramidal law. In either case, you *will* remain here until I am satisfied in my full investigation of the matter at hand. Now, take a seat, madam." Aethelgard looked down his crooked nose at Silgish and adjusted the writheblade in its ceramic scabbard on his hip, eliciting a whiff of ozone that quickly permeated the compact cabin.

The artifact hunter recoiled and buzzed anew. "How could you know me a woman?" She thought twice about her actions after sniffing the ozone and sat down in a seat.

"Your gait, for one, is characteristic of a woman – the greater rotation of your ankles as you walk when compared to a man. The manner in which you stand is also a clear giveaway," explained Aethelgard. "The hunched shoulders are indicative of breastfeeding and the rotation of your hips would tell of a baby that was carried on your right hip for an extended period. You've corrected some of your posture. Would I be correct in surmising that your son or daughter is seven or so years of age by now?"

Silgish was silent for a long time, shaking her head and regarding the Knight Investigator through her mirrored goggles. When she finally spoke, she reached up to tap something at her throat which deactivated the voice modification artifact. "Very well," she said in a feminine voice. "But your identification of my gender means nothing. Lauryn killed Japhus. She threatened to put his guts all over the inside of the Tubeways just before he was killed. And I'd put bits on her hitting the debris on purpose to get him outside of the slug."

"Due time. Due time, Madam Silgish. I shall make that determination after the full gathering of information is complete." Aethelgard stepped farther into the room and grasped Actaeon's hand. "Good to see you, my friend. It is quite the conundrum you have found yourself in."

"It is indeed, is it not?" Actaeon embraced his friend and grinned nervously.

"Do not despair though. For I have already concluded that Engineer Lauryn did not commit the crime," said Aethelgard.

"See?" Silgish leaned back in her seat, exasperated. "Just as I said, Prince Engineer. You've got your man on the inside in order to clear your protégé."

"On the contrary, Silgish. If Lauryn is guilty, I will hold her accountable to the fullest extent of Arbiter justice. By the end of my investigation, I will prove to everyone here who the killer is," promised Aethelgard.

"Now this I must see," said Silgish.

"A bit of a change in attitude now, eh?" said Valissa.

Naimeth laughed at his fellow apprentice's words.

Aethelgard ignored them. "Next I shall need everyone's story of what transpired. Each of you will join me in the control room for questioning – one at a time."

"An odd reaction for you."

Aethelgard was interviewing Lauryn and she had just finished her account of the events to Actaeon and him in the pilot house of the metal slug.

"To vomit after Japhus' death. There's another similar incident in your past –"

"Brigert," admitted Lauryn.

"Actaeon told me about him. And yet you did not vomit when he died. Why?" Aethelgard pushed the lenses up along the bridge of his nose.

Lauryn looked at him, dumbfounded. She looked like she was about to cry.

"Is that not a bit harsh?" asked Actaeon, displeased.

Lauryn's expression hardened then, and she shot daggers at the Knight Investigator with her blue eyes. "Perhaps because his guts didn't get splattered all over a window in front of me? You're supposed to be an investigator – you tell me."

"And yet, they still blew all over the place, if the accounts I have heard are correct," said Aethelgard. "Are you certain you didn't hit the debris on purpose? Get Japhus to go outside so you could shut him up for good?"

Lauryn glared at him and bit her lip until it bled, using every bit of self-control to keep herself from throttling the Arbiter. Then she burst into tears.

"That is enough!" shouted Actaeon. The Prince Engineer rarely raised his voice, but the complete lack of compassion in the line of questioning was getting to him. He stepped between Lauryn and Aethelgard.

The Knight Investigator withdrew a pipe from his cloak and sprinkled some bits of guaraja root shavings into it. A practiced strike from his knife drew a spark from the flint inset into the shank of the pipe and the lit contents glowed to life in the dim room. Aethelgard took a drag from it. "Indeed, it is enough. I have learned all I need to know here. You may leave, Engineer Lauryn."

Lauryn tossed her braid over her shoulder and huffed her displeasure as she stormed out of the room, stifling a sob.

"Was that wholly necessary?" Actaeon leaned heavily against his halberd and scrutinized his friend.

"Do you know me to be a practitioner of superfluity?" asked Aethelgard, blowing a ring of smoke across the pilot house.

Actaeon waved some of the errant smoke from the drug away from his face. "Then what was the purpose?"

The Arbiter spread his hands. "The making of a few pestiferous comments has allowed me to more quickly draw conclusions. Lauryn is innocent. Of that I have no doubt. You did the right thing in summoning me here, despite the insufferable pain it brought to life in my knee after that infernal walk out here. Your Companion Yanelle was insistent that we continue forth even when I wished to pause for a break."

Actaeon dug in a pocket of his leather jacket and tossed him a half-through vial. "Take this. You should have told me you ran out. So, tell me why you are convinced Lauryn is innocent."

After quaffing the contents of the vial and tossing the empty container back, Aethelgard took another drag from his pipe and winced as he flexed his knee from where he sat on one of the benches at the back of the room. "A person guilty of the crime we suspect would not be so argumentative, even in the face of an upsetting line of questioning. Especially when they were not contentious about it in the first place. No, she is not guilty. Upset, yes. But not guilty. At least not for the murder. Though I believe she suffers no small amount of guilt for failing to realize that he was not aboard before she started up through the Tubeways again. It is safe to say that she feels responsible for his death. That much I gathered from her retelling of the events. Let us next speak with your two young apprentices. They were both with Japhus. Perhaps one of them will be able to explain why he never returned to the craft after their check."

"What do you mean?" asked Actaeon, confused. "Lauryn said that she saw him come back aboard. First Valissa, then Japhus, and then Naimeth. The only possibility is that he exited the vehicle after Lauryn witnessed him climb aboard."

Aethelgard puffed on his pipe and blew another ring of smoke that traveled quite far in the still air. "That cannot be the only possibility, for I have eliminated it. Which means that the only possibility that remains, however strange it is, must be true. Japhus never returned to your metal slug."

"But the projection showed his return. You yourself said that Lauryn is innocent in this crime. Why would she lie about this?" Actaeon scratched his right hand through its fingerless glove.

"I agree that she wouldn't lie about it. However, the oil and metal shavings on his boots would certainly not have the ability to tell a lie. And I traced the prints from where he worked on a workpiece to when he exited the craft to where he met his end. At no point did he come back aboard."

"Then what?"

"I am surprised, my engineer friend. You, who work every day with the broken artifacts of the Ancients... That you would so readily trust their veracity is surprising." Aethelgard offered him a thin smile and stroked his short beard.

"I..." Actaeon started, about to argue with the Knight. He paused and reconsidered. After a moment, his mouth twisted into a broad grin. "Interesting theory. But a difficult one to prove. You mean to say what Lauryn saw was inauthentic."

"Precisely," said Aethelgard, snapping his fingers. "I expect your apprentices may shed further light on the matter – if you would be so kind as to bring them both in."

"At the same time?" asked Actaeon.

"Yes. I think so. It will tell us more than with each alone."

The sharp-eyed young man with the pinpoint nose and the mop of blond hair came in first. A round-faced young woman with short, wavy locks of hair the color of coal stepped in behind him, observant eyes darting between Actaeon and Aethelgard.

"How may I help you, sir?" Naimeth asked, his voice quavering.

"Relax, young man." Aethelgard smiled and patted the air in front of him reassuringly. "I just need to ask you a few questions."

"I swear I didn't kill Japhus!" Naimeth blurted out.

Aethelgard laughed at that. "Well, thank you. You've ruled out one of my suspects then."

"I did?" asked Naimeth, his voice a combination of relief and confusion.

"What is the first thing I taught you to do when you encounter a new problem to be solved, Naimeth?" asked Actaeon with a grin.

"Uhm..." The young apprentice crossed one foot over his other and nearly stumbled in the process. "Ask the right questions to better understand it? Ah... aha! That's what the Knight Investigator is doing now, right? That's what you mean?"

Actaeon nodded approvingly. "Exactly."

Aethelgard arched a brow and stroked his beard as he regarded Valissa. "I see that you're not as quick to profess your innocence, young lady."

"Isn't that just what the guilty party would do?" she asked with a chuckle and a skeptical glance toward her fellow apprentice.

"Clever one you've got here, Act," said the Knight Investigator.

"Oh, I know," said Actaeon.

Both apprentices turned red, for completely different reasons. Naimeth cast a look at Valissa and mouthed some words at her, confusion writ upon his brow.

"Tell me about what happened after the three of you exited the craft," requested Aethelgard. "Unless there is any other information you'd like to volunteer first." He offered the lad a thin smile.

"Oh, ah... no no. I'll tell you what you asked to hear about." Naimeth leaned on a nearby console and triggered a projection. He quickly slapped the symbol on the console again to shut it off. "Sorry, ah. Yes, so you want to know what happened outside of the craft."

"If you would be so kind as to indulge my curiosity," said Aethelgard. He crossed his bad leg over the good one so he could massage his throbbing knee while he puffed on his pipe and listened.

"Well, let's see..." began Naimeth.

"When we got out into the Tubeway," Valissa interrupted. "I remember that Japhus muttered something to Naimeth about how a woman couldn't be trusted to do the job. He took Naimeth ahead with him to check for damage to the slug and further obstructions. He said to me: 'Clean up the debris back here, girl. We'll check on your work when we get back.' Then they were gone. I didn't see them again until I was back aboard. I heard him call back that I could tell His Grace over the communication port that they were all clear up front and that we were coming back aboard. Naimeth came back to the pilot house, but I didn't see Japhus again until Engineer Lauryn killed him."

Naimeth opened his mouth several times but no words came out.

"Anything to add to her account, Naimeth?" asked Aethelgard.

Naimeth blinked and backed away from the other apprentice. "What are you talking about, Valissa? You went with Japhus – not... not me!"

Valissa offered him an incredulous look. "You mustn't be serious, Naimeth."

"I... I... I went back to clean up the debris. Y- you asked me to do that. You lying bitch!" Naimeth balled his hands into fists and began to step back toward her.

Aethelgard stood and stepped forward quickly. "Compose yourself, Naimeth. If your –" But his words were cut short as he tripped over his cane and stumbled forward, crying out in pain. He nearly fell flat on his face, but at the last moment, he struck out an arm and caught himself on one of the artifact consoles. An Ancient symbol was inadvertently pressed by his hand and the metal slug began to glide forward along the Tubeway.

Valissa shrieked and stumbled backward under the sudden acceleration, catching herself against the rear wall.

Naimeth leapt forward over the fallen Knight Investigator and punched the correct symbol to bring the craft to a stop. After that was done, he reached down to help Aethelgard to his feet once again.

"Thank you, lad," Aethelgard said.

"I... I swear she's lying," said Naimeth.

"I've heard all I need to hear from you both," the Knight said. "You may leave."

"But..." Naimeth began.

"Believe me, I know where to find you if I have more questions," said Aethelgard, making a shooing gesture with his free hand.

Valissa glared at Naimeth and then left the pilot house. Naimeth hesitated and when he saw that the Knight Investigator wasn't going to heed his argument further, he followed her out.

Aethelgard sat down heavily on a bench at the back of the room and rubbed his knee. "With any luck the pair of them won't kill one another before we are finished."

"Yanelle is out there," said Actaeon. "She will keep them in line. You fell like that on purpose. Why?"

Aethelgard nodded and relit his pipe, offering his friend a wink as he released another puff of guaraja smoke. "I have this case solved."

"Were the projections accurate that we saw, I would have to conclude that Naimeth was responsible, being the last person back aboard after Japhus. However, I know better than to trust any part of something that has been proven patently false." Actaeon sat down beside his friend and leaned forward heavily against the shaft of his halberd.

"Quite so," agreed Aethelgard. "Just one last thing to do now. Bring in the Lost translator. Darbin, was his name?"

When the three of them emerged from the small pilot house, they entered a deathly quiet room steeped in suspicion. The two apprentices were sitting as far apart as possible on opposite sides of the passenger compartment. Silgish paced the room to one side, pausing from time to time to direct a long gaze toward Lauryn from behind her goggles. As for Lauryn, she sat in the center of the room, arms folded defensively as she eyed the other three with mistrust.

Amidst them all, and standing over Lauryn in the very center, was Yanelle. Her hands rested comfortably on her swordbelt, ready to take action if needed.

Everyone looked over expectantly as the Knight Investigator strode back into the room, his cane clicking on the metal floor.

Darbin walked over to take a seat beside Lauryn. Lowering his head into his hands, he began to tap his temples rhythmically.

"Are we done here?" asked Silgish with her artifact augmented buzz of a voice. She paused her pacing and tapped a foot impatiently. "We all know she did it." Lifting a finger, she cast it toward Lauryn as if delivering a punishment.

"On the contrary, Madam Silgish," said Aethelgard. "I know who the real person responsible for Japhus' death is, and I can prove it."

"Who then?" asked the enshrouded artifact hunter.

"Care to share with everyone, Valissa?" asked Aethelgard. His cobalt eyes burned as he gazed down his crooked nose at her.

The apprentice jumped in her seat, surprised to be addressed. "It was clearly Naimeth. He went off with Japhus and then lied about it."

Naimeth stood suddenly from his seat, his hands balled into fists again.

One hand moving to the hilt of her sword, Yanelle lifted her other hand to caution him.

"Your little game is over," said Aethelgard. "You killed Japhus, Valissa. Perhaps not directly. It was indeed Lauryn who was piloting the craft when he was struck and killed. However, I am now certain that all the events leading up to that moment were fully orchestrated by you."

Valissa shook her head, her black locks of hair bouncing back and forth. "You're a lunatic."

"Regardless of whatever my mental state might be, the evidence speaks for itself," said the Arbiter.

"What evidence?" asked Valissa, her voice raised now. She drew to her feet and waved a hand at Lauryn. "She's the one that wanted him dead. If not Naimeth, then her. Maybe he covered up for her for all we know."

"If you refuse to tell the truth, then I will," said Aethelgard. With both hands clasped behind his back, he began to pace to and fro across the room. "You first altered the detection system of the craft so that Lauryn would not see the debris ahead. You've been in this section of the Tubeway before, so you knew it would be enough to give reason for a stop, but not enough of an obstruction to do any serious damage to the vehicle."

"This is outrageous," she began.

"Shut up and let him talk," shouted Naimeth, his voice cracking. Yanelle's outstretched hand was the only thing that stopped him from approaching Valissa.

"Once your plan was underway you were sent to join Japhus outside. You knew he had to be out there since the master metalsmith needed to weigh in on any repairs that might be required. Naimeth was in the way though, so you told him to clean up the tunnel at the back of the car while you went forward to join Japhus. There you offered him sexual favors, knowing that would delay his return to the metal slug."

"That's ridiculous!" said Valissa.

"The scene of the crime doesn't lie." Aethelgard tugged at his short beard. "The shuffling of Japhus' oily bootprints in one spot was quite telling after he'd spent some effort moving one of the pieces of debris that had become lodged in the side of the vehicle. You see, I've never before seen a belt unbuckle due to blunt trauma. And I sincerely doubt that a metalsmith normally so skilled with his hands would have buttoned up his shirt incorrectly. Which led me to believe that Japhus had adequate motivation to unbuckle his belt and unbutton his shirt. Both things that a young woman – or a young man – might accomplish. In his rush to get back to the metal slug that left him behind, he hastily failed to buckle his pants and buttoned his shirt up wrong as he ran to catch up. Of course, he must've been left in somewhat of a daze as you reentered the vehicle in order to miss it himself."

"I'd never have offered that misogynist sexual favors. That's disgusting," asserted Valissa. "I'd never have lowered myself to that. It could only have been Naimeth."

Aethelgard dismissed her comment with a wave and continued pacing. "Once you were back aboard, you fully anticipated Lauryn would turn the slug around and smash into Japhus. That's why you were ready to use her console to stop the craft after he died, hoping to impress your Prince Engineer with your quick thinking. You see, you don't normally react so quickly. When I fell against the console earlier, it was Naimeth who reacted quickly to stop it, while you just fell against the back wall."

"This is naught but conjecture and nonsense," said Valissa in exasperation.

"That much could potentially be arguable, if not for the final piece of evidence," said the Knight.

"And what is that?" she asked, her tone dripping with skepticism.

"Darbin, if you would be so kind as to pull up the recording from just before the murder on this room's central projector?" Aethelgard offered his suspect a thin smile as the Lost translator stood and approached the nearest console.

The first images that flickered to life showed the entry room where Valissa climbed aboard and did something to the console.

"Pause it," said the Knight Investigator. The projection froze in place with Valissa's hand touching the console.

As she watched, the color left her face. Naimeth blurted out a laugh.

"Nervous now, I see." Aethelgard waved his cane back and forth through her projection. "This is the moment where you instructed the console to impose a completely different image upon the moment. Instead of seeing what really happened – Naimeth returning to the metal slug alone – we instead see this." He nodded to Darbin. When Darbin didn't respond, he snapped his fingers.

Darbin blinked and snapped out of a Lost episode. The projection resumed. In it, Valissa left the room to enter the rest of the vehicle. A short time later, Japhus climbed in, followed by Naimeth.

"Darbin, replay it if you will. And everyone please take note of how Japhus lifts his right arm over his head to stretch it after entering. And also, before leaving the room Naimeth glances back as if to look at someone. As it turns out, he *is* looking at someone. That will all become apparent." Aethelgard stroked his beard and waited.

The projection replayed and everything occurred exactly as described.

"I don't see how this proves anything," said Silgish.

Aethelgard held up a finger. "Next, Darbin will launch a projection that was recorded three days prior."

It flickered to life in the center of the room, with the translucent details tinged with silver-green edges. Two people walked in first: Actaeon and Lauryn having an enthusiastic discussion. After they walked out, the blacksmith came in and stretched his arm identically to the other time. Next arrived Naimeth, who paused before entering the rest of the slug to look back at the entry portal, just as he had in the projection from right before Japhus' death.

What happened next caused many in the room to gasp. Within the projection, Valissa entered and immediately approached the console to tap it several times. The projection flickered and disappeared.

"It ends there because you ended it. Undoubtedly to save the portion you planned to use later on," said Aethelgard.

"I'd wondered why you fell so far behind us," said Naimeth, sudden understanding dawning on him. "You were right next to me before we reboarded."

"This proves nothing," said Valissa, tears filling her angry eyes.

"This proves everything," said Actaeon.

"For days she meant to do it," exclaimed Silgish. "Days! Who else were you planning to kill?"

"Fine," snapped Valissa. She leaned forward and withdrew something from under her seat. Grasping it tightly in one hand, she strode forward awash with a sudden calm. "I guess you figured it all out, old man. Too bad you'll never leave this place alive."

Actaeon recognized the item in her hand immediately. It was cylindrical, and a small pin hung from it by a string. A grenado of his own making. And she had armed it. All that was needed now was the impact. The detonation would destroy most of the metal slug and kill them all instantly at this range. "Valissa, do not do anything stupid," he hazarded.

Yanelle drew her sword and Aethelgard drew his writheblade as the young woman approached more closely.

"Stupid?" Valissa lifted the grenado up in front of her face and smiled at it. "The only stupid thing I ever did was thinking that you'd realize my value here. I should've been leading this project. Not her." She pointed with her free hand at Lauryn.

Lauryn stood and spread her hands. "We're engineers, Valissa. We all work together. The best ideas are made when everyone pools their ideas. You were as much a part of this as any of us."

Actaeon moved behind Aethelgard and whispered in the Arbiter's ear. "Keep her talking as long as possible." The longer they kept her occupied, the longer he had to figure out a solution to this problem.

"Sure I was," spat Valissa. "Admit it. I was your lackey. Your flunkey. A drudge that you could dump off the dirty work on."

Aethelgard returned his writheblade to its ceramic scabbard and spread his hands. "That's one thing I hadn't figured out."

"What's that?" asked Valissa, her head spinning to settle her hard gaze upon him.

"I just don't know why such an intelligent young lady as yourself would lower yourself to murder someone and frame Engineer Lauryn. It would appear to me that you had a good situation here," said Aethelgard. "Two highly accomplished engineers willing to train you and involve you in what I'd say is the most exciting technological discovery of our lifetimes. Why risk throwing that away?"

Valissa tensed up as the Arbiter challenged her. She raised her voice as she responded until she was practically yelling. "I'm the smartest one here. Even the great Prince Engineer wasn't able to figure out the Ancients' consoles as well as I could. And I figured it out without that idiot Lost that they brought on. If anything, I should've been Actaeon's protégé, not Lauryn."

"And so, you thought," said Aethelgard in a soothing voice that he hoped would calm the explosive-wielding woman, "that if Lauryn was no longer in the way, you would be the likely replacement as the manager of this project and his new protégé."

"Not just that," said Valissa. "Of course I'd do better. But Lauryn was doing just terribly. For every idea I brought up, she had a reason not to go ahead with it. For every daring new plan that would've advanced this project by leaps and bounds in a matter of hours, she instead slowed things down to an absolute crawl."

"Even the boldest engineering efforts must be tempered with reasonable caution," said Actaeon. "We deal with artifacts and technologies at just the very fringe of our knowledge and capability. An incomplete understanding, a wrong assumption, or even uncertain circumstances could cost someone their life."

"She cares nothing about that last thing, Act," said Lauryn. "Valissa's just a bratty little girl that wants to be the center of attention. Even if she has to kill someone to get there."

"And now she's willing to kill all of us," added Naimeth. "A true zero sum."

Valissa's lips twisted into a scowl and she drew back the grenado as if to throw it at one of them.

Actaeon leapt between her and the others. He held his halberd before him horizontally. "Wait, Valissa. You do not want to do this. There is too much at stake."

"Not for me," she responded with a shake of her head. "Not anymore."

"That is not true," he insisted. "Even if the Arbiters were to sentence you to some sort of captivity, your mind is still valuable to Redemption. Think of the difference you could make in the world. There is every chance that you could eventually redeem yourself from your mistakes here today. Do not throw away all your potential."

Hope crossed Valissa's features for just a moment, but then her face hardened and she shook her head. "That's not how justice in this backward place works. I know better than that. In the next life perhaps?"

The killer scowled then and threw the grenado right at Actaeon's head.

Actaeon dropped his halberd and positioned his hands to catch the grenado. If only he could cushion the impact enough...

All of the lights went off in the vehicle. Their world plunged into darkness.

The grenado slammed into his hands and he felt a click within the device as he closed his fingers around it. The drop trigger must've cracked the luminary within the grenado's shell in half.

And yet, they were still here – alive. The grenado hadn't exploded.

Redemption's Darkest Hour had saved them. Without power, the broken luminary inside had lost the volatility it needed to ignite the slug slime within and trigger the deadly reaction.

That didn't mean that once the Darkest Hour was over it wouldn't explode. And despite its name, the duration of the Darkest Hour was ever uncertain.

And so, as a commotion broke out all around him, Actaeon knelt to retrieve his halberd and crawled his way out of the passenger compartment and toward the engine room.

To his right there was a struggle. It was most likely Aethelgard and Yanelle trying to restrain Valissa.

Deadly burden in hand, Actaeon managed to find the entryway to the engine compartment. There he found one of Japhus' metal boxes. He dumped the contents on the floor and stuck the grenado inside before continuing on his way to the entry room. From there, he climbed down to the floor of the Tubeway and began to run forward into the pitch black of the tunnel.

At least if the mysterious power of the Ancients came back on now, everyone aboard the metal slug wouldn't die – just him.

Into the darkness he ran, counting his paces as he did. He didn't stop until he reached one thousand. Then he knelt down, placing halberd and box on the bottom of the cylindrical tunnel. He pulled the grenado from the box and pulled his dagger from his belt. The housing of the grenado was an interference fit. During assembly, the inner shell was kept cooler than the outer shell so that they would slide together easily. Once a homogenous temperature was reached, the housing would lock together. The design included grooves on the inner housing in case disassembly was required.

It was into one of these grooves that he worked the edge of his dagger. Thusly, he was able to pry the housings apart. It took a long while, but soon enough the two halves were separated. He fished out two large pieces of the broken luminary and threw them ahead down the Tubeway. He tucked the remainder of the grenado into the metal box and closed it again.

It was at that point that he heard what sounded like breathing behind him. It was a huffing sound, like someone winded, but quite low.

With care not to make any noise, he felt on the ground until his fingers touched the shaft of his halberd. He lifted it by the end and swung it in a large arc around himself.

There came a yelp and a cascade of sparks revealed a momentary figure that bowled him over. In the darkness, he hit the ground hard. A warmth spread over the side of his face: blood.

With care, he climbed unsteadily to his feet. Several more times he swung the halberd. This time there was no yelp, but he could swear he heard breathing ahead of him along the tunnel. It was away from the metal slug though. He considered saying something, but doing so would give away his location in the darkness. If it was Valissa, who knew what other weapons she might have?

Instead, he began to back away slowly down the Tubeway toward the slug, careful to step softly. He counted a hundred steps that way. Then two hundred. Then he turned and ran, staying on track by feeling out the bottom of the Tubeway's cylinder. When he hit nine hundred and fifty steps, he slowed down and began to wave his halberd back and forth slowly.

It connected with something on step nine hundred and seventy-nine. He crept forward and found the bulk of the metal slug. The hatch was still open from when he had left, and so he entered and sealed it behind him.

Hands were upon him immediately and wrestled the halberd from his hands. He went limp and put his hands above his head. Another set of hands patted him down before a feminine voice spoke. "Act?"

"Yanelle?" Actaeon hugged her. "Am I glad to see you. Since you are here, I would surmise that you did not capture her."

Yanelle hugged him back for a moment before she stood and pulled her charge to his feet. "You're right, Your Grace. In the confusion, Silgish lunged forward to attack Valissa. Aethelgard and I pounced, of course. But when we managed to subdue and restrain her, it wasn't Valissa. It was the artifact hunter. After that, we all searched the craft and found no one, but the rear hatch was open and you both were missing. So, I stood guard."

"Smart," said Actaeon.

"We searched for the grenado..." started Yanelle.

"I caught it," said Actaeon. "I ran it down the tunnel and disassembled it. Hopefully, I did an adequate job."

"Is that you, Actaeon?" came another voice – Aethelgard's.

"Aye, it is," said Actaeon.

"Very smart plan to keep her talking until the Darkest Hour," said the Knight.

"I wish I had so much foresight," admitted Actaeon. "I had only hoped to delay her for long enough to come up with a workable plan."

"Either way, your plan worked. Well done, Engineer," said Aethelgard.

Just then, the lights flickered back on and an explosion shook the metal slug.

The three of them stood, all of them disheveled from their chaotic time in the darkness, and looked at one another in bewilderment.

"What was that?" asked Aethelgard.

"It was close," said Yanelle.

"Let us go see," said Actaeon.

Out in the Tubeway tunnel just outside the metal slug they found the remains of Valissa beside the twisted remnants of Japhus' metal box. She had brought it all the way back to kill them.

"It must have had a fragment of the luminary in it still," said Actaeon. "What terrible luck for her."

"Good luck for us, though," said Yanelle.

"The guilty cannot hide from the hands of justice," said Aethelgard with a thin smile.

His Final Act

THE SCREAMS COULD BE HEARD from as far away as the Sun Chamber. They were even more audible from Saint Torin's Hold, where Actaeon and Eisandre hosted Raedelle's Lords and Ladies of the Conclave. Husband and wife shared a look and then both of them were up and running through the Mirrorholds, toward the sounds of distress.

"It's coming from the Garden of Dancing Water," said the Princess. Her old Arbiter arming sword was in her hand as she ran.

"Aye," said Actaeon, breathing heavily as he rushed to keep up with his wife's pace. He gripped the shaft of his halberd tightly, anticipating battle.

Instead of battle, they found something completely different.

The open air garden just beneath the huge, multi-tiered Garden Terraces was alive with its various patterns of shooting water. Bursts of liquid fired off in satisfying sequences in some fountains, while, in others, streams of water writhed like serpents locked in a mating dance. The room was alive with the phenomena, but not much else.

Actaeon was the first to realize that something was off. He wrapped an arm around Eisandre and held her back. "Wait, love. Something is wrong."

Eisandre shrugged free of his grasp to make sure she could defend herself unimpeded, but she knew well enough to heed his words.

The dark blue gas that clung to the floor in patches came to both of their attention at once. It drifted lazily between the elderstone walls of the various fountains and raised garden beds. The next thing they noticed was the pile of bodies that lay motionless in the center of the water displays. There were ten of them. It was difficult to tell if any were still alive.

Lord Aethelred Ackart of Southward slid to a stop beside them, with Lady Neryl Vanora of Whiterose just several steps behind him. The two members of the Conclave had chased after while the others had sat in surprise.

"Keep everyone out of this room," commanded Eisandre.

Ackart nodded and rushed off to do just so.

The Princess looked to Actaeon for what to do next, at a loss with the situation before her.

Actaeon grinned and chewed his lip as he regarded the scene. "Lady Vanora, have the cooks bring all the raw cliffshard intestines they have."

"Intestines, Your Grace?" Neryl asked.

"Aye," said Actaeon. "They will have them for sausages. We can use them here – they are stronger than pig intestines, or, at least, I hope so. Oh, and have them bring the bellows for the oven hearths. That and..." he considered for a moment, "send someone to fetch as many Altheans as can be found. Tell them to bring all of their thread and wound closure needles. We shall need it. And bowls. Have the cooks bring a few bowls – wooden, if possible."

Neryl's eyes narrowed and the Lady from Whiterose examined the scene before her, with its still bodies and lingering dark blue gas, as if trying to figure out why such a strange collection of things would be needed.

"You heard him," said Eisandre.

Neryl Vanora saluted, fist to chest, and rushed off to follow the fulfill the request.

Together, the Princess and Prince Engineer retreated to the entrance of the room.

When a squad of Arbiters arrived, Actaeon had them stretch their capes across the doorway to prevent any of the deadly, dark blue gas from finding its way back into the Pyramid.

Grabbing one of the Arbiters who had relinquished his cape, Actaeon spoke quickly. "Bring a team down to the open market below and evacuate the lowest lying sections of the marketplace. The gas in there is heavier than air. If any spilled over, it will go there and poison people."

There was fear in the young Arbiter's eyes, but he nodded and rushed off.

A crowd began to gather farther along both sides of the eastern tunnels. Eisandre fell into her old habits and directed the Arbiters who didn't have their hands full with the cape barrier to help her keep the gawkers at bay.

Amidst the chaos, Actaeon hefted his halberd, regarding it in a new light. "Aye, this will do."

With a grin, he knelt and laid the polearm before him before unstrapping his recurve bow from the back of his jacket. He stepped between the string and the limbs and used his body to bend the wood and slip the string into place. Once done, he laid the bow across the shaft of the halberd so that it was perpendicular to it. Then he pulled a coil of glass rope from his lower right jacket pocket and lashed the two together before cutting the excess cordage with his dagger.

"Bring that top cape over here," he called out.

The two Arbiters stretching the top cape across the doorway into the gardens looked at one another before bringing it over to the Prince Engineer. Wasting no time, Actaeon stabbed the bottom center of the cape with the halberd's blade and then tied the bottom corners to the ends of the recurve bow. Finally, he tied the narrow top of the cape as close to the butt of the weapon as he could.

As he was finishing, Lady Vanora arrived with a pair of Altheans and the rest of the items he'd requested. To the healers' consternation, he set them upon stitching the intestines together carefully, after nesting one end inside the other. "Pick a direction and then put that end inside the next consistently. The far end of that will be the side that goes into the room."

As they started, Actaeon grabbed a bowl.

"I'm not sure what you're doing, Your Grace," said Lady Vanora, wrinkling her nose, "but it sure does stink like a slug monster."

"That it does," said Actaeon, as he worked to carve a hole into the bottom of the wooden bowl. "Unfortunately, it is the quickest thing I can think of to save the people in there. It will be a difficult stench to breathe in."

Once he finished the large hole, he used the tip of the dagger to hastily carve four more holes – a pair on either side of the bowl's perimeter. Through these he laced the remaining section of glass rope, tying knots to lock it into place. From there, he grabbed the end of the intestine length and fed it through the larger hole in the bowl bottom. He split the intestinal wall inside the bowl and tied the ends through two of the edge holes. He pulled some lenses wrapped in a felt cloth from his top left jacket pocket, freeing them from the cloth and dumping them back into the pocket. The cloth he used to cover the intestinal opening and pad the edges of the bowl. It would have to do as a filter. He unstoppered his flask of water and used it to dampen the cloth around the edges and the place where the intestines entered the bowl.

"What are you doing?" asked Eisandre, who had returned to his side.

"With any luck, this will help me breath clean... well, not clean, but, at least, not poisonous air until I can extricate the victims from their unfortunate circumstance," Actaeon explained. "Can you pump the bellows, Eis? We should not leave them in there any longer or they will not have a chance."

"Show me what to do," she said.

Actaeon shoved the bellows tip in the other end of the intestine chain and began to pump. He had to squeeze the material against the tip while he pumped to prevent air from leaking out around the edges. Once he handed it her, Eisandre began to pump and he lifted the bowl to his face to test it out. The first breath of air nearly caused him to vomit inside the thing, tears streaming down his face.

"By the Fallen, this is going to be horrendous," he said, pulling his goggles down over his eyes.

"First time I've ever seen someone try to save someone by breathing cliffshard shit," said Neryl Vanora. "Saints guide you."

With a grimace, Actaeon slipped the bowl over his head and drew the glass rope straps tight. Lifting his improvised halberd fan, he turned to Eisandre, who nodded. He bit his lip to provide a counter sensation to the waves of nausea he felt from breathing the foul air.

Without delay, he waved the last pair of Arbiters aside. They pulled the cape back and Actaeon began to fan the dark blue, toxic gas with his halberd fan. The gas swirled and cascaded away, and into the room behind it he pushed forth.

Behind him, the Arbiters pulled the cape back across the doorway while the lengths of intestines fed underneath them, following the Prince Engineer into the room.

Fanning the deadly gas away and toward the outer wall, Actaeon advanced as quickly as he was able. Tears streamed from his eyes to pool at the base of his goggles as he somehow resisted the urge to vomit.

When he reached the nearest victim, he snagged the man's belt with the hooked end of his halberd and turned to bring him out. The Arbiters reached in to pull the man to safety once he reached the doorway, and Actaeon turned back for the others.

Most of the victims had something he was able to snag with the hooked end of the halberd blade. A dress hem, a belt, a cuffed trouser leg, or even the laces of a boot. One way or another, he dragged all ten of the lifeless bodies to safety.

Then he stepped through the doorway as the Arbiters restored the protective cape barrier behind him, removed his improvised mask and promptly vomited the contents of his lunch all over the floor of the eastern tunnels. That done, he stepped clear of the mess and rolled onto his back, tears continuing to fill his goggles.

Eisandre rushed over to check on him. "Are you alright, Act?"

Actaeon took a deep breath of fresh air. "Aye, Eis. Now that I can breathe clean air again."

A pair of boots came to a stop next to his head. "Fine work here, my engineer friend." Above him stood the Knight Investigator, stroking his beard with one hand as he regarded Actaeon. "I have the culprit in custody already. He used the Pyramid's ventilation system to deliver the poison in plain view of dozens of people. Care to join me in questioning him?" He offered a hand to help Actaeon to his feet.

Actaeon grinned up at his friend weakly and accepted his hand.

Seraeta caught up with Actaeon and Aethelgard just before they made it to the Rainbow Room. The old Althean reached out to touch Actaeon's hand. "I thought you'd like to know that we may be able to save three of them thanks to your quick thinking. It'll be touch and go for a while, but with any luck they'll make some sort of recovery."

"Thank you for letting me know," said Actaeon, scratching the back of his right hand through his fingerless glove. "No hope for the other seven then?"

"Too much damage to their airway. I don't have to tell you it was a caustic gas," said Seraeta, matter-of-factly. "There's naught else you could've done."

"There's something else we can do right this moment," said Aethelgard, gesturing to the doorway. "If you'll please excuse us, Matron."

The Althean huffed at the Arbiter. "Oh, don't let me bother you then." She turned back to Actaeon. "If you learn what was used in the attack, get me the information. It may well help us."

"Aye, Matron. No bother at all." Actaeon grinned.

The old Althean let out a guffaw and turned on her heel to head off.

"What is it?" Aethelgard arched a brow when Actaeon fixed him with a look. When his friend just smirked, he tugged his short beard and shrugged. "Come, come. There's no time to waste. If our saboteur has more traps set to spring, I intend to find out before they can be sprung."

A posted Arbiter stepped aside, and the door slid open to admit them.

In the center of the conical chamber sat a fat, disheveled man in a plain wooden chair. He looked up nervously as the pair of investigators walked in.

The walls were flickering between dull green and sky blue in a sickening manner.

"I am the Knight Investigator in charge of this case," said Aethelgard. "My associate and I have questions for you, which you will answer succinctly and honestly. If you aren't being straightforward with us, we will know. Let's start with your name."

The bewildered man leaned forward against the bindings that held him to the chair. "I..." His eyes bulged as he looked all around at the flashing room before his eyes settled back on the Knight Investigator. "I... don't know." His eyes drifted down to the back of one hand that was bound to the armrest and he bit his lip and flexed his fingers, shaking his head.

"Nonsense," said Aethelgard. "A quick call into the Thyrian embassy and I shall have your identity. Hiding it is futile. I already know you're a sailor given the rope calluses on your hands and the unique wear on the soles of your boots that shows you're no stranger to climbing rigging."

The man opened and closed his hand, staring at it like he'd never seen it before. Around them, the room continued to flash. Blue then green, blue then green. "A sailor?"

"Quit playing stupid," snapped Aethelgard. "A sailor indeed, and a bosun at that. The marks on your teeth show where you're chewing on that damned ear-piercing whistle all day. How long do you think it'll take for the Supreme Captain to tell me who's the fattest bosun in his fleet?"

The man looked down at his ponderous gut as though seeing it for the first time. The room kept flashing.

"My gods, man," said Aethelgard. "You really don't know, do you?" He cracked the knuckles of one hand. "Well, perhaps you can tell me why you killed all those people in the garden then?"

"Ahhh..." The man's cry of despair coincided with the room's hue shifting to a deep purple. He squeezed his eyes shut and tears pooled at the corners. "I... don't know. I did though, didn't I? I killed them. I killed them? Why would I do such a thing?!" The last sentence was a shout.

The interrogation was interrupted when the door slid open and another Knight Arbiter rushed in. Bergum sof Matine saluted Aethelgard sharply and frowned. "Sorry to interrupt, sir. There's been another murder."

Aethelgard clicked his tongue. "Outside, please."

When the door slid shut behind the three of them, Aethelgard scolded him. "You know better than to say anything pertinent in front of a suspect." Before the other Arbiter could muster an apology, he said, "Don't make that mistake again. Now explain to us what happened."

"Uh, right, sir," blustered Bergum. "A woman walked right into Arbiter Pyramid Command covered in blood. She stabbed two people to death in the baths. She even brought the murder weapon with her."

Aethelgard arched a brow and glanced at Actaeon, who shrugged. "Her disposition?" he asked the other Arbiter.

"Honestly?" asked Bergum. "She was really confused. Couldn't answer any of our questions. We took the dagger from her and put her in your office."

Aethelgard pulled the lenses from his face and his eyes bulged out in bewilderment as he regarded Bergum. He bit his tongue and restored the lenses to his face before taking a deep breath. "You put the bloody woman in *my office?*"

"Under guard," said Bergum, quickly. "So you could speak to her."

"Could he not speak to her just as well in a holding room?" inquired Actaeon with a grin.

Bergum lifted a hand and slapped his forehead before dragging his palm down his face. "Right, sir. Yes, so... I'm really quite sorry."

Aethelgard offered him a thin smile. "Lead the way then, Knight

Arbiter. And don't be quick to leave when we're done. You'll be mopping the floors in there."

"I must have killed them," said the woman from her perch atop a chair in the corner of Aethelgard's utilitarian office. She was dressed in the silken red robes of an Ajmani priestess and the front was dark with drying blood. "I don't know if it's true – gods only know. But I was holding the bloody blade. And so, I came here as quickly as I could to turn myself in."

"Do you have any memory of who you are or why you would kill those people?" asked Aethelgard.

The woman pressed her blood-stained hands together and touched them to her lips, squeezing her eyes shut. "By my clothing, I might be a priestess? I don't recall. Everything is so hazy. It's horrifying to think that I took those lives. How could one possibly atone for such an act?"

Actaeon leaned over to whisper to his friend. "What were those green and blue flashes in the Rainbow Room?"

Aethelgard led him to the opposite side of the office and spoke in a hushed tone. "Confusion like I've never before witnessed in there. Mild or moderate confusion I've seen in there, but that man was experiencing such severe confusion that it pained and even frightened him."

"Then there is something going on that relates these two cases?" suggested Actaeon.

"Precisely my thoughts as well," said Aethelgard.

A knock on the door interrupted them.

When Aethelgard opened it, Sentinel Arbiter Corvin sof Haringar stood there. "What is it, Sentinel?"

"You must come with me at once, Knight Investigator. An Arbiter has been poisoned," said Corvin.

"You must be kidding me," said Aethelgard. "This is getting ridiculous."

"Related?" asked Actaeon.

Before Aethelgard could reply, Corvin continued. "It was the Matron. She poisoned the Sea Lounge guard and is up in the control room above. Somehow she accessed the lift." He turned to Actaeon then. "It's a good thing you're here, Your Grace. We might need your help with this."

"The Matron?" asked Actaeon. Now it was his turn to feel confused. "You mean Seraeta?"

"Is there another Matron?" Corvin spread his hands.

"And even broader this web weaves," said Aethelgard. "Let's go then."

When they arrived in the Sea Lounge, they were met by two more Arbiters who tended to another of their comrades, who writhed in agony on the floor, clutching his stomach.

Actaeon led the way to the scaffolding that brought them up through the broken elderstone opening to the corridor that led to a massive chamber above.

It was raining outside, and it poured in through the broken ceiling on the northern side of the room. The giant pillars and pipes in that area gleamed with a sheen of water upon them.

Lines of luminaries inset into the floor led through ancient slagged metal to a square column in the center of the room. Atop the column was the little control room that Actaeon was all too familiar with. The lift was already up there, and was in a locked out state – he could tell by the dull red glow of the luminaries.

"Seraeta!" Actaeon called up as he slid to a stop at the base of the column with Corvin and Aethelgard several paces behind. "What are you doing up there?"

"That's not Seraeta right now," muttered Aethelgard.

Actaeon nodded. "Worth a shot though. We must get up there. There is no telling how many people she could kill if she can decipher the consoles in that room."

"So, how can we get up there?" asked the Sentinel Arbiter as the three of them gazed up at the cube far above their heads.

As if in answer to Actaeon's fears, one of the pressure relief valves on the other side of the chamber sputtered and whistled before it began to spew an invisible jet of steam that shot across the open room until it hit the opposite angled wall where it turned to a white gas that began to fill that side of the chamber.

"Would it be prudent to evacuate the Pyramid?" asked Corvin.

Actaeon pulled his goggles down over his eyes. "Aye. That would be advisable. Though I doubt we have enough time."

The Sentinel Arbiter nodded and started back toward the Sea Lounge at a sprint. Seconds after he disappeared down into the tunnel below, an iris opened in the far wall, and boiling hot water began to pour into the room.

"What's your plan, Engineer?" asked Aethelgard, taking a few steps to the side as the first rush of boiling water rolled against the toe of his boot. The water began to circle the hole that led down to the tunnel that Corvin had gone into like the drain of a giant bath. "A lot of lives depend on you now."

"Have I mentioned that I am extremely tired of this room?" asked Actaeon with a grin. He scratched the back of his right hand through its fingerless glove and stared up at the cube that topped the column high above him.

"Even so," said Aethelgard. "It would be best to come up with a plan sooner rather than later."

Actaeon's eyes flicked about as he considered all of his options. "It would be preferable not to kill Seraeta." Killing the leader of the Altheans wouldn't be the best move – though he already knew she'd be okay with the sacrifice. No, there had to be a better option. "Give me your writheblade," he concluded.

Aethelgard knew better than to ask, and he pulled his belt free and handed the scabbard to Actaeon.

Taking the artifact weapon, Actaeon unsheathed it from its ceramic scabbard to reveal a crackling blade that reeked of ozone. He wasted no time in cutting into the luminary line at his feet. With precision, he cut through the material perpendicularly in two different places sending up gouts of steam from the thin layer of boiling water that now covered the floor. He kicked it on one side with his boot, which cantilevered the broken material upward so he could grasp it and fling it aside. Beneath was what he'd hoped for – a thick glass rope that glowed with the luminary material inset within it. He assessed the height of the control room column and then began to cut a gauge through one side of the top layer of material that encased the luminary rope into the floor. He followed along, cutting as he went with the violently crackling artifact weapon. All the way to where the inset luminary line disappeared under the metal slag, he went along, cutting his line. When he hit the slag, he cut a deep perpendicular slice to sever the cable beneath. Once that was done, he started back in the other direction, this time slicing through the other side of the floor inset.

Once he reached Aethelgard again, he grinned and made another deep, perpendicular cut. Next to this, he quickly plunged his hand down to grab the luminary rope beneath. He winced as his hand made contact with the scalding water, but he came away with the end of the luminary glass rope. Sticking the free end over his shoulder, he shook his hand dry.

He handed the writheblade back to Aethelgard. "Gather the cable and bring it over here." From his shoulder, he pulled the recurve bow free, and, flexing it slightly, he stepped between the arms and the string to slip the string into place for use. That done, he drew a single arrow from the quiver built into the back of his jacket and fished a roll of thread out from his lower right pocket. This he tied to the rear of the arrow just in front of the fletching, using a pair of constrictor knots. After unspooling the full length of thread, he tied the other end around his thigh.

Stepping back, Actaeon narrowed his eyes to size up the shot and, after nocking the arrow, fired it in a gentle arc that passed over the lift just beneath one of the railings. The arrow jerked and then swung downward to crash into the floor after it reached the end of the thread's length.

"Here is your coil," said Aethelgard, arriving at his side to hand it over. "Best hurry. At first I was appreciating the warmth on my toes, but it grows difficult to breathe in here."

"With any luck, this will get me up there," said Actaeon, as he removed the thread from his thigh and tied it to the end of the glass rope with a sheet bend. "After that, I will have to figure out something on the fly to disable her."

"Please don't tell me you're relying on luck for this," said the Knight Investigator.

"Every endeavor has a level of uncertainty to it," explained Actaeon as he handed the rope coil back to Aethelgard. "A proper analysis can reduce the risk, but in situations such as these, there just is not the time for it. Here, hold this high and feed it out as I pull the other end. It will help keep weight off the knot as much as we are able."

"Right..." said Aethelgard, eyeing the Prince Engineer with skepticism.

Retrieving the arrow, Actaeon began to pull the thread downward, careful not to jerk or tug it excessively. On Aethelgard's side, the glass rope began to raise and he did his part to feed the coil out slowly above his head.

Once the sheet bend was at the top, it snagged against the bottom lip of the lift. "Walk it a distance out and whip your end to try to clear the knot," Actaeon instructed.

"Aye, I'm already on it." The Knight Investigator whipped the glass rope and a wave rolled up along it that didn't reach the lift. He tried again and it got closer. The third time was a charm though, and the knot jumped up and landed on the lift's surface.

The two men looked at one another and grinned. "Well done," said Actaeon.

Then the thread snapped and both ends came tumbling back down.

"Well, by all cracked Redemption," swore Aethelgard. "By the Fallen – we just had it." He threw the rope to the floor with a steaming splash. "What next then?"

"Time for the backup plan," said Actaeon, gazing up at the control room with hands on his hips. The water was so high that it was filling their boots now.

"Which is?" asked Aethelgard.

"May I borrow your writheblade again?"

Aethelgard handed it over. "For what this time?"

"I will use it to cut the control room tower down," explained Actaeon, letting out a sharp crackle as he unsheathed the weapon.

Aethelgard tugged at his short beard and arched a brow at his friend. "Doesn't that violate your 'not kill the Matron' plan?"

Actaeon hefted the writheblade in his hand and considered the square column that the control room sat upon. "Right – that is a problem."

"So, what then?" asked Aethelgard.

Raising the writheblade over his shoulder, Actaeon then hurled it up at the control room.

"What the –" started the Knight Investigator, but then he was running away to avoid getting hit by the deadly artifact weapon when it came back down.

Instead of coming back down, it flew through the window of the doorway to land inside the control room proper. Sparks showered back out from the writheblade's impact with the floor.

Aethelgard ran back to Actaeon, who was still standing there gazing up at the control room and grinning like a complete idiot. He grabbed him by the collar of his jacket and shook him hard. "Are you out of your damned mind, man? That could've come right back down and killed one of us! What were you thinking?"

"Wait for it," said Actaeon, the stupid grin still plastered upon his face as his emerald gaze was still transfixed upon the control room above their heads.

"Wait for what?" snapped Aethelgard, shaking him again. "What has happened to the others – is it happening to you too? Answer me, damn it! Or I'll strike that damned grin right off your face."

"You'll do nothing of the sort!"

The voice of the Matron came from far above their heads.

Aethelgard let go and spun about to join Actaeon in staring upward.

"That's better," said Seraeta, from where she peered over the edge of the lift. "Now, can you please tell me how to get down? And why I'm up here in the first place? And where did this writheblade come from? And who am I, even?"

Aethelgard offered Actaeon an incredulous look before sudden understanding dawned on his features.

"She was possessed by an artifact," said Actaeon.

"Darkest Hour take you," said Aethelgard, dumbfounded. "You're a genius, Act." This time when he reached out, he embraced his friend. "I had suspected as such, but I didn't think to interrupt it like that."

"Not a genius," said Actaeon, patting his friend on the back and grinning. "Just a person with the right past experiences to deal with the situation at hand. It is all very much like how Yonniker and the Veiled One took over the minds of people, excepting their manipulations never removed the memories of their enslaved hosts." He turned back to Seraeta. "I am glad you are okay, Matron Seraeta. Now listen carefully – I will walk you through the sequence of steps you will need to take to put an end to this disaster."

Once disaster was averted and the remainder of the steaming water was draining down into the tunnels below, Seraeta descended down the lift to join them. She handed Aethelgard back the writheblade, the weapon awkward in her hands. The Arbiter gladly returned the artifact back to its protective scabbard. Then his face went white.

Over the healer's white robes hung a pendant that he'd never seen before on an Althean. And yet, it was deadly familiar to him.

Seraeta reached out to feel his forehead. "You look as though you might pass out. We'd best get you to a place you can lie down." Despite having no memory of who she was, the Matron's healing instincts still kicked in.

Reaching out, the Knight Investigator lifted her pendant in his hand.

"What's that?" asked Seraeta.

Actaeon's breath caught as well as he saw what was in Aethelgard's hand. "Ruinlock…"

It was a broken artifact lock. In fact, it was the very type used to lock away access panels such as the one up in the control room.

"That name?" The Matron laughed. "Don't tell me the pair of you are afraid of a children's bogeyman bedtime story."

"A bedtime story," said Aethelgard, his eyes haunted. "Right."

Actaeon had to practically run to keep up with the Knight Investigator on the way back to Arbiter Pyramid Command. "There has been no trace of him for nine years now. Suddenly he resurfaces and is taking over people like the Starborn did? Are you certain it is him?"

"It's him," said Aethelgard. "I felt something strange in my gut when we first started working this case and now it's all clear."

"But why all these different attacks?" Actaeon struggled to keep up with his friend, who didn't seem to feel the normal pain in his knee as he raced ahead. "What was the motive?"

"To flush us out, of course," said Aethelgard with certainty. "Ruinlock wants the ones who took him down. Consider the circumstances – all cleverly designed to guide us to this point. The poison gas incident near Saint Torin's Hold that he knew would draw your swift response. Then, while we were still involved in the first incident, a second one to keep us from getting too far along in our conclusions. And finally, before we could draw any solid evidence from the second, a third incident to bring us to one of his tests – one that he undoubtedly hoped would best us, though you thwarted him again, Actaeon." Aethelgard slowed a bit so that Actaeon could catch up and walk side by side with him. "Even now, I'm certain he's getting ready to spring the next trap upon us."

When they arrived back at his office, Aethelgard wasted no time in tearing open the bloody priestess' robes to reveal another broken artifact lock hiding beneath, against her brassiere.

And, when they arrived back at the Rainbow Room to visit the sailor, Aethelgard found yet another calling card to Ruinlock beneath the sailor's threadbare tunic.

"Give me some time, Act," said Aethelgard, after they'd exited the interrogation room. "Don't go too far though. I shall send word to the Raedellean Hold once I find something."

"Would it not be better if I accompanied you?" asked Actaeon.

Aethelgard waved his hand dismissively. "Not at all. I work better on my own for these tasks. You'd only get in my way. I mustn't have a distraction. Now it is time for me to operate within my expertise. Trust me, and I shall contact you shortly."

Actaeon returned to Saint Torin's Hold to update Eisandre. That night, they slept together in their private quarters, and she comforted him from his concerns in the way only his wife could.

A knock at the door woke them both before dawn.

Eisandre insisted on answering, her sword in hand, just in case.

Before her stood Aethelgard. The Knight Investigator looked worse for the wear. Dried mud was caked on up to his knees and clung to the bottom fringe of his cloak. Dirt was even smeared across one of his cheeks.

The Princess eyed the man before her. "You look like you fell into a pig pen."

"No matter," said the Arbiter with a dismissive wave of his hand. "Is the Engineer here?"

Eisandre nodded and Aethelgard stepped in past her to enter the room before she could react. She grunted in disapproval, but closed the door behind him.

"Act, wake up," he said, his cobalt eyes shaking with excitement behind their lenses. "I've sniffed out the trail. I know where to find Ruinlock."

"Oh?" Actaeon sat up in bed, bare-chested, and arched a brow at his friend. "Where?"

"None other than the Song of Sisters," he explained. "Every one of our hapless, lock-necklaced criminals frequented the establishment earlier in the day."

"I had not released how muddy the Song was these days," said Actaeon, pulling a tunic over his head.

"Muddy?" A glance down at his clothes brought a thin smile to

Aethelgard's face. "That you mean. Right. One never knows where investigative paths might take them."

Retrieving his halberd and throwing on his jacket, Actaeon grinned. "A muddy Song then. Understood."

"The preferences of the nobility have changed," noted Eisandre with amusement.

"Hurry up, now. We must strike while the iron's hot with this one."

"And what if it is a trap?" Actaeon ran a hand through his bed hair to straighten it out and, in the process, let out a big yawn.

"Of course it is a trap," said Aethelgard.

Everyone in the Song of the Sisters slept as the pair of investigators crept in.

Aethelgard had instructed the small squad of Arbiters along with Eisandre and her Companions to remain outside until they were called for. "Be prepared to respond with haste when one of us summons you."

Inside, the confused bellhop was sent to retrieve the proprietor after entering a note into his log.

When a flustered Cassanthia arrived, Aethelgard explained the situation and demanded a keycard, which she begrudgingly handed over. "You had best be correct about this – lest I lose all the trust my customers have in me."

"There lies no doubt in my mind." Aethelgard pocketed the key.

"How could you know the exact room?" whispered Actaeon. "Did you track them right to the door, without going in?"

"It was all much simpler than that, my engineer friend," said Aethelgard, lifting a flint to his pipe. "Mind if I borrow your dagger?"

Actaeon arched a brow. "Forget your own?" He drew his and passed it over.

Aethelgard shrugged. "Must've lost it in the mud." He struck the flint several times and then puffed on the guaraja before handing the dagger back. That done, he led the way down the hallway toward the room in question, puffing from his pipe as he went. "We must be exceedingly quiet now." His voice was hushed.

The inset luminaries were dimmed to their lowest setting for the nighttime. The hall ahead was interrupted only by an occasional lounge that shared part of the sloped outer glass of the Pyramid's pinnacle. At this time of night, all the lounges were empty.

"Tell me what was so simple about determining the room," whispered Actaeon. "I know you well enough by now to know there is an interesting method to everything you do. I would much like to understand how you came to the conclusion."

Aethelgard's chuckle was barely audible. "Did you not notice the bellhop making note in his logbook? Well, all three of our offenders were logged with a description and the room they were visiting. You see, in a reputable business like this one, all visitors are logged. After I tracked them all here, that gave me the final location without having to scrutinize the halls and risk giving myself away."

"Of course," said Actaeon. "Obvious…"

Aethelgard shushed him and drew to a stop before the room.

"Ready your boltcaster," he advised. "And don't be afraid to use my writheblade if you need to."

"Why would I –" Actaeon's question was interrupted as the Knight Investigator tapped the keycard against the lock and slid the door open.

The scene within looked like it had encountered one of Actaeon's grenados. Down feathers from the ripped up mattress were scattered everywhere. A cold breeze blew into the room from a perfect circle that had somehow been cut through the thick elderglass. Most of the furniture was toppled and pushed up against the walls. In the center of the room, the bed frame was tipped up on its head and a person was bound upside-down to the bottom of it. Her long red hair hung down to mingle with the feathers on the carpet.

It took Actaeon a moment to realize that it was Yanelle. "By the Fallen…" It was all he had time to say before Aethelgard reached beneath his cloak to draw his knife. The Arbiter pulled Actaeon roughly toward him and stabbed him multiple times in the chest before throwing him to the floor in the room below the bound Companion.

Each blow brought a bloom of pain and, when he hit the ground, Actaeon's breath was knocked from his body.

The Knight Investigator didn't give him a moment of reprieve though. Aethelgard slammed the door shut and took three steps forward to kick Actaeon solidly in the face.

Pain flared to life in his jaw and he let go of his halberd. Tears in his eyes, Actaeon tried to climb to his feet, but was caught by another boot in the ribs.

Shouts sounded from out in the corridor. The banging on the door that followed was loud enough to wake everyone in the Song.

Aethelgard stood over him and laughed in a way that made Actaeon certain his friend was not himself. "Well, well, Actaeon Rellios Caliburn... The Prince Engineer... eh? I don't see your engineering helping you now. Do you?" He lifted the dagger to his eyes and poked it with his other hand. The blade flexed, made from some sort of rubber material. "Aethel thought he was so clever." Tossing the fake blade aside, he knelt easily to retrieve the halberd, testing the heft of it in his hands before turning the blade on Actaeon. "Too bad it didn't make a difference. Fitting, huh? To meet your end on the blade of your own weapon?"

Pain flared throughout Actaeon's body and his vision was filled with stars. Despite that, out of his periphery, he caught Yanelle's wink just beyond Aethelgard's legs.

"I suppose you figure this ends it, Ruinlock?" Actaeon said, in an effort to delay the inevitable.

"That's about how I see it," said Aethelgard. "You've done quite enough damage. There is an order to things that you nearly toppled. But all that is past now. My control of this will resume and your meddling will be naught but a bad memory. One that shall be erased soon enough – you see, it is the winners who write the histories, and history will not remember the Actaeon who genocided an entire Dominion well."

"You know that is not true," said Actaeon with a frown that sent a sharp pain lancing down his neck. "The Veiled One activated the artifact that destroyed Czeryn."

Aethelgard laughed someone else's laugh once more. "And yet, you were instrumental in its activation. You may trust in one truth – the people of the future will learn the histories that I *decide* they will learn. Bye, Actaeon Rellios Caliburn. You were useful once, but your time is over." He lifted the halberd and thrust it forward to open Actaeon's throat with its blade.

Before the killing blow could land, the Companion shifted her hips forward and the entire bedframe toppled down atop the Arbiter, striking him in the head and sending him sprawling across the carpet before the frame, Companion and all, landed atop him with a thud.

With the frame pinning him against the floor, Aethelgard reached out to grab the halberd that had tumbled to the side. Before he could, Actaeon climbed to his feet and stomped down on his hand. "Nobody," started Actaeon, rubbing his jaw, "has a monopoly on the truth. Not even you, Ruinlock. No matter how deeply it is hidden. No matter how blanketed it might be with lies. No matter how many have been incensed against it."

With a grin, Actaeon reached down to Aethelgard's left hip, which stuck out from the side of the bedframe. "Whether you like it or not, the truth always comes into the light." Wrapping his fingers around the hilt, he pulled the writheblade from its ceramic scabbard.

It crackled to life in Actaeon's hand and suddenly Aethelgard was free of Ruinlock's possession. The Knight Investigator brought his hand to his forehead and howled in pain.

Setting the writheblade down, Actaeon winced at the pain throughout his body as he bent to lift the bedframe up onto its side. It revealed Yanelle, now bound sideways to the frame, looking dazed after she landed on her head.

Wasting no time, Actaeon cut her loose and knelt beside the woman who served as his protector. "Thank you. Even when restrained, you manage to save my life."

"Back at you," she said with an awkward smile. "Though, maybe you can tell me why I'm here? And... who I am?"

Actaeon frowned and nodded. "Do not worry, Yanelle. I will help you through this."

The door slid open with a shriek as the group of Arbiters and Companions outside finally forced their way in. Eisandre led them forward and they canvassed the room, swords drawn.

Actaeon looked up at her as he worked his sore jaw. "It was definitely a trap."

"And you're surprised?" Eisandre eyed him.

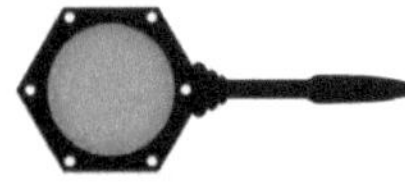

As the morning sun began to trickle through the prisms built into the Pyramid's pinnacle and refracted down into the vast Sun Chamber below, everyone gathered on semi-circular elderstone benches that were set into the thick, translucent floor where one of the big staircases terminated.

"And you're saying I'm some sort of investigator?" Aethelgard rubbed his head where it had slammed into the ground and winced at the fresh bruise on his hand.

"A Knight Investigator," said Actaeon, seated next to his friend. "We are working together to pursue a deadly criminal who calls himself Ruinlock."

"Right," said Aethelgard. "Now that name sounds familiar. It scares the piss out of me."

Farther along the curve of the bench, Eisandre and the other two Companions sat with Yanelle, trying to jar her memories.

Arrayed about them, in a rough circle, were the Knight Arbiters who had accompanied them up into the Song of the Sisters. They were, one and all, keeping a look out for any signs of attack from someone controlled by Ruinlock, including among one another.

"Keep your piss inside you," said Actaeon with a grin that he quickly traded for a wince. "We need to have you sharp again in order to track him down and put a stop to this."

"Tracking!" Aethelgard's face lit up with delight. "Now there's a topic I *know* something about. There are clues everywhere. Care to bring me back to this place where you say I became possessed and attacked you? If there's something to be found, I'll find it for you." The Knight Investigator climbed eagerly to his feet.

After Actaeon shared a look with Eisandre, she nodded for him to go and returned her attention to Yanelle.

Once in front of the room that was the scene of the crime, Aethelgard wasted no time in throwing himself down to the carpet. He peered at the floor intently.

Actaeon knelt and reached into the man's vest to find his magnifier. He handed it over to him after demonstrating how the inset luminaries could be flicked on and off – the Prince Engineer's own design.

"Right... thanks," said Aethelgard. "Feels familiar in my hand now that I hold it."

Actaeon used the keycard on the room lock and slid the door open.

After crawling around some more, both inside and out, Aethelgard clicked his tongue and sat against the wall to inspect the soles of his boots. "Yours now..." When Actaeon offered his own boots, the Arbiter scrutinized them similarly. "Hmm... I can tell it wasn't Companion Yanelle. The signs were nowhere near her."

"What signs?" asked Actaeon.

Snapping his fingers, Aethelgard raced along at a half crawl, half stoop. "Follow me!" He forgot his cane beside the door and Actaeon snatched it up before chasing after him.

The owner of the Song, Cassanthia, was at the front desk when they arrived. She let out a frustrated sigh when the Knight Investigator crawled up to it. "We have standards here you know..."

"Oh?" said Aethelgard, glancing up. He adjusted the lenses on his face. "Well, they don't appear to apply to your carpet – it's right filthy down here. I'd suppose the guests don't notice given the elaborate pattern, but you know all this gets kicked up and people breathe it in, right?"

Cassanthia huffed, her angular features burning red. "You may show yourself out at once!"

Waving his hands before him, Aethelgard blinked up at her. "Oh, I'm not complaining by any means. You see, my friend here and I, we're tracking someone down. The dirty carpets in the room and the corridors were both a great help. Had you swept them regularly, I might not have found as obvious a trace of the person we're searching for, or even that they had been frequenting the room for the better part of an arc of the moon. Please, do continue your current cleaning regimen. It will prove quite helpful if we have to come back here."

A coterie of Niwian nobility arrived behind them as Aethelgard was speaking. The leader, a woman in a dress that threatened to swallow up the Knight if she stepped any closer, murmured to her followers in undisguised disgust.

"Ah, madam..." Aethelgard spun to face the new arrivals from his place down on the carpet. "Please keep your distance. The giant broom you call a dress is disturbing the evidence. If you are looking for something to do with it, perhaps you can take a few passes down the room corridors. Shattered Redemption knows, they could use it – absolutely filthy."

The Niwian woman gasped in horror at the insult. "Come," she said, turning to her group. "We shall find a room to rent in the Hives rather than spend one more lifebeat here!" That said, she marched out with her followers in tow.

That was it for Cassanthia. She rounded the desk like a woman possessed to stand before Aethelgard. Her arm snapped up to point at the door. "Get! Out!"

Barely containing his laughter, Actaeon nodded and ushered Aethelgard along. "Come on, now. See if you can pick up the trail outside."

The Arbiter nodded and scurried his way along like an animal on three limbs, his free hand holding the magnifier lens between his eye and the floor ahead. "Gotta say, this pain in my right knee is unworldly. Makes this all quite difficult."

Reaching into his jacket, Actaeon withdrew a small half-through bottle and passed it down. "Drink this. It will help with the pain. Come to think of it..." He unstoppered it and swigged half of it himself. "Here, you can have half. Thank yourself for kicking me in the face for my taking the other half." He rubbed his sore jaw that had begun to swell.

"If I understand correctly, it wasn't me who kicked you in the face though, was it?" Aethelgard accepted the medicine and quaffed it anyway before handing the empty bottle back. "No matter. Any help is appreciated." With a wince, he drew to his feet. "The pulls at the rug changed to nicks in the floor. By my estimation – and I've no idea how much that's worth – the person in question, this Ruinlock, if you will, has some sort of sharp metal component that is either attached, or broke through one of the soles of their shoes. Does that mean anything to you?"

Despite the pain, Actaeon grinned. "Aye. During our last encounter with Ruinlock in the palace at Rust, he lost a leg while using one of his artifacts to escape us."

Aethelgard whistled and snapped his fingers. "Perfect. So then I would figure that you surmise he has some sort of prosthetic leg?"

"Right," agreed Actaeon. "And I would bet it is an artifact leg at that, knowing Ruinlock and his capabilities."

Snapping his fingers again, Aethelgard nodded. "Right. Now you're talking. The strides didn't quite seem right to me for a prosthetic. Fake limbs don't tend to trace the same walking path as real ones do. But now, an artifact one could, right?"

"Indeed, it could," Actaeon agreed, leaning heavily upon his halberd. He held out the cane and Aethelgard took it, examining it awkwardly, before tucking it over one of his shoulders.

"Carry on then. We're on his most recent path," said Aethelgard. "You say you're an engineer, right?" He led the way at a walk. They were out of the Song and into the greater Pyramid beyond now. Still, he used the luminaries built into his magnifier lens to shine light upon the floor, looking for the telltale nicks and scratches as he followed the trail.

"That is correct," said Actaeon, following a few paces behind.

"How long have we been friends, did you say?" asked Aethelgard.

That took Actaeon a moment, thinking back to their first case together, when the Knight Investigator had sought him out for help figuring out how a suspect had flown away from the Pyramid after committing murder. "For about fifteen years, I would guess."

Aethelgard chuckled. "Fifteen years, eh? Some friend you've been..."

Actaeon arched a brow. "What do you mean? We have been through a lot together – the pair of us."

The Knight Investigator shrugged and patted his bad knee. "Friends with an engineer for fifteen years. Hrm. I dunno – you'd figure he'd offer to design you some sort of knee brace at some point..."

"By the Fallen..." managed Actaeon. "I made you that magnifier!"

"Aren't you supposed to be some sort of solver of problems?" teased Aethelgard. "Fifteen years is a long time. You'd think, seeing me in pain every day, that a problem would've been evident."

Actaeon grinned and jabbed him in the ribs with a finger. "You pain in the ass. Once we are done with this case, I will fashion something for you. It might give you a shock on random occasion though. You know, most these artifacts are somewhat broken after all."

Jumping at the jab, Aethelgard offered him a thin smile. "Let's move fast. Judging by the freshness of the pulls in the carpet of the Song, I don't think he's too far ahead."

The trail brought them all the way down the Pyramid's Northern Descent and into the ruin pile known as the Boneyards.

"We should wait for some of the Arbiters to follow," suggested Actaeon. "I will message Eisandre to see if she can alert them."

"How can you do that?" asked Aethelgard, confused.

Actaeon tapped the small artifact clipped to his ear. "The Thoughtlink allows me to share thoughts with her at any time."

"Intriguing..." said Aethelgard. He held the back of his hand out to his friend. There was a droplet on it. "There's no time to waste. We wouldn't wish to lose this track to rain. It's fresh – within the day. This Ruinlock character can't be too far ahead. If it begins to rain hard though, much of the trail will be washed away."

"So, you are saying..."

"There's no time like the present," said Aethelgard. "And, it indeed may be the only time we get."

Using the butt of his halberd, Actaeon gouged out an arrow shape into the dirt. "Very well. The Princess knows. She, the Companions, and the Arbiters will be but a few steps behind us."

"A good plan," said Aethelgard with his thin smile. "Almost as though I remember what in cracked Redemption I'm supposed to be doing."

Actaeon grinned. "I have faith in your abilities. Memory or no. And I do believe that your memory is gradually returning to you."

"How do you suppose?" asked Aethelgard.

"Well, you started using your cane normally again." The Prince Engineer pointed at it. "That is a start."

"Right," said Aethelgard, looking down at the object in his hand. "Let's hope it all comes back before we must come face to face with our old nemesis." He smiled at that. "Our old nemesis... Indeed, certain things begin to trickle back in."

"That they do."

"Shall we carry on then?"

"Indeed."

The trail Aethelgard followed was not a straightforward one. It wound throughout the Boneyards as if Ruinlock had known they might follow and was trying to lose them. Despite that, and the occasional light drizzle, the Knight Investigator continued to follow the trail with expert skill, tracking their enemy through the ruins.

Even though the ruin pile just appeared to be a chaotic mess to Actaeon, it actually helped Aethelgard follow the path. It wasn't just nicks, and scuffs, and footprints any longer. In addition, there was recently disturbed scree and trampled vegetation that grew out of the disaster zone. If that weren't enough, the possibilities were vastly simplified – there were limited options for a reasonable person traversing the ruins to continue along. Despite it being evident that Ruinlock was trying to lose anyone tailing him, most of the time he chose the easiest path forward and to the northwest. Only on occasion did the trail disappear and the Knight Investigator had to double back to find the signs that Ruinlock had climbed some difficult structure, or slid into a pit of debris. The entire way, Actaeon would either use his halberd to trace arrows or build them out of various pieces of detritus to continue to point the way for those following them.

In time, the path led out from the Boneyards to skirt along the southwestern border of Craters. The Hold had once belonged to the Czeryn Dominion, but after the people in it all vanished following the activation of a blue sphere artifact by the Veiled One nearly twenty years ago, the Raja of the Ajman Dominion had laid claim to it, following a brief conflict with Shield over its possession.

"It makes sense that he'd be in this area. The former Portent of the Raja would be quite familiar with this region." Aethelgard paused to catch his breath.

"Some more of your memories appear to be returning." Actaeon grinned.

"Indeed, they are," said Aethelgard. "With any luck, I'll have enough of my facets that we can successfully face our quarry once we reach the end of this track. It is fascinating, the unfolding – like hearing a story out of legend for the first time. Only, it's my own story."

The path never led into Craters though – it simply skirted around the edges of the Hold. In the end, it led then to the sea caves.

For Actaeon, it was a familiar place. It was the location of the final battle with the Veiled One, and he would have died there had it not been for Eisandre's heroics.

The sea caves.

The natural sandstone structures topped the cliffs ahead, dotted with numerous openings like the giant version of anthills Actaeon remembered seeing along the river in his childhood. Only, these openings were big enough for humans. To the left of the caves, their south, a number of tremendous, rusted beams curled into the water like the claws of some Ancient terror. From their vantage point above the caves, hundreds of transparent domes in various states of disrepair marred the angry waters of the Great Sea beyond like a pox.

"It figures that it would be here," said Actaeon, scratching the back of his right hand through his fingerless glove.

Aethelgard noticed the movement and narrowed his cobalt eyes upon Actaeon, cocking his head to the side. "You fought some sort of battle here, right? Against something bad. Something powerful." He snapped his fingers as he racked his brain. "It's on the tip of my tongue, I swear it."

"The Veiled One." Even all these years later, speaking the name aloud made Actaeon shudder.

The Knight Investigator offered a thin smile. "You bested one foe here. Why not vanquish a second together?" He stuck out a hand.

Actaeon grasped his arm so that they stood forearm to forearm. He looked his friend in the eye and nodded. "With any luck and ingenuity."

"It's all very hazy," said Aethelgard. "But I do believe we've had both of those things in abundance in the past. Anyway, I feel comfortable tackling this thing with you. Shall we proceed?"

The first bolt of lightning cut across the sky above the sea caves to strike an upright portion of the massive metal claw. The resulting shower of sparks cascaded downward to disappear beyond the cliff's edge. Less than a lifebeat later, the crack resounded all around them, causing them both to jump.

"A storm's incoming." Aethelgard turned to face it. "Let's finish this before the rain washes Ruinlock's tracks away."

"Lead the way," said Actaeon. He sent a message to Eisandre over his Thoughtlink and used the butt of his halberd to scrape another arrow into the dirt. This one he cut even more deeply in the hopes that the rain wouldn't completely wash it away.

The ruins gave way to dirt and the dirt gave way to sand as they drew closer. The trail led them to a small mound of sand that drew Aethelgard's eye. He stooped to examine it and kicked the sand aside. It revealed a still smoldering campfire. Using the tip of his cane, he scattered them about, then knelt to fish something out of the ashes using the edge of his cloak to protect his fingers. He turned the scorched object over in his hand, examining it.

"What did you find?" asked Actaeon, leaning forward on the shaft of his halberd to see more closely.

When his friend held it out, he recognized the artifact lock at once, even in its blackened state.

It was the lock from his own workshop, surgically removed from the heavy wood door. The charred remnant of the edge of one of Lauryn's carved reliefs was even visible.

"By the Fallen. He toys with us." The color drained from Actaeon's face.

He sent another message through the Thoughtlink for Eisandre to dispatch some of her pursuing forces back to the workshop to check on Lauryn and any of the academy apprentices who might be there. "This is naught but a game to him. Everything…"

"As if he's anticipating our every move," said Aethelgard. "So, what might we do to subvert his expectations? Think, Engineer. We cannot allow him to beat us."

"It is clear he knew we would follow him if we survived the trap in the Song. Even knowing that your memory would be impacted, he correctly surmised that we would track him all the way out this far. So sure he was, that he planted a lock in the fire – the very lock from my own workshop. To show us he is not afraid and he knows what we will do." Actaeon narrowed his eyes on the caves ahead, as if considering.

"Keep going, Act," the Arbiter encouraged. "You've learned much since we've started working together. Finish your train of thought."

Another crack of thunder jarred them both.

"And so, he knows we will approach. He knows we must. He showed us in the Song of the Sisters that he was willing to take a hostage – someone dear to us. And with the lock from my workshop, it shows that he may well have done it again. Thus, he expects that we have no choice but to rush in brazenly to come to the rescue. That is when the trap will be sprung. It will be an artifact trap, as is his wont. And, after what we did to him last time, he will make sure it is our last."

Aethelgard adjusted the lenses on his nose and smiled. "So, what should we do about this development?"

"Let us follow him in," said Actaeon. "But I will lag behind. Once you trigger the trap, I can sneak around to find and disable its power source. The sea caves are a maze. We can use that to our advantage. He cannot have accounted for every direction. Can he?"

Aethelgard arched a brow. "Time will tell. I trust you, Engineer. It's a good plan. Don't let me die."

"I will not," said Actaeon with a grin.

The trail was easy to follow from there, almost confirming their suspicions that their quarry wanted them to pursue him.

The moment came when they were less than a hundred paces from the nearest entrance. They could hear the relentless pounding of the waves against the sandstone cliffs far below. That was when they saw him.

The stout figure with the tattered tan cloak drawn across his body neatly blended in with the sandstone caves behind him. The cloak whipped like a flag in the growing wind of the storm that was practically upon them. Half of his face was covered with a crude metal mask. The former Portent no longer had any hair. Instead, his pate was shaved to the skin, and straps crisscrossed it to hold the mask against his face.

"Ruinlock!" screamed Aethelgard, pointing his cane at the man.

Ruinlock turned his back on them, and was gone.

"After him!" The Knight Investigator shoved something into Actaeon's free hand and then he was off.

Actaeon lifted the object and saw that it was the Knight's writheblade. He took off after him at a sprint.

The crack of lightning took the sound from the world and left ghost images in their vision as it blasted apart a natural sandstone pillar just to the right of where Ruinlock had been standing.

By the time Actaeon caught up, Aethelgard was already halfway down stairs that he'd uncovered next to where the man had disappeared.

A shout brought the Knight Investigator around. Aethelgard shook his head – he didn't want Actaeon to follow. Responding with a slight nod, Actaeon tossed him his halberd, and then turned to find another way in.

The sense of being began to return to Aethelgard as he descended the roughly hewn sandstone stairs. That recognition of self only served to bring a biting terror to the pit of his stomach. Somewhere ahead was the criminal who had threatened him his entire career. The only one elusive enough that even his powers of deduction were insufficient to catch. A certain death awaited him at the end of this pursuit, unless his friend could find a way to stop the trap that Ruinlock had undoubtedly set for him.

It was a risk, but one that would be necessary to take down his nemesis once and for all. With the familiar aspects of his self seeping back in, the knowledge of the trust he had in the Prince Engineer also returned, along with a welcome realization: this was his own plan coming together. As long as Actaeon could figure out a way to shut the power to whatever trap Ruinlock had set for them, the rest would be elementary.

And so, he plunged ahead through broken sandstone caves and the narrow causeways between them. The scrapings of Ruinlock's artifact leg were quite clear here. Even in the darkness, some light shed from his magnifier luminary quickly revealed the path he needed to follow – the path into a trap certain to kill him if Actaeon failed.

Holes here and there in the caves revealed angry waves far below. Normally, he'd be more careful with his footing, but he was certain that Ruinlock wouldn't be satisfied with that sort of end for him. No, the madman would want to be responsible for killing him with one of his machinations.

Rivulets of water along the walls gleamed in his luminary light as heavy rain from the storm outside began to trickle down into the caves.

Though the trap ahead was fully anticipated, what happened next caught him completely off guard.

The change in direction of the little streams of water was the first herald of the change in local physics. The next step caused his stomach to lurch and the lack of the normal, comforting pressure against his feet was a definitive sign. He was floating.

"What sorcery is this?" He began to flail about, looking for something, anything, to grab onto.

Releasing his cane, he extended the engineer's halberd to try and reach something with its hooked blade, but the movement just sent him into an uncontrolled spin.

A tsking sound came from all around him, and the voice that followed it did also. "Aethel, Aethel, Aethel... Foolishly you stumble along right into my trap. Have you learnt nothing? Or..."   A beam of green light flickered to life from somewhere above him, then from his left as he continued to spiral in zero gravity. The shimmering beam struck a wall in the cavern and fanned out to project a featureless green face. The face stayed stationary as he rotated – in the darkness it gave him the perspective that it was spinning before him. He remembered that face from long ago, in Canal Keep. It was the face that Ruinlock had first appeared to them with.

The now upside-down apparition kept speaking. "...perhaps that is your plan. Let the Caliburn Engineer lag behind and try to disarm my machinations. Don't worry, I'll deal with him separately. Just worry about yourself now – the Fallen know you'll need to!" The face twisted in laughter that echoed throughout the chamber before it disappeared.

A line of yellow light appeared to his side. He twisted to look, and his neck cracked as he craned it to follow the line as it spun around him. At its end was a large artifact that looked like some sort of pod. At the front of it was a window, lit from behind with a dull blue glow. When Aethelgard adjusted the lenses on his face, he gasped as the face behind the artifact window came into focus.

The laughter came again – a lunatic's cackle. "I thought long and hard who might actually matter to you – enough to teach a lesson, at least. I'd considered some of the Arbiters you've mentored, but they're just so... disposable, right? Fat Elmerth, or dopey Schlefer, or even stubborn, ugly Matine. I even thought about using the woman you'd swooned over. What was her name? You remember..." When the Arbiter didn't answer, Ruinlock continued. "Myridia, of course. But I decided she'd be a nice trophy for me after all's said and done. So, instead, I decided to pick a blast from your past, Aethel sof Leaf. Oh, how you wanted answers. And since you're so desperate for answers about me, I thought it only fitting to permanently take away answers you seek from another. A fitting punishment for Redemption's most persistent fool."

Inside the artifact pod, Arvin sof Balur's eyes opened. Aethelgard's once mentor looked around in a panic, until he spotted the Knight Investigator spinning in the center of the cavern room. He yelled something that went unheard within the artifact and pounded his fists against the elderglass window. Leaf was the man's nickname, given to him after he'd abandoned the Arbiters for another cause. A cause that he'd abandoned Aethelgard for when the Knight Investigator was still just an Arbiter Initiate.

A chill ran down Aethelgard's spine. For fourteen years, ever since Leaf had been unfrozen from the capsule artifact and had subsequently disappeared, he had searched for his old mentor, not completely knowing why, but he searched anyway. Ruinlock was right – he wanted answers. And now those answers were right in front of him, locked inside some artifact.

What really shook Aethelgard to his core was that where for all these years he had failed, Ruinlock had succeeded.

A humming sound began. Behind the window, Leaf screamed and his face began to fade, turning transparent. The back of the pod was slowly becoming visible as his once mentor continued to fade.

Stretching his arms out, Aethelgard attempted to strike the artifact pod with the halberd. A spark lit the cave as the blade struck the pod's side, sending the Knight Investigator spinning faster in a second direction.

Leaf's face continued to fade until it was gone completely. In the last moments, Aethelgard caught a glimpse of Arvin looking at him in terror. The yellow line flickered and shut off, plunging the chamber into darkness once more.

"What have you done with him?" demanded Aethelgard, as he spun through the air, clutching the engineer's halberd. He pulled out his illuminated magnifier and used it to cast some light upon the room.

Ruinlock's laughter filled the cavern again. "A gift for the Starborn. Another trap, if you will. There's a reason behind everything, after all."

Spheres of water shimmered in the luminary light as the rainfall spilling in from above began to coalesce in the zero gravity zone. The hundreds of floating bubbles splashed against one another, combining and separating in a dance that was, at once, nauseating and beautiful. With the back of his sleeve, he wiped his own spheres of water that had, unbidden, begun to accumulate at the corners of his eyes.

The things that entered the sandstone room next looked like giant spiders, except that they each had five legs. Their metal carapaces gleamed in the light. There were three of them, he counted as he spun. Each one had a stalk that turned to peer at him with cold, glowing blue eyes.

"These friends of mine will help you follow in Leaf's footsteps. Fitting, don't you think?" Ruinlock chuckled again. "Now, if you'll excuse me, I must go deal with the Caliburn Engineer."

Aethelgard's head snapped from artifact machine to artifact machine to artifact machine as he spun. In that way, he watched them all tense and leap toward him at the same moment.

One of Actaeon's ramblings came to him in that moment – one where the Engineer described rotational inertia. With a thin smile, the Arbiter pulled the halberd against his body and tucked himself into a tight, little ball. The speed at which he rotated threatened to loose the contents of his stomach, but he bit the impulse down and waited until the many-legged artifact monsters were nearly upon him. Then he extended the halberd.

It slammed into the side of the first machine with a crack and a shower of sparks.

The window that Actaeon found wasn't quite wide enough.

Aethelgard's writheblade made short work of that problem. Once the dust cleared and the sandstone was cool enough, he climbed down into the chamber and scanned the surrounds using the luminary strapped into his goggles.

The power detector artifact that Kryo had given him vibrated the strongest outside of this chamber.

With any luck, Ruinlock wouldn't expect him to find the power source from the outside and cut his way in through a window.

The artifact buzzed with a higher intensity when he lowered it to the floor. Unfortunately, there was not a staircase or any obvious way downward.

Fortunately, he held a way down right in his hand. With a grin, he plunged the writheblade into the sandstone floor and carved out a circle that was wider than his shoulder width. Once the hole was cut, the freed material fell with a thump against the floor below and shattered into a thousand pieces.

After the stone had a chance to cool, he lowered himself down and dropped to the floor below. He landed awkwardly on one of the broken parts of the floor and stumbled backward to land hard on his tailbone. The pain from the impact radiated all the way up his back and he felt everything tighten there. A decade ago, Actaeon would've shrugged it off and just kept moving. Now, in his forties, everything had a lasting effect on his body. With a wince, he pushed through the pain and the tightening muscles in his back to continue his hunt for a power source. Aethelgard was counting on him.

The investigation warranted another hole – this one cut into a wall. It led to another cavern chamber that had an entire wall missing facing the Great Sea. The angry waves below were illuminated with frequent flashes of lightning. The resulting thunder shook the sea caves beneath his feet in a manner that would have worried him of collapse if they hadn't been here for thousands of years before. Irregular gusts of wind that brought a combination of rain and sea spray blew into the chamber and chilled Actaeon even through the thick leather of his jacket.

A quick inspection found that this chamber once had a stairway cut into the stone that led upward, but the stairway was no longer tenable, having been filled with the fragments of a collapse.

The power detector led him to a wall at the back of the chamber. When he pressed his ear to the wall, he could make out the telltale hum of a powered device.

There was no direct way to reach it, of course, but he held a solution right in his hand.

With a grin, he cut into the wall with the writheblade. This time, it wasn't so simple though. Even sunken to the hilt, the artifact blade couldn't cut through the thickness of the wall to the next chamber. Once he realized this, he abandoned the square he'd been cutting and started to cut out wedges of stone.

The operation generated so much dust that he was forced to pull down his goggles and wrap a bandage, which he soaked in some rainwater, around his mouth and nose to protect against the heavy sandstone dust. When he cut slower through the substrate, it didn't throw up any dust at all, but he needed to move fast in case Aethelgard was already in whatever trap Ruinlock had set for them.

And so, he quickly cut wedges of sandstone out, throwing off plumes of dust and cutting deeper and deeper into the wall toward the source of the humming.

The wall turned out to be eight times thicker than the previous one he'd cut through. It was a relief when the next cut broke free into the open air of the room beyond and the wedge tumbled outward to crash down to a floor that was several feet below.

The thin red lines of light that lanced out were brief and barely visible in the dust and darkness of the small tunnel he'd created, but Actaeon saw them, nonetheless.

After cutting another chunk of sandstone free, he tossed it down into the room beyond and watched as the red, pencil-thin light beam lanced across the stone several times before it rolled to a stop. The light left deep cuts through the stone.

"Fascinating…" breathed Actaeon. "Thin light that can damage."

It reminded him of a light lance, but this beam of light was narrower, and when it didn't strike its target, it continued past to strike the wall beyond. It also didn't cut through the sandstone completely. A light lance would have sliced easily through the stone in an instant. Ruinlock must've anticipated their plan and left it as a means to guard this room.

Actaeon tested the theory by drawing an arrow from his quiver and holding it out vane first. The red light shot through one of the feathers to hit the sandstone behind it. A narrow flame grew from that part of the feather to lick the air above. Withdrawing the arrow, he blew it out.

After repeating the test by sticking the arrow out in several other locations, he concluded that the apparatus emitting the deadly light was in a consistent location in the chamber beyond. Judging by the separation of the burn marks on the wall of his crude tunnel, he was pretty certain he could guess exactly where it was located too. Imaginary lines from the marks to where the arrow vane had been would all intersect there.

Next, he took a handful of sandstone dust that had gathered in one corner of the opening and blew it into the chamber before sticking the arrow on the other side of the dust that hung in the air. The light speckled across the floating particles and played along some strands of the feather, but the effect was diminished and the fletching didn't catch fire immediately. After the dust began to dissipate, the feather burst into flame.

With a solution clear in his mind, he set to work.

First, he strung his recurve bow and set it aside against the wall next to the hole. Beside it, he placed one of his special overload arrows.

An invention of his, the arrow shaft was modified with copper wires that wound around from a compact luminary strapped beside the fletching to the metal arrowhead, which was designed for maximum piercing. Once a switch was twisted just before the luminary, the infinite energy of the artifact would begin to pour into the arrowhead, heating it up until it glowed. Upon piercing an artifact, all that energy would be delivered into it, permanently disabling it with any luck. It was an arrow he hated to use, as all artifacts were worthy of further study and utility, but in this case, where an artifact was trying to kill him, he'd have to make an exception.

Once his bow was at the ready, he cut into the opening more with the writheblade, shaving the bare minimum off – just enough to create sandstone dust, and lots of it. He sliced along at the top of the hole, so that the dust would fall downward and be driven by the gusts of wind into the chamber beyond.

When the room with the deadly light was filled with dozens of puffs of dust, he returned the writheblade to its scabbard and snatched up his recurve and the arrow.

Setting the overload arrow to string, he twisted the switch and laid down sideways inside the hole until he could just barely see the flickering red light through the haze. With the room thick with dust, it was difficult to see where he was aiming as he pulled back on the string. Fortunately, the arrowhead began to glow red hot as the energy of the luminary poured into it. He lined up the light of the luminary with the glow of the arrowhead and loosed the arrow at his target.

The overload arrow struck home and, with a crack and snap, the frantic red light ceased.

Shouldering the bow, he drew the crackling writheblade from its scabbard and rushed into the chamber to slice the artifact in half. That done, he crouched and waited for the dust to settle.

With the gusts from outside driving into the room, it took some time, but eventually the air cleared enough for him to see.

A hexagonal frustum made from elderglass stood half his height near the wall at the opposite side of the cavern chamber. Inside of the transparent artifact was a black cylinder with several rings around it that lit up sequentially in a dull red glow that rose up from the floor.

Actaeon frowned. There was so much to learn from this device of the Ancients, but more to lose. So, he wasted no time in bringing down the writheblade to slice the thing in half.

Two of the spider-like machines launched themselves at Aethelgard again, this time aiming to skewer him between the points of their legs.

The Knight Investigator was bleeding from several wounds the machines had already caused. The blood droplets floated all around him – evidence that he wouldn't last much longer under this assault. Still, he wasn't ready to give up just yet. He had to give Actaeon more time.

The spin he'd started when he first entered the room was still underway, but he'd managed to slow it somewhat. Now, he attempted to rotate the halberd so that it would impale both arriving machines before their legs could do the same to him.

It was a struggle to keep the tips of the halberd aligned with the machines, and, as they neared, he realized that he wasn't going to be able to do it.

But before the sharp tips of their legs could tear into his body, he fell.

As what he could've sworn had been the ceiling rushed toward his head, he stretched an arm out to protect himself and felt a pop as his shoulder dislocated and he tumbled against the rough sandstone. He grunted as fresh pain shot up his arm.

The five-legged machines crashed into one another below him – or was it above him? They were yanked against the same surface as him and crashed against the sandstone less than a hand's breadth away. The artifact monsters were tangled in one another and, in their struggle to free themselves, they rolled away from him.

The third machine, severely damaged from his earlier strike, chose that moment to pounce upon him. He felt the sharp edges of its legs bite into flesh on the sides of his chest as it lifted its other remaining leg to deliver a death blow.

Aethelgard was faster though, and he jammed the butt of the halberd into its body between the disc and the stalk. The machine twitched and jerked to one side, yanking the halberd from his grip as it stumbled away.

While all the machines were occupied, he winced where he lay and then lifted his dislocated arm over his head. He reached first to the back of his neck and then to the opposite shoulder. The clunk that followed told Aethelgard that he'd reduced the injury correctly. But it also made him pass out.

The loss of consciousness was brief, but when he came to, the pair of machines had disentangled near one of the doorways and were angling to attack him again. Their stalks tilted forward to allow their eerie, glowing blue eyes to peer at him as they advanced. The third machine laid lifeless upon the ceiling a short distance away, with the engineer's halberd jutting from its metal carapace.

Before they could attack, the Prince Engineer entered through the doorway behind them and leapt from the floor to the ceiling as gravity reversed. The writheblade scrapped the first machine before it even noticed. The second machine spun to face him, but Actaeon was already slicing through it. It crumpled to the ceiling in a shower of sparks.

With a grin, Actaeon sheathed the artifact weapon in its ceramic scabbard and started toward Aethelgard to help him to his feet.

A weighted leather sack struck him in the head, and he crumpled down against the sandstone.

Behind him was a wild man, eyes wide, with half his face hidden behind a metal mask strapped to his head. To Aethelgard, he was just barely recognizable as the person that was once known as Gaemri Ip Monjata. Ruinlock's crazed eyes settled upon him and he knelt to draw the writheblade that Actaeon had dropped. "Time, at last, to die, Aethel." He stomped forward with his artifact leg and swung the weapon down toward the Arbiter.

Aethelgard was already rolling backward though, and he regained his feet upon the ceiling. He ducked under a wild slash from Ruinlock and leapt backward away from another. There was an open portal behind him, and he scrambled toward it. Even though he anticipated the reversal of gravity, he still stumbled and twisted his bad knee painfully as he landed.

With Ruinlock hot on his heels, he bit his lip against the pain and took off through the caverns ahead.

The flight took him through winding corridors, down twisting stairwells, and into dozens of different chambers that each served a role in some ancient society.

The final chamber was either a school or a place of worship. There were a multitude of sandstone podiums that were carved into the very room. They were all arrayed around a raised dais that served as their focal point. Beyond the dais, the wall of the cave was gone, revealing the angry lightning of the storm and the violent waves below.

With nowhere else to go, Aethelgard came to a stop upon the dais, and spun to face his pursuer.

"Finally," rasped Ruinlock. Wild-eyed, the madman approached the podium, holding aloft the crackling writheblade. "Fun though it's been, at last, we've reached the end. I'll miss our games, old Aethel. But, not to worry, I won't miss them enough to prevent me from ending you here."

"There's one last thing I finally figured out," said Aethelgard. He shrugged. "Of course, you probably don't have the patience to hear about it."

"Oh?" Ruinlock scratched his face near the edge of his mask with his free hand and regarded the investigator. "Do tell."

"It's about the Baron Thrist," explained Aethelgard. "I finally figured out what you were looking for from him."

Ruinlock bared his teeth in something between a grin and a snarl. "Okay, clever Aethel. I'll tell you if you were correct before I spill your blood into the Great Sea below."

Aethelgard offered him a thin smile. At some point his lens frame had become bent in the struggle and he pushed it back up his nose. "The Baron of Suncrest had located one of your greatest artifact stashes and stolen it. The secret of its location is what he brought to his grave – to your great frustration. Perhaps, you'd even have beaten me here today, if only you hadn't lost it."

"Very clever, Aethel," said Ruinlock. "Only, I don't need it, do I?" He raised the artifact blade. "I have your sword."

"Don't be so sure," said the Knight Investigator, narrowing his shrewd cobalt eyes upon something beyond his nemesis.

Actaeon arrived just a moment too late.

In horror, he watched as Ruinlock swung the writheblade at his friend. The scene unfolded in slow motion before him as Aethelgard ducked under the artifact blade. The Knight Investigator smirked and snatched at Ruinlock's throat. The enemy was too fast though, and Ruinlock's kick caught Aethelgard square in the chest, knocking the lenses from his face.

As Actaeon watched, his friend tumbled out into the air beyond the cavern. He could've sworn Aethelgard smiled at him, but then the Knight Investigator was gone into the dark tumult of the sea far below.

"Noooo!" Actaeon cried out in rage.

Ruinlock spun to face him and raised the writheblade.

The bolt that struck him dead in the chest forestalled that effort, blooming into a burst of red upon his tunic. The writheblade fell from the hands of the criminal mastermind and Ruinlock staggered backward until he fell from the cavern chamber to join Aethelgard in the Great Sea below.

Actaeon blinked at the boltcaster in his hand. Hand shaking, he dropped the device and yanked the luminary from the strap of his goggles.

"Aethelgard!" he shouted into the darkness below. The Prince Engineer threw himself down to his belly and shimmied over to the edge of the dais. He shined the luminary into the angry waters below and shouted his friend's name again.

Far below the waves roiled and churned.

Beside him, at the edge of the broken floor, lay the twisted lens frame — one of the glass lenses cracked within

Actaeon scanned the water until Eisandre finally arrived with reinforcements.

There was no sign of either man down among the waves.

A week later, he laid his friend to rest.

Even though they never managed to find a body, the Knight Investigator would still be memorialized.

And thus, a crowd now gathered around the cairn in the Stone Gardens south of Pyramid. Among them were those that had worked with him, those who had been helped by him, and those who had called him friend.

"As a member of the Order of the Arbiters of Redemption," recited Sentinel Arbiter Corvin sof Haringar. "Aethelgard sof Leaf devoted himself to the pure vision of a civilized society, in which all the people of Redemption work together toward their common goals of survival, prosperity, and happiness. He believed there to be a fundamental worth in all men, women, and children. And in their collective ability to create a society in which cultural and personal differences are embraced in the light of a greater and more unified whole.

"Unity of vision for a better future," continued the Sentinel. "Clarity of purpose – always assisting those who are in need. Honor and civility, in which he always earned the respect of those around him. Personal modesty, where he always remembered that he served a purpose greater than himself. Purity of focus, more than any who came before, to concentrate on protecting those who needed him. Beyond even this world, may he have the enduring strength, integrity, and conviction to remain true to this difficult path, that all might know a brighter future. Rest easy now, brother. With your everlasting guidance, we shall take it from here.

"If, at this time, anyone else wishes to speak, let them do so." Corvin turned his eyes to Actaeon.

Flanked on one side by his wife, Eisandre, and on the other by Companion Yanelle, Actaeon nodded to the Sentinel. Both women reached out to squeeze his hands as he spoke. "There may never be another man who sees as clearly as the Knight Investigator of the Order of Arbiters. He was a man who truly cared about the people of Redemption. A lifetime was spent honing skills that would solve crimes to protect the future of us all. From his diligence and determination, we all find ourselves in a safer world. In the end, he gave his very life to protect all of us against one of the most evil men of our time." He paused to look around at those present. "Aethelgard was a dear friend, and he will be missed."

Releasing their hands, he stepped forward to place the Knight Investigator's newly repaired lens frame upon the cairn. "Rest well, my friend. Into a safer world we stride forth, thanks to you."

It wasn't until over a year later that the letter arrived at the workshop.

Your urgent help is required, Engineer. Meet me at Blacksands Beach. Come alone!

There was no signature, but none was needed. Actaeon would have recognized that handwriting anywhere.

"Carry on the project, Lauryn," he instructed. "I have a matter I must attend to."

When his colleague smiled and nodded, he threw on his jacket and grabbed his halberd.

As he walked along, the first drops of rain landed upon his face, and he smiled up at the sky.

Another mystery was afoot!

Afterword

UNTIL MY BOSS, FRIEND, FELLOW engineer, and mentor, Ed Barkan, encouraged me to read Sir Arthur Conan Doyle's Sherlock Holmes series, I was never really a fan of the mystery genre. Before then, I'd always thought of mysteries as "whodunnit" stories where the reader has to guess who the killer is based on little tidbits scattered throughout the tale. With that sort of story, many authors strive to spring the most incredible twists upon the reader so that most won't see the conclusion coming, but, when paying enough attention to detail, the cleverest of the bunch might figure out who the culprit is. I've found that I can pretty easily solve many of these "whodunnits" often by simply thinking like a writer. By paying attention to the characters that the author tries to divert you from, many times you will be led directly to the culprit – do not pass GO, do not collect $200. Reading or watching mysteries always felt like a tropey, eye-rolling experience, where the author plants certain things throughout the story just to mislead the reader, or to drop tiny, subtle hints for them. Sir Doyle's mysteries about Holmes and Watson were entirely different in a way that I found delightful.

In my work as an engineer, I'm oft confronted with a technical mystery, frequently a failure. I have to decipher what the root cause of the failure is and figure out a solution to prevent it. In these situations, there are no little hints or misleading crumbs littered about by an author. Instead, it is just your mind versus the uncertainty at hand. Even with years of schooling and many more years of experience on the job, it can be quite intimidating to be confronted with a fresh problem where the solution isn't readily apparent and there's no trail of bread crumbs to point me in the right direction. Instead, it comes down to one's true powers of deduction. One's ability to look at all of the details, to consider every single possibility, to recognize the pertinent signs, and to draw from a wealth of experience are all critical to solving a given problem. It really is a feat of, not just wisdom, but of perseverance and scrutiny of the tiniest details that will lead to a successful conclusion. Once it is had, that conclusion is immensely satisfying. That holds true whether it be deciphering the cause of a failure, inventing a new product to solve a problem, or solving a crime.

Sir Doyle really captures that feeling with Sherlock Holmes. Most of the stories aren't meant for the reader to figure out. For the most part, they aren't "whodunnits". The point of the story is the detailed diligence that Holmes undergoes in order to solve the mystery. It is in seeing how that is accomplished that is the great joy of reading those stories – just like watching a video about how something complicated is made, or why events unfolded a certain way in history.

It is that feeling of joy – of decrypting the details of a great mystery – that inspired me to write these stories. Only, I didn't just want to write about crime-solving. I wanted to show that investigative process, and, indeed, even an inventive process, from the perspective of an engineer. That's why Actaeon was really the perfect character to bring into a story about sci-fi tech investigations alongside the more traditional Holmes-like Aethelgard. Plus, it hadn't been unheard of for Actaeon to investigate mysteries when he was bored on the grid of Redemption MUSH, the text-based game which my wife, Stefanie Handshaw, and her friend, Simon Svensson, created. I remember one particular mystery that Actaeon investigated which was created by my friend and fellow plot director, Pauline Holman (who also played Enrion Zar), where Act had to break cyphers, solve riddles, and search for clues in the text-based world. It was great fun! I even remember one of the Knight Arbiter characters asking Actaeon for help with one of the crimes that was committed in the Pyramid. So this series of mystery cases was really perfect for Actaeon.

There's also a fun juxtaposition when you compare Actaeon and Aethelgard to Watson and Holmes. Watson was there to witness the unbelievable conclusions of Holmes and act as an agent of skepticism and disbelief, in contrast to Holmes' confidence and certainty in everything he does. You see, Sherlock Holmes is just incredibly good at noticing all those details, and seeing how everything worked together, in concert, to result in the situation at hand.

Act and Aeth are a bit different in that regard. Both are part Watson and part Holmes. Where crime is concerned – human behavior and movement, trace evidence, motivation, and emotion – Aethelgard is Holmes. But when technology comes into play, Actaeon becomes Holmes. Thus, in a way, both of them act as the Watson to the other's Holmes. When writing the stories, it was fun to play those two characters off of one another. I hope you enjoyed reading it as much as I enjoyed writing it.

Creating the character of Ruinlock was another interesting exercise. Of course, there's Holmes' mysterious arch-nemesis Moriarty. But I wanted their foil to be more than just a copycat character. I've always thought of Actaeon as a sort of medieval MacGyver. In several of the stories you've read, he must invent a clever way for them to escape with very limited time. Well, MacGyver fans might remember his nemesis: Murdoc. Murdoc liked to set up elaborate traps for MacGyver in order to capture him in the moment of death. Thus, Ruinlock is a sort of rough combination of Moriarty and Murdoc, which I felt was fitting. In the MacGyver TV series (the 1980s one, not the 2016 one), Murdoc is frequently killed off only to reappear in future episodes because he miraculously survived. Perhaps there's a conclusion you can draw there...

I owe a number of people my gratitude for this collection. Of course, at the foremost, I have to thank Stefanie Handshaw and Simon Svensson for creating the world of Redemption and allowing me to write these stories in it to continue to explore and grow the world. I do hope I have done it the justice that it deserves. A big thank you also to my friend and neighbor, Ernestine Franco, for editing and beta reading all these stories (and encouraging me to keep writing them). Thank you to the character of MacGyver, who, even decades later, continues to inspire and drive both me and the character Actaeon, and to Mac's creator, Henry Winkler, and Mac's actor, Richard Dean Anderson. I also owe a big thanks to Sir Arthur Conan Doyle for the inspiration of Sherlock Holmes.

Lastly, I'd like to thank Ed Barkan for introducing me to the real Holmes of literature and who taught me to never cease being curious. As a prolific inventor with somewhere around 400 patents (among them the first handheld barcode scanner and the earliest capacitive touch circuits), Ed is an inspiration for me in the engineering field and life in general. I'll ever be impressed with his own stories of how he not only invented products that solve real life problems, but continued to refine and advance them diligently for decades. It has been an absolute honor to be a part of that for this past decade. Thank you for all that you've taught me over the years, Ed!

About the Author

Darran M. Handshaw is the author of The Engineer and The Dark Heart of Redemption. In addition to writing, Darran works as an R&D Concept Engineer at a technology company where he invents and designs new products. He holds more than 110 patents in data capture, vision systems, and emergency services. Darran also volunteers as a firefighter with his local fire department, where he serves as an Ex-Chief and active firefighter and teaches fire prevention to the children of his community. Darran hails from Long Island, NY, where he lives with his beautiful wife, Stefanie, and incredible son, Corwin, who fill his life with love, wisdom, and endless adventures.

Follow Darran below:

 fb.me/ActaeonRellios/

 goodreads.com/TheEngineer

 twitter.com/Engineer7601

 amazon.com/author/engineer

Also by the Author

The Engineer,
A Chronicles of Actaeon Story
http://getbook.at/engineer

The Dark Heart of Redemption,
A Chronicles of Actaeon Story
http://mybook.to/darkheart

The Machine in the Mountain,
A Chronicles of Actaeon Tale
A short story in The Quantum Soul: A Sci Fi Roundtable Anthology
http://getbook.at/quantum